T0188761

On the ROYLE RANGE

On the ROYLE RANGE

WILLIAM W. JOHNSTONE

AND J.A. JOHNSTONE

KENSINGTON
PUBLISHING CORP.

www.kensingtonbooks.com

KENSINGTON BOOKS are published by

Kensington Publishing Corp.
900 Third Avenue
New York, NY 10022

ISBN: 978-1-4967-4586-6

ISBN: 978-0-7860-5060-1 (ebook)

First Kensington Trade Paperback Printing: September 2024

10 9 8 7 6 5 4 3 2 1

Printed in the United States of America

On the ROYLE RANGE

Chapter 1

Conversation around the campfire at Royle Ranch was light, and everyone felt buoyed by bowls full of warm stew. The day's work had been long and successful, which put Jarvis "Bone" McGraw, erstwhile Texas Ranger and current overseer of the men and ranch manager, in a good mood.

Bone had been wearing himself thin with full days of work at the Royle Ranch. Then he'd ride on home to his own smaller ranch a couple of days a week some miles north of the Royle Range.

When Regis Royle himself was present at the ranch, his men were wary and not a little skittish. He had a tendency to ramrod everything. The man would pop up in the most unlikely of spots, and it was unnerving.

Just when you think you earned a quick moment to lean on a shovel and wipe the sweat from your brow, there'd be Regis Royle. He'd not say a thing, but cast his tall, wide-shouldered shadow on whatever task you were up to, be it sinking fence posts or digging out a perimeter to lay stone for a new building's foundation.

It seemed they were forever building some structure or another. They certainly were needed, especially the small houses for workers, because the Royle Ranch was a growing place.

It also seemed that every time someone in a boss position about the place—usually Regis or Bone, but sometimes Cormac, Regis's partner in the steamship freighting business—opened up their mouths to speak, the ranch hands knew what they were going to say.

And it usually was something about Regis having bought more land. And that was a never-ending source of conversational fodder for the boys come meal time.

"Honestly," one or another hand would say. "Is there any more land for sale in Texas?"

That brought a breezy laugh from the cluster of haggard men. They were knackered, having spent the day working under Bone's watchful eye.

Even though Bone could be a hard man to please, he would dole out a nod or grunt of approval to the men when they tried at whatever task it happened to be, from fence building to carpentering to brush popping for wayward cattle. A man didn't always have to complete a task successfully to get one of those hard-earned but powerful grunts or nods from the man.

He was willing to see you fail . . . once, though he rarely tolerated a second time. He'd call a fellow off to one side for a low-volume conversation. Even the most hardened cowboy could be dressed down by Bone McGraw and come away red-faced but grateful for the talk, and feeling bad about having let down the big, mustachioed ranger.

He'd also work right by your side to show you a better way to do a thing. Could be smithery, fixing a snapped shovel or banging out another batch of nails. Or it could be riding down broncs or repairing and maintaining tack, it didn't matter, it seemed Bone had done it all.

And if you happened to know a thing that he did not know, he was not shy about asking you to repeat your instructions so that he might learn a new task by your side.

Yes, Bone McGraw was a man the rest of the growing number

of men at the Royle Ranch agreed was hard as stone, but a good fellow to work for.

Their feelings did not run in quite the same direction when it came to ranch owner and top boss, Regis Royle.

Oh, he, too, was a solid man, but he was not afraid to bellow a man down right in front of everyone else, and then he'd storm off when he'd reached the end of his tether, leaving an embarrassed hand and a throng of equally embarrassed nearby men. And that seemed to be happening a whole lot more these days.

There were a number of men, the old-timers, who had been around several years before when Regis first began carving a ranch out of this vast, sometimes beautiful, sometimes brutal country of far southeastern Texas.

And those old-timers, though some of them weren't yet thirty, and a few of them even younger than that, were always quick to point out to the newcomers that the ranch they hired on to today was a whole lot finer than it had been in the early days.

"See that reservoir there?" a youthful old-timer would say, sipping a cup of coffee.

"Yes, sir," the newcomer would reply.

"Hand-dug."

"All of it? You mean it wasn't here?"

That common reaction was always met with headshakes and sneers of pity by the old-timers. And then one of the bosses would show up, and the day's work would commence. Or resume.

Frequently they began their long days well before sunup. Before breakfast, there was plenty to do—tending the stock, rounding up chicken and goose and duck eggs, and in the process seeing what damage the night's coyote raids had inflicted on the poultry.

If there were carcasses of birds, and they weren't too badly mangled, they would be fetched back to Percy Grimlaw, the cook, and his assistant of the week. (They never lasted long be-

fore being rotated out to other duty. Any duty, if they had a say
in the matter. Percy could be touchy, and exacting, and cantankerous.)

If the poultry carcasses were too far gone, the pigs got the
meat. Same thing with any of the seemingly endless supply of
rattlers the men shot. Pigs, they found, would eat just about anything.

"How is it a pig can eat such a thing as a snake and piles of
food scraps and roll around in dust and shade all day and still end
up tasting so dang good?"

It was a question Burton Shanks, the blacksmith, always asked
with a chuckle as he fed the pigs. It was a chore he enjoyed, and
he always spent time scratching the snouts and ears of the grateful critters.

"Burton, you talk to them as if they can understand you,"
Chubby John "Tut" Tuttle, another hand from the ranch's early
days, said, shaking his head as if he'd just witnessed something
mighty strange.

"Who's to say they can't?" Burton would always say. "I, for
one, believe all God's creatures understand one another in some
way we dumb humans can't even understand yet."

Tut shrugged and sipped his coffee while he watched Burton
dump a stewpot of peelings and bone scraps into the hewn log
trough. "Okay, then, by that logic, next you'll tell me that trees
and grass and flowers and such are chatty with each other, too."

Burton leaned his head to the side. "Who's to say . . ."

"I know, I know. Who's to say they aren't." Again, Tut shook
his head and turned to head back to the kitchens, eager for a second cup of coffee, strong and black and hot, just the way his best
friend, Percy, made it and just the way the men had better well
like it. "All I know is you talk that talk too loud, and the men are
liable to haul you off to some place they keep the crazies."

Burton smiled and gave a pig one last scratch on the snout,
then fell in line behind Tut. "Who's to say we aren't already
there?"

Tut laughed. "Burton, you beat all, I swear."

As one of the seasoned hands, Tut had earned the right to get to work a pinch later, which gave him time to welcome the new day with his young wife, ranch schoolmarm, formerly known as Miss Belinda Orton. On this morning, Tut was filling in on early shift duties because of the lack of new hires of late, a trend becoming more of a worry as talk of war in various parts of the country at large began fomenting.

Tut and Percy had, in fact, been among the first men hired on by Regis Royle back when there was nothing but snakes and grass on the spot now occupied by a range of impressive shacks, shanties, and proper sheds, stables, and homes that helped make up what Regis called the "ranch proper."

Tut and Burton made it back to the grub house as other men stumbled and grumbled and yawned and scratched on in. One of the things that made the single ranch hands' lives easier these days was the fact that the families they'd helped relocate to this side of the border were no longer crowding around waiting for their own feed.

Those days had been a pain, because everyone had to eat in shifts at each meal and you had to get yourself in line early to get a place at the table.

Most of the families were Mexican villagers that Regis brought over the border to live here and work the ranch—laboring men, as well as their wives, children, old folks, burros, chickens, goats, the works. Now that they mostly all had houses with their own outdoor ovens that they shared, they were able to feed themselves and take the pressure off of Percy and his various helpers at the ranch grub shack.

And the men no longer had to eat in shifts. That didn't mean there wasn't jostling in line to get at the table.

That morning, as with all mornings, Percy was surly and in a dark mood. But as with all other mornings, the men ignored his steaming ways, because for all that, Percival Grimlaw was one mighty fine cook. And for such a young man, too.

Yes, sir, the ranch had taken shape in these last few years, from a sea of grass and rock and scrub and mesquite teeming with snakes and birds and coyotes. It was also home to herds of bawling, brawling, brush-rat cattle with horns aching to hook a man's horse wide open. They were cattle that stood their ground, snorting and bellowing and raking earth with chipped, stomping hooves.

And there were herds of mad-eye, snorting wild horses that took a whole lot of catching and even more working and coaxing before they broke. And some of them didn't, at least not before they broke many a cowhand's bones.

The place that stood today made for an impressive change in the landscape. It boasted a whole lot of man-built structures and refinements, including water containments and canals, gardens, crops, fences, corrals and barns, adobe and log homes for the Mexican villagers, a church and schoolhouse, again for the villagers, as well as a smithy and wheelwright shop, and a cook shack with a dog run for cooking outdoors, which Percy got up to most of the time, save for the windiest days of the year, and the cold ones, too.

But it was the herds of cattle that Regis was most concerned with—and most counted on. The aggressive breeding efforts that he and Bone had set in place had begun to pay off. They'd mated the rangy, small, tough-as-nails longhorns with thicker, slower, but fatter beef animals from bulls Regis had bought for fees that some of the men swore equaled ten times what they made in a meager wage in a whole year's time.

Removed from the rest of the ranch proper's constant hubbub, there was also a genuine house in a slow but constant state of expansion. It was built with genuine lumber, ferried in by wagon, and it was Regis Royle's home, and had been shared by his troublesome younger brother, Shepley, before he left for the second time to join the US Army.

Everybody liked Shep, as he was all the things his older brother,

Regis, was not. Namely, the younger Royle brother was a smiler who never had a cross word for the men. He'd also always been willing to tuck in and help when they really needed the help.

Trouble was, he was just as prone to loping off in the middle of the day and finding a shady spot to nap away a few hours where a breeze would keep him snoring and smiling. Until his brother found him, anyway.

Most of the men just shook their heads and chuckled at the young man's exploits. They all wished they could get away with such actions, but they'd be out of a job the first time they tried.

But Shep, as the baby brother of the ranch owner—and rumor had it, part owner himself—was able to get away with a whole lot most men would never dream of doing. It did not mean he was immune from the brutal tongue lashings of Regis.

Indeed, he got chewed out so regularly by his older brother that the men bet each other chore duties as to how long Shepley Royle would take his brother's bellowing rages before he up and left for good. Not that anyone thought he really would.

Then the kid did just that. He'd pulled up stakes on his eighteenth birthday. But the kid, being a fool, and as green as a spring shoot, never made his escape past Corpus Christi, where he was knifed nearly to death in an alley behind the bar he was getting legless in.

Before he got intimate with that blade, however, but after he'd downed a whole lot of whiskey, he'd signed on with the US Army.

It had taken Regis, so they were told, a whole lot of fancy talking, and some folks even said a big ol' wad of cash, to keep the kid's enlistment in the army from going ahead.

Instead, and barely into Shep's convalescence, Regis had hauled the kid back to the ranch, and kept him all but locked up in his old room until Regis decided Shep was well enough to resume his ranch duties.

But Burton had overheard them arguing one evening, and

he'd learned that Shepley Royle had other plans, and they didn't include living on the Royle Ranch. "It's always been your dream, Regis, not my dream. Yours."

And that's when they all knew that as soon as he'd healed up, Regis was going to make life a big ol' pain once more for his kid brother.

But Shep beat him to the punch by leaving one day while Regis was off on one of his forays for land, cattle, supplies, or to tend to matters at the shipping office he shared with his shipping business partner, Cormac Delany.

The oddest thing, all the men agreed, was that Regis did not chase after him this time. Instead, he let him go. But at the same time, it had seemed that something about the man had changed, and that showed itself about the ranch, too.

There were rumblings and rumors that Regis, whose coin pouch had always seemed bottomless, was strapped for cash. Some men said they'd heard in Brownsville that the shipping business was all but dead, and all because of Regis's thirst for land.

Cormac's visits to the ranch had been infrequent in the past, but nowadays they had become downright nonexistent. It was rumored he was too busy in town courting banks and drumming up shipping business for their fleet of steamers.

And Regis Royle himself, never what you'd call a full-bore, gregarious, chatty fellow, had grown more sullen and surly, barking at men for slim, and sometimes no, reasons at all. And then Regis had met a woman, and his attitude had begun to shift, barely, to be sure, but enough that the men caught glimpses of light shafting in through his dark moods and these dark times for the ranch.

And the more seasoned of the Royle Ranch hands knew who this mysterious woman was. And their wry grins and sly head-shakes showed their approval at this choice of a paramour for Regis Royle.

For she was none other than the true and proper heir—or rather heiress—to the Valdez land grant, the land on which much of the heart of the Royle Ranch sat.

It made sense, they explained to the newcomers, on purely practical grounds. But what sort of woman wouldn't see through such a wooing? Sure, Regis Royle was a big, handsome, wide-shouldered, square-chinned fellow, but still . . .

Chapter 2

Every time Shepley Royle, well into his eighteenth year, felt like throwing up his hands and giving in to his urges to quit, he thought of his brother, Regis, and the smug look on the man's face.

It was a look Shep had long wanted to pummel with a flurry of hard fists. He'd set his jaw just thinking about it, feeling his molars beginning to powder and his jaw muscles twitching and jouncing and bulging.

"Boy, what ails you?"

Shep jerked out of his reverie and spun to look in the eye of the man who'd spoken to him. It was his commanding officer, Sergeant Cowley. Despite what the various recruits said, sniggering in secret with the lamps blown out for the night after a long ol' day of training, there was nothing 'cowlike' about Cowley. If anything, the man was all bull.

"Sorry, sir!"

"You best be, Royle." The man leaned forward and nearly touched his nose tip to Shep's. In a low voice, he said, "And don't you think because your name sounds like something the Queen of England wears that you're going to get special treatment in this here army, you understand?"

"Yes, sir!"

"Now answer my question, Royle." He'd resumed his normal near-shout, still only a hand's distance from Shep's face. It was loud enough that the five other men Shep had been working with most definitely heard.

And as he cast a quick glance their way, he saw the relief and telltale reddening on their faces. He'd been caught daydreaming again when he should have been digging the hole he'd been assigned to dig. They were digging latrine hole pits to be filled with dung, nothing more.

This, he thought, was what he'd left the ranch, Regis's cursed ranch, for so long ago. He'd left twice, in fact, and had been nearly done in by that vicious cat from Hades, Tomasina Valdez.

And now here he was, thinking a life in the army would . . . would what, Shep? Would prove he was a man. To whom? To Regis? Regis didn't care. No, Shepley, my boy, he told himself, you went and did it again. You played the fool without thinking through the consequences of your actions, as Regis had reminded him to do over and over these last few years.

"I'm waiting, Private Royle!"

Shep's eyes grew as wide as they'd ever been. Oh no, he did it again! He felt himself shaking, and he said, "I . . . it's my brother, sir."

"And what about your brother, Royle?"

"I . . ." What about Regis, Shep? he asked himself, licking his lips. Go ahead and tell the man that you didn't like how he was treating you. How he wanted to give you part of the biggest ranch the world had ever seen, at least according to Regis. And he had to hand it to his brother, the Royle Ranch, and Royle Range, was huge, and if Regis had anything to say about it, it was only getting bigger. "He's dead, sir."

He had really had no intention of saying that, but there it was, he thought, like half the things he'd said and done in his life, but it had happened anyways. Almost as if Shep could not control himself or his thoughts or actions or words. He was a mess, as Regis had said more than once.

If, deep down, Shep had thought he might receive some amount of sympathy from Cowley, he was sorely mistaken.

"So what, Royle? My sainted mama's dead, my long-suffering pa is dead, my two sisters are dead. I'm the only one left of my family. You see me tearing up and looking past that hill thinking of good times and tea parties? No!"

And then, as that last word drove into Shep's face like a hard slap, Cowley walked into him hard and fast. Cowley was built like an oak barrel filled with lead and rage, and his arms and legs were as close as human flesh and bone could get to steel.

He rammed that brutal pointer finger into Shep's chest and backed him up as he bulled forward. Shep stepped backward, had no choice, and his second step back kept going.

Cowley stopped, but Shep didn't. He shrieked like a small child. Somehow his shovel fetched up behind his right boot. He tripped over it and fell backward, arms flailing.

He ended up on his back, his head slamming into the craggy rough hold he'd dug, his backside and legs collapsing him into a sprawl at the bottom. His long-handled shovel dropped down on him, the ash shaft smacking him atop his pate.

Shep looked up, dazed, into the sun, squinting, and Cowley shifted to his left, blocking out the sun. The two men stared at each other again, Cowley shaking his head slowly, Shep shaking his, too, but only to dispel the buzzing and ringing he felt there.

"Next time you daydream on army time, Royle, you will spend a whole lot longer than a few minutes in a hole. You'll be in the hole, you got me, boy? And I'll make sure it's for at least thirty days. At the end of that, you'll have to start your training all over again, you hear me?" He leaned down, not quite kneeling, and said, "I'll see to it personally."

"Yes, sir."

"What?"

Shep scrambled to an upright position, still down in the hole, and saluted a quick, smart gesture as he'd been taught, over and over again. He couldn't seem to do much right in the US Army, but he could, by gum, offer up a snappy salute.

"Yes, sir!"

Cowley straightened, his eyes narrowing as he looked down at Shep and shaking his head as if he smelled something vile dangling off the heel of his boot. "For a fella so close to finishing his training, you sure act like a fool. This is your last chance, Royle."

"Yes, sir!" Another salute.

"Overdo that and you'll be in the hole, too." Cowley walked away, down the line of holes being dug with renewed fervor by Shepley's fellow privates.

As he scrambled up out of the hole, Shep kept his gaze on the task at hand. He knew if he looked up, he'd see one of the others smirking at him, which he knew they all wanted to do, he just knew it. He also knew he was liable to bolt for them and give each and every one of them what-for. And that would sure as anything land him in the hole.

His face was hot, blazing red, as were his ears. It took a whole lot to embarrass him, and yet he'd spent a good amount of his life putting himself in embarrassing situations, and he was sick of it.

The more he dug, the more he thought, and the more he thought, the worse it all became. He recognized he was putting himself right back in that situation he didn't want to be in, the one where he was daydreaming, and that would bring Cowley running. The man was looking for the chance to clip him off at the knees.

He sucked in a breath through his tight-set teeth and glanced up as he worked the shovel deep into the side of his hole. This was going to be the best darn latrine hole anyone in the history of the US Army had ever dug.

Cowley was gone, nowhere in sight, but Shep knew he'd gone on down the line, inspecting the others. They were all the newest recruits, but the others, to a young man, were, from what Shep could gather, wet behind the ears in almost all ways.

And there wasn't a single one who knew how to wield a shovel like he could. And for what it was worth, at that moment, Shep couldn't help but to half smile. "Thanks, Regis," he grunted as he scooped and slung more earth.

And then he heard a rifle shot, followed by two more. And then a man's shout: "Hey now!" growled the big voice. It was Cowley . . .

Shep used the shovel to vault up out of his hole. The other five were all down in their holes with their hands on their heads; two of them prairie-dogged up when Shep tore by. He snarled, ducking as he ran. "Keep down!"

They did.

He made for the shots, which continued at random intervals, but he no longer heard Cowley's voice.

Shep reached out of raw instinct to his waist, clawing for a sidearm, but where it normally rode, at least back on the ranch. There was nothing but sweat-sodden wool trousers and braces.

He cursed, remembering as soon as his fingertips felt nothing that he was in the army now. And it felt as though he was as far from Texas as a man could get—back East at the US Army training ground in Virginia.

So why was someone shooting? Gunfire happened all the time here, but this time, there was something about it, in addition to Cowley's shout, that had made them all look up. It was close, and they were definitely not at the rifle shooting range—nowhere near it. They were behind the barracks.

Then he had no time for further speculation, because his scurrying, low-walking strides brought him to the nearest large thing behind which to take shelter, the bunkhouse of his company.

He could dart inside and rummage in his gear until he found his revolver and knife. But why? They'd taken his bullets when he'd arrived. And the knife? As nice a piece as it was—a gift from

Regis, who'd had it made especially for him—it would be nearly useless against a gun-armed enemy. If that's what was up ahead.

As if in response to this thought, two more shots cranked out, one ricocheting off something. He'd heard plenty of bullets spanging off rock to know what it was.

But it was the third sound that chilled him and told him to keep moving, come what may. Somebody had shouted, and was in distress. And that meant he had to help.

He and Regis had both learned that bit of selflessness from their mama, dead these past few years, but as good-hearted a person as Shep knew he was ever likely to meet.

The sound he'd heard was a yelp, the very same one he'd heard men make when they'd been wounded, mostly shot, back in Texas. He'd been through a number of rough scrapes down there, from an attack by a band of rogue Apache to not infrequent and random raids by border pirates looking to thieve cattle and horses and anything else of value. And then there was Señorita Valdez, the brute killer and her deadly gang, who'd kept him prisoner, chained to a rock wall in a cave. Again, Regis and his men had ridden to Shep's rescue.

He bit back the bitter thoughts rising in his gorge. He was more beholden to his older brother than any man ought to be, but he needed to get over it.

The sound brought him back to the present. The yelp. It sounded like it could be any man. And yet it had to be Cowley; somehow, he knew it was Cowley.

Had the man been shot? If so, how badly?

Too many nervous-making thoughts skittered in and out of his mind as he edged closer to the end of the building. Once he got there, he'd have to poke his head around the corner, risking a look.

Shep felt sweat slip into his eyes, then slide down his face. He scrunched his eyes quickly and opened them again.

Before he got to the corner of the building, he glanced back to his right, far behind toward where he'd loped from. His latrine-digging companions were still there, cowering, but emboldened enough to poke their faces out of their holes.

He cut his gaze back to the task at hand. And shook his head. Keep moving, Shep, he told himself. To heck with those other fools. Cowley—or someone—needed help. He heard no other voices. Where was everyone?

He made the corner and, keeping low, dropped down onto his left knee. If the shooter was looking in his direction, he'd be safer down low, and not poking his face out where it might be expected to appear.

He kept himself tucked low, his palms flat against the sun-puckered planking of the long, low building. He smelled the old, piney scent rippling off the wood in the noonday sun. His boots scuffed gravel and, keeping low, he planted them with more care, making his way to his left toward the end of the structure.

Beyond lay the commons—the parade ground in the center of the entire place, where they gathered at dawn for reveille to welcome the day and raise the colors.

Shep licked his sweaty top lip again and held his breath. Here goes, he thought, and edged his face, left cheek tight to the wood, and peered around the corner.

The first thing he did not expect to see was a man, not twenty feet away, sprawled on his side, his back to Shep. He knew it was Cowley. The man was not moving. And owing to the dark blue of the man's uniform coat, it was difficult to tell if he'd been shot. He was too far from the nearest building, two structures down to Shep's left, to crawl to safety.

But Shep had to get out there.

The next thing he saw was a figure, far across the way, moving from behind a parked, horseless wagon, to another wagon beside it. The figure flashed into the light as it moved.

"Sergeant!"

Shep didn't think his hoarse, shouted whisper could be heard all the way across the parade grounds to the wagons, but he had to try.

"Sergeant, it's Royle. If you can hear me, move the toe of your top boot!"

There was a long, sickening moment when the man didn't move; nothing happened, save for a fleeting swirl of dust eddying off into nothing to Shep's right.

Then Cowley's boot moved up, down once.

"Thank God," said Shep to himself. Now what, Shep? Now, he thought, now we get over there.

He pulled in a breath through his nose, let it out, and dashed, keeping low. He made it across the few yards separating him from the big, gruff man who seemed to have it in for him.

"Sergeant!" Shep whispered.

"What on earth are you doing?" said the big man, without looking at the young man who'd just collided with him, hunkering low and resting a hand on the big man's topmost shoulder.

"Are you okay?"

"No, shot through the meat of my left leg, the one beneath me. Folded me up like a dropped doll; something must have got severed inside. Don't hurt much, and I can't feel a lot of blood. But I don't think I can walk on it."

"Your gun . . ."

"Yeah, dropped it when I fell. I'm a fool for letting it go. Got no way to cover us now."

"I'll get it." And before Cowley could protest, Shep dropped to his belly and slithered the few feet to the revolver. He laid a hand on it when a shot pinged out, furrowing in the dirt about four feet before him.

Shep kept low and snatched the gun to him, amazed he'd not been shot. He hadn't seen the shooter leave the safety of the wagons. There were stacked supplies beyond it. So why wasn't someone closing in on this crazy man?

"Soldier, I think," said Shep, raking his ragged cuff across his eyes quickly.

"Why?" said Cowley.

"No idea," said Shep, "just a guess, sir." Though he knew it was more of a question from Cowley to himself. It occurred to Shep that to a man such as Cowley, a career Army man, the notion of a soldier opening fire on others of his kind was unimaginable.

"Can you shift enough to crawl backward?"

"Don't know . . . might draw him out."

"Good," said Shep, keeping the revolver half-raised in the direction of the man. "All I need is one clear shot."

"Too far, Royle. No man with a revolver can shoot decent at that distance."

"I can. Or at least I can try. You game?"

"Yeah, okay. Better than sitting out here waiting to get shot again. Might as well try to save ourselves."

Shep palmed the half-cocked gun and thumbed the hammer back the rest of the way and pinched off a shot, all in one motion. It pocked the wagon. Even as it hit, Shep was skittering backward to Cowley.

"Fool boy!" growled the older soldier. He'd shoved himself up onto his elbow and reached out for the gun. Shep ignored him.

"Sir, I am a good shot. Let me cover you and you can get back to safety."

"I told you I can't walk!"

"Nobody said a thing about walking. Just drag yourself back there. Belly down or on your back with your good foot and elbows, I don't know. But I'll cover you."

"Boy, you don't need to do this. You're risking your neck."

"You eat at the mess hall, right?" Shep grinned at the man, then swiveled his gaze back toward the wagon. "Same thing."

Cowley groaned. Shep could not tell if it was because of his joke or the pain. Then Shep saw the blood beneath the big man's

ON THE ROYLE RANGE

left leg. No wonder he couldn't feel blood; it was all leaching into the gritty packed earth of the marching grounds.

"I'll help you, sir."

Cowley snorted, and Shep saw that the big man's face had taken on a grim, gray color. "How?"

"Like this," he said, skirting around the man's head, keeping his eye as much as he was able on the parked wagon. No more shots drilled out. Shep positioned himself behind the sergeant's shoulders and head and, with the revolver in his right hand, he looped his left beneath the big man's upper armpit.

Cowley said, "Fool boy!" But he went with it nonetheless. Shep knew it was the only way, despite the big man's grunts and gasps of pain. If he didn't get Cowley help soon, or at least to a place in hiding where he could tourniquet the leg, the man might bleed to death.

"Time, no time," said Shep.

"Huh?"

Shep ignored it and said, "Can you jam in with your good foot? I'll drag you on your back. We can do it, sir!"

And they did, but not without another bullet whistling in from the rogue shooter, chasing them. It came close enough that gravel sprayed at them.

They both offered low yelps of surprise, but the shot hastened them.

With the speed of a snake strike, Shep sent a shot in return. It didn't strike wood, so he assumed it went beyond, wasted. But hopefully it bought them enough fear time from the shooter to get to the safety of the building he'd emerged from, away from the sights of the rogue.

It worked, and they each held their breath as Shep set down the pistol behind the barracks. He helped the big man, who was clearly losing strength, to drag back behind the wall, beyond the corner, and to safety. They each held their breath until the sergeant's last inch of boot was pulled to safety.

Just then a low running sound came up behind Shep, along the side of the building. He snatched up the revolver and spun, ready to fire.

"Royle! Don't shoot, it's me!"

The *me* happened to be one of Shep's latrine-digging fellows, a decent, if fey, young lad named Wilkins.

"Wilkins! Sarge has been hit. Go get help as fast as you are able. Medics, a stretcher." Wilkins nodded and began to race toward the corner of the building.

"Not that way, man!" Shep pointed with the revolver. "Behind! Go around! And run as fast as you've ever run in your life!"

"Yes, sir!" said Wilkins, his eyes as big as coffee cups. He bolted and was soon gone from sight.

"Sir, I have to tourniquet that leg of yours. It's bleeding something fierce."

"Okay . . . you know what you're doing?"

"Yep, had similar troubles back down in Texas."

"Okay, then. Have at it. I am in no mood to die today."

"Yes, sir. Not on my watch, sir." Shep kept chatting like that, forcing responses from the man, who, Shep thought, seemed to be in decent enough shape, considering the situation.

He stripped off his own leather braces and used them to cinch the wound, halfway up the sergeant's beefy left leg. "This is going to hurt, sir." Shep didn't wait for the man to nod approval, but pulled hard, the flesh bulging to either side of the leather.

Cowley's teeth ground tight together, and he breathed hard, spittling through his teeth. He nodded. "Okay, okay."

And they waited for long moments. No sounds rose up from across the field. And then they did—the voices of a dozen soldiers from all directions descended on the shooter's hiding place. Shep and Cowley watched the proceedings with increasing confidence that the ordeal was over, the shooter taken in hand.

Oddly, they didn't see anyone being led on out of there in

manacles. And then they saw a body being hauled away on a stretcher. From the sagged, flopping arm and wagging boots, they saw two things: the shooter wore soldier's garb, and he was likely dead.

"Looks like that second shot found its target, Royle. That's some shooting."

Shep let out a long sigh, not wholly pleased that he'd taken a life. "No more good times and tea parties for him, eh, Sergeant?"

Shep regretted saying it even before he gave voice to the thought. It sounded petty and childish, though he'd only meant it as a bit of a joke, something he always did in a grim situation to ease the tension. But now Shep regretted every single little sound of it. And yet there it was, out and running around the world.

"I'm sorry, sir," said Shep in a gasping whisper, certain of what would come of it already tracing lines of deep fear and agony on his face. "It just slipped out!"

To Shep's great surprise, Cowley smirked and shook his head. "I know, I know."

"You do?"

"Sure thing, boy. You think I was always this kind, caring person? Nah, was a time when I joined up, I was just like you."

"You . . . you were?"

"Sure. I was an idiot, too. Only thing that kept me from keeping on being one was Sergeant Driscoll, as I recall. He cared enough to keep me fearful and walking the line."

"Yes, sir. I'm so sorry about saying that, sir."

"That's another thing, Royle. Stop apologizing so much. Once in a while, it shows a man has a conscience and some kindness in his bones. But all the time and it just tells everybody he's weak in the head. You weak in the head, boy?"

"No, sir."

Cowley nodded. "I know you aren't."

"Yes, sir. Thank you, sir."

Cowley stretched his good leg, moving both feet and wincing, then rolling his shoulders and flexing his fingers.

"May I ask, sir . . . what happened to him?"

"What happened to who?"

"Driscoll, sir."

Cowley smiled and looked past Shep's shoulder at the medics hot-footing toward them, carrying a stretcher. "Oh, he's still kicking, far as we know. Retired from army life. Went out west, Colorado way, I believe, looking for gold or some such fool thing. But you didn't hear that from me. Man might be older now, but he can still kick my backside, you hear? And I need to keep on his good side."

"Why's that, if you don't mind me asking."

Again, Cowley grinned. "Because I up and married his daughter, that's why."

Shep's raised eyebrows were his only response. Then Cowley's eyes narrowed again, and he flicked that big sausage finger out once more, ramming it into Shep's chest. "Don't you ever play me false again, you hear? You stick to the routine, learn everything that needs learning, and you'll get through this okay, and hopefully with something more to show for it than that bitter look on your face. You hear?"

"Yes, sir."

"Good. Now, I expect the captain will want to talk to you. Until they send for you, I want you and those other tenderfeet to get back to work!"

Shep stood fast and nodding, walked backward a few steps, then saluted and spun and bolted for the half-dug hole he'd left behind.

A few minutes later, as he dug, squaring up the sides and making a proper job of it, he wondered, right before he chastised himself for daydreaming again, if Cowley had a daughter. The thought of what she might look like caused a shiver of fear to ripple up his spine.

He focused on slicing out dirt and scooping it up and out of his hole. His perfect latrine hole.

Two days later, having been quizzed and lauded in equal measure for his part in the unfortunate incident, Private Shepley Royle made his way toward the infirmary to visit Sergeant Cowley. He mused on the last few days with the wide-eyed wonder that follows strange circumstances.

He'd learned that the shooter had been a fellow private, a man named Hugh Lanser, no one Shep had been acquainted with. The man had never adjusted to life in the army, and had displayed increasingly odd behavior until he finally did not show up for work duty that day.

Instead, Lanser had stolen a rifle and bullets and hidden himself in the midst of that stack of crates and wagons. And then he'd begun shooting, apparently trying to kill anyone he saw. It was Sergeant Cowley's poor luck to be that first person the shooter sighted on.

When Shep arrived at the infirmary, he noticed the sergeant was the only man in the sick ward. Shep also noticed a pretty young woman, just about his age, standing at Cowley's bedside.

She held the big man's hand and kissed the scarred knuckles. Then Cowley patted her arm and said, "Oh, I'm all right, child. Tell your mama. You two need to stop worrying so. And tell her I appreciate the pie, but I can't eat that in here!" He chuckled; then his eyes fell on Shep standing in the doorway.

The girl followed Cowley's gaze and turned. She looked at Shep, and their eyes met across the fifteen or so feet between them. They stood like that for a long moment; then Cowley cleared his throat.

The two youngsters both jerked as if awakened from a reverie.

"Private Royle, this is my daughter, Philomena Cowley. And Philly, dear, this is the young man who saved my crusty old hide."

Shep felt himself reddening. "Oh, no, sir. You didn't need me. You were—"

"Nonsense, Royle. Now, what do you want?"

"Papa!" said the pretty young woman, her eyebrows rising. "That's a terrible thing to say to this young man."

Shep shook his head. "It wasn't anything anyone else would have done."

"Nonsense," said Miss Cowley. "That shot was impressive."

Shep didn't think his face could get any redder. He mumbled, "Thank you, ma'am," and looked away as she bent to kiss her father's cheek. "I'll be back later to play cards, Papa. Until then, you rest. Or I'll send Mama."

"Oh, no, not that. She'll start telling everybody what to do, change my dressing, all of it. I'll never heal!"

The young woman, her pretty dark eyes and equally dark hair long and pulled back in a fashionable style on both sides of her head, walked by Shep.

He saw that her neck was beautiful, but paled in comparison with her face . . . and everything else about her. She offered him a slight smile and nod of the head, and he bowed and mumbled, "Ma'am," as she walked.

He watched her walk down the hallway toward the front door and out into the bright day. He wondered what it would be like to walk in the sunshine with her. A loud, low growl snapped him from his daydream, and he turned to see Sergeant Cowley glaring at him from his bed and curling a big finger, beckoning him closer.

Shep walked over, redder than ever. Cowley kept beckoning him until Shep's face was bent close to the big man's own narrow-eyed face.

The sergeant grabbed him by the front of his tunic and yanked him close, balling his shirtfront in a big fist. He poked a big finger in Shep's face.

"Don't even think it, boy. No, no, and never."

Shep gulped. "Sir?"

"Don't 'sir' me. You know and I know and . . . no!"

Their chat was a brief one, during which Shep tried his best to listen. He heard something about thanks, about getting a commendation from the Army, and other bits of information that he'd nodded and said, "Sir, yes, sir," to, and then he left.

Once outside, he looked left and right and left and right again. Much to Shep's disappointment, he saw nobody who looked even a little bit like Sergeant Cowley's pretty daughter.

Still, on his way back to the barracks, he smiled and whistled a low, jaunty tune and rubbed his chin. He might just have to shower and shave a little more often.

Chapter 3

"How long has it been?" asked Regis, looking to his right at the tall, lithe woman who walked beside him. Her long black dress fit her well, and even her veil, something he'd only ever seen her wear, somehow seemed just right on her.

She shrugged. "Some time, I don't know how long. I . . . I don't measure life in terms of time like that."

Regis stopped. They were walking side by side along the river through one of his favorite stretches on the ranch. A low, pleasant breeze ruffled the long seed heads of the gamma grass, silvering the landscape as it traveled over the rolling land.

"What does that mean?" He looked at her, intrigued by this strange, bewitching woman who, to date, had not let him do much more than take her hand in his twice.

She stopped as well, and, as was her way, as Regis had begun to realize, she walked ahead by a half step and looked out across the same vista. What was she seeing there that he wasn't?

"I mean"—she turned to face him—"that as I was raised largely in the convent, time ceased to mean much. Time in the traditional sense, that is."

"Hmm," he said. "I don't know as I could function from day to day without at least taking a look at the sky to get a sense of where the sun is. If I don't get the men up and out and doing their chores and then back for breakfast and then getting their day's assignments, why, I'm not so certain anything would get done."

As usual in her presence, as soon as he spoke, Regis began combing through the words he'd just uttered. What had he really said, and how would she take it?

She did not mock him, but regarded him through her veil.

"I did not seek you out, Regis. Remember that—you came seeking something, and I was there. And despite what you have found in me, you sought me out again and again."

"Not despite what I found. Because of what I found, Marietta."

Again he reached for her hand, the left, and held it but a moment before she pulled it away and half-turned from him once more. "You are a strange man, Regis."

Hearing her say his name still gave him a little zing up his back. He said nothing, as again he was uncertain what she meant. Every conversation with her was a pleasure and a challenge, and whenever they parted, he always felt slightly hollowed out, as if she had tired him. And he supposed she had, for she made him think like no other person he had ever met. She made him look at himself, inside himself, and wonder what he was doing.

"Why, Regis?" She faced him. "Why do you seek me out?"

This was one of the first times he could recall that she asked him a question in so straightforward a manner. Her statements and occasional questions were usually more cryptic.

"I thought that had become obvious, Marietta."

"No," she said, and shook her head. "No, I do not think so. Not to me."

He drew in a deep breath, aware that the words he had long wondered if he would ever say to a woman were about to come forth. "I . . . have become in love with you."

"Become?" She almost sounded as if she were laughing. "That is a curious way of wording such a sentiment."

For once, Regis did not know how to react, did not know what to say.

"Regis, why do you say this to me? You do not know me."

"I feel as though I do. I know enough about you to say so."

She shook her head. "You cannot know me. Not this way."

"I . . . Marietta, I want to. I want to know you more."

She did not walk away, did not shake her head, but looked at him. At least, as he always wondered, he thought she was looking at him. She faced him, but the long, black veil that obscured most of her features, even in sunlight, was, as always, pulled down.

"There is one thing that will put this talk to a stop," she said, in her endearing way of speaking that was, to his ears, perfect. It was obvious she had been highly educated, yet also was a child of the Spanish language first, and of English second, though barely.

"Foolish talk," she said, quieter, as if to herself. Then she half-turned from him once more and did the thing he had longed for her to do since he had met her in that cave so many months before.

Since then, their meetings had been occasional and, as she had said, instigated by him. But not only because he sought what he had quickly learned was her wise counsel, but because he was intrigued by her.

And all that without having so much as seen her face, let alone kiss her. That she was possessed of a comely body, he already knew. Her dresses, though black, and unadorned with frills or much more than lace accents, were nonetheless fitting to her long, slender form.

She spoke well, carried herself well, and was still a complete mystery to him.

To make matters even stranger, regarding business she was, as he and his business partner, Cormac Delany, had learned through their lawyer's digging into the roots of the Spanish Land Grants on his ranch, the sole heir to that land, what he had considered his land, his beloved ranch.

But soon after meeting her, he realized she was fast becoming as important to him, perhaps more so, than the ranch. The thought frightened him, unnerved him, bothered him to his roots, and yes, it even thrilled him.

And now, here she was, about to do the very thing he had longed for her to do—reveal her face to him, a face he had learned had been damaged by the kick of a horse when she was but a young girl.

Despite the fact that she had been the eldest child in the family, and thus the sole heir to the Valdez family's fortunes, waxing and waning as they had over the years, they had been shamed by her malformed presence and had sent her to be raised in a nunnery, a convent.

She had left there of her own volition and had, as he had read of St. Francis, taken up residence in a not-uninviting cave. It offered her a grotto and a small oasis with a clear, bubbling, spring-fed pool in a basin of rock. That was where he had found her the first time he returned there to seek her out.

And now, standing here before him, some distance from that cave ground, she was raising her arms to lift the veil from her face. Did he want this? Would it ruin something that existed only in his head, in his heart? That very heart thumped in his chest. Was this something that might forever change their budding relationship? For it was not something she had wanted to do.

She stopped, her hands half raised. "This will tell me truly."

He reached out and touched her near arm. "Marietta, no. If you're not ready, then no. I can wait."

"Wait for what? Until you have convinced me you love me enough to own the Santa Calina? And then what? Then you will discard me."

He jerked, taking a stumbling step back, as if she had slapped him hard across the face. "Is that what you think this is? Is that what you think I have been doing—seeking you out only to gain control of the ranch?"

"Is it not?" she said.

A welter of raw feelings bubbled up inside Regis Royle's mind, his breast, his mouth. Words struggled to escape, hot words that would sting her as he had been stung. But no, he could not do that to her.

He shook his head and walked away, striding a good ten paces or more. Then he slowed to a stop and he stood that way, with his back to her. He did not know what to do now. He had bared himself as he had never before with a woman, with anyone, really, and it had not gone at all as he had imagined. Or as he had hoped.

Regis expected that when he turned around, she would have vanished, as she had proven to be most capable of, silent and cat-like. He might never see her again. That sudden, awful thought gripped him inside, and he turned quickly.

She still stood there, but now she was not veiled. The left side of her face angled toward him. Her arms were crossed, and with the breeze ruffling the veil out behind her slightly, she turned her head to face him in full.

The right side of her face was indeed disfigured, but time and scarring had left her as they needed to. A long, pink, raised scar stretched along its length, ran from high on her cheekbone and curved down along her jawline to meet the right corner of her mouth.

"I did not want to show you . . . this." She gestured with long fingers toward her face, taking care to keep her left side to him. Even then he saw the glistening of tears forming.

"But you did," he said softly. "That means you trust me. And that is all I could ask for. Forever, in fact. Perhaps you might come to love me."

"Love?" she stifled a little snort of mockery, a tone he'd not heard from her.

Again, a warring, potent mix of emotions bubbled in him. He looked down at her. "Woman," he said, his nostrils flexing. "Take the ranch, take everything I have, and you are welcome to it. I'll sign it all to you. As for me, I will be content to one day earn your love."

Regis let his big hands fall to his sides, and he shrugged. "That is all I have, all I can offer you."

She did something then that he could not have imagined so strong a woman such as this might do. She took that half step toward him and leaned her forehead against his broad chest.

Instinct brought his big hands up to wrap around her. Though he knew her as a strong, bold woman, in stature and in conviction, he was surprised, too, at how slender and slight she felt beneath his arms. He also was amazed at how very right holding her in such an embrace felt. He could stay that way forever and never tire of it, that much he was certain of.

"Why?" she said.

Her voice was barely a whisper, and he knew from the sound of it that she was sobbing.

"Why?" he repeated her question. "Marietta, no one in all of the world's long history has ever been able to explain the why of love. All I know is that I don't need an answer to it, any more than to say that I love you. And that is enough."

She said nothing, but he sensed that she had relaxed into him, into his embrace. Her tenseness had abated, and she turned her face to one side, still not pulling away from him or looking up at him.

"Might I dare to hope that one day you, too, might feel the same toward me?" His voice was hoarse, a low, crude whisper.

She nodded. "I already do." Her words, too, were whispered.

Regis let his eyes close, and he let go a breath he had not realized he'd held. He lightly rested his chin on the top of her head and held her close. Never, never had he felt such happiness. No, that was too weak a word. Elation, perhaps. Come what may in life, he thought, we will have this moment.

Sometime later, she pulled away gently from him and, perhaps out of instinct, turned the unmarred side of her face toward him.

Regis touched her chin and gently turned her head so that she faced him in full once more. He looked into her eyes. "Marietta, you are the most beautiful woman I have ever known."

"Then you have not known many women."

To this, Regis said nothing. He just gazed into her eyes. He reckoned he was learning.

Chapter 4

"For the last time, I tell you there isn't going to be any cursed war! At least not any time soon." Cormac Delany growled and chewed the soggy end of his cigar until it turned to mush in his mouth.

"Bah!" he growled again and spat the sodden remnants into the spittoon by his feet behind the desk.

Regis sat in his usual spot before the desk, big arms folded, and he gazed at his longtime business partner. The grizzled older fellow he saw before him now had changed these past couple of years. This man—a father figure to him more so than anyone had ever been—looked just plain rough.

Regis knew for certain that he himself had had a whole lot to do with this transformation in his friend. It pained him to see it, and it pained him even more to admit to himself that he was largely responsible for this change. And it wasn't just Cormac's appearance. The slightly paunched man had always seemed a bit tattered about the edges, even back some years when they were both captaining vessels in their growing line of steamship traders, coast hugging and river riding.

Some years back, they had set up an office and had hired other men, capable men all, to do the day-to-day shipping and cruising. Cormac and Regis still kept a hand in and would, periodically, take to the water once more. Though they never did this with any regularity, in part so they might catch their crews off guard.

It was important to keep an honest eye on proceedings. Yet as the business grew, Regis found himself gravitating less and less to the water and more and more inland. He reckoned it was that innate, inner urge that led him to seek such things.

There was that word again that Marietta had used. And it was true, Regis was always seeking something, in life, be it wisdom or place. He craved new experiences, new insights, something that might make his next minute, hour, day, week, month, or year more exciting.

He'd come to realize that Shep was built the same way.

"Look, Cormac, I never said I thought we were headed for a war, though I think we are. Might not be next month, but in time it's bound to happen. What I said was that in the past, when men have been fighting, whether we agreed with it or not, our shipping business did well, money-wise."

The older man looked up from the ledger and stared hard at Regis as if he'd never seen the man before. "What did you say?"

"Come on, Cormac, you heard me."

Cormac rubbed his face and stood, his fingers steepled on the cluttered desktop. "I thought that's what you said." He leaned forward. "Is that all you're concerned with? That we make money? I know we're in it up to here!" He held a pudgy hand about a foot above his head. "And I know it's largely your doing."

Regis felt his face redden. What the man was saying was all true, but that didn't mean he had to sit here and take it. They'd been down this road too many times before. "I thought we already traveled this path, Cormac. And I thought we'd come to an agreement. I told you I would not risk any more of our money on buying land around the ranch."

"Good! It's already the biggest ranch I've ever heard of. Now we just have to figure out a way to pay for it without going belly up." He shook his head.

"That's the only reason I mentioned that during wars, freighting transport outfits such as ours tend to make money."

"I know that! You don't think I don't know that? Heck, Regis Royle, I taught you everything you know about shipping, didn't I? I didn't get to where I am by being a fool!"

"Look, Cormac, I didn't come here to argue with you. I—"

"Then why did you show up? I hope it's to tell me you figured out a way to make more money, to help pay for your outlandish spending of our money—our money—on land."

Regis stood before the desk. His eyes were closed, but his jaw muscles bunched and jumped as he fought down the urge to bellow in his senior partner's face. He did deserve this sort of treatment, after all. But he'd received it in full three times now, and he wondered how many more times he would have to do so.

"Yes," said Cormac, as if reading Regis's mind. "We should be through with this discussion, but as you can tell, I'm still steamed about it all. I thought I could keep my mouth shut, and if the crazy spending ceased, I'd be okay. But it hasn't worked out that way." Cormac shook his head.

Regis softened his voice. "How bad is it, Cormac?"

Cormac, too, paused, and then rubbed his face again, as if he were washing it up and down with his palms. "It's not good. That's why I'm so worked up."

"I figured, yeah."

"Yeah, well, did you make any headway with that woman?"

"I told you, Cormac, we can talk about most anything, but not her."

Cormac snorted and shook his head. "Look, far be it from me

to tell you how to spend your time or who to spend it with. But this infatuation you have with the Valdez woman . . . Regis, it can't end well, you know that, don't you?"

"No, actually, I don't."

"Look, I don't know her."

"That's right, you don't."

"But I do know that she's the rightful heir to the property you bought on our behalf."

"So?"

"So"—Cormac held up a hand to placate the large younger man—"now hear me out. Just suppose she was the one taking you for a stroll."

"What does that even mean?"

"It means what if she's stringing you along."

"For what reason would she do that, Cormac?"

"Just answer the question."

Regis bit back hard and fast by leaning over the desk and sticking a big ol' digit right in Cormac's face. "Not acceptable, man, and you know it."

"Maybe not, but you didn't answer the question."

"Why would she do that? What would she gain? If she's the true heir, and if our ownership is null, then she'll have the land anyway."

"Oh, Regis," said Cormac, sinking back into his chair with a sigh.

Regis walked to the door. "I have some things to tend to here in town. I'll stop back in an hour. Do me one favor—have a figure for me."

"A figure?"

"Yeah," said Regis. "A dollar amount of what it will take for the next three months to cover our expenses. And I'll get the money to you as soon as I can. Okay?"

Instead of waiting for an answer, Regis walked out, closing the door firmly behind him. Out on the street, he breathed in deeply of the dust, the dung, and the sun-puckered boards that made up Brownsville, Texas.

How he was going to pull this off, he had no idea. But he had to do it. Or risk losing Cormac, the ranch, and Marietta. And of all of them, if it came down to a choice, he would not lose the last of them. No way.

Chapter 5

Jarvis "Bone" McGraw, a famous former, and now again, Texas Ranger, shook his head and wondered how in the heck he got himself into this mess. He nudged his horse, a big gray gelding named Bub, down a steep embankment. The horse did not want to go and balked, stiff-legged, kicking up gravel and sending fist-sized rocks tumbling down to the bottom of the dry gulch.

His old ranch hand, Ramon, affable, morose, and kind all at once, had been out walking with his donkey, Tomatillo, and had spied cougar tracks down this way. Bone knew if he let that stand, he would end up with dead beeves and a full-bellied cat roaming his property who thought it could get away with this sort of behavior any ol' time it wanted to.

"Not a prayer," mumbled Bone, trying and not succeeding to forget, if only for the moment, the dang fool thing he did recently. He'd agreed to head up the newly reformed Texas Rangers.

He had no intention of doing so when he'd set out with the young Texas Ranger Howard Strickland, but a few months before to do his old friend, Captain Sam Fiedler, uncle to the young man, a favor. He and Fiedler had served together, years before, as Rangers back when the outfit was a ragtag mess with more gut and spit than experience.

But the mission with young Strickland, which was supposed to have been a brief scouting job, had been a mistake from the moment he'd warily agreed to go. Margaret had all but forced him to go, her logic being that it sounded like a simple enough mission, and he'd be doing an old friend a mighty favor.

And hopefully, she said, he'd get this Rangering stuff out of his blood for good. She had talked about wanting a child, something Bone, who was a few years her senior, had never thought would be possible for him.

But she was keen, and he wouldn't mind having a little version of either of them scampering around the place. Heck, he'd said just this morning, why stop at one? He'd said that to her, and she gave him a stern look. "You thinking of carrying a herd of them around in your belly, then?"

He'd turned red and kissed her on the forehead. "Ramon's waiting on me. I hope I won't be too late, but I have to go look for that big cat he saw tracks of off in the northwest corner of the spread once we're finished cobbling together that corral."

"That's fine," she'd said, "I'll have warm food for you."

"And a warm bed?"

"Start with the food and see how far you get, mister."

And now, on the trail, and making for the clutter of big boulders that almost perfectly pinpointed the northwest corner of his ranch, Bone pulled up short at the bottom of the draw and let the big horse get his wits back.

He had to keep reminding himself that Bub was not Buck, his big grulla that was shot from under him by unseen, vicious varmints, the very gang who laid low young Strickland.

He sat the horse and let the memory of that awful day wash over him once more, as it had nearly every day since then. Time was working its mysterious balm on his mind, but too slowly to prevent the grief that came with even the slimmest of those memories.

Bone had found the boy dead, humped on his side in the dirt, not where he'd told the young man to stay and wait for him. He'd gone to scout and had expected the kid, the junior ranger among them, to listen to Bone and to heed him. But he hadn't.

Then Bone had been pinned down, forced to finish off his beloved Buck, a horse he'd ridden with for many long years. In all that time, they'd come to know each other so well. And then he'd had to huddle behind good old Buck's corpse for a day, then two.

He still had no clear recollection of that time. He'd had no water, the canteen having been blasted apart by the malicious shooter. And then Regis Royle, his old friend, had ridden out that way after Margaret had told him where he might find Bone.

Regis had only expected to find Bone riding casually back from their scouting mission. Not pinned by death dealers and knocking on the gates of Hades himself.

After a day of rest and healing, far shorter than Margaret and Regis wanted for him, Bone shook his head and insisted on telling the boy's uncle, Sam Fiedler, Bone's old Rangering friend, as well as the boy's mother, the wife of another old Ranger Bone had ridden with—until he'd been killed in the line of duty, as well. And now her son was dead.

What was that poor woman to do? The thought continued to torment Bone. He'd told her the awful news, insisting that it was his own fault, for that's what Bone chose to believe, told himself he had to believe, in the deepest, dankest chambers of his heart.

Mired in these thoughts, Bone nudged the big horse onward, toward the base of the upthrust of boulders and raw, jutting sandstone.

It was the horse's low whicker that pulled him back from within his reverie of pity. But not in time to prepare for the near-silent, sidelong leap of the big, tawny cat.

Its shadow presaged its brute collision with him, its claws raking at him before it collided into him. And when it did, the spasming, muscled beast slammed into Bone's right side, having leapt from a broad rock slope beneath a shaded declivity six feet above where Bub chose his path with deliberation.

Bone barely had time to yelp an oath of shock before he was shoved from the saddle, jerking to his left as if a wide loop had settled over him and then tugged hard by five burly men.

Before he slammed to the dusty earth, his head smacked a clot of fist-sized rocks inches from a boulder that would have rendered his pate a smashed thing beyond any possibility of healing.

The impact of the pounce carried the lion a dozen feet beyond Bone and the horse, and it slammed into rock and gravel, rolling headfirst over itself, but not hard enough to lay it low. Instead, it spun and lunged, clawing gravel and giving voice to a buzzing, low, chesty growl that bust out of its fanged maw as a cold, scraping scream. Then it landed once more on Bone.

Even in the midst of this brute struggle, he was grateful. For the fall, as brutal as it had been, had not killed him. He knew he was still very much alive, because he felt the relentless beast slam into him once more, heard its freakish scream, felt its bristling whiskers swipe his face as its brutal claws raked over him, digging in, popping his flesh through his canvas chore coat, his neck, and the left side of his head.

He'd lost his hat in the fall. And his horse. Bub had bolted as soon as the cat collided with them, taking with him Bone's rifle slamming in its scabbard, and the rest of his gear.

The smacking his head took dizzied him, but did not render him unconscious. He cursed himself for a fool as he fought, felt the beast have its way with him, slamming him, jerking him this way and that as though he were nothing more than a child's rag-stuffed doll.

His efforts to protect himself grew weaker, and the thought came to him that he might well die right there and then. And would that be so bad? Was he even of use to anyone anymore? Had he not gotten that young man killed? No, Bone told himself, he was an old ranger, little more, with a small ranch and an old Mexican working for him.

And then Margaret's beautiful face came to him, and he recalled how much grief she'd had in her life already, how she'd been lured West by a brute who beat her mercilessly. She'd escaped his clutches only to be kidnapped by murderous slavers. Bone and the men were on their way to sell her and other women in Mexico.

No, man, no! He would not, could not be the thing to crush the last of that wonderful woman's life, her soul, her kindness from her. He cursed himself and bit back his bitter wad of pity and bile, and though the cat continued to claw and lash at him, he now fought back with everything his battered ranger body had.

The only thing he could think of doing to best the creature was to match it fang for fang, claw for claw. And as he was a paltry human equipped with blunt teeth and pathetic claws, Bone had to rely on a tool for the job.

The beast raked him and screamed at him and kept trying to bite his neck and his head. Bone knew that if the vicious creature managed to clamp its jaws anywhere near his neck and sink fang in the doing, then he was a dead man. So he risked freeing one hand from the struggle to keep the beast away from his vitals and raked at his own claw, in the form of his sheath knife.

It hung at his right side, and the handle, a ridged, hefty thing made of antler and steel, was secured with a leather thong. He cursed himself for securing it too tightly, rendering it nearly useless now in this dicey situation.

He wrapped his steely fingers around the handle and jerked at it once, twice to free it from the sheath, and on the third, when he jerked the knife upward, he shouted even louder than he had been bellowing.

At the sound of his shout, for a hair of a second, startled the mauling cat, though that resulted in little more than the cat jerking its head back, eyes wide, for another lunge.

The attempt was also the one that worked, for the knife was now free of the sheath.

Bone wasted no precious moments, and no movements, but drove the blade upward at the jerking, writhing, thrashing, tawny body of the beast.

It hit bone, ribs, and would have bounced off, causing a gash in the beast's skin, but little more, had the rancher not sensed this was going to happen, felt it beginning to happen. He flexed his tight grip forward, twisting the knife slightly, and kept shoving.

The blade, a long thing, and wide, and kept keen-edged, slid into the animal's chest, angling in from the side, all the way to the hilt.

In the time it takes to pull in a breath, the frenzied cat seized, a low growl ripping skyward, rising higher into a scream.

The bloodied, thick-bristled face jerked upward, as if the cat were looking to the sky for a reason behind this sudden, mortal pain inflicted on it.

The cat spasmed, tremors rippling up and down its long body; then it stiffened and collapsed. Atop Bone McGraw.

The action forced out the last of what breath there was in Bone's chest, and he wheezed, gasping, shoving at the dead animal. Alive, it had been frightening and filled with bloodlust and rage. And dead, it felt twice as big and twice as weighty. He knew if he didn't get it off himself, he might die beneath it, weakened as he had become in the tearing, thrashing, brutal fight.

Later, he could recall but snatches of memories, as if he'd pieced them together from someone else's retelling. He remembered shoving the beast from him. Then he had a memory of trying to free the knife, but of it not budging. Then he crawled, saw the big, skittish horse some distance away, but it would not let him get near it, so frightening did he seem to it.

Then he remembered the inky darkness of nighttime, and coldness. He heard coyotes all around, but saw none. Shivering as if his entire body might rattle apart. And he remembered hot, searing pain overtaking his body in wave after wave, unending.

Then he remembered voices, shouting, boots crunching gravel, the glow of a light swinging. Maybe this is heaven, he thought, feeling confused because he had always assumed it would be bright, like a fine day in spring. If it's not heaven, then maybe help has come, he thought. He tried to shout, but the effort yanked a flaming barbed chain up through him, from his guts to his head. He kept trying. And then the voices and light grew louder, brighter.

The next thing he knew, he was waking up at home, in the little pretty ranch house, pretty because Margaret had made it so. And it was now a home because of her, too. And there she was, her serious face close to his peering at him, with concern.

"Hi," he said, wincing in pain as he did so.

"Hi you," she whispered. And then she did something that he'd rarely seen her do, despite everything she'd been through in life.

She wept, and Bone knew he was going to make it.

"My word, Bone." Regis looked over at his bedridden friend. "You've had a rough run of luck these past few months, no lie."

Bone looked over at his old friend, Regis Royle, and something niggled at the back of his mind. He knew this man better than a whole lot of other folks knew him. Regis wanted something. And sure enough, Regis didn't disappoint . . .

"Look, Bone, I'll come right out with it. I need help."

Bone smirked and looked at the white-painted plank ceiling. "I don't doubt that, Regis. And you will recall I told you after you brought me back that I'd give you and your ranch what time I could, but that I had too much to do for it to last. Besides, you have Tut and Lockjaw and Fergus and Percy. And plenty other capable men. I should know. I trained them."

"Yeah, but Bone, I . . . I need your help." Regis held up a big hand and slid the chair closer to the bed, then glanced toward the open door. "You see . . ."

Bone gazed at his old friend through narrowed eyes. He'd seen this look on Regis Royle's face before. Many times. It always came just before a big announcement that nearly always cost somebody a whole lot of something, usually time, money, and more.

Regis couldn't help but smile. "Here's what I intend to do."

"Why am I feeling worried, all sudden like?"

"No, no, it's not like that. See, I'm planning on sending a herd up to the rail head."

Bone waited a few moments. "Uh-huh, that sounds about right. Not a new idea, though. You said you were going to do that six months ago come spring."

"Right," said Regis, nodding. "But I'm going to send them to the rail head . . . in Schiller, Colorado Territory."

"Colorado Territory?" said Bone. "Why that far?"

"The cursed Army has put a lockdown on the rail lines moving in and out of the big rail hubs anywhere closer. Besides, I've corresponded with a buyer who's interested in long-term contracts."

"So you're going to send your herd with one of the other big boys?"

"Nope," said Regis. His smiled widened. "Going to do it ourselves."

"Oh, really."

"Yep."

"Regis, have you ever been on a cattle drive before?"

"Nope," said Regis, folding his arms and smiling and leaning back in the chair. It creaked a little.

"Well, I have," said Bone, shaking his head.

"I know." Regis kept his eyes on Bone and his smile in place.

"What? Oh no, no. Now you don't think I'm—"

"Who else can do it, Bone?"

"Anybody else who has a little experience, that's all."

"Nope. I want you to ramrod the entire thing." He said it as if he were bestowing on his laid-up friend one heck of a life-altering favor.

Bone leaned back and held his tongue for a moment. Finally, he spoke. But first he grinned, a wry look pulling his mouth into a half-frown that seemed to match his demeanor. He slowly shook his head. "Not going to happen, Regis."

The big rancher's smile slipped a little. "What do you mean?"

"Regis." Bone chuckled and stiffened, touching his side with a bandaged arm. Those busted ribs pained him whenever he moved. "Have you seen me here?" He raised his arm slightly. "I can barely move without wincing and whining."

"Yeah, but you're the toughest man I know. You heal fast. I've seen it! Besides, I need you, Bone. I can't run the ranch without having somebody I trust driving the cattle."

"Regis, the only person you've ever trusted is yourself. So why don't you just up and do it on your own!"

"Very funny, Bone. Look, you're not hearing me. If I don't get those cattle to the rail head, I will be sunk, don't you understand? I need this done, and you're the man for the job. Think of it—" He leaned closer and lowered his voice. "A couple of months away from the little woman, out there on the trail with the boys. Why, I'm almost envious of it, myself."

Again, Bone stared at Regis for long moments while Regis continued to give him that too-big smile, as if he had just offered Bone the keys to a mansion filled with gold doubloons.

"Regis, listen and listen hard to me. Between my own ranch, and being so lame I can barely move, and my commitment to helping the rangers in whatever way I am able as soon as I can get back up to normal moving speed, and most of all, because I most definitely do not want to spend even one night away from my wife, let alone what will likely be three months or more, there and back . . . there's no way I can even begin to think of anyone else's cattle. Don't you see that, man?"

As he spoke, Bone saw the smile slide from Regis's face. It was a look he'd seen a few times in the past; sometimes he'd been the one to cause it, sometimes others. It was the look of a man not accustomed to hearing the word *no*, and when Regis did hear it, he did not like it. Not one little bit.

Then Regis surprised him. "You said your 'wife.'"

Bone nodded. "Yeah, yeah I did."

"You didn't tell me you were going to wed."

"Didn't tell much of anybody. But you're wrong. I did try to tell you, back on one of your visits, but you were all worked up about the same thing you're always worked up about—money and not having enough of it to buy whatever it is you think you need to buy. Usually land."

"When was this?"

"Does it really matter, Regis?"

"No." He stood, fidgeting with his hat. "No, I guess not. Well, you got somebody to stand up for you, then."

Bone nodded. "Ramon."

"Good man. Well, um, okay then, Bone, I'll leave you be for now." Regis walked to the door, then stopped. "Oh, congratulations."

"Thank you, Regis."

"And you both . . . are you happy?"

Bone looked confused, but said, "Yeah, of course. Happiest I believe I have ever been."

"Good, that's good, Bone. Okay, then, well, I'll be seeing you."

He walked out, down the short hallway, and into the kitchen. ""Ma'am, I . . . congratulations to you. Your wedding. He's a good man."

"Thank you. I know." Margaret stood before the breadboard, a mound of floured dough before her.

"And he's lucky, too. I wish you both the very best."

"Thank you, Regis."

He offered her a weak smile, plunked his hat on his head, and shoved through the door.

Once she'd worked the dough and covered it to rise, Margaret leaned in and looked at Bone. "Jarvis, is he all right?"

Bone looked at the wall as if he could see the dooryard beyond and the slowly departing figure of the man on horseback. "I honestly don't know, my dear. But I wish him well."

Chapter 6

The next three weeks were among the most difficult of Regis Royle's life. And it was all because of his conversation with Bone McGraw, one of his oldest friends.

And the fact that the man who had always been there for him, the man who could always be counted on to do a thing when Regis needed it done, the man who always put everything else in his own life aside to attend to whatever it was Regis needed doing, had told him no. Flat-out no.

And that had been one heck of a slap to the face for Regis. And then Bone had told him that he was married.

Regis had assumed they would tie the knot, but he thought he'd be invited. And then he remembered that Bone had indeed tried to tell him. But . . . well, that brought Regis back to where he was, feeling hangdog guilty all over again for any number of reasons.

He'd run his and Cormac's business into the ground, taken out far too much credit in its name, and ticked off his old friend in the process. He'd run his one and only brother, Shepley, out of his life just when they were getting to know each other again after years of living separate lives. And all the men on his ranch—which might not even be his ranch, after all—nearly shook and quivered when he showed up. Was there anyone happy to see him anymore?

And then his thoughts turned to the mysterious Marietta. He was pretty certain she felt about him as he did about her. But it was so complicated, wasn't it? Here she was, the heiress to the land grant that owned the land on which his ranch sat. If she exerted her legal rights, Regis and Cormac could be set out on their ears, whistling in the dark, without a penny between them.

In the distance, he saw two, three lights, one of them low, the intermittent flicker of a campfire. That would be the boys, his men, eating their grub around the campfire. They still preferred that to sitting at the long tables they'd built under the ramada out front of the cook shack.

For some reason, the sight of that, and knowing that many of the several dozen men in his employ were there around that fire, enjoying brotherhood, filled him with a bold budding of his old confidence. But now, instead of stomping all over anybody and anything in his way to get what he wished for, he felt something like humility tempering it. And he didn't mind it.

As he walked through the low fog and dusky night from his cottage toward that campfire of Royle Ranch, the feeling grew. By the time he reached it, he had decided just what it was he would do, what he had to do. He would send cattle to market, yes, but he was the one who had to, who needed to ramrod the drive. Himself. All the way.

And if he failed, he could blame no one but himself. And if it succeeded, then so be it. It was no guarantee he'd save the ranch, but it would be a start.

The cook's wagon was anything but ready, and Percy Grimlaw, the best ranch cook Regis had ever come across, was not impressed. He'd come to know Percy when he and John "Tut" Tuttle had ridden in one day looking for work, back in the early days of the ranch.

It was hard to believe that was a mere few years back, thought Regis. Percy and Tut were pards, on the drift from another ranch and looking for work. They were lean (well, Percy was. Tut, on the other hand, was and always would be on the husky side) and keen and eager for work. They tucked in and showed more spit and gumption than a lot of men Regis had known. So they'd stayed.

Trouble was, Percy was not much interested in wrangling rangy cattle and spending his days a-horseback. Oh, he was capable of it and did as he was requested in those days, but his true gift was in how he cooked and what he could do with a paltry pile of ingredients.

Percy was also a prickly sort, quick-witted, sure, but sharp-tongued, too. It was all tolerable, because his food was so darned tasty. The rest of the men had put up with him for the same reasons Regis did.

But his surliness had, at times, caused Regis to reluctantly have a talk with the scowling young man. For a few days following their wee chats, Percy would be almost civil, but it wouldn't last. Trouble was, when he was at his orneriest, his culinary offerings were at their tastiest.

Regis had hoped when he'd approached Percy about the trail drive that he would put up a fight and tell him he did not want to go. But Percy had surprised him by almost smiling. "You bet, sure, I suppose I could come along. How many men will I be cooking for? I'll need a wagon and a helper. I can't be expected to lug water and chop wood and do all the driving and cooking, now can I?"

He shook his head and slid a bubbling pot of beans to one side of the big outdoor fire he cooked at. "And just who's going to sling grub for the ones left back here tending the ranch, huh?"

Regis realized he hadn't thought this through properly before talking with Percy. And then, as was always the case with Percy, Regis recalled a few moments too late that he was the boss of this outfit anyway.

He pulled in a deep breath and said, "Now look, Percy, don't push your luck!" He pointed a finger at the young man. "You don't like the way things are run here, you are welcome to hit the trail!"

"Bah, boss. Bah! You tried that one last time. Work on something new. And you're in my way, shift aside, will you? And find me a decent wagon. I'll need a way to keep everything tidy inside, too. I'll take care of that, though. You can't be trusted."

Regis had just growled, glared, then strode off rubbing his head and glancing about, thankful to see nobody else had witnessed this exchange. That Percy was going to go too far one of these days. Even if he was a good cook.

He made his way to the stables and found men all busy enough, shoeing and mucking out, and one vaquero breaking green horses in the corral out front.

The fellow, José, was a Mexican, his skin brown as a cured tobacco leaf, and eyes that glinted like black diamonds. And he was the best horseman Regis had ever met.

At least Regis had suspected he was darn good, and then Bone had told him the man was indeed, one of the best Bone had ever seen in action. That made Regis feel as though he was gaining knowledge about the ranching life.

Chapter 7

"**D**oes that mean I'm stuck running this place?" said Cormac, flicking an impatient hand before him as if shooing a fly.

Regis ground his teeth. "No, Tut will be around."

"You're not taking him with you? He's the one man on your crew, other than Bone, I'd trust."

"That's exactly why I'm leaving him behind. He's needed on the ranch."

Cormac nodded and sighed. "All right. I see." The unspoken accusation hung between them. Regis knew Cormac blamed him for Bone not remaining part of the ranch. And if he were honest with himself, Regis guessed that was true, in part, anyway. But Bone's life was more complicated than that.

"So where do I fit into your plans, then, Regis?"

"Well, I realize this isn't your ideal place to be, but if you could come out every couple of weeks, just to see that there hasn't been mutiny and Tut hasn't been hoisted high, kicking and screaming."

Cormac's eyes widened. "You think that's a possibility?"

Regis tried to maintain a poker face, but the raw terror on Cormac's grizzled face was too convincing, and a hearty laugh burst out of his mouth.

"What's funny?" said the Irishman.

"Your face, Cormac. You had convinced yourself that the entire place was in dire need of a constant, watchful eye."

"I'm still not unconvinced." Then his scowl became a rueful sneer and a headshake. "I tell you what I would like from you, though."

"What's that?" said Regis.

"Just come back."

Regis smiled. "And?"

"No 'and,' said Cormac. "Just make it back safe and whole."

"I'll do my best," said Regis.

"I know." Cormac smacked his hands together. "All right, now show me whatever else it is I need to know about the magical Royle Ranch in your absence."

Chapter 8

Cormac had told Regis the week before that he'd do his best to try to make it out to the ranch on the morning they left. But that would necessitate him coming out the night before, a problem because Cormac was becoming increasingly set in his ways and rarely liked to travel beyond Brownsville.

In fact, he had nearly worn a groove in the pavers between their office along the waterfront and his own home, on a side street. With side journeys to Millie's Hash House and the Double Dare Saloon.

He rarely cooked for himself. And when at the ranch, on the few occasions when he'd made the journey inland, cooking was never an issue, because he always tucked in with the men.

Cormac was voluble and enjoyed the company of the ranch hands and their families. They all knew who he was and liked him a whole lot, that much was obvious to Regis.

Whereas with Regis they were pleasant and deferential, with Cormac they were, well, if Regis had to choose a word for it, friendly. And relaxed. Around him, the same folks were tense.

He'd talked with Marietta about this, and she had nodded. "Yes, I have seen this on the few occasions I have accompanied you to the ranch."

"How might I change that?" he said.

As was her way, she thought for a moment. "It will not be as you wish—not a quick solution." She snapped a finger to indicate what she knew, and so did Regis, was his preferred method of solving problems.

"It will take time and much work on your part."

That had been the day before their departure. She had refused his invitation to stay at the ranch while he was gone, but she did agree to see him off. After that, she would ride the horse he had given her, a fine, sleek, and gentle mare, black all over save for a shock of white in the midst of the mane. A truly stunning horse for a woman he thought of as the same.

He knew she would ride this horse back to the small, humble adobe casita she had had built close by the grotto in the caves. Regis supposed that her fondness for such a simple life was gained through her years of living in the convent.

In a way, he could understand that a quiet, contemplative life such as she led was ideal. But the ranch, oh, the ranch. His thoughts always returned to the wonders of the Royle Range. And he knew he could never give it up.

That's why he had decided to ramrod the trail drive himself.

Trouble was, he was starting out with a dozen men in all, and more than 350 head of half-ornery cattle. He could have taken more, but he wasn't certain, despite his intentions, that he would succeed on this drive.

If the worst happened and he should fail, the cattle he left, along with what other meager stock and assets he'd managed to accumulate at the ranch, would perhaps be able to pay Cormac something. He would leave it to Cormac to figure out how to care for the Mexican families in the ranch's care.

The dust boiled up and nearly choked them all long before the departing herd left the ranch proper. Already a half dozen of his men were whooping and hollering to either side of the herd, as if they had done this very thing every day of their lives. Regis wondered how long they'd keep it up.

The cows, for the most part, were reluctant to leave the rich grasses in which they walked, most of them having been gathered from all points of the compass about the ranch. It had been a grueling couple of weeks leading up to the departure day.

Regis was still barking orders to Tut, the man he'd left in charge of the ranch's day-to-day operation while he was away. He wished Tut could be with them on the trail, but he needed him here on the Royle Range.

The young man was fast becoming a much-relied-upon rancher, and Regis had bumped him up in the pecking order of the ranch, making him acting ranch foreman. He figured he'd keep the word *acting* there for a spell, so as not to give the young man a swelled head. Not too soon, anyway.

Besides, Tut had a new wife himself, the pretty and capable Miss Belinda, the ranch schoolmarm. She was also up for anything else that might be required of her. They were a solid and happy young couple, and it warmed him to think that in a way, they'd be ramrodding the place in his absence.

And then came the time when he had to say goodbye to Marietta. Regis rode over to her; she sat her horse as though she was born to ride that way, forked and wearing a black dress that she had modified for riding.

The wind played devil with her long, black veil. He rode alongside and squinted at her from beneath his hat. It was not but seven of the clock, but already it was nearly as bright as midday, and down here on the wild southlands of Texas, it was nearly as hot, too.

The departure came about sooner than Regis had expected, his part in it at least. Cyril, a young English fellow, keen and decent enough as a worker that he'd stick with a job, rode back from the herd toward Regis at a hard clip. He shouted before he even reached Regis at the rear. "Boss! Boss! Mr. Royle!"

Regis's left hand slid down to his holster out of caution. "What now?" he said aloud. "Can you see anything that's wrong up there, Marietta?"

The veiled woman offered Regis a slight nod.

58 William W. Johnstone and J.A. Johnstone

"Mr. Royle! Mr. Royle!" And then Cyril was upon them, his eyes wide and his mouth dry, given the rate at which he was trying to swallow and lick his lips.

"What is it, Cyril?"

"Ma'am," said the young man with a blush and a head nod. "It's one of the cows, boss. She got herself fetched up somehow and stumbled. Then another one went down and landed square on the head of the first one!"

Cyril sat there breathing hard, even tough his horse had done the running.

"And?" said Regis.

"And the one that fell second, well, sir, she's . . ." He angled a hand over one side of his mouth and leaned toward Regis as if what he was about to say was too awful for Marietta to hear.

"Out with it, Cyril!"

The words came out hot and loud, bellowed far louder than he'd intended them, but the kid was annoying the heck out of him.

Cyril nodded fast. "The second one got herself impaled on that first. She's in an awful fix. And the first one, she's dead. Neck snapped when the second one fell on her."

"The second one died, too?"

"Well, no, not yet, but she's awful bloody. And the front of the herd, well they got wind of the blood, and they took off running!"

"How many?"

"How many what?" said Cyril, his eyes still wide.

"Good lord, man! How many cows are running?"

"Oh, about fifty or more, I reckon. Anyway, Fergus sent me back to fetch others. He said we need to tell you that we are going to need some of the men from the ranch to bring the herd back into control, and then we can start all over again!"

At that moment, Tut rode up from the stables. "What's the problem, boss?"

"Glad you're here. Listen, Cyril, you take Tut with you and make for the front of the herd, and I'll go wrangle up more men."

The two men took off for the herd. By then, even the rear of the herd, closest to them, was beginning to move faster.

This didn't look good to Regis. He rode back toward the heart of the ranch, buildings and the hustling and bustling he thought he'd not see again this close up for months. Marietta rode with him. As usual, she said nothing, but beneath her veil, he could tell she was waiting for him to speak.

By the time Regis found three more men, all of it taking far longer than he wished it would, Tut met him and the men when they were halfway to the herd.

"What are you doing, Tut?" Regis hadn't wanted to, but he barked the question.

The jovial Tut winced, but he said, "It's okay, boss. By the time I got up to the front of the herd, that fella, Ferg, you know, the older one? He had the men dealing with it just fine. I tell you, he's worth his weight in gold, is that one."

Regis slowed his horse, as did the other three men.

Tut continued, "I asked him where he learned to work cattle like that, and he shrugged, said he'd been on a drive or two in his day." Tut's smile had resumed its perennial place beneath the mustaches he was trying to grow. "I reckon you'll be glad you have him along before the drive is through."

"From the sounds of it," said Marietta. "He's already proved himself, no, Regis?"

Regis glanced at her, quelled his urge to offer a flippant remark, then nodded. She was correct, of course, and he just needed to take that moment of thought before replying. "Indeed," he said, forcing a smile. "I'm grateful to him, and I'll tell him so. As soon as we get everything back on course, that is."

If the previous weeks had been difficult, leaving Marietta a second time in an hour was to prove nearly impossible for the big man. "You certain you wouldn't like to tag along?" he said, knowing the answer but half-hoping she'd take him up on it. Heck, he thought, gazing at her. If she asked him to, he would postpone the drive just to outfit her for it.

She offered him a rare full smile. "I can be of much more use to you here than I can be out there, wherever it is your cattle drive takes you, and however long it takes you."

He reached for her hand and kissed it, not caring who saw. "I promise you I will return, and I promise you I will take only as long as I need to, no longer."

"No." She shook her head. "Do not make such promises. Instead, tell me that you will do the best that you can for yourself and for your men and for the cattle. Everyone is important, Regis Royle, and we all have our parts to play."

"You will be here?"

"I will be here . . . unless someone else comes along."

His eyebrows rose. If she was making a joke, it was startling, because it was not what he wished to hear and because she rarely cracked wise. And then her headshake and small chuckle told him not to worry.

Some minutes later, when he had lingered as long as he dared, they parted. Regis rode forward to catch up with the herd, not daring to look back for a last glance at his friend and partner, Cormac, who stood off to one side, nor to see his beloved ranch, and not for a last glimpse at Marietta, his newfound love.

It was going to be a long drive, but the sooner he started, the sooner he'd return.

Chapter 9

"I thought all these tribes hated each other."

Regis looked over at the kid who'd spoken. It was Chancy. The kid was a jittery mess, and he was pouring himself another cup of coffee. Tell the kid to lay off the coffee or let him be?

Might be wiser to let him have the comforts of a cup of hot coffee in his hands. Even if it meant he was a little more skittish. As to Chancy's comment, Regis couldn't say much. He'd wondered the same thing.

They'd been out on the trail northward for a few weeks, and they'd met with little hardship. The cattle had been relatively docile and had taken herding well, all things considered. The weather had been sunny, the sky blue, and the nights star-filled and dark.

Heck, even Percy had been, if not jovial, at least two shades less than surly. But the biggest relief and comfort to Regis, who had spent the first three days and nights barely sleeping, so nerved up was he, had been the calm, jovial, reassuring presence of Fergus, the seasoned cowhand.

The man had come to them not long before, and while he had been acquainted with Bone from some work in the past, it was Tut who had hired the man on. All the other men had taken to

Fergus and his quiet, friendly, confident ways, and now Regis saw why.

In fact, he'd come to rely more and more on the man's opinions and suggestions, only offered when Regis asked, of course, but eminently useful and appreciated. Yes, sir, Regis had mused just that morning. If this was life on a cattle drive, he could not see what the fuss was about them being dangerous, problem-riddled affairs.

And then, hours before, they'd spotted the Indians.

Each of the four men, plus Percy, sat in silence, sipping from their cups, letting the warm meal do its work to their innards, and wondering what it all meant. The "it" being, of course, what young Telos, the Greek fisherman, who had by far the best eyesight of any of them, had seen before noontime that day.

Regis had noticed the young man visoring his eyes beneath the short brim of that small black fisherman's cap he wore. He'd been looking northeastward toward the long, low hills that snaked a quarter-mile away. They were close enough that once Regis followed the man's sight line, he, too, sat rapt, staring at the thing he suspected they'd see sooner or later on this venture.

A whole line of riders, looking to be Indians, from the jutting of lances among them, stood skylined along the ridgetop in an irregular but daunting line. Eighteen or more of them.

By the time Regis pulled his gaze back down, Telos had trotted his horse on over to him. "Mister Regis, you see them, then?"

"I do, Telos. What do you make of them?" Regis asked the man, because in addition to possessing tremendous eyesight, the Greek was also a living library of information about most any topic. Regis found himself wondering at times just where the young man might end up once he shook off the dust of the trail. If he ever did. Telos seemed to love the life of a freelance cowboy.

Without hesitation, the young man said, "They look to be a pirate band, maybe of Kiowa, Apache, some Comanche, and of course half-breeds and whites."

Telos said this with a nonchalance that made Regis feel as if he should have known this himself.

Regis had kept the herd moving, but had stayed riding drag and had sent the young man forward to tell the others.

"And make certain they don't gawk too long at them. We have to keep the herd moving. I want to make that river by nightfall."

As Telos had prepared to depart, he said, "There will be precious little sleep for the Royle crew tonight, then." He smiled and touched the brim of his funny little black cap, and rode ahead as if he had seen nothing more than a distant coyote.

"Precious little, that's right," said Regis to himself as he cast another look toward the ridge. The odd collective of watchers was gone.

And so the day's long, hot hours passed with nothing to break them up save for taking the midday meal in the saddle. Percy, for once, had no gripes or sharp comments, and Regis noticed that he had strapped on his sidearm, as had all the men, in addition to rifles in scabbards on each mount.

Instead of a rifle, Percy kept a short-barrel shotgun beside him, leaning within reach against the wagon's seat, nestled in a groove to prevent the gun from sliding. Regis had seen the younger man wield guns in a fracas with border rats a year or so earlier, so he knew that Percy was more than capable of holding his own in a squabble.

He hoped the sighting of the strangers wouldn't lead to a fight, but deep down in his gut and bones, Regis knew better. Establishing the Royle Ranch had come at a high cost in lives not only on his side, but also measured in the number of thieves and brigands they'd been forced to lay low.

Sure, those brutes had asked for it, looking for easy thievings, hoping to plunder and pillage and set fire to everything they might, and then ride on. But for most, it hadn't worked out that way.

Regis had more respect for, if not agreement with, the tribes and Mexicans who had used that range forever, at least long, long before whites such as he rode in and laid claim to it. But times change, and while he would have preferred to explain this and figure out some way to live and work the place in somewhat harmony, they had chosen the path of violence. And he with his hired men and superior weapons, had bested them at every turn. Sometimes at a high cost.

He recalled the faces of men he had known who had been shot, gutted, beaten to death at the hands of border bandits. That's when any sympathy he might have felt, albeit the thinnest of slivers, powdered into dust. He'd been in so many cursed skirmishes, since those earliest days of establishing the ranch. Most recently, he and other large ranchers had had to deal with cattle rustlers.

There had been a particularly bold and aggressive band of them, and he and his men had ridden point, run them to the ground, and wiped out the sorry lot of them. Those they didn't shoot in fighting they had strung up, and a few luckier rustlers had pleaded persuasively enough or been young and stupid enough that Regis had felt the twinges of small pities.

Those men, he'd trussed and brought in to Corpus Christi for the law to deal with. Last he heard, those rustlers had had the poor luck to come up against Hardnose Hanlon, the toughest, no-quarter-given circuit judge a wayward Texican had the poor luck to meet. They'd all danced at the end of fresh hemp ropes within a week of being brought in.

Going into this cattle drive, Regis had known it wasn't going to be a straightforward affair, especially because he was so inexperienced. He had two men on the crew who'd been on drives, and only one of them, Fergus, had done so over any distance.

The other had been a green kid and had gone along as the remuda wrangler's assistant.

The rest of the day Regis had spent swiveling his head, looking for sign of invaders bent on killing them and stealing their cattle. But by nightfall, no further sign of the mysterious distant men had been seen.

Chapter 10

When the attack came, two nights later, it happened fast, with fingersnap speed, as the scream of a horse ripped open the night. It was followed with the snapping of gunfire, several rounds.

For a quick moment, Regis had no idea where he was or what might be happening. He kicked away his blanket and shoved to his feet, realizing he had slipped into a too-deep doze. There was no mystery as to why—he'd been awake more than he'd been asleep for days, ever since those brutes had begun trailing them.

And that, as he now saw, was precisely why they had trailed them—to disturb him and his men, to wear them down and make them skittish, anxious, and nervous. And it worked. All of his men were feeling much the same as he was.

But no matter now, he thought, sliding his rifle from its scabbard. He bent low and ran toward the campfire, now a dull glow. He skirted that and made for the wagon beyond. "Percy! Where are you?"

"Boss?" said the cook. "Port side of the wagon."

Regis appreciated that Percy peppered conversation with nautical words. They were something Regis was quite used to, having spent so much of his life in and around ships, first as a stowaway discovered by Cormac, and then, as he grew, as a deck hand and later, captain.

Regis found Percy, hunkered and with his revolver drawn. Another gunshot, then several more, split the dark, far to their left, from the far side of the herd. They were followed by a rumbling.

Regis knew what it was before he could even shout the warning. "Stampede!"

And that's just what it was.

One moment, the herd was a quiet, sleepy mass of low snorting and rumbling, and the next, it sounded as if each beast had received a scream right in an ear. Regis could not see any more than a dark mass beneath the purpled sky above, but that dark mass was on the move.

He heard a scream then, from a man, and hoped it was not one of his. "Who was that?" he shouted. As he ran toward the remuda, with the passing frenzied cattle a couple of dozen yards away and boiling northward, he heard Percy shout, "Sounded like the far side of the herd, boss!"

That's where Fergus might well be, nighthawking, he thought. No use thinking of who it might be; he had to get King saddled and ready to ride.

He was halfway through the task when fast-scudding clouds slid beyond the half-moon to reveal something he'd not expected, and never could have: a man, running and naked to the waist, bearing down on him at full speed. Their eyes met, and the attacker screamed, a raw, guttural howl that sent a fingernail of ice raking up Regis's spine.

He had reholstered his revolver and had slid his rifle into its scabbard slung on the saddle of the big, stamping horse. King was more agitated than ever, and Regis could barely contain the horse's spinning, jerking moves.

He gave up blindly grabbing for the rifle from where it slapped and thumped and instead clawed his revolver free, cocking it and drawing on the running man. But the man had had the same notion and, though still stomping toward Regis, he had raised a rifle to his shoulder. Despite the awkwardness of it, he managed to send a shot sizzling close by Regis's right cheek.

The big rancher dropped to his left knee as the man hustled forward, rifle held before him and ready to send another shot, now less than five yards distant and closing the gap fast. Regis didn't dither—he delivered a bullet to the man. It caught the fiend on the left shoulder, not in the chest, where Regis was aiming, but it would do. And it did.

The man screamed once more, this time as an animal in pain. The bullet halted his run and instead spun him to his left as if jerked from behind.

He dropped his rifle and snatched at the wound as the clouds closed ranks once more. Though the man was close, he was all but lost to Regis visually.

But Regis marked the spot and he made his move, figuring that while the fool was still moaning and clawing at his fresh wound, he would be unlikely, at least for a few short moments more, to resume the fight.

With his revolver ready and riding in one hand, Regis dashed forward, keeping low and cutting to his right. He kept his eyes fixed on where the man had been and one, two big strides more brought him to within sight.

He thumbed the thong free holding the staghorn handle of his big hip knife and slid the keen blade free of its sheath. In the same motion, he pulled it back, waist-height, and drove it forward as he collided with his attacker.

The man had bent low, and though Regis could barely see him, he glimpsed enough to see that the brute was scrabbling for the rifle. He had no time for more, because the big rancher's blade slammed into his side, a sloppy strike that nonetheless did the intended job. Perhaps too well.

The blade itself was nearly as wide as a man's wrist, and the point was fine enough to part the hair on a frog, as Tut had said when Regis had lent him the blade months before. Tut had admired the well-kept blade, hefting it and turning it over to see the sunlight glint off the honed steel. Then he'd handed it back.

"What's the matter with it?" said Regis, mildly offended. He had, after all, spent a good amount of cash on that custom-made knife.

"Nothing at all," said Tut. "But . . . well . . ." Then Tut did as he always did in conversation with Regis: he turned red and offered a half-smile. "It's just that it's far too fancy, I mean nice, to use cutting old rope like this." Tut held up the knobby ragged clot of knotted hemp rope.

The only reason Tut had asked to borrow a knife was because he'd forgotten his trusty Barlow folder back at the bunkhouse.

Regis had rummaged in his own trouser pocket and handed over his own folding knife. He'd also learned a lesson then— just because his money bought a big, fancy knife didn't mean it was a useful, functional tool. At least not until it proved itself on jobs. And so he'd vowed to not own anything so fancy that he wouldn't be afraid to use it. After all, he reasoned, what good was a blade if it was babied and not used as a knife?

Regis thought of that as his fancy knife, much used and honed since Tut's encounter with it, slid into the strange, howling enemy's side. Regis felt it nick bone and continue inward, popping vitals and slicing a hole wide enough that the big man's wide hand rammed up to his knuckles inside the shrieking man's gut.

With his other hand, Regis shoved at the already-slumping man and spun away, partly out of disgust, partly because close-in, quick gunfire began to echo and flash, mingling with the guttural growls of men struggling with other men, with screams of horses and men and the frantic, wild-throated bellows of night-crazed cattle.

Regis left his victim mewling and writhing on the earth and spun to run back to King, but his way was blocked.

A tall, dark shadow, that of a man on a horse, stood pawing and prancing in place. The mass of shifting blackness began to laugh, a low, coarse sound that grated on Regis's thrumming nerves more than it frightened him. He once more lifted his revolver and prepared to pull the trigger when the mass was on him. It had been far closer than he'd thought.

Flashes of light from close-by gunfire offered him snatches of sight in the gloom. And the last Regis saw before being run down was the wild-eyed, hot, snorting face of a hulking horse ridden by a kicking, shouting man.

No demon and hell-steed they, he thought as he was slammed to earth, his revolver flying from his grasp.

But as his head buzzed and clanged with the discordant peals of one hundred bells, Regis retained enough sense to pull his limbs in and curl up on his side, arms and legs tucked in tight, as if he were mimicking a newborn napping.

As soon as he knew the thundering beast stomped past, he rolled to his left, closer to where King had stood, for Regis was uncertain if the big horse was still there. If he were King, he would have thundered on out of there by now.

The darkness held between gun flashes and the one or two swinging lanterns someone from camp had managed to conjure light from. But it was that darkness that saved Regis, his one ally as he sought to be anywhere but where that crazed rider hoped he'd still find him.

Regis reckoned he'd rolled at least ten feet when he felt something jam him hard in the ribs. It was no rock—it was his revolver. He wanted to hold it up and kiss it, but there would be time for foolishness later, he hoped. And prayers of thanks. Right then, he had business to tend to—and a sneaking suspicion that the dark rider wasn't through with him.

And then his suspicions were proven correct. The rider had

jerked his mount's reins and pounded back. By then, Regis had gained one knee and waited, squinting into the darkness, trusting his side-sight instead of looking straight on at whatever it was that he needed to render into defeat.

"Boss!"

It might be Percy, he thought; though the voice was that of a young man, it was hoarse, as though it were being choked out.

Regis sucked in a quick breath and was about to race to help whoever it was who had shouted to him from some yards behind. But then the darkness before him shifted enough that he saw the tall shape aboard the horse once more. The man was looking for him as much as Regis was looking for the intruder.

Who would see the other first?

Regis held his breath, leveled off with the gun, and squeezed, dropping down to his left again, in case the man was counting on just that in order to see where he was.

Regis was rewarded with a high-pitched yip, cut off in mid-shout, as if the man had chosen the very moment Regis had touched his trigger to shout some sort of deranged war cry. It would be his last, for Regis heard the finality of it pinching out. Then he heard something slop and flump to the tromped earth.

Then came the harsh, irregular stomping of a horse, the very beast that had held up his foe. It was running off once more, this time without a rider to jerk the reins. But something was a bit off with it.

As Regis spun to find whoever it was who needed help, he knew why the horse sounds were odd—he bet that though his shot hit home and knocked the man to the ground, one of his feet had fetched and fouled in a stirrup. And then the crazed horse kicked and dragged and snorted and slammed that poor fool the rest of the way to death. At least that was Regis's hope.

He felt not one pinch of pity for these thieving killers. And he vowed if he survived this mess that he'd track them all down and drive bullets into each of their foul, hate-filled heads.

But that desire would have to wait, for ahead, back by the cook's wagon, he saw figures of men struggling. Why could he see them he thought. And then he knew—Percy had lit a lantern, and in doing so, he attracted attention to himself, the wrong attention, as it turned out.

For Regis saw that one of the fighting men was indeed the young, surly cook. And while he was still upright, doling out lunges and punches in a close-in fight, he would not be for long, because Regis saw not one opponent laying into his cook, but two foes. And one of them was a big whopper of a man.

Regis was no wilting daisy in the size department himself, but he knew it would be foolish to barrel in when he had the opportunity to take at least one of them by surprise. He cut to his right, beyond the reach of the meager honey-glow of the swinging lantern—it hung off its hook, jutting from the middle wagon rib it usually hung from during nighttime camps.

"You . . . filth!" growled Percy, bending low and driving his head, battering-ram-like, at the smaller, closer of his two opponents. The man he'd rammed gagged and doubled over, letting loose a long, moaning sound interrupted by wet coughs.

Apparently, none of the men were in possession of knives or any other weapon suitable for close-in fighting.

"Howl, you demon!" growled Percy as he landed another punch, even as he was jerking his head back from the man's gut.

That was all the invitation the newly arrived big brute needed, for he snagged Percy by the scruff of his vest and shirt and lifted him, swinging, swearing, and kicking.

Regis reached the big man, darting in from the side with his knife, intending to land a hard driving blow just behind the man's left side, aiming down low on the man's back, where bone would do little to interrupt the blade's intended route.

But at the last moment, the man, whose left arm was free, swung it, clublike, down and straight into Regis's left arm, slamming into the rancher and knocking him off his stride. His savage knife blow arced harmlessly past the man's body, barely, but it was enough to spare the brute the killing slice.

But not for long, as Regis regained his balance and lunged, low this time, wrapping his arms about the man's meaty thighs and jerking him to his left. It worked, and the man let out a snarl of surprise, even as his knees buckled.

He still held Percy, but as he toppled, the cook's collar slipped free of his thick fingers and Percy hit the ground moving. He didn't wait, but redoubled his efforts and slammed once again into the smaller of the two opponents, the one he'd already attacked.

The man had just about recovered and gained his wind back from being driven into by the crazed cook, but Percy's renewed efforts overwhelmed him. Soon the crazed cook had the man down, slammed flat on his back.

As he struggled to sink his blade into the big man, Regis saw that Percy's foe, the small, wiry, swarthy-looking character, bore scars crisscrossing his half-shaved head. Then he noticed no more, for the big man had wriggled enough that he was able to half-turn to face his enemy.

His ham-sized fists slammed downward at Regis's head. The first drove into Regis's left shoulder, as if he'd been clubbed with a stone axe.

"No, you don't!" Regis forced the low words, a promise, through gritted teeth and once more drove the blade into a fresh enemy.

The big man squealed as if he'd dropped a big rock on his toe. But the cause of his shock was far worse than a rock; it was Regis's blade tickling bone high up on the outside of the man's left thigh. Regis had driven it in at an angle, unplanned, as it was the only direction he could send it.

The big brute flailed his massive arms and tore free of Regis's grasp, wrenching the knife from the rancher's fingers.

Regis lunged for it and felt the polished grip beneath his fin-

gertips, but the man twisted, in part out of agony and in part because he saw Regis redoubling his efforts. With his big right
hand, he swatted at Regis, landing another clubbing blow, this
time on Regis's head, and with the other, he snatched the knife
and jerked it free of his leg.

Given the shrieking howl he emitted, Regis wondered if the
blade hurt worse coming out than going in. He had no more time
for speculation, because the big man was once more on him.
Regis ducked low, and lost his footing.

And then a clunk and a crash of glass was followed by darkness—the dim light they'd been using to guide their movements
in this freakish dance pinched out.

For a brief moment, all four combatants paused in their efforts, and then each moved, the same thought in their minds:
evade their opponent and attack where they might least expect.

And each man was successful in this, as Percy, who was already
down on one knee and preparing for a sudden rush by his swarthy
foe, dropped all the way to his left, rolling onto his shoulder and
regaining his footing to the right of the enemy.

The enemy, apparently not gifted with an intellect offering
more than basic breathing and reacting skills, tucked low and
prepared to ram forward, much as Percy had done to him. But the
swarthy fellow dithered a moment too long after the lantern's
light extinguished.

That was all the time Percy needed. He emerged from his
tuck-and-roll and laid hard into his foe, first with a hard, swift fist
that he drove into the flat plane between the man's eye and ear
on the right side.

It had been a blow more owing to luck than skill, but he did
not care. He followed it with another, but his fist glanced off the
top of the man's bizarre, scarred head. The man was either shrinking, thought Percy, or dropping.

Percy did the same and dropped to his right knee, and drove
both fists, right, left, right, but they touched nothing save for

dark night air. He hustled forward, shuffling on both knees now, fists still before him, and felt with caution. He was rewarded with the feel of his enemy in a sloppy heap, bent at the waist, legs folded beneath him, all of him unmoving.

This was worse, thought Percy, than having killed the man. For then, he could move on and do his best to put the brute out of his mind. But now? Now he had a choice, a decision—truss up the pig, leave him be, or snap his neck?

Before deciding, Percy cocked an ear and heard the sounds close by of two men scuffling, the heavy, rasping breathing and dull thuds of fists smacking flesh, growling yells that were no more words than a bear's guttural bellows. Good, Regis was still in the game. Now Percy could continue to deal with his opponent.

Killing the man, despite the situation brought on by his filthy ilk, immediately turned Percy's gut cold—the taking from a creature its most valuable thing was no small matter. Regis had once said this, and it had struck home for Percy, who regarded it as a point well expressed, and he'd not forgotten it. It also said much about Regis.

There was precious little reverence for life in this world, thought Percy then, and once more now, in the heat of the vicious battle, he still heard and felt waging all about him. For shouts and gunshots and thundering hooves and screams and maniacal laughs told him it was bound to be a long night.

Yet to kill the brute, no matter how foul or ill-intended, was something he could simply not justify, not except in the heat of battle, when the man was awake and doing his best to do the same to him. Then it was different. But to snap the neck of an unconscious man? That was murder.

So Percy, knowing he was but six feet or so from the back of his cook wagon, dashed low over to it and rummaged, laying a hand on the thing he knew was there because he had put it there—a hank of rope.

He yanked it out and, stumbling in the dark, made his way back to the man who, he felt, was slowly coming around. Percy felt the man's face with a slapping palm, and when he'd located it, he let the bum have another hard fist, to the same spot. That dulled the man's efforts at rousing, and once again he lay still.

Percy trussed him as he would a roped calf ready for castration. Now that was something he'd likely not have trouble doing to the evil little seed, thought the grim cook with a wry grin, but he had no time.

He had enough rope left over to drag the savage a few feet closer to the wagon, just enough to tie him off to the wheel. He thought it might help keep the man there until Percy could get back to him. Perhaps he could be useful to them somehow— ransom? Information? It was doubtful, but it was better than nothing.

All this took a minute or more, and in that time Regis, who, from the sounds of it, was still fighting with that big beast of a man, was somehow still alive and holding his own.

Regis knew he'd soon have help, for Percy, who by now had become accustomed to the near darkness about them, walked forward, low, with his arms out.

He half thought about weapons, but didn't want to waste time feeling for his shotgun or a cleaver from his cooking gear when Regis was so close and no doubt suffering harm at the hands of the big man, though Percy was quick to note that Regis Royle was no tiny fellow himself.

A mighty heaving bellow sounded, followed with a toppling, thudding sound. It was several yards to Percy's right. He halted and heard no more sound, save for that of one big man breathing heavily, rasping harsh breaths, each earned with a hard pull.

Percy was not accustomed to not being decisive. He could decide in a fingersnap of time what he would make the men for any meal, and with a glance at his stores could tell if he had enough to do the job or no. But he found himself standing there in the dark wavering for a moment about what to do. Who had won?

Finally, after long seconds, Percy remained crouching and said, "Boss? That you?"

Again, long seconds passed, he repeated himself, stepping to his left in case the man had decided to come for him based on his voice's location.

"Regis Royle!" he said.

"Yeah, yeah," the man said, struggling for breath as if he'd run a great distance and needed water. "That you, Percy?"

"Yep."

"Good."

"The big one?"

"Dead. I hope."

Percy moved forward; within feet, his left boot struck something that did not feel like a rock. He bent down and felt a big foot, a boot.

"He didn't seem like an Indian," said Regis, now but a foot or so to Percy's right.

The cook stood. This close, they could just make out each other. All about them, the sounds of intermittent scuffling still sounded. Cattle bawled, horses thundered this way and that, gunshots cracked the night, and whoops and shouts rose up here and there.

"Don't know what they are," said Percy. "The Greek said they were a mix of just about everything. I guess this one's all bear."

Regis chuckled. "I have to figure out what to do here. See if you can't find a horse, one for each of us. I'm going to do the same over where I left King. I can't imagine he's still there."

Both men groped in the dark; then, as if they'd been granted a favor from on high, the inky black night began to take on shape and form and distance. Regis glanced up. The thick clouds had parted once more. Who knew for how long, so he used it to his advantage and took in as much as he could with his eyes.

From what he could see, given the night and the feeble but welcome moonglow lighting the scene, Regis's trail drive had become, in a matter of what he felt was far less than an hour, a ruptured mess. Humped forms lay here and there, smaller ones between larger—cattle and men? Horses? He didn't have that many men to begin with. How many had lost their precious lives?

But the most shocking sight of all were the cattle, for they had not stampeded, merely thundered as a group a short distance to the northeast. And from what Regis could see, they had come to a standstill, despite being circled by riders firing random shots into the sky. Regis hoped the bullets came straight back down and drilled the shooters square on their thieving pates.

"No such luck," he muttered, and strode forward, hunching a bit, and keeping a wary eye to both sides of himself.

The big shock was finding King not but a dozen feet from where he'd left him. The big horse cropped already gnawed brittle grasses, as if he lived in a world of quiet and calm.

Regis walked up, and King whickered low until he satisfied himself that this approaching man was someone he knew. Regis was relieved to find that his horse was cool and calm, much as he himself felt. Except for that fact that there was a battle being waged all about them.

He was about to swing into the saddle when a mounted rider trotted up. Regis bent behind King's left side and fumbled for his revolver.

"Boss!"

It was Percy. Thin relief washed over him, and he mounted up on King. Urging the big horse around to face the herd, and without looking at Percy, Regis said, "You have a gun?"

"Yep, found my shotgun."

"Good, let's make for that nearest cluster of cattle. I saw two strangers circling northward counterclockwise, your side. We'll meet them around the far side."

"Or someone," said Percy, urging his horse up alongside Regis.

"Keep apart a good twenty feet. One of us gets picked off, the other will have a better chance to flee."

"Good thinking," said Percy, mulling over the gruesome thought of being picked off. It sounded like something someone did to a tick on a hound or a scab.

They parted a bit and rode wide around the clot of cattle, the near-dark doing as much to shield them as it did to prevent them from seeing attackers. But of those, they saw few.

Percy gave voice to the same thought Regis had—perhaps the attackers wanted to cut out cattle and run for the hills? If so, why were some bent on attacking?

All these questions and more rippled through his mind as he guided King around the lowing herd.

The moonglow had been more with them than not for some time, and he'd grown used to it. He glanced up and saw stars winking here and there. Finally, he thought. That meant those annoying clouds were spreading apart and out. Good riddance.

They rode on, armed, wary and spread out, circling wide around the smaller block of seemingly placid cattle. They found no one they did not know, and only one other of the Royle men. It was Cyril, a young Englishman whose desire to see the world had gotten him as far as the American West, where he had, as he put it, fallen head over heels for the land and its denizens.

He was windy and liked to bloviate, but Regis liked him nonetheless. He had all the endearing qualities of his younger brother, Shep, with few of the annoying traits.

Cyril seemed to genuinely enjoy the long, grinding hours in the saddle, and was always up for a game of poker for raisins at night. And he was often the first to volunteer for nighthawk duties. Regis had few complaints about the young man. Another of Bone's hires.

As he rode, Regis wondered about his old ranger pard and

hoped he was well on the mend from that cat attack. He also
hoped he was not out rangering. Too old for that foolishness, especially when he had a woman at home who obviously thought
the world of him. And he her, if Regis was any judge of another
man's emotions and intentions.

"Boss!" said Cyril. "Good to see you."

"Cyril, are you hurt?"

"Oh, this?"

As Regis rode closer, he saw that the young Englishman held a
hand to the side of his head. "I'll be fine. A mere scratch. On the
other hand, you should see the fellow I found myself matched up
with. We were engaged in true fisticuffs, I tell you! He escaped,
in the end, the brute, but I'll wager I gave him a good hiding
nonetheless."

Even ailing, the Englishman was chipper. Regis indulged in a
slight smile. "Okay, then. When daylight comes, we'll tend to
that wound. You fit to ride until then?"

"You can count on it, sir."

"Good. Percy is with me. We're trying to assess the damage."

"Right, sir. I don't want to assume too much, but I think
they've left us."

"Why do you say that?" said Percy.

"Haven't you noticed? We've not heard a peep from those
howling buffoons in long minutes now. And the cattle seem
much quieter. Horses, too."

"He's right," said Regis, cocking an ear. He'd been doing the
thing he always did that got him nowhere fast. He'd been thinking three steps ahead of himself, trying to figure out what to do
next, and not paying attention to the most important things—
namely what was going on, or not going on, around him at the
present moment.

"Let's split up and ride further apart, see how many of our
men are left." He knew as soon as he said it how grim that would
sound, but it was the truth. It had been a barbaric, odd attack, un-

provoked, to be sure, but the intention seemed plain to Regis—to kill Regis and his men.

But if that were so, he asked himself, why stop? The attackers seemed to have superior numbers, though barely. Unless there were more of them they hadn't seen on the ridge two days before.

As they rode, none of the three men met with any more trouble from attackers. It took nearly an hour before Regis and Cyril found the other Royle Ranch men, and when they did, they were all up by the largest group of the herd, keeping them milling and calm. It was working. It was also growing light, as the sky to the east offered them the first faint twinges of purple that slowly bloomed into pink.

After they'd passed around the smaller group of cattle, Percy had continued his circuit, intending to do what he could to keep that batch of rangy longhorns from wandering too far.

He'd angled north of the beeves and urged his horse eastward for a few steps, and took time to glance upward and admire the lightening morning sky. He felt a flutter of relief, tempered with a little dread at what daylight would show them. And then he looked down to see a dead Royle ranch hand.

It was Telos, the Greek. Percy recognized the man's little black fishing hat, which lay a couple of feet away from the man's earthbound, unmoving form. He slid down from his horse, glancing about in the early morning gloom for sign of any attackers, but of anyone else, save for the cattle some yards to the south, he saw no other creature.

"Telos," said Percy, bending low and nudging the man's shoulder. The form jostled but offered no response.

The Greek looked to have been smacked hard in the head with something heavy and blunt, perhaps the butt of a rifle or a belt axe.

He lay curled on his side, with no stones jutting from the soil within a dozen feet of him. It didn't mean he hadn't fallen from his horse and hit his head, then staggered to this spot and collapsed, but that seemed unlikely, given the deepness and angle of the wound.

Percy knelt beside the man and sat back on his heels and sighed. "What a night," he said, shaking his head. "What was the point of it all?"

He looked around him again, not convinced he was truly alone, and knowing he could well be picked off by a long shot from someone with a rifle who sat in hiding somewhere behind one of the few boulders scattered about the gently rolling landscape. Or even from one of the not-too-distant hills.

To the northeast, Percy saw something moving; then it grew, separated, and became two somethings, both moving, far too distant to be a threat, or so he hoped. Nonetheless, he kept a firm hand on his revolver, which he had pulled from his holster and cocked before he inspected Telos's body.

The things he saw grew smaller. Then one cut away from the other and moved northward, and at a quick enough clip that even at his distance of roughly a quarter mile, perhaps farther, Percy guessed it was a man on horseback.

Now whether it was one of the Royle Ranch men or one of the attackers, he knew not. Nor, at that moment, did Percy much care. He was tired, bone tired. Violence had never sat well with him.

He was by nature a quiet fellow who had long known he preferred his own company to that of all the yammering men he was surrounded with at the ranch and even out here on the plains and prairies of the West.

You stay away from others, your odds of ending up in a violent situation are greatly reduced, he'd long thought. But none of that was true, and none of it mattered now. He was thinking like a fool. He sighed again.

The night had been awful for all, worse for some. His eyes rested on the dead, slumped body of his comrade, the Greek.

"You'll never lay your eyes on your beloved Greece again, Telos. I am sorry for that. Heartily sorry."

Percy stood and glanced about again. His horse had not strayed, so he walked to it, slowly, just in case he spooked it, and gathered up the reins. There wasn't much he could do except load up the Greek and carry him north to where he saw the rest of the herd and a few taller figures, men on horseback, moving slowly around them. Had to be his compadres.

Then he looked once again at the smaller bunch of cattle behind him and decided to continue his intended task of tending, to the best of his ability, to the cattle close by, since he saw nobody else about. One of the other men would come around eventually.

As he rode by the Greek, he said, "I'll be back, chum. I promise. I need a little help to hoist you up." As he said it, he knew it was the truth. He was indeed that tired. He angled the horse east, cutting wide of the flank of the bunched cattle, then southward along the length of the strung-out group.

He guessed there were sixty or seventy head in the group, and luckily, they were satisfied at the present with nibbling the sparse grasses. The light bloomed brighter, just as it does every morning, he thought.

And he was able to see farther. Far to the southeast, he saw his cook wagon and a few random, lone forms of horses, content to do the same as the cattle and nibble the dusty, sparse grasses thereabouts.

He also saw three, no four, low dark forms along the ground. He knew at least one of them was that big brute Regis had laid low. And then he remembered the odd, scarred man he'd clubbed and tied up. He'd surely be revived by now. Perhaps he was fidgeting and gnawing at the ropes.

For some reason, the thought of that bizarre, swarthy, bald man nibbling at ropes that Percy had cinched as tight as he was able struck Percy as funny, and he let out a quick snort of exhausted laughter. Then the image of the Greek, dead and never to talk again of his beloved homeland, clipped off that newborn laugh as if Percy had used a scissors.

He continued to ride along the east flank of the small patch of cattle and glanced at them as he went. The beasts looked as tired as he did, which, in his experience, didn't matter much, because a cow was a deranged thing that would bolt and run right off a cliff with little or no prompting.

He'd remained wary of the cursed things, particularly given the fact that most of them wore long horns that jutted from their heads at right angles and looked to him to be sharpened on stone as they walked along.

He knew that was absurd, but he didn't care. Longhorn cattle or no, and even if they were crossbred with other breeds to make them fatter, they all were still a hazard and not right between their ears.

Almost as soon as he thought that, Percy spied an opening in the mass of cattle, as if they were keeping their distance from whatever it was. In his experience, cows were not like horses and would just as gladly stomp all over a fellow.

"What could that be?" said Percy to himself and to his horse, patting the trudging beast on the neck. He squinted, but it was still too dim out to see clearly. It might well be an attacker hunched and lying in wait, perhaps a man who had seen him coming and wished to get a sight on him.

The surly cook held his revolver out and, as much as he did not want to do it, he angled the horse closer to the cattle. The beast tensed, knowing what unpredictable beasts the longhorns could be. But it complied with his urging, and they walked closer.

The open space was perhaps twenty-five feet in from the near edge of the herd. Percy stood in his stirrups to get a better view, and he saw what looked like a man's legs. Whoever it was, he was laid out on the ground. Face up or down, he could not yet tell. They rode closer, the cattle drifting apart before them.

Percy kept the horse moving slowly, so as to not spook the beeves. He did not want to feel a hooking horn in the leg, or worse, in the horse. Not only would that be dire for the horse, it would likely put him afoot, and in the midst of the unpredictable, wild-eyed, ornery longhorns.

He stood higher in the saddle, as tall as he was able, while still gripping the reins with one hand and the pistol in the other. Now he saw much of the rest of the fellow. He was facedown and so dusty that Percy did not know if he was one of them or one of the rogues.

And then he looked familiar.

"Oh no," whispered Percy as he guided the horse through the gauntlet of dagger horns. He did his best at the same time to keep his eyes on them when he noticed one of the man's feet move. "Praise be," whispered the cook, trying not to hurry the horse too much. They were so close then that he wanted to slip down out of the saddle and run to the man, but the cows were once more pressing close.

In another few moments, they reached the prone man in the clearing made by the beeves, and Percy saw then that it was Fergus Jones, a man who kept to himself but was always polite and generous with a head nod and a smile. He was also one of the few men, Percy had noticed, that Regis Royle never lost his temper with, because Fergus was reliable and a true seasoned cattle drive hand.

Percy respected Fergus for all those reasons and wished he could be more like the man instead of the moody, somber grousing fellow he knew everyone thought he was.

He wasted no time in dismounting and dropping to the man's side and jostling him gently on the shoulder. Fergus groaned.

"Mr. Jones!" said Percy.

One of the man's arms lay stretched downward, along his right side. Fergus's left hand, closest to Percy, clawed in the dirt, as if he were searching for something buried there. Then the fingers straightened, and the rangy man shoved himself over onto his back with a tremendous gasp and groan. The movement caught Percy by surprise, and he jerked backward.

"Mr. Jones, you're alive!" Percy didn't quite know what else to say to the man who now lay on his back, eyes gazing skyward up into the brightening dawn sky.

"Percy . . ." The man's voice was its usual deep tone.

The cook leaned closer. "Yes, Mr. Jones?"

"Please call me Fergus. And help me up."

"Oh, okay, okay, easy now." Percy stood himself and bent low to help the man stand. It was then that he noticed the dark stain low on the man's left side, above the belt.

"Mr. Jones . . . I mean Fergus, you've been shot."

Fergus leaned heavily against Percy, and they rose together. "Yeah, twice over the years. First time was . . . oh, that's better, get my pins under me. First time was on the street in Julep Springs, Arkansas, some years back. A drunkard was threatening a woman and her little child. He wanted something, money or favors, I expect. I was lucky enough to be there."

"I'm not so certain I'd call that lucky, Mr. Jones. You got shot, after all."

"Fergus," he said. "And if I hadn't been where I figured I needed to be, that bullet would have hit the little girl."

"Oh, yes, sir. I see that. And the second?"

The man wheezed and groaned a little. "Second what?"

"Second time you were shot."

"Why, that seems obvious, doesn't it?" Fergus tried to smile, but his face pinched, and he clutched at his side. "I think it's still in there. How'd everyone else fare?"

Percy led him to the horse, and Fergus stood there. "Why, it's Molly."

"Molly, sir?"

"My horse."

"Oh, she was close by the wagon. After the fight, I just hopped on her. I hope that was all right."

"Course it is. She doesn't mind, do you, Moll?" Fergus patted her neck. "Been together a long ol' time, we have. She's a smart one; when I toppled, she made for the wagon. I'd like to think if she could speak human tongue, she'd have told you I was out here."

"That bullet, Mr. Jones. Fergus, I mean. We have to get it out."

"I know. You can do it."

"Here?"

"No, back at your wagon. I see it yonder." Fergus squinted southeast of them. "Looks like there's a man there, too. He's rolling around on the ground."

Percy looked in that direction but could only make out the dark shape of the wagon. "Oh, him. After our fight, I trussed him up." Percy kept looking at the wagon but saw no one. In truth, he couldn't see much of anything. He'd worn spectacles since he was as a child, but even with them, his sight was not impressive. "You have good sight, sir."

Fergus chuckled. "About the only thing I do have that hasn't broke down yet."

"Give it time," said Percy, and then regretted it. He'd not meant to say it; it just popped into his head.

Fergus smiled and patted the fellow on the arm. "There's the Percy we all know."

"I'm so sorry. It just slipped out."

"I know. It's just your way. You have a good sense of humor, son. Never lose that." He held the saddle horn and made ready to hoist himself up into the saddle. "Though you may want to temper it with a laugh now and again so the men know you're not angry."

"Oh, yes, sir."

"And Percy?"

"Yes, sir."

"It's Fergus, not sir. Make me sound like a dandy or some such." Again, Fergus smiled.

Percy nodded and helped the older cowboy hoist himself up into the saddle. Fergus sat, left hand on his wound, eyes closed and gray-faced for a moment, then pulled in a deep breath. "Okay. Moll can take both of us, no worries. Give me your hand."

"No, sir. I'll walk alongside. It's not far." Percy eyed the cattle, who were curious and had closed in on them, tightening the circle.

"Don't mind them, son. They're just nosy. All cows are. It's their way."

"I don't like them. Big and dumb, that's what they are." They began walking through, and the beeves parted before them, though still standing spraddle-legged, heads down, and eyeing them.

"Naw. They're no dumber than people. They just know different things. Problem is that folks are always trying to get critters to do things they aren't suited to doing. Then when the critters balk, people call them dumb. I'd say it's the other way around."

Percy nodded. This was the most he'd heard Fergus talk all at once in the entire time he'd known him. He was also not entirely in agreement with the man's estimation of cows. It stood to reason a fellow who spent all his time around cattle might defend their intelligence, but cows to Percy were . . . cows.

Within a few moments, they were out of the clot of cattle, and though a few of them seemed eager to follow, the rest continued slowly ambling northward toward the larger herd. Soon enough, the nosy beeves left off and moved along with their kind.

"Are you . . ." Percy didn't know what he was asking, but he saw that Fergus had gone tight-lipped and grim-faced again.

"What? Am I going to die?" Fergus had meant it as a joke, but it came out too forced and pained sounding.

"No, well. I . . ."

"Well, we're all set to die at some point, Percy. Even the fanciest of gentlemen and ladies. But if it'll put your mind to rest, it's not a bad wound, nothing vital has been hit, I don't believe. So no, I'd say this bullet will not be my undoing." He looked down, straight-faced. "As long as you yarn it out of there for me."

"Oh, of course I will. Yes, sir. Fergus, I mean."

"Good. And I hope you don't have the shakes. You don't, do you, Percy?"

Percy's eyes widened; then he realized the man was joshing him. "Only if I've been drinking. And I never stop that, not even for an attack such as this."

Fergus smiled and readjusted his seat in the saddle. "Okay now, tell me—how did the other men fare? I see some northward with the cattle."

"Yes, sir. Regis is up there, and Cyril. And there were others, I don't know who, or how many, but I made my way toward those beeves so they wouldn't wander off. Then I found Telos."

"Dead?"

"Yes, sir. I'm afraid so."

"Oh no. No, no. That's a pity. He was a good man, a kind man. I sure liked to hear him tell of his homeland of Greece."

Percy nodded, but said nothing. It had been, he thought, feeling not a little guilty, a gift to have forgotten for the moment that the Greek had been killed.

"Sounded like the sort of place it'd be nice to see one of these days. But that is as likely as me sprouting wings." Fergus followed this unusual somber comment with a wry chuckle.

They spoke no more for a few minutes. As they drew closer to the wagon, Percy saw that Fergus had indeed seen a man rolling around on the ground. It was the same rascal he'd tangled with, and the man was still tied. He was on his front, working his way in a flailing, rolling motion first to one side, then back toward the other.

"I'd say he's trying to break free, but you tied him too well. Look at his hands."

Percy had already seen the man's hands, which he'd tied behind the man's back. They were three times their normal size, purpled and puffed as if they might burst. And the man was moaning. Despite the fight and the attack in general, Percy felt badly about it. But what could he do now? Cut the man loose? Perhaps, and then retie him.

They reached the wagon, and Fergus dismounted with slow effort. He leaned against the tall front wheel, massaging his tender left side with both hands. "Your pistol work, Percy?"

"Yes, I believe so."

"Good. Give it here," said Fergus. "Mine's spent. Didn't have enough bullets with me, more's the fool I am."

"What are you going to do?"

"Calm yourself, Percy. I'm going to make certain he doesn't turn on you while you loosen his bonds. Can't leave the man like that. He must be in agony. Listen to him moaning."

"That's what I wanted to do, yes."

"Good."

Percy fetched his slender boning knife from the wagon, figuring it would be the best tool to get in there between the man's puffed wrists to slice the rope.

He straddled the man, and for the first time, the man's moaning ceased and he looked up at Percy with a sweaty, sand-caked face. He whimpered something, his teary eyes pleading for relief.

"Oh, I am sorry, mister. I didn't think much about your comfort. Now, hold still." He bent low and pointed with the knife toward Fergus, who had ambled closer. And who, despite his wound, held the revolver aimed square on the man's head.

"No fooling around, you," said Fergus, his big, bushy eyebrows drawn together in a hard V.

The man must have understood, for he nodded with vigor and groaned as Percy set to work on the scar-headed fool. The cook could not help but wince at the smell of the man, as if he'd soiled himself steadily for a week. He reeked of campfire smoke, the sour tang of whiskey sweat, meat gone green in the sun, and fresh, fly-swarmed dung.

"Good Lord," whispered Percy as he probed with care the thin crack between the trussed hands. They looked like hams he'd seen years before in a butcher's shop in St. Louis. "It's no use," he said, wincing as the man groaned and seethed and squealed.

"I can't see what I'm cutting, and I might slice him open. Lots of veins in the arms."

"I know. But you have to do something, because I need you to yarn this bullet out so I can get back out there to help the boss and the others."

"Okay, okay. Keep your trousers on," said Percy, then remembered who he was talking to and glanced up.

Fergus was grinning at him. "That's better."

Percy ended up slicing the rope free where it trailed down to the man's ankles and sorting it out from there. Much to his surprise, it loosened enough that he was able to make a few surgical cuts, and the entire affair loosened.

The man lay there groaning and panting.

"You going to keep for much longer, Fergus?" said Percy, looking up at the rangy older cowboy.

"Not much longer enough for you to retie that fool. Only thing I can think of to do with him for now."

Meanwhile, Regis had lost count of the number of times he tried to count the head of cattle in the herd. He knew it was a fool's errand, but he couldn't seem to help himself. He also knew that his business, his profit, was, or should be, the last thing on his mind.

Instead, he tried to alter his thoughts to take in the odd situation, not only the results of it, namely the loss of men, but the intention behind it. He still didn't understand what it was all about, what had been the motivation behind such a bizarre dealing.

The only thing he could come up with—and this had been verified as a good possibility by Cyril—was that the attackers, while stronger in number, wanted everything. And would continue to conduct such attacks until they succeeded in their chosen task—the cattle stolen and the cowboys dead.

Regis set his jaw hard at the notion. It wouldn't happen until he was good and dead. And he'd do everything in his power to see that day didn't come any time soon.

"Cyril!"

The young blond Englishman looked over at him from his spot half-hidden behind a bush. He was urinating, and Regis had waited for him rather than risk losing track of him again. The young man had an unnerving habit of galloping off to inspect something that had caught his eye.

"Yes, boss!"

"When you're finished, we need to head back to the rest of the men. We need a plan. I have a few notions, but we're facing superior numbers, so we need a superior plan."

"You want ideas from the men, sir?" said Cyril, climbing back into the saddle.

"Of course," said Regis. "I'm not so conceited . . . yet . . . to think that my plans are the only ones worth considering."

"That's admirable, sir. And good to hear," said Cyril.

Regis shrugged, and they rode on, circling the herd, making for the far northeast corner, where they saw at least three other Royle Ranch riders clustered. "I'm not looking for admiration.

Not any more, anyway, but I am looking to get the rest of us through this alive, and if we can, with the herd, too."

They rode on in silence. The day was "hotting up," as Bone would say, and Regis still didn't have any more answers to the endless cannonade of questions filling his mind.

Then he recalled words from the wisest man he ever knew, Cormac. When Regis, as a much younger man, had been faced with a task that seemed far too big to wrap his arms about, Cormac had once told him, "When you find yourself in a hole, for heaven's sake, put down the shovel and stop digging. That will only ever end up with you in a deeper hole."

Another thing Cormac had taught him was to think of each big task as something akin to eating an elephant. Of course, Regis knew what an elephant was. He'd attended the performance of a small traveling circus some years back. He had felt bad for the big, sad-eyed, slow-moving beast chained by the foot and forced to perform inane tricks so that awestruck folks could gawp and stare.

But of course, Cormac's point was that the only way a fellow could eat an elephant was one bite at a time. And so Regis rode along, half trying to keep an eye on the surrounding countryside for sign of the attackers closing in for a renewed fight. He was also assessing his options. To his best reckoning, two, perhaps three, men were as yet unaccounted for.

He had what looked like roughly the same size herd they'd had yesterday, perhaps a dozen head fewer. Was that all the attackers wanted? If so, he'd consider the Royle drive lucky and bid the brutes good riddance. But both he and Cyril had agreed that there had to be more to it than that.

There seemed to be no tribal pride in the attack, as the attackers were of apparent mixed-breeding and a hodgepodge of cast-offs.

By the time Cyril and Regis reached the cluster of men, he felt himself getting lathered up once more, this time because the herd had continued to spread out, the individual beeves ranging away from the main clot of cattle in search of tastier grass.

He was about to shout at the men to ask what in the blazes they thought they were up to, sitting on their horses and gabbing when there were men down. There were likely some of their own men dead, for heaven's sake, with the enemy not likely far off, perhaps watching them all at that very moment.

And their cattle, the sole reason for them all to be out on the trail in the first place, were now walking away without anyone tending them, or whooping and shooing them back into the herd itself.

Even as stinging words nearly flew from between Regis's lips, one of his men, Benito, the remuda wrangler, a barrel-shaped fellow with a lisp, sidestepped to reveal the form of a man on the ground. He was hunched and bleeding. And though the largest puddle of blood glistened in the growing daylight, it had begun to sheen over with a dull look.

The fallen man was Asa, an amiable young man who was perpetually out of breath and always smiling. He was a good sport, perhaps not the sharpest knife in the kitchen, but in Regis's estimation, one didn't need to be a genius to follow the orders of someone else.

None of that mattered, because he was dead. That much was obvious, for protruding from betwixt the man's shoulder blades stood a lance, angled. Feathers high up on the shaft riffled ever so slightly from an unfelt breeze.

Regis rode up and slid from the saddle, his eyes fixed on the awful sight before him. His own brutal feelings warred within him, knowing he was the cause of this man's death; all arguments in the world to the contrary could not dissuade him from that gruesome thought.

One of the men was weeping; the others looked far too spent

to expend even that much effort, though Regis knew that none of them felt any less awful about it than did he or the man crying.

He was about to speak, to say something, anything to interrupt the terrible stillness of the scene, when Benito said, "Oh, no . . ."

Everyone looked up at him, but he was looking behind them, to the east, toward the long, low ridge a quarter mile away. They all glanced in that direction, as well.

"Boys," said Regis, not taking his eyes off the line of riders strung out on the ridgetop. "We know they mean business, so two of you gather up young Asa. Take him back to the wagon and help Percy rig up his team. We have to make tracks. By my maps, there's a town, Fishville, or some such, ahead. We make it there, and we'll pick up more men, get some help from townsfolk."

"How far ahead, Boss?"

That was something Regis did have an answer for, and it wasn't something he wanted to tell them. But there was no use in life in sweetening bad news. "It's a good two days of hard pushing."

"A lot can happen in two days."

"Yes, it can. But moaning about it won't get us there any quicker. Now let's go. I'll circle around westward and bring up that bunch of laggers."

The men set to the sad task of dealing with Asa's body. As he was riding out, they paused again, with Benito resting one hand on the lance. They were unsure what to do.

Regis hated to do it, but he barked, more to get them to snap out of their hesitant reverie than anything. "Pull it out and let's go! Those killers will not let us be!"

As the herd slowly moved forward, Regis's instructions were the same to all the men he rode up alongside: "Everyone keep an eye out for them, in all directions; we don't know how many of them there are, but they know how many of us there are."

"Yes," said Cyril. "Unfortunately, not many."

"Can't disagree," said Regis, riding off to talk with others. "But we can't change that now."

"The boss sent me back here to help with the wagon," said Benito.

"How many did we lose?" said Percy, visoring his eyes as the young man rode up. "Who's that?" said Percy, not waiting for an answer to his first question.

"It's Asa."

"Oh no." It was all he could say. Everyone liked Asa. Heck, he thought, there wasn't a poke among them anybody disliked. A few were prickly, but Percy reckoned he was the worst of the lot, an assessment he'd make if he were any of the other men.

"I'm going to need help with Fergus."

"What's the matter with Ferg?" Benito rode closer and dismounted, the horse carrying Asa trailing behind him, the reins in his right hand. Then he saw the tall, older cowboy leaning against the wagon. "Ferg?"

"I'm all right, son, a graze. Percy's going to yarn the bullet on out of there as soon as he quits jawing with you." Fergus tried to smile, but he was too pained.

"Oh, okay, Ferg. I'm sorry."

"No . . . I'm funning you, boy."

"Get my team, Benito. And then tend the remuda. Just leave Asa here. Lay him out by the wagon."

The wrangler nodded and rode off.

"You can do this alone?"

"I can if you don't hit me. It's going to be rough, Fergus."

"I know, but I'm about out of time, son."

Percy had the tall man lie down on a tarpaulin along the left side of the wagon, still shaded from the sun.

"Here," said Percy, handing Fergus a brown bottle stoppered with a cork. "Medicinal."

"I thought this was a dry drive."

"It is. That's strictly for emergencies."

"Uh-huh, I don't recall having many before now, yet this here bottle appears to be half full."

"You think tending to you lot day after day isn't a sore trial bordering on agonizing every day of this drive for me?"

Fergus forced a grin. "I forgot who I was talking with." He swigged and sighed. "Ah, almost worth getting shot to taste that."

"Don't spare yourself. This will hurt."

"Oh, so this isn't the lot of it?"

"Might be. Might not." Percy allowed a grin of his own and checked the water he'd set on the boil. "Now lift that shirt if you can, and I'll clean the wound."

"How you going to get in there? Feels as if it's in my side meat pretty good."

Percy rummaged in a box he'd rigged up at the back of the wagon to hold his utensils and seasonings. "Ah," he said, and tugged free a long, narrow pair of wooden pinchers.

Thy measured a good eight to ten inches. He slid out his folding knife and narrowed the tweezing ends, shaving careful curls from the wood.

"They look like they'll do the trick nicely," said Fergus, becoming more relaxed with each swig of Percy's medicinal tincture.

"I hope so. I made them myself. Saw some in a shop one day and thought they'd be just the thing to fish out unwanted stray items from my stew. You wouldn't believe what all floats on in there when I'm cooking."

"Not so sure I want to know."

Percy nodded and plunged the freshly whittled working end of the pinchers in the pan of steaming water. Then he dipped some of the same hot water into a small basin and washed his hands.

"What are you doing that for?" said Fergus.

"You want me to rummage in your innards with grimy mitts?" Percy shook his head as if he'd been asked the most absurd question of his life.

"Huh, I'll be."

"We'll see about that," said Percy; then he plucked the long, wooden tweezers from the water. He rolled up a rag into a cigar-like tube shape. "Bite down on this. I'm about to commence."

Fergus did as he was told, right after he'd swigged again. No sooner had he stuffed the rag into his mouth than Percy, gently but quickly, wiped the barely bleeding wound with another wet rag.

It did seem as if the wound was far enough to the outer edge of the man's side that it had missed anything vital inside. He plunged the tweezers into the wound, and Fergus's eyes widened.

He made a harsh, deep, quick bellowing sound into the rag and clutched the nearly empty brown bottle so hard that his fingers and knuckles whitened. Percy thought the man might crack the glass.

But he didn't writhe and buck, for which the cook was grateful.

It was then that the prisoner, who they'd both forgotten about, began to come around once more. He, too, made groaning sounds.

Three, then four inches of the wooden utensil disappeared inside the cowboy's side. Percy squinted and angled his head to better see into the wound. As gently as he was able, Percy dug and moved the tool left, right, then a bit deeper. Each time, Fergus groaned and bellowed into the rag stoppering his mouth. His cheeks puffed and dropped in rapid succession with the effort.

Finally, Percy was convinced that perhaps the bullet had gone in deeper than he'd suspected when the wooden tips touched something hard. He hoped it wasn't bone. Didn't seem to be, as it was off to the side where any bones should reside in the man's side, still a hand width below the bottom of the man's jutting rib cage.

"I think I found it," he said, in a quiet voice. He'd been squinting and looking upward, across the plain to the west, but not seeing anything. He widened the tool's jaws and tried to get the thing out of Fergus. He thought it might be working, and he prepared to lift it free when the prisoner again moaned louder and Percy paused, holding the tool still.

"Shut up!" he snapped, glaring at the man seated in the sun, trussed and sweating and looking, by the jerking of his head and his drooping eyes, rather sickly.

The cook's harsh directive worked, and the man sat still, his head wobbling.

Percy glanced up at Fergus, who was wide-eyed and staring at him. "I meant that for him, not you."

Fergus kept his eyes wide but had reduced his own moaning to a soft growl.

Great, thought Percy. That'll do nothing to change the man's opinion of me. He kept the tweezered bullet held pinched tightly between the wooden jaws of the tool and kept slowly lifting it free. It worked, and he held up the glistening red and gray thing, gore slicking the sides of the wood.

He smiled and held it closer to Fergus, who had spit out the rag. "Lordy, boy, you have got a career as a doctor in your future."

"Me? No thank you. Too much whining for my taste." He smiled at Fergus. "How are you feeling?"

"About like you'd feel if somebody jammed lead and logs into you and then rooted around in there for a while."

Percy stood. "You want this," he said, holding the bullet up.

"Sure. Make me a fine keepsake, I reckon."

"You could make it into a ring for some lucky lady one day."

"No, not this chicken. I've outlived that stretch of my days. I aim to rope and ride and die in the saddle. A lone wolf."

"Well, you nearly got your wish today." Percy rummaged in the back of the wagon.

"Not a wish I was making when I woke."

Percy walked back with a fresh bottle, the same as the other but full. He uncorked it and without warning glugged a goodly amount into Fergus's wound.

The rangy cowboy barked like a scalded coyote. When he got his wind back, he said, "Boy, you give a man a warning before you commence to terrorize him like that!"

Percy turned red and pulled back as if he'd been slapped across the face. "Sorry, Fergus."

"It's all right. It needed it, I guess. Oh, but that smarts."

Right about then, Regis rode up from southward, having angled around the nearest cluster of the herd.

"Ferg? You all right?"

"I will be now. Thanks to Percy. He dragged this here out of me." Fergus held up the bullet between grimy, bloody fingers, then took a hit on the bottle.

Regis nodded. "Good, good. You be okay to ride?"

"I sure can try."

"Not until I stitch you up. Otherwise you'll bleed and be of no use to anyone."

"How long will that take?" said Regis, eyeballing the ridge to the east. The attackers were gone again.

"I can be ready to roll in a half an hour."

"Well, they're still out there, appearing and then disappearing on the horizon. You have fifteen minutes," said Regis, jerking the reins to keep moving. Then he looked down by the end of the wagon. "He's still alive?"

The prisoner had leaned back against the wagon. Only his chest and belly rising and falling with quick, short breaths showed he was still with them.

"Yep," said Percy. "Too tough to die, I guess."

"Too bad. Now we have to deal with him."

"I'll think of something," said Percy. "Go on and let me get to work!"

As he rode out, Regis realized that once again, he had been chastised by his cook. The young man had no problem doling out directives. He'd make a fine boss of an outfit one of these days.

He was bothered that Fergus had been wounded, as Fergus was a senior member of the team and had more cattle drive experience than any of the others put together, Regis included. "Don't be so selfish, Royle," he mumbled to himself. "At least Ferg is alive."

Chapter 11

"So what will you call it?"

"Pardon me?" Marietta Valdez turned to see who it was that had crept up on her. If there was one thing she wished she could change about herself, it was the intensity and focus she slipped into when she found herself immersed in a task, particularly one new to her.

The ranch, Regis's ranch, was no exception. Despite what she had told him, she now knew that her presence here at the ranch, run by a thin, overworked crew in his absence, was useful. And so she had, with reluctance, stayed on at the ranch to help Tut with what she might.

She had, from the start of becoming acquainted with Regis Royle, disliked the notion of a ranch being here on this vast swath of land she had known her entire life.

She was still not backing down from not wanting to cede ownership of the place to him, not one bit. But the idea that something so foreign, something so very in keeping with the white conquerors' mentality, could ever take over this place had until recently seemed absurd. And yet now here she was, working, in Regis's absence, to help keep his dream alive. Which part of herself was she allowing to die? Perhaps that was the wrong way to think of it. Perhaps it was, as with all things in life, merely a time of much change.

Early on in getting to know him, she had not cared one bit about his ranch. She had, in fact, felt it would be fine if it failed, and dried up and blew away like dust on a hot, windy day.

But then she had come to see the place up close and for herself, giving in to his requests that she at least come to tour it, see what he and his men had done. He had been like a little boy, almost pleading with her, and there was something about his manner that made her agree.

And so she had allowed him to take her on a tour. It had been on a day in early spring, when daisies and primrose had begun blooming, revealing their colorful selves before the gamma grass grew up, taller and thicker, and silvered by summer in gentle breezes across the land. And now, she realized, it was that day that had changed her mind.

Marietta turned to see who it was who had spoken behind her. It was Cormac Delany, Regis's business partner and, from what Regis had told her, likely his best friend, as well, despite their hardships of late.

And yet there was also the Texas Ranger known as Bone. She had yet to meet that man and was uncertain if she wanted to. He sounded like one of those men who Mexicans had come to fear and hate, for reasons not unfounded. And yet she tried to keep such judgments to herself until she met someone. As the nuns had told her, the opinions of others did not mean they were yours. Judge for yourself. And then don't judge—instead, be kind.

"Mr. Delany," she said, resting on the hoe handle. She had hitched up her long, black dress slightly to keep the bottom from dragging. Dresses were so impractical for real sweat labor, but she was a woman, and the expectation was that she and her kind must dwell well within convention. And it rankled her.

"Cormac, please."

She nodded, aware that the morning light was angling such that, despite her veil, he could probably see some of her face. Her scarred, hideous face.

It was the one thing about herself she hated. But even that was somehow changing—barely, yet she knew it was. In coming to know Regis, and in allowing him to see her face in full, and not flinching, not revealing a fib behind his eyes when he saw her face fully for the first time, in all that, she had come to hope that she might one day not need the veil.

This, she doubted, but still, it had been an exciting fantasy to dwell upon, nothing more.

"What did you mean when you said that?"

"Oh, what will you call it? I meant the ranch."

"I do not understand."

"The ranch. I assume you and Regis are . . . oh." Cormac's face reddened. "I have overstepped the mark, I am afraid. My apologies, ma'am."

"I still do not understand."

Cormac sighed. "I had assumed, wrongly, I am sure, or perhaps prematurely, at any rate, that you and Regis were to be wed. At some point."

"Oh." Such a notion was impossible to her. Still, when she let her foolish thoughts trail off on their own while drifting to sleep at night, she dreamt that, if life had only worked out differently, they might well have . . .

"I am sorry, ma'am. It was thoughtless of me to presume."

"No, it is all right, Cormac. It cannot be, but you were not to know that."

"Oh. Well, I know that Regis is very fond of you. These past few weeks before the trail drive, you were about the only thing he wanted to talk about. Of course, preparing for that blasted drive took over every conversation and all our spare change, I don't mind saying, but still . . ."

Marietta could not help but smile. It was nice to hear. She wanted to believe with all her heart of hearts that Regis Royle felt toward her as she wanted him to feel. Perhaps as she, too felt, but . . . of what use would it be?

"This garden will not weed itself," she said, perhaps a bit too suddenly, turning back to her task. Then she thought of something and looked at him once more. "Mr. Delany, or Cormac, rather. Why are you here?"

He chuckled. "I could ask you the same thing. We both know that you and I are on opposite sides of this ranch situation. Who owns what, that sort of thing. But right now, Regis and I have about everything we own, and then some, tied up in this place. We can't afford to let it go belly up. But you? Are you protecting your property just in case the tide turns in your favor?"

Marietta felt her face heating up. She did not wish to allow herself to feel the obvious anger this man had kept quelled below the surface of his initial false niceties. Cormac Delany was resentful of her being here and fearful of her presence, too.

Finally, she said, "Mr. Delany, I am not here to undermine anything you and Regis have built. I am not here to overthrow or usurp any investments you have made. I am here merely because I promised Regis I would keep an eye on things, as he put it."

"Well, all right, then. That's what I'm here for, too," said Cormac. "So if you have commitments, I can look after things."

"Before he left, Regis confided in me that he did not think you would visit the ranch much while he was gone."

"Why would he say that?" said Cormac, his jaw muscles working.

"Because you have not been here very much, at least that is what Regis tells me."

The Irishman was about to respond with barely controlled, slow-boil anger when a Mexican boy rode toward them.

Marietta recognized him as one of the youths living on the ranch with his family, a family Regis had introduced her to about a week before he left. The boy halted his head-shaking pony and glanced at Cormac, but spoke to Marietta in Spanish. "Señora! Senora! Mama has sent me to find help! There are banditos by the river. They are taking our goats and trampling the crops!"

Marietta grabbed her hoe halfway down the long haft. "Show

me!" And without looking at Cormac, she mounted her black horse and rode close behind the barefoot youth on his pony.

They made for the southern edge of what Regis called the Ranch Proper, of what she had come to realize was the heart of what they had thus far built. Beyond the ranch houses and barns and corrals and cook shed and bunk houses sat Royle Ranch village, relocated from across the border, to become rebuilt here, better and cleaner.

In return for moving everyone to Royle Ranch range, Regis had told Marietta that he expected each member to put their shoulder to the wheel that was the growing ranch. In return, furthermore, he would build the homes, a church, a school, and support them.

Marietta rode up behind the boy and jumped down from her horse, the hoe still gripped in her hand, her skirts gathered and pinned below her knees, her feet clad in black boots.

She was a tall woman and veiled, her head topped with a flat-crown, broad-brim hat, and she looked as one in command as she strode to the small group of women headed by Belinda Tuttle, Tut's wife and village schoolteacher, herding children running about, scared as rabbits by the situation playing out at the river. Soon she had them wrangled and ushered into the schoolhouse.

The rest of the villagers, young and old, men and women, all clad in the white, rough-spun cloth of people of the land, were spread out, some armed with guns, most with cudgels and farming implements—hoes, rakes, forks, shovels, axes.

They were doing their best to defend their vast crops, their farm animals, including goats, cattle, donkeys, chickens, and geese. All about them, yipping, shouting men on horseback wearing tall-crown, broad-brim hats weaved in and out among them. The raiders taunted the angry villagers, lashing ropes and long reins and whips at them, all the while other bandits worked to scatter and herd livestock and crush and stomp their ragged way through crops.

Marietta took all this in with wide, sweeping glances, and then Cormac hustled over to her side, his hands filled with a rifle and a revolver. "We have to stop this."

"Cormac . . . yes, we do. I am uncertain how, but that does not mean I can do nothing."

"I feel the same. I'm going to ride out, meet them head on."

"Lupita!" shouted the boy who had escorted them back. He pointed toward the crops.

Marietta and Cormac glanced that way and saw a young woman, no older than fourteen, it seemed to Cormac, stranded in the midst of a crop, a long-handled implement in her grasp.

The riders closed in on her, whooping it up and shouting words that Cormac and Marietta assumed were lewd and vile. The girl, even from their distance of perhaps 150 feet, seemed frightened, her shoulders drawn up as she spun in a circle, trying but not succeeding because of their numbers, to keep the riders in view.

"This cannot stand!" With that, Cormac was off, running back to his horse. He climbed aboard, slower than he would have liked, but he was, after all, a man of a certain age, and a river man, at that, more used to the rocking and rolling of vessels than he was that of horses.

Within moments, he was heeling the horse hard, beelining for the girl. He threaded through and past a handful of running, shouting men and women. He reined up at the edge of the crop, a well-tended field of squash and peppers, the field in which the girl was trapped.

His abrupt halt almost seemed as if he were afraid to trample the crop. But no, Cormac raised his rifle to his shoulder and took aim on one of the invading riders. With no shout of warning, he pulled the trigger, and the man screamed, not a yelp of antici-pated glee this time, but one of shock and pain.

The shot rider hung on, jerking back on his reins, his big, broad-brim hat flopping back off his head, but retained by its chinstrap. It bounced against his shoulder blades in counterpoint to his horse's frantic bucking.

More carefully tended crops surrendered to the beast's lunges, but Cormac paid this no heed. He delivered another shot to another of the rogues, and landed a solid hit to the brute's chest, possibly his shoulder, it was difficult for Cormac to tell.

Again, this man stayed in the saddle, but not for long. Clutching at his wound, he lost his balance and slipped to the side, his own gun, a revolver, pinwheeled from his grasp. He slopped to the earth and did not rise.

The first man Cormac shot looked about ready to do the same, his body slamming up and down in the saddle.

By then, the other three riders who had also been closing in on the terrified young woman had halted their efforts and had instead begun sending lead toward the irate Irishman. Instinct drove Cormac to hunker low in the saddle, but he kept on with returning fire, matching theirs shot for shot, and advancing on the retreating riders.

By then, other bandits had ceased their destructive tactics and had begun milling, some sending poorly aimed shots toward Cormac, some heeling their horses and heading southward. As each one made that choice, the advancing Royle Ranch villagers grew emboldened. Those that carried guns, only three that Cormac could see, also sent bullets toward the bandits.

One of them landed a solid shot, and the man stiffened in the saddle, his arms whipping skyward as if he were warding off crows. Then he slammed once, twice, and his right boot slipped from the stirrup. His horse churned even harder, jamming the still-screaming rider to the earth, and landing a series of stomps to the thumping, flailing body.

The villagers wasted no time in rescuing the young girl, and then in descending on the three attackers left behind. They gained two horses and gear out of it, and a total of six guns.

Cormac vowed to make certain the villagers were given more

weapons. They hadn't needed them, because more of the ranch hands had been around before this.

He was certain Regis would have outfitted them better with weapons had he suspected the border raiders would be so bold as to attack Royle Ranch in his absence.

Regis and the other local ranchers of the region had spent previous seasons enforcing their own brand of vigilante justice—entirely justified, in Cormac's opinion—on what had been a spreading vile sickness of rustling rings. They had been made up largely of whites and rogue half-breed thieves who would have rather stolen from hardworking ranchers and farmers than work for their own living.

In response, Regis and the others had formed what they called the Cattlemen's Justice Consortium which, among other tasks, had succeeded in stamping out most of that vile rustling scourge. But now, there was apparently a new threat bubbling along the border.

"They will be back, and we must be prepared," said Marietta.

"But how?" said one bedraggled man with an angry red weal across his face and slashed shirt. He had been whipped by the attackers, and the blow had, by thin good fortune, cut to the outside of his left eye. "There are not enough of the ranch men about. Those who Señor Royle left behind are too busy tending to the ranch to protect what we should be able to defend ourselves."

"No," said Marietta. "That is not the deal that was struck with Señor Royle. You should have the protection you need if you are to farm on this side of the river."

"Sí, sí, but as I said, there are not enough of us, or the gringo ranch hands. Oh, it is hopeless. They will be back, and they will take the rest of our stock, trample the rest of our crops."

"No," said Cormac. "I will not let that happen."

"But how? How can you prevent this, Señor Delany?"

He turned to Marietta. "We mustn't forget the Texas Rangers. They are stretched thin these days, given their low numbers and the rampant border troubles such as we've seen here, but it can't hurt to try to find them. With or without their help, I have an idea, but I will need a little time. I believe I can get men from our warehouse and from the docks in Brownsville. Perhaps others."

"How will you pay them?"

"I . . . I will skip paying the lawyers' fees just now, and see if I can get one more loan. Oh, I pray to God that Regis had luck with selling the herd. Without that money, we are lost. All lost."

Marietta looked at him, then at the villagers gathered about them. "No," she said in a quiet voice that only he could hear. "We will not let that happen, Cormac. We cannot."

The men of the village had been the only able-bodied men Regis had not called on when the drive came about. He had needed a skeleton crew to run the ranch while he was away with what few cowhands could be spared. The rest, most of them sorely green, were placed under Tut's management. Green or no, most of them had some experience wrangling cattle and ranching.

The Mexicans had precious little such experience, but they did know how to keep a place going, and knew far more than anyone else about crops, critters, and growing food.

"Are there others?" said Cormac.

"Not many, no; what vaqueros there are have either gone with Regis on the trail drive or are here but are out working the range. Regis was hoping the villagers would be able to keep the place alive until his return."

"The drive must be a success, or all of these people will have to move on."

"Why?" said Marietta. "Just because Regis Royle's vision of a ranch for this place may die does not mean these people will die with it. They will live here much the same as they have lived elsewhere. It is the people who must make that decision and not

someone who wishes to possess this place. As if such a place"—
she waved her long arms wide, taking in the entirety of the beautiful, rolling land—"could be owned by someone." She shook
her head at the folly of it.

"I'm beginning to see what you mean," said Cormac, nodding
and squinting about him, taking it all in. "And so help me, I'm
beginning to see what it is Regis loves about this place."

"Yes," she said, and Cormac realized she was looking at him.
"I believe you are, Cormac Delany."

He could not be certain, but it almost looked as if, beneath her
veil, Marietta Valdez was smiling at him. Perhaps there was more
to this ranch than he had been willing to admit to Regis. More
than he had been willing, been allowing himself, to see.

As they talked, hoofbeats from eastward grabbed their attention. Three riders pounding hard made straight for them. Guns
were raised, but Cormac held up a hand. "Hold! They're our men!"

It was Tut and two of his ranch hands. They thundered to a
halt beside them, dust billowing up about them. "We heard shots!"
said Tut, searching their faces for answers.

Cormac nodded. "Border bandits—we drove them off, but they
made a whale of a mess." He waved an arm toward the fields,
where the villagers were already roving among the trampled
crops, doing their best to repair damage. Others were frantically
chasing and rounding up their scattered livestock.

"Is Belinda . . . my wife . . . is she all right?" Tut searched the
fields with his eyes.

Marietta nodded. "She took the youngest children to the
school to keep them safe."

"Oh, thank God," said Tut, sagging in relief and exhaustion.
"We were off working on the east gathering pens. Cormac," he
said. "Can I talk with you in private?"

"Sure, son," said the older man. "But whatever you have to
say, you might want to include Señorita Valdez, too."

"Oh, oh, yes, you bet. Just wondering if you might be able to track down the rangers. I can't spare anybody here to ride for Bone's place. I don't even know if he's there just now, anyway."

Cormac nodded. "We were just discussing that. I'll track down those blasted rangers, don't worry. And I'm going to try to get more men from town to help out."

"All right, thanks," said Tut. "But if they don't have any ranch experience, I just don't know if I have the time to train them. If you see what I mean."

"I do. And I'll make sure not to saddle you with any clunkers." Cormac smiled, trying to keep the young man's burdens as light as he was able. A tall order, he thought. But I have to try.

Chapter 12

Jarvis "Bone" McGraw stood in the dooryard before his modest ranch house, his broad hat tipped back on his head, and he squinted toward the woman on the porch. He would hold her and hug her and kiss her and then, he knew, he would take his leave of this place.

If all worked out, it would be a short time away. He did not even want to be gone from here. Not ever again. He'd always loved the place, certainly as a younger man when he'd visited the old couple who owned it. Then, when they had left the place to him, his fondness for the modest but excellent ranch had only grown.

Then Margaret had come into his life, one of the women captured by slavers and forced to endure beastly abuse and more, all for the sick greed and desires of evil men. But he and a few of the boys at the ranch had rescued the women from those foul men, and killed them in the process. Bone and the others had shed no tears for the vermin they had dispatched.

And now Margaret was the biggest, most important part of his life. She had done the one thing that no other woman had ever done—she had captured his heart, and he hers. And neither of them had sought this. But there it was. And now they were married and talking of having a brood of their own, and he did not want to leave her ever again.

But he had to. He was, and had been for far longer than he had ever been anything in his life, a Texas Ranger. And now he was a senior ranger, one of the original and old guard, training up the new crop of keen young men. But there were precious few of them these days, and at a time, once again, when they were sorely needed, especially along the border with Old Mexico.

Would border trash, from both sides, ever dry up and die? He did not think so. There had been a time, many years before, when he had been far more hopeful about such things, but not now. Now, he saw the world for what it was.

It was populated with good people, to be sure, but also with a whole lot of filth, mostly men who wished to do as little as possible and yet have handed to them as much as they desired. Kindness mattered not to these brutes. Yes, there was a time when Bone had said, "We have them on the run, and their kind will be wiped out soon."

That did not happen. Instead, the vermin gained the upper hand, and the rangers lost men and became stretched too thin and fought evil-minded folks within the borders of Texas. And now here it was again, one of those spiky times when Rangers were needed. And he could not let them down.

Particularly not when one of their own, Howard Strickland, that young, fresh-faced ranger, had been killed while investigating a rail line camp with Bone. No, Bone thought, he owed the Rangers time. How much of his time to give them was still something he had yet to determine.

But now he looked at Margaret standing there on the top step of their home, drying her already dry, red hands on her freshly laundered apron, looking extra spiffed, he knew, just for him and his departure. When he saw this and everything else about the place, even old Ramon, his longtime help, Bone was nearly unable to walk to her and do what needed doing.

Finally, she said, "The sooner you leave, the sooner you will be back."

Bone wanted more than anything to believe this. He moved toward the steps and stood at the base, looking up. He cleared his throat. "Margaret, I—"

But she cut him off by stepping down so that they looked in each other's eyes. "Everything is fine. Ramon and I will care for it all, and we will be fine. You had best do the same. Come back when you can." She hugged him then, burying her face in his chest. "As soon as you can."

They stood that way for long, long minutes, and then she pushed away from him, smiling up at him. He kissed her forehead, smiled though he hardly felt it was possible, and she did the same. Then she turned and walked into the darkness of the kitchen, the screened door closing softly behind her.

Riding on out of there aboard Bub was the most difficult thing Bone had ever done, in all his long days.

It took many miles before the man could come to appreciate the fine day he had been given to take his leave of his ranch and his wife. But finally, he was able to gaze up, up into the brightest of blue skies and see the wonder of the perfect day there. He pulled in a deep breath and slowly let it out.

"Bub," he said to his trusted horse. "Let's do as Margaret said—make tracks for Corpus Christi. The sooner we get this foolishness over with, the sooner we can return."

And they did just that, letting the sun soak into his tired body. He'd been all but killed in that awful fracas with the band of killers at the rail camp, the same brutes who'd laid low the young ranger. And then he'd been mauled by that mountain cat while roving his own property. He surely didn't think he'd live through either of those episodes.

He did not want to tempt the fates, but the rangers were in need. And he was obliged to help, curse him.

Bone made it halfway to the coast, making straight for Corpus Christi, where he had been told in a dispatch that he would meet up with several other seasoned Texas Rangers. He'd made it but halfway, and had been thinking of calling it a day as he'd gotten a later start than he would have liked, but in truth, he didn't much care.

He'd get there when he got there. He knew for certain nobody was going to begin any sort of training or mission without him. He wasn't certain if he should feel good about that notion or old. He settled on not caring a whit, and instead looked for a place to brew up a pot of trail coffee.

He wasn't certain if he was going to camp early, then get up early and make it to town with much of the day ahead of him, or end up spending the night in town itself. That would mean he'd finish off this day in the dark, arriving there with the nightlife kicking into full trot.

Bone thought on this as he kindled a small coffee fire and fed the hungry little flames. And then, just like that, he decided that no, he was not up to seeing and hearing so many people so dang close to him.

He had never been one for crowds and such, and the notion of facing that in a few hours did not sit well within him. No, sir, he'd camp here and buy himself more hours of reprieve.

He knew he was merely postponing the inevitable, but that was all right with him. It would give him more time to think about his life, and other topics that demanded consideration, such as his infuriating friend, Regis Royle.

He'd not heard from the man in a number of weeks, not since Regis left him while Bone was laid up recovering from the lion attack. And frankly, the hubris—one of those useful words that Margaret had taught him just by using it now and again—of the man had been enough to keep Bone from thinking about him, and gladly so. He had plenty of his own affairs to tend to.

He didn't really think that Regis was about to head up a cattle drive on his own, anyway. But the man might just hire on somebody he'd trust as well as he trusted Bone to do the job. Trouble was, and Bone knew this himself, getting men to work at the ranch, at any ranch, was a dicey proposition these days.

It was the rumblings of war that were to blame. It seemed that was all men were eager to do these days—fight, fight, and fight, down south, up north, in the east, over to the southeast. And then he'd heard there was fighting waging here and there in Europe, too.

"When isn't there?" he said out loud, to Bub, who stood but eight or so feet away, cropping a patch of greening grasses.

"When isn't there what?" said a voice.

Bone spun, his big pistol palmed and cocked and leveled on whoever it was who had crept up on him.

"Easy now, man! Easy with that thing . . ."

A dozen feet from him stood a whip-thin black man in threadbare clothes. His hands were held high, and his eyes were open wide. "Don't shoot me, please."

Bone eyed him for a long moment, and kept the gun trained on him as he glanced past the fellow. He didn't see sign of anyone else, but he knew that road agents often worked in pairs, and sometimes more than two.

Finally, Bone said, in a big, deep voice that he gladly emphasized, "Who are you and why did you sneak up on me?"

The man began to smile and lower his hands.

"If the hands are too heavy, I'll gladly make them lighter for you and shoot them off."

The man lost the fledgling smile and hoisted his hands once more. "You are a cold one, mister."

"Nope. Just don't like being caught unawares."

"Well now, that's hardly my doing. I been walking in this direction all day."

"I didn't see you."

"That doesn't surprise me."

"What do you mean by that?" said Bone.

"Aw, take it easy, man, I meant that I come from a join-up trail a half mile or so back. Making for Corpus Christi, I am."

"You didn't answer my questions."

"You're right. But I will now. I'm Jervis Latham. Late of points west of here. And as for why I crept up on you, well, I didn't try to. But you were busy making your fire and talking to yourself. I scuffed on up, and here I am."

Bone eased the hammer to half-cock. "I see that."

Jervis Latham nodded. "That fire could use more tending."

Bone did not glance at it, though he knew the man was correct. "Come over here so you're before me." He made a quick motion to the left with his head.

Latham complied. "Can I put my hands down now?"

"No." With reluctance, Bone used one hand to tend the fire and kept his gaze flicking between the flames and the stranger. "Where are your things?"

"Things?"

"Yeah," said Bone. "Clothes and food and such."

"Oh, well now, Jervis Latham travels light. Mostly because I have been robbed."

"You don't say."

"I do. But I don't think you much care."

"You are correct."

Bone continued to alternate his gaze between the growing fire and Jervis Latham. The man did indeed look to have little more on his person than raggy clothes.

Bone poked at the fire. He'd grown tired of holding the heavy weapon and wagged the barrel. "Sit down, Mr. Latham."

The man did. "And my arms?"

"Rest them, too."

The lanky man rubbed his limbs. "You don't mind me saying, you are not a little surly."

"That so?"

"Mm-hmm."

Bone let the moment hang for a bit, then said, "You always so forward with folks holding a gun on you?"

"Sometimes. It's a trait that got me this far."

"And where exactly is it you are headed?"

"I told you, I'm making for Corpus Christi."

"So you did. But I meant in life. Where is it you are headed, Jervis Latham?"

For the first time in their brief encounter, the black man didn't respond right away. After a few moments, he said, "Well now, that's an odd question, you don't mind me saying. I can't decide if it's too personal or not."

Bone shrugged. "Suit yourself; I wasn't necessarily looking for an answer. In fact, it was rude of me to ask. I'm tired and undecided about a few things, and I am going to have a cup of coffee. There will be enough for a second cup if you'd like some."

Latham's raised eyebrows showed that he would indeed like a cup. They each waited in silence for long moments while the coffee bubbled and rolled. Bone rummaged in his saddlebag beside him and pulled out a tin cup. He filled it and handed it, handle first, to Jervis.

"Oh, I can't take your cup, mister."

"I'm the host, so you have no say in the matter." Bone extended the cup closer. Jervis took it and nodded. "I thank you kindly."

Bone grunted. "You bet." He made busy with his bag so as not to make the man feel as though he had to rush drinking the coffee and burn himself. But Jervis was doing just that, making pained faces as he sipped.

"Take your time, take your time. Hot coffee should be enjoyed, not rushed."

"But it's your cup. I'm sure you'd like some, too."

"I look like I'm going anywhere? Take 'er easy."

"Appreciate that, mister."

"They call me Bone."

"Bone?"

"Yep."

Latham nodded, sipped. "Odd name."

"I said that's what I'm called. Doesn't mean it's my name."

"Oh."

Bone couldn't help but smile. Latham noticed and offered a small one himself. "Interesting to me that your name is Jervis."

Latham stiffened and sipped, then said, "It's a good name."

"You bet it is. Mine's Jarvis."

"No! Is it?"

Bone nodded.

Latham sipped his coffee. "Why'd you pull that gun on me?"

"I drew down on you because you surprised me and I was, and still am, annoyed because I allowed myself to be sneaked up on."

"Well, I wasn't exactly sneaking." Latham nodded. "But I see your point. I'm harmless enough. Can't offer any more than that. I have a broke-blade pocketknife and a fishhook and some twine. That's about it. No guns on me."

"Good to hear it."

Latham upended the cup and drained the last drop. "As to your question, I am making for Corpus Christi because a man some time back told me that's where I could find the Texas Rangers."

Bone gave Latham a hard stare. "Why do you want the Rangers?"

Bone saw the flinty look in Latham's eyes. The man gazed westward, as if he could see whatever it was that dogged him. But Bone knew that the sorts of things that truly haunt a man are not visible. They are phantoms from the past, and the best a haunted man can do is face the unseen and take them in and figure out a way to exist with them.

For some men, that is to burrow down deep into a bottle; for others, it's to sweat like a beast until hard work cripples them and kills them far too early. For others still, it is perhaps enough to mete out hard justice, lawful or otherwise, to those who have committed the grievous wrongs a soul can't forget or forgive.

Bone reckoned that Jervis Latham was one of the latter. It was the man's miles-long stare that tipped off Bone.

"You cook, Jervis?"

That roused the man from his reverie. He looked at Bone. "Can I cook, you say. Look here, never was a child born to Maudie Latham who did not know his way around a fry pan."

"Good." Bone unpacked a saddlebag and laid out the contents on the earth beside the fire. "Prove it."

Jervis glanced at the items: a small skillet, a sack of corn meal, slab bacon, a packet of dried apple slices, and a sack of fresh-that-morning biscuits. His eyes lingered on the biscuits.

"I . . . um . . ." He looked aside and ran long fingers over his stubbled, jutting chin.

"I'd have more, but I wasn't certain I'd be encamped tonight on my way to Christi."

"I see," said Jervis, still not looking back at either Bone or the food.

"In fact," said Bone, "my Margaret made these biscuits fresh this morning, and I fear if they don't get et soon, they'll spoil in this heat. You'd be doing me a favor to give some of them a home."

That brought Latham's gaze back. Bone plucked a couple out of the sack and shoved the rest over to Jervis. "Have at them. They'll go good with more coffee. I'll set some on the boil while you tend to vittles."

"You are a poor liar, sir. Those biscuits would keep for a few days, I bet. Still, you certain?"

"Why sure," said Bone. "One thing I can't stand is to see good food gone to waste."

Latham handed Bone the cup and Bone filled it with the last of the coffee, then commenced to sip it down. Still good and hot.

"You . . . you didn't wash it out."

Bone paused, the cup in the air. "I need to?"

"No, no. It's just that we're different, you and me."

"Not so much that I can see," said Bone. "Both like coffee, and we're both on the road to Corpus Christi."

Latham nodded and said nothing. He set to the task of preparing to cook, and seemed to know what he was doing. In short order, he had thick slices of bacon sizzling and corn cakes popping alongside. And, as Bone had suspected, the younger man began to talk.

"You say you have a wife. That's good," said Latham. "A man ought to have family."

Bone nodded and sipped. "You?"

That's when Jervis clammed up. He kept prodding the bacon with the wooden spoon Bone had handed him. After a few long moments of silence, in a low voice, he said, "Had one. A family."

He looked up, then back down at his task. "West of Texas. We holed up there, me and, well, me and my wife, Tilly. Had a small patch all to ourselves. Grew melons and corn, the works. Even had chickens. I tell you, never has there been a man more proud. Except when Tilly whelped one of each, a boy and a girl." He smiled then, and shook his head at what was to him a most amazing adventure.

"Where are they now?" said Bone, who nearly regretted saying so right away.

Latham did not respond right away, and Bone said nothing more, but he saw that the man's eyes had teared.

"Again, I have said something that was rude. I apologize, Jervis. Blame it on me being sour today."

"No, it's all right." Latham sighed and prodded the sizzling bacon and browning corn cakes. "It happened in the night, as such things will. My Tilly grabbed my arm and shook me hard. 'Jervis!' she said. 'You wake up! There's somebody out there!'"

"I slept like a dropped tree in those days. I was working hard then, you see. With the farm and all, trying to make a go of it for my family. But that got me awake. Sure enough, I heard sounds out there, horses and low, coarse shouts, then I heard the chickens get all riled, as chickens will do. So I rolled out of bed and snatched up my hardwood club. I had no gun, you see, but I can swing a mighty club. Even more in those days. I was stronger then, all that field work."

Latham nibbled the inside of his lip as if considering something; then he nodded once, and while he stirred around the food, he resumed his story. "I saw two men, one on horseback, one had jumped down and he was killing the chickens, and quick, like he was familiar with the task. Now, those chickens were my Tilly's pride, you see, because I never wanted them from the start, but she was determined to have some.

"Wanted a big flock, said we could end up selling eggs. And she was right. They were good to have. We ate some, too, which was fine, just fine. Tilly was one cook you'd never forget. So good. So when those men commenced to killing our chickens, I pulled on my trousers and took my club outdoors and stood as big as I could before my home. 'Look here!' I said. 'You hungry, you knock on my door and I'll find you some food! But to steal from a man ain't right!' Well, that's about all I got out, because another of those men I never did see come up on me from behind, and he whomped me good."

Latham rubbed the back of his head and shook it slowly side to side. "Should have known. Before I dropped, I got a look at them. Even the one who clubbed me, because he looked down at me and said something in Spanish as I was fading out. Then he laughed. They all did. They laughed even louder when my Tilly came running out of the house shouting and cursing at them. She dropped down beside me and held my head. I tried to tell her it would be okay, to get back in the house, but I couldn't seem to make my mouth work. About the only time in my life that ever happened."

He rubbed his jaw and slid the skillet off the fire, onto a couple of rocks.

Bone knew that as painful as it was for Latham to tell the story, he needed to finish it out.

"If ever there was a man who needed to not pass out of his

waking self and into a blasted stupor, it was me, and it was that night. Oh, but I have gone over that time that night, those moments when Tilly looked into my eyes, over and over again. And every time I come up with the black, blank ghost face of death and nothing more. Nothing more."

Jervis shuddered and stared into the fire.

Bone knew he wasn't even there, with him at that moment. He was off by himself, deep in his own past, deep in his own mind, reliving a hell no man should have to, but that he would never escape.

"I came to hours later. It was raining, a rare thing in those parts, but something always cherished by the folks thereabouts. In fact, it was them folks, our neighbors there in New Hope, who found me. They saw the fire. Burning even in the rain. Imagine that." He nodded his head in wonder.

"There was commotion and running around, and they all thought I was dead, but I rose up, not quite like Lazarus. Would that I was dead, but no, I was alive. But not my Tilly." Jervis shook his head slowly.

"She was . . . she was gone. They found her . . . naked and . . . savaged, that's the only word to describe it. She had fought so hard, she ripped out some of her fingernails. Imagine that?"

Jervis looked at Bone for the first time then, but again, the ranger doubted the man was really seeing him.

Jervis also wasn't crying. His eyes did not glisten, his cheeks were dry, but Bone knew that was only because he'd shed his tears long, long ago. He guessed the man was truly cried out.

"I could hardly stand, but I managed to stagger on over to where one of the neighbors had covered Tilly over with a singed blanket from the fired house. Those men had set fire to my house after they'd finished with Tilly and set it alight. With my babies inside. This I know because the neighbors come running when they saw the fire in the night sky.

"But it's a fair piece, and they got there far too late. My babies, the boy and the girl, they burned alive in their beds. Neighbors found them that way. Smoke and flame got them before the neighbors could.

"Imagine that. There I was, knocked cold and addled and unable to do a thing while my Tilly was savaged and killed and my babies burned in their beds. Imagine that, will you. What kind of a man am I?" Latham sat there, shaking his head and staring at the glowing fire.

"Oh, I was crazy for a time. Didn't know what to do. Kept thinking even after we buried my family that I might somehow find them in the cinders and ash. But they weren't there. Neighbors tried, bless them, but nobody could help me. I come around to understand it was up to me to help myself. Tilly always said just that, that folks want something, they have to do it for themselves, that hoping someone else would do a thing for you was a waste of good hopes."

He pulled in a deep breath and let it out slowly. "So I realized after a few days that they weren't in the burned house. They weren't even in their graves. But they were in here." He tapped his head and flashed a glance at Bone. "And in here. Still are." He thumped his thin chest hard enough that Bone heard it.

"I tracked the filth down, pieced together clues, ate just enough to keep my body moving forward. My mind could not be stopped even when I slipped into sleep. But I kept on. Found the first of the three a couple of weeks later, down Sonora way. He was whoopin' it up in a cantina, yammering and yowling in Spanish. I looked in the open door and as it was night, nobody saw me watching. That . . . that man was beating on a woman who worked there, but nobody seemed to care.

"Even the woman looked to be too far down that road to care herself. But I cared. Because when I saw her getting cuffed about the face by that brute, I saw my Tilly, clear as a spring freshet, looking down at me. And she was saying, with her mind, not her voice, she was saying, 'Jervis, honey, you had best do something about this and do it now. That woman does not need to suffer as I did.' And so I did.

"Luck was with me then, I guess, because the man grunted and lurched on out the back door to relieve himself. I waited until he was busy and then I come up behind him and I held his arms tight and I said, 'You remember me, Sonny Jim?' He squawked and tried to get all manly on me and spin and fight, which was just what I wanted.

"I squeezed him tighter and said, 'No, no, not this time,' and though I had intended to ask him where his friends were, I guess I squeezed too hard. Something inside him cracked, I expect it was his neck. I dropped him where he stood, and stripped off his guns, his hat, his knife, and his serape, and I moved on.

"I found the next one the very next day, camped beyond town. I was guided to that one the same as I was the first, something I still credit to Tilly's presence in my mind, you see. The second maybe was my little girl guiding me. Led me right to him, she did. I trusted that and nothing else. Trusted in it, if you know what I mean. And this one, he put up more of a fight, which was satisfying. I fought him, but it didn't matter because I knew I was going to win. And I did, as you see. But before that, he fought like a cornered lion."

That word gave Bone pause, and he thought back in a flash to the lion that had attacked him mere weeks before. How quickly a life can be altered, how quickly a life can be pinched out, like a candle flame between two licked fingers. And then Jervis Latham continued his piece, and Bone once more listened.

"He heard me walking up. I did not creep, but strode on in like I owned the place. It was a nice little camp he had, too.

"We fought, as I said. Then I gutted him then and there like a banked fish, with the knife belonging to the first one. Then I dropped him where he lay, ate his bread and cheese, drank his coffee, and left the gear off that first one with him, and took the gear of that second one, another gun and knife and hat and poncho, and I walked on. Them two came easy, but that third one, he might have had a notion he was being stalked, because it took me three, four months to find him.

"He led me, as they say, on a merry chase. But there wasn't a merry thing about it. I walked on and on, following what my heart and head told me. It was my boy, this time, who guided me. He was my son, and I could not let him down. I moved when and where he told me, and I found that man. And as much as I trusted my wife and daughter and son to lead me to those men, it was the same type of force that told me with no doubt that each of those men were the ones I sought. The ones who wronged us in the worst way that one man can wrong another, one human can wrong another. Plus, I recalled their foul faces.

"That vile killer was hired on as a cowboy on a little ranch up in the hills of Arizona. Him and another man had gone on up into the high country to tend to the fair-weather cattle. So I waited. I felt bad about what I was going to do, not because I cared about the one I was going to kill, but because that other fellow might get the blame.

"I needn't have worried, because he was gone down at the home ranch fetching supplies and he come back with another man while my victim was still limp. That one, he fought the most of all three of those cowards. He come at me with a gun, cranked off two shots. One slid right through my shirt. See here"—Jervis poked a long, bony finger through a hole in his left sleeve and wiggled it.

"The other bullet whanged off a rock way over my head. I kept moving toward the man, walking steady, I didn't draw a gun nor knife, but walked. He didn't know me, I don't think, because he kept shouting, 'Who are you, man?' in English, but with a Spanish accent."

"I told him I was a man him and his friends should have killed when they had the chance. I walked on up to him, and he was so fearful he stood right there, bullets still to go and everything. He dropped his gun and ran. I walked after him. He was only in his socks, and I was in boots.

"He stumbled and ran and tried to climb a scree slope. No man in his right mind would do such a thing. I think maybe at the end he recognized the gear of the second man I'd done for. 'What did you do? What did you do?' He kept asking me that as he looked me over, backed up to the sliding gravel. Finally he fell backward and sat there looking up at me with big ol' wide eyes.

"'Same thing you did. And I am about to do it again.' I didn't have to shoot him nor gut him. It was almost as if he was expecting me. He made sounds like a child in the midst of a bad dream will make, whimperings and such, but by then, that was all he was good for.

"I reached around and put one hand behind his head, and with the other I grabbed his chin. And as I looked into his eyes, I twisted his head quick and fast and hard, and there was a popping, snapping sound inside his neck, I felt it through my hands, and that was it. He flopped and I let him. Then I dropped the gun and knife and hat and serape on him and walked on."

Jervis Latham paused a moment; then he said, in a quieter voice, "With none of them did I bother to explain much. I figured the only ones who needed to know the deeds were being taken care of were those who sent me—my dear Tilly and my two babies. The diseased wrecks who killed my life knew, too. Deep down they knew, at the very moment life went away from them, they knew."

He sat in silence.

After a few minutes, Bone said, "How long ago was that, Jervis?"

In that same low voice, Latham said, "That was near a year since that last one."

"And you've been walking since?"

Latham nodded. Then he offered a weary half-smile. "I look it, too, don't I?"

Bone smiled. "I have seen better fed men, it's a fact."

At that mention, Jervis looked down at the bacon and corn cakes, slightly crispy, and beginning to go cold. "I am afraid I have jawed away the goodness out of that food, mister."

"It's Bone. And nah." The ranger leaned forward and shoved a few sticks into the coals and blew on them. "It'll reheat just fine. Same with the coffee."

And within minutes, Latham was dishing up the warmed food.

They ate in silence, each taking his time. When they had finished, Bone leaned back and ran his tongue over his teeth. "And that's why you're seeking the Rangers?"

Latham shrugged. "In a manner of speaking, yeah. I want to join up."

"Join the Rangers?"

Latham nodded.

"It's not an outfit for revenge, you know."

"It's not revenge I am seeking. I already took care of that part." Latham's jaw flexed, and he nodded as if conversing with himself.

"Why, then?" said Bone.

"Figure the least I can do now is keep others from losing everything to killers and thieves. It's little enough. I was spared for a reason."

After a quiet few moments, Bone said, "I respect that."

Latham let out a breath and stretched his long legs. "So, yeah, that's why I need to find me a Texas Ranger."

"Well, you found one." Bone extended a hand for a shake.

Latham, for a long moment, looked from the hand to Bone's face. "One what?" he said.

Bone reached in his vest pocket and lifted out his old badge. "A Texas Ranger."

Latham's eyebrows rose, but he shook Bone's hand. Each man offered a firm, but not foolish, crushing grip.

"Okay now," said Bone. "Let's get this camp tidied. We have

sleep to find, and I'd like to make an early start so we can get to town and get you signed up."

"But . . ."

"I thought that's what you wanted?"

"It is," said Jervis. "But . . ."

"I'll vouch for you, no worry there."

"I appreciate that . . ."

"But?" said Bone.

"But I'm a black man."

Bone leaned forward. "Huh, I reckon you are. So?"

"They'll take me?"

"You bet they will. I expect they'll even pay a bonus if a man can cook some on the trail, too."

"Oh, Jervis Latham can cook, don't you worry about that."

"Good. And you can make the coffee in the morning, too," said Bone.

"Now, now," said Jervis. "There is such a thing as tasking a man too hard."

Bone smiled. "You just let me know when you start to feel overworked and underpaid. That's when you'll know you're a Texas Ranger."

Chapter 13

In the long weeks following the shooting attack at the fort by a crazed, angry private who wanted nothing more than to express his rage by killing people, Shepley Royle was summoned to the office of the slowly healing Sergeant Cowley.

"I have an assignment for you, Royle."

"Sir?"

"An assignment. You will provide escort services to a small band of very important people, Corporal Royle."

Shep said, "Yes, sir," and offered a quick snap of a salute. Only after the words sunk in, and Sergeant Cowley had stared at him for a long moment, did Shepley Royle comprehend what had just happened.

"Yes, sir," Shep said again, not knowing what to think. He wasn't even certain he was finished with his training. All he really knew was that he was confused . . .

"Sir . . ." Shep knew his face was reddening like a vine-ripe tomato in the sun, but he didn't care. Was what he heard the truth? Could it possibly be?

Cowley nodded, beaming. "It's true, son. You are promoted."

"But . . . how. I mean, thank you, sir, but . . . how?"

"Do I need to spell it out for you, boy?" Cowley's big face squinted down at him. "You saved my backside out there." He pointed a big, meaty finger toward the window of his office, and beyond it, the parade ground.

"The reason you haven't been told in the usual way, is because I wanted to tell you myself. So as to thank you properly."

"Oh, there isn't a need . . ."

"Don't interrupt me, boy!"

"Sir . . . yes, sir!"

"That's better. And also because I have to give you the full news, good, bad, you take it any way you like."

"Oh, it's good news, sir."

"What'd I say about interrupting me, boy? Now, the part that you might not consider good news depends on how you view such things. This means that your training here has been short-ened, I reckon. Just a bit. As I said before, you've been handed an assignment. Oh, now, don't fret, you won't be the man in charge. That lucky assignment goes to me. But your experience as a man from Texas will be most useful in this venture."

Cowley waited a long moment. "Well?"

Shep turned red again, not certain he'd been allowed the op-portunity to speak. "Yes, sir. I don't understand fully just yet. But . . . as to Texas, sir. I have lived there, it's true, but not for long. I didn't live there for long, that is."

"But you have more experience with that country than anyone else here at present. We'll be making for southeastern Texas, in-itially."

He slid a large, folded wad of paper from atop a stack and opened it to reveal a map of the United States. He spun it around and tapped on it. "We're here, which I hope you know."

"Yes, sir."

"Good. And we'll be making for . . . here." He slid the tip of his index finger westward, then down. "And we're headed for here." Again, he tapped the map. "I have been asked, which in the army means ordered, to help set up a base of operations down there. Something the army wants to do before it decides where exactly in the region to establish a fort. Trouble is, until we get down there and scout around, we won't know exactly what we'll find. That's where you come in."

"Me, sir?"

"Yep. Since you are more familiar with that country than anyone we have on hand at present, you'll be coming along. The tricky part comes in when I tell you who else is going."

"Other soldiers, sir?"

Cowley sighed. "I doubt I can convince the captain to let me have them. We'll be riding lean, I'm afraid."

"Who else . . ."

"Don't speed the plow, son. I'm getting to it. But yes, also my wife and my daughter."

"Your wife and daughter!"

"Yes," Cowley nodded, and then shook his head. "I felt about the same way. I told Mrs. Cowley this is not any place for women, but you know how women can be."

"Yes, sir. I mean, no sir, I don't. Not yet. I mean—"

"Royle?"

"Yes, sir?"

"Shut your mouth until you have something intelligent to offer a conversation."

"Yes, sir."

"Good. Now, my wife told me she is in no way going to stay back east while I travel out west. And if I knew what was good for me, I'd mind her. Well"—he rasped a big hand over his chin—"all I care about is getting the two of them out there safely. I'm going to try to leave them in northern Mississippi."

"Why is that, sir?"

"My wife, she had kin there. Hasn't seen any of them in, oh, eighteen years. Since before our Philly was born."

Shep made quick, nimble calculations. That meant that the lovely Philomena was but a year younger than him. He thought about this because, since he'd exchanged greetings with her at the infirmary, Shep had been unable to shake the girl from his mind.

But instead of happiness over the prospect of spending what might well be a whole lot of time with her in close proximity, he was instead filled with fear and dread. And that feeling came full throttle when he looked into Cowley's big, drawn eyes.

The man was watching him now for a reaction and would be watching him even harder and more diligently on the trail west. Oh, boy, thought Shep. Why does life have to come in such big waves of good and bad? Oh, boy.

Chapter 14

No matter how many times in a day Regis consulted his small pocket journal, and tugged out the pencil from its loop, carved away the end for a fine point, and then licked it, the days didn't advance any faster than the hours on the trail. And it was getting him downright worked up.

He knew that about himself, could feel it coming on, but in the past and of late, he'd begun to think in terms of the past as the time before he met Marietta. And in that past, he'd rarely been aware of his rising agitation, which nearly always ended up in him moving faster and shoving aside whoever wasn't working hard and fast enough to suit his tastes.

But now, as on this day, he sat still, pulled in a deep breath, and thought of that woman, that beautiful, infuriating woman in the veil. And he smiled and nodded and closed the notebook—after double-checking the date was indeed the same as it had been two hours earlier.

He glanced at the wide, low horizon to the north, dead ahead, and didn't like what he saw. They'd slowly made their way into territory that was largely strange to him these past few days, and flat and wide and . . . flat.

Sure, there were mountains, but they were far to the north-west. Too far, for his liking. He wasn't certain why, but the mountains represented a slice of safety, a way to mark progress.

So far, in the many weeks they'd been on the trail, they hadn't encountered much in the way of dicey weather. But he knew it was a matter of time. And those clouds—actually a wide, deep-looking band of blackness slowly growing taller and closer, didn't impress him.

And it was wide, wide enough that there was no way on earth they could alter their course to avoid it. They were headed right for the middle of it—or the middle of it was making for them.

Regis tucked the notebook back into his inner pocket and peeled away to the right, angling down the herd to reconnoiter with Fergus Jones, the one man on the crew who had had experience driving cattle great distances. In fact, Regis figured Fergus had more experience in the saddle than all the men combined.

Fergus had recovered pretty well from the shooting during that bizarre attack, and hadn't once asked for special treatment due to it. He was a solid sort, and Regis had come to rely on the man's quiet ways and subtle suggestions quite a lot. And he was grateful for it.

As far as Regis was concerned, Fergus already earned himself a bonus. And Regis was about to pester him again.

"Fergus!" Regis rode on over to the man.

"Hello, Mr. Royle."

"I told you before," said Regis with a smile. "Call me Regis. And as you can imagine, I have a question for you."

The lanky man, with the rangy dragoon mustaches and otherwise clean-shaved face, smiled and raised his eyebrows. That was as much of a response as Regis knew he would get.

"That raft of clouds ahead." Regis nodded toward the dark gloom to the north. "It worry you?"

The man scratched his chin as if considering a purchase. "It isn't something I would like to see, that's true enough."

"Any thoughts about it? Anything we can do to avoid it or at least see that it doesn't cause us more headache than we'd like?"

"Hmm. Yes, as a matter of fact, I've been thinking on that.

Was going to talk with you in a bit about it. You saved me the trouble." He smiled. "If I recall correctly, we'll be coming to a river, a feeder fork of the Sandy. If we make it to that before that storm greets us, we'll be better off."

"Is it possible today, do you think?"

"If we get the boys to step more lively, we might stand a chance."

"And if we don't make it before then?"

Fergus shrugged. "Could be worse. But what we don't want is to be crossing them in the middle of it. Or right after it."

"What are the dangers?"

The cowboy shifted in his saddle, and they rode a few paces before he responded. "If it's as big a storm as it looks, it'll likely flood. That river could stay bigger than we'd like for a day or two, maybe longer."

Regis thought about this for a moment. "That would slow us down too much."

"Yep. And the cattle won't like it. They'll have nubbed the grass down on this side quick. And when they get hungry, which a cow always is . . ." Fergus let that thought hang.

"Then," said Regis, finishing the unspoken threat. "They'll be restless and more apt to bolt."

Fergus nodded. "A hungry cow is a stupid cow. And that's saying something." He squinted and smiled.

"So our best bet is to make it across before the storm floods the river."

"I'd say so, yes."

"Think we can do it?"

Fergus pooched out his lower lip. "It's worth trying."

Regis nodded. "I'd say we have no choice. I'll cut around and tell Percy, then Cyril, who's riding drag, then I'll cut on up the left flank. Maybe you could cut up this side and do the same?"

"You bet, Mister . . . ah, Regis."

"Thank you, Fergus. I appreciate it. And your wisdom."

"Oh, boy. Don't thank me until we're safe across."

Regis turned his horse southward. "We'll make it, you'll see." But as he rode toward Percy's wagon and the remuda behind, Regis glanced once again at the clouds, which looked closer and more menacing than ever, and he wasn't so certain.

"At least we have to try," he whispered to himself.

The storm advanced on them quicker than anybody had anticipated. Soon enough, all the men had broken out their slickers and grabbed a cold trail lunch of biscuits and bacon and dried apple slices from Percy. There would be no time for him to halt and brew up a few gallons of hot coffee in the midst of this day.

The wind reached them first. Fergus thought they still had a chance if they could get the boys to drive the laggards quicker. But the boys were doing their best, and it looked like it still wasn't going to be enough.

With collars tugged high, hats jammed low, stampede straps cinched beneath chins, and gloves pulled tight, the men rode the cattle hard, not letting the willful hook-horned beasts have their way. It was a rough run, for though the river was not far ahead, perhaps a quarter mile, by Regis's best reckoning, the storm was moving in quicker.

He'd wanted to lob a few more questions at Fergus, but he knew the answers already, namely that they still had a little time to cross the herd before the river swelled. Or at least he hoped so.

Regis did know water, being first and foremost a steamship captain, and he knew that creeks, rivers, and such could fill to brimming as a man watched. He guessed that was because they were such narrow channels. He hoped the flow ahead was not too wide, nor too deep.

He raced King up the left flank, shouting "Hoo-rah! Get up there!" As they galloped forward, and at the sight of each man he came abreast, Regis shouted over the wind, "Don't spare them now! Get to the river! Then get them across and keep them there!"

The men nodded and continued doing exactly that. Regis topped the herd and crossed to the right flank, making for Percy's clanking, blundering wagon. It was the loudest thing on the drive, most days. But on this day, even its odd clanking, slamming bulk rolled forward with as much grace as the cumbersome thing could, and Regis thought he might just beat the cattle to the river.

"That thing flows west," Regis shouted to Percy.

The cook nodded and kept his wagon on trail. "You want me to drop back and pass downstream or up?"

"Stay on course and cross upstream. Dangerous for you, I think, but only if you swamp. If you do, you'll wash into the cattle. But if you're downstream of the herd, and some of them lose their footing and wash into you, why . . ."

And then something occurred to him, and he looked before and aft Percy's wagon. "Where's that cursed prisoner of yours?"

Percy looked straight ahead and snapped the lines on the backs of his horses.

"Percy! I said . . ."

"I heard you! I turned him loose!"

"You what?" Regis stood in the saddle, eyeing the wagon once more, expecting to see the deranged little half-naked prisoner pop out of the back.

"I couldn't very well kill him! Besides, I sent him packing southeastward. Kept a gun on him the whole time, at least until he was out of sight!"

Regis shook his head. He didn't know whether to laugh or curse. "I suppose you fed him, too."

Percy shrugged. "Might be he had a few biscuits. I don't recall."

Regis kept on shaking his head as he rode back into the thick of the action.

And then the rain began, driving at them from the north, before them. At first, it whipped in on the wind, tentative pellets spaced wide and not too forceful. But soon the drops multiplied, and spit almost horizontally at them, lashing in with increasing intensity.

The drops stung like sand, and even the cattle, who were so knob-headed they often blundered and slammed into painful situations with abandon, began wincing and shying, trying to turn tail to the wind.

This made the cowboys' job even more difficult.

Percy reached the river first, and he heard the racket behind him and winced with each clang and crash. He'd secured everything in and on the wagon as best he could, but he felt certain he was going to find a whole lot of his goods and gear either smashed and leaking or mangled, or just plain gone, having floated away on those infernal rising waters.

And then he saw the riverbank and slowed the two-horse team. "Whoa! Whoa, now!" He angled the wagon slightly so as not to keep taking the rain in the eyes. He needed to see what it was he faced, and decided there was nothing for it. He'd have to give it all he could.

Upstream, a dozen yards from where he sat, the bank had been chewed away in previous storms enough that it looked to afford him a wide, sloping drop instead of the severe, narrow mess before him. He'd try it there.

"Get up there! Git Git!" And the team, not impressed with this situation in the least, nonetheless complied, jerking their heads like pump handles and blowing and snorting. None of it did them any good, for Percy's whip, which he hated using, tickled their backsides and flanks with as much fury as did the rain on their faces.

Down the embankment they stepped. Halfway to the river's edge, the wagon slewed to the left, and Percy felt the entire contraption begin that sickening feeling as the right side of the wagon lifted.

He shouted, "No! No! No!" and crawled up the rising side of the seat, toward the right, and forced his not-too-hefty weight as far over the side as he could, while still holding the lines ands keeping his legs wedged within the seat's well.

It nearly did the trick, so he began jumping up and down in place, all the while jerking the lines to the left to get those blasted horses to turn back toward the water they were doing their level best to avoid.

That, too, did the trick, and the rising right side of the wagon slammed back down to the moistening, mucky riverbank. Percy grunted a thanks to the heavens and figured he'd celebrate properly later.

Right then, he had to lay into those mangy beasts with the hated lash once more, keeping the lines coiled tight around his left fist to force the steeds straight down into the water. All the while he turned the sizzling air blue with cursed oaths and threats such that horses and men had never heard.

He even mumbled an apology to his mother and any other spirit that might be listening in, but he reckoned once again he'd beg forgiveness and offer thanks later, in equal measure.

"Get on there! Cross it now, I tell you! Do it, do it!" He shouted any words that came to mind, and he didn't much care who or what heard. As long as it helped to move the horses forward, it was worth shouting into the blistering, rain-filled wind.

They made it into the water, and the shock slowed the beasts once more. He doubled his brutal shouts and lashes and snapping of the lines, and soon the entire wagon was up to its hubs in the river.

A thought came to him then that he hadn't considered before—what if the bottom was silty and soft? What then? He'd be stuck out in the middle of the swelling flow with crazed horses and a wagon broadside to the river.

"Broadside! No, no, no!" he shouted, and jerked the lines harder to the left, as if he were going to turn the apparatus around. He had no intention of doing so. Instead, he was angling the wagon so as to cross the river at an angle instead of straight on over to the beckoning far bank.

And after what felt a double lifetime, Percy was able to right the ship, as he thought of his successful maneuvering with a smug, grim grin.

It was then that Percy noticed the river's flow, specifically the swelling of the flow upstream of him. It looked through the graying daylight and pummeling, slashing, wind-shoved rain that the river was growing taller, wider—bigger all around.

"Can't be . . ." said Percy, his eyes wide.

Even the horses appeared to cease their knob-headed struggles and pause to swing their heads upstream.

Not only was the flow growing, but it was growing in sound, too. In addition to the hissing spatter of the rain on the roiled surface of the river, the momentarily bewildered cook and his horses became aware that there was another sound, a deeper, rumbling, crushing sort of sound, also oddly enough from upstream.

But the moment was short-lived, for they all saw, or rather grasped, the reason why the river had become louder. It was the storm that swelled the river. And it showed no sign of decreasing anytime soon.

It was also because there was a massive log, from who knew where or how far upstream, since there were no trees of significant size for what looked to be a mile or two upstream. But the river, as Percy had come to know about so much in the non-human world, was forever moving, changing, growing, shrinking, thriving, and dying. All at once.

That big tree was coming on strong. And it was wide in the trunk and long, perhaps thirty feet in length, and it still wore a number of branches that hadn't yet snagged on something in the river.

"You have to be joking me . . ." said Percy, working his mouth like a banked fish. Already the team began its jerking, thrashing dance all over again, but this time Percy showed no hesitancy and laid the lash onto their straining rumps and backs. The horses felt it and dug in, slashing the churning, foam-topped water with their newfound efforts.

The tree, which looked to Percy to be twice the size it had been moments before, bobbed and spun and lurched closer. Percy stood in the boot well and howled to the horses, to the heavens, to himself, to anything that might respond and be of use to him in this moment of need.

And it almost worked.

The horses emerged from the river as quickly as their legs could manage the task, and dug hard into the long, sandy slope of the riverbank, with Percy flailing hard the entire time. He glanced back once and saw the log, riding the crest of the building swell, almost as if the dead tree were holding back the water.

Then the water overtook the surging log, and for a moment the big stick disappeared, leaving a wall of frothing brown water the only thing in Percy's view.

The wagon kept jerking forward as the horses dug into the bank, and then the water was on them, shoving hard against the wagon, the angled bulk of which still sat in the water, the rear wheels up to their hubs. But it wasn't enough to escape the pounding flow, and as it hit, it knocked Percy hard.

His right arm, which held the long buggy whip, flailed upward, the whip flying free and disappearing into the pelting rain. He lost his balance and ended up on the toes of his right foot.

Then another something slammed into the still-moving wagon, knocking it sideways, downstream, and knocking Percy to his right knee, his right hand grabbing for anything he could feel to steady himself.

The lines wrapped about his left fist were the only thing that saved him, because when the tree slammed into the lurching rear of the wagon, Percy was leaning upstream, reaching in a blind grope for something, anything to grab. His flexing fingers found nothing but air. And then the tree's slam knocked him over the side, out of the driver's seat, and into the water.

The rain had already soaked him to the skin, and though it had been cold, it had at first been a welcome sensation, since the day had been a hot one. But the full-body crush of the slamming brown water seized him with shock. He didn't have time to do anything but gasp, for the driving water slammed his legs against the front right wheel and pinned him there.

The only thing that prevented his head from being pulled beneath the bubbling surface was the fact that the lines were still wrapped about his left hand. He realized this and held on.

The trouble was, now he was fighting the thrashing horses as they continued to lurch up the sopping, sodden riverbank.

The wagon continued to move; Percy held on, trying to shout even as he knew it would do little good, as nobody would be around to hear him. The rest of the crew would be downstream of him, crossing the cattle, hopefully having better luck than he.

His head rapped over and over against the side of the wagon just before the wheel. He struggled to move his legs, to free one of the crushing force of the boiling river, trying to use the wheel to shove against.

And then he felt the wheel move again. The horses were still at it, still trying, had to be them. Or else it was the river itself, carrying them away.

For the briefest of moments, Percy pictured his team and wagon, with him entangled in it, beneath it in a web of leather harness and lines. They would be carried away in the mammoth brown flow, tumbling and turning forever. Or at least until they ended up in the ocean somewhere far away; then they would continue on, floating far out to sea.

Somehow, in this bizarre fantasy, Percy, though trapped beneath the wagon and thus underwater, would still be alive and able to see what was happening. A fate, he sensed, that would continue forever.

A shout roused him from his foolish reverie, and he realized it was his own voice, a gagging, spluttering sound, because his head was being jerked up and down in the water, the level of the vicious brown flow rising with each moment that passed.

"Gaah!" he shouted, struggling to get his free right arm closer to the wagon. He did, and fighting the pummeling flow, managed to snag a clawhold on the top plank forming the boot well of the seat. It was enough to allow him to pull himself up to draw in a stuttering, water-filled breath. He coughed and gagged and breathed.

All the while he was aware that the horses had managed to drag the wagon halfway up the slope in one, two great strides, it seemed, before jerking to a halt.

Much of Percy's body was still underwater, and he flailed until he was able, slowly and with more effort than he'd ever put into anything, pull himself up, up even as the river continued to pummel the wagon, not with repeated blows but with a near-constant drumming force that felt relentless.

Percy was certain that if he ever made it out of this alive, he would be unable to walk, for the river's power would have somehow battered the bones in his legs to powder.

Now that he had a useful grip with his right hand, he used the left, even though it was jerking hard on the lines that he hoped were still attached to his horses, and dragged himself upward, out of the water.

The wagon, he realized in mid grunt and groan, had ceased to move. He would worry about that later. Right then, he had to get out of that water before he lost strength and slipped back in. He was certain if that happened, he would never again be able to drag himself out.

He heard, as his head begin to rise slowly above the wagon's battered, soaked planking, the shouts of a man, not himself this time, bellowing curses and words that made no sense. What was he saying? And then he recognized it as shouts at the horses, to get them moving again.

He wanted to tell whoever it was that they were mostly out of danger, he was certain of it, even though he really wasn't, and that the poor horses were likely played out. They needed to rest. Just like he did.

But the voice would not let up. It was one of the men. He thought he knew the voice, but which one? Did it matter?

And then Percy was up, up enough that he wedged his rib cage over the planking and, with a mighty last grunt and shove, forced himself up to pitch forward, face-first, into the boot well of the driver's seat once more.

His left arm was partially pinned beneath his chest, and it throbbed worse than a hangover or a toothache. Maybe both together.

"Percy! Percy!"

Someone was shouting to him. He wanted to tell them to shut up. Leave him alone, go away and let him rest. He just needed a minute or two to get his wind back.

"Percy! There you are!" shouted whoever it was. Then the man kept right on shouting, close up, it seemed to Percy.

"Thought we'd lost you—saw your legs sticking up there out of the side of the wagon! Good thing you're a tall drink! I'd never have seen you if you had stumpy legs . . ."

It went on like that while somebody laid hands on him and jerked him over so that his face stared skyward. It was worse than before, because the rain had not let up, maybe only gotten bolder, and now it pelted his face like hot sand.

He sputtered and tried to turn his head to the side, but whoever it was kept fighting him. "Let me get these lines off your hand. It's all blue and swelled up! Busted, I expect!"

"The wagon—horses . . ." That was all Percy could manage to say, but if the man heard him, he did not say so. He kept on fidgeting and fussing and annoying Percy worse than ever.

"Get away!" Percy finally managed to shout. He thought the man heard him that time, for he paused in his jerking and lifting, and Percy thought he heard a laugh.

"That'll do, then! You're going to live if you're back to your old self!"

And then the man did laugh, and Percy knew who it was—Cyril. Only man on the crew from England. At least with that odd accent of his. And the only man who always seemed so darn chipper all the time.

Percy didn't trust a fellow who was always happy. Hiding something, he thought. But for the life of him, he could never tell what it was Cyril was hiding.

Then Percy was dragged deeper into the cramped boot well and shoved a little bit more. "There! Now stay put!" said Cyril.

Then he began shouting, "Hee yah! Get on there! Get get!" And Percy felt the wagon rumble and slam and crash and lurch and do that some more and some more. It seemed to go on forever.

It was the worst wagon ride of Percy's life, but he couldn't seem to get his eyes to rise to the challenge of opening in the rain, and his mouth wouldn't do much more speaking, and his arm and leg just plain hurt.

Not to mention the rest of him. He felt himself slipping backward, as if he had tipped into a big hole while walking in the forest in the middle of the night. And he kept right on falling.

Chapter 15

Regis saw, far to his left, eastward, Percy maneuver his team and cook wagon toward the river, but upstream of where the men were angling the bulk of the herd. He was pleased that the surly cook had done so, since a cow struggling against the current might easily separate from the herd and drift downstream.

And having a petrified and belligerent longhorn smack broadside into a horse team and wagon would be a very bad thing. And if one could do it, there would be others. And the results could be a whole lot worse if more than one beef got pulled downstream.

He gave no more thought to the cook and his charges, because he had bigger problems before him.

The herd had, despite the earnest efforts of the men, separated into two groups, uneven in number. The men were doing their best to keep the cattle from drifting and separating, especially difficult since the lashing rain had only increased in intensity.

Regis spotted a lone steer trotting westward away from the herd, tail up and head high, as if the rain gave the beast a jolt of excitement. He growled, "No you don't," and cut his King hard in that direction, but Fergus rode back to him from the herd, shaking his head and waving an arm at him.

"Let it go!" shouted the seasoned cowboy.

"But . . ."

"We'll get him later. Best to help get everyone to put the crush on these cows, drive them hard and tight, keep these fools from continuing to split in two. Never get them across like this!"

"Okay," shouted Regis. "What would you like me to do first?"

"Ride the perimeter and tell everyone to push them hard, squeeze them right at the river. One group only! Got to do it!"

"Okay!"

Regis did as he was told, grateful that Fergus was experienced enough to know what they needed to do next. Regis rode hard, hat tilted forward to help keep the lashing rain from pelting his eyes. He spotted one of the men, he didn't know just who, and he didn't much care at that moment.

The man seemed more concerned with fiddling with his slicker and tugging his hat low than in riding after strays and, according to Fergus, tending to the most important job at hand of driving the herd back together into one big, roiling, bawling, wet mass and forcing them all toward the river.

They were still hundreds of yards from the riverbank, but the slight rise Regis had topped afforded him a look at the river itself, and what he saw did not impress him. It was already flooding, which he assumed was due to the fact that this stretch of the river, which ran in a southwesterly direction, had already experienced some of the coming storm from the north on its way down here.

None of that mattered to Regis; all he wanted to do was get the critters across that river as quickly as possible.

"Hey!" he shouted to the lone cowboy fiddling with his gear. Regis rode up, and the man looked sufficiently cowed, his head bent, but he didn't ride off. "What are you doing . . . Chancy, that you?"

"Yes, sir!"

"Well, get on back to the herd if you aren't going to ride down the strays! We have to cross them and quick! That river's rising!"

Still the kid hesitated.

"What's wrong with you, man?"

"Can't swim, sir!"

Regis gritted his teeth. "You don't have to! Your horse does! Half the men here can't swim! Cows can barely swim! Get on over there, now!"

The man nodded and heeled his mount into a hard lope back to the herd, some twenty yards away. Regis continued on along the west flank. He knew it had been a harsh way to treat the man, but his fears were going to get someone hurt, or worse.

He'd been around plenty of sailors who couldn't swim, and a good many of them lost their lives to the fact, a fact some of the fools clung to as if it were a point of pride.

Point of stupidity, he'd heard Cormac mumble more than once. The Irishman had made certain that Regis knew how to swim before he'd allow him to call himself a "sailor."

It had been an easy thing for Regis to master, seeing as how he'd spent hot afternoons of his youth back in the hills of Maine, swimming on hot days at the river there, which emptied into a millpond. Still, he was forever grateful to Cormac for his insistence on such matters, making self-preservation of top importance to a fellow.

"If a man can't take care of himself, how in the world can he expect to be of use to the ship or his fellow sailors when the time comes? And it will come. It always does."

His partner's sage words echoed in his ears as he rode toward the next trail hand who, unlike Chancy, was doing his best, fairly effectively, to keep the straggling line of cattle from straying and spreading.

Regis glanced back and to the east. It was difficult to see, but he thought maybe the rest of the herd, thanks to Fergus's efforts, was beginning to come together and move forward. This flank was the worst of the lot, and so he would stay with this fellow to bend the line of cattle northward.

He rode up nearly abreast of the man. It was Benito, he now saw. Good, the man was solid. "We have to work faster! Bunch them and make for the river. No time to waste!"

Benny nodded and raced to rein in another steer bucking off away from the rest. Regis spun King and raced back part of the way he had come, crowding the herd as much as he dared, shouting and whistling and trying to sound menacing, and as if there were six of him.

What had he been thinking, deciding to take the herd so far north with so few men? Don't think like that, he told himself as he raced through the rain, growling curses and threats at the frantic cattle. He had made the only choice he was able to.

If he sat at home, he would surely have lost his shirt, and then some, in whatever paltry deal he might get for the herd. But if he succeeded, despite odds that were stacking up taller with each day, they might just manage to get to the rail head in Schiller. Then he might be able to save the ranch. Or at least buy enough time to keep busy until next year's drives.

It was one mighty task, but it was all he had left, all that Regis could count on.

He raced to head off a hornless but headstrong young beast, muscles lean and quivering beneath its rain-slick hide, devil in its eyes and a half a mind bent on escape—to anywhere but that cursed river.

"I sympathize," growled Regis. "I don't want to go for a swim in that flow, either, but like the rest of us, you don't have a choice!"

He herded the ranging creature hard back into the mass of jostling flanks and hooves and horns and hide, and bellowing, wide, wild-eyed beeves. They were the cattle of Royle Ranch. And with the unrelenting pressure from far too few cowboys, they were making their way toward the now-thundering river.

Fergus ranged fast and wide at the drag end of things, somehow, Regis noted, suturing together the two bunches of cattle as if he were wielding a huge, invisible needle and thread. Now that, thought the boss, is a vaquero who knows his job.

He did not ruminate long on this, because he saw that he could mimic to the best of his meager abilities the man's behavior. He jerked the horse left, tight to the jostling beasts, and he kept up his shouting. As soon as he made progress and got them moving even faster, he spun tight and thundered back the other way.

And thunder was the right word for it, for the storm, already dark, seemed to sense what they were trying to do and appeared to want to prevent them from crossing the boiling flowage.

The leading edge of the black-clouded mass from the north now sailed low and tight over them, its front curling, clawing, raking down at the racing figures arrayed wide along the river.

It brought with it a blast of frigid, corpse-like air, lending the lashing rain an even more foreboding feeling. It was this dark, storming mess that gave the still-hesitant herd the kick to the backside it needed by delivering a series of bright-as-the-sun racers of lightning, lancing down from the center of the blackness low overhead.

The sizzling bolts snagged along the ground behind the cowboys, as if to say they were no longer allowed back the way they'd come. That they must move on.

Regis knew the worst place to be in a lightning storm was in the water or anywhere near it, but trapped they were, with no choice but to scream at the reluctant cattle and haze them forward. The shouts and threats and gunshots of the cowboys were somewhat effective, but it was the storm itself that hastened the job—as thunder snapped and crackled like whip strikes from heaven.

The front edge of the herd, now once more a collective of boiling, riled beasts, felt the desperation rippling through the herd as it reached them and forced them at last into the rising river.

"Drive them without mercy!" shouted Fergus.

Regis had no idea how the man, in the midst of the storm,

could sound so clear to them all, but the normally quiet cowboy's voice was given full throat, and he exercised it.

The herd, cow by cow, plunged down the embankment, some stretches of it steep, others not as harsh, but all of it wide open, unfettered by the low, scraggly scrub bushes that much of the riverbank wore.

This was obviously a wide, popular spot to cross herds. But how many of them had had to do it under such trying circumstances? Regis continued racing along the rear edge, along with his men, urging the cattle forward, downward into the river.

He glanced to his right, upstream, and saw something he did not believe he was seeing, could not believe it. But yes, it was true—Percy's cook wagon was nearly side-to in the river, not all the way across yet. He'd angled it a bit, but somehow he had managed to get the wagon wedged, it seemed, in the boiling river. The horses stomped and thrashed and churned but didn't seem to be making headway.

And then, as Regis watched, a shout of horror lodged in his throat, he saw Percy, standing in the wagon, lines in one hand, and the whip lashing the team with the other. Then the wagon rose as the water surged up and around it, and he saw Percy rise up with it, attempt to compensate, and then the man lost his balance.

The whip flew from his grasp and, as Regis watched, already turning his horse to race upstream, he saw Percy topple over the upstream side of the wagon and fall from sight.

"No!" shouted Regis.

But as Regis watched, the two of his men closest, along the upriver edge of the herd and nearest to the riverbank, peeled away from the herd and thundered down into the river, one cutting straight across river and angling upstream a bit, the other cutting upstream behind the wagon.

Regis still rode hard for the site, but Fergus rode before him.

"Hold there, boss! They got him! You need to stay with the herd or we'll lose it, sure as I'm wet to the skin!"

Regis ground his teeth, but saw the man's logic, though he cursed about it as he nodded and swung back around, keeping an eye on the wagon every few feet as he and King pounded back along the herd's edge.

If it hadn't been fully evident before, the brute gravity of the situation slopped down hard and fast on Regis. No man's life was worth the entire herd of cows. He was certain the cows might disagree, but he had a responsibility, first and foremost, to Percy, Cyril, Chancy, Benito, Fergus, and all the others. And to their families, wherever back home to each man might be.

The idea that he didn't really know where these men called home struck Regis then. He bet they each knew more about one another than he did about any of them. He was not an attentive boss, but more to the point, he saw himself as the boss. Not as a man who had hired these capable men, some of them barely out of the boyhood phase of their lives, to do a task for him in exchange for pay.

He vowed when they got through the foolishness of this storm that he would reconsider the way he conducted himself with the men. But first he had to get them and the cattle all across the river without any of them dying in the doing of it.

Regis rode left, right, then back again, whooping it up and waving and shouting. He heard occasional gunshots cracking off, something he did not approve of. A bullet sent skyward had to come down somewhere, and these fools, he thought, were sending them straight up into the rainstorm above their heads.

A fleeting thought almost made Regis smile, despite the situation: were his shooting trail hands trying to kill the storm troubling them so? It was a notion he'd mull over later, hopefully sipping a cup of hot coffee laced with a splash from Percy's stashed bottles of medicinal whiskey.

As he rode and shouted and crowded the cattle ever closer to the riverbank, he glanced up again. He hoped to see Percy's situation resolved and not the brutal likelihood of the wagon being pummeled by the river. If it succumbed to the flow, then what? They'd lose the wagon and its contents. But what of the lives?

Try as he might, Regis was unable to see with any clarity through the smear of pounding rain. The drops felt as big as fists, each landing a solid blow on his body.

All of them, the cattle, the men, the horses, each and every one got soaked to the bone, pummeled by the rain, and rattled by the thunder and lightning.

As if to emphasize that fleeting thought, another of the random, sizzling lightning strikes zapped the earth not fifty feet from where the herd had been three minutes before.

Regis screamed, a thing he had not done, to his knowledge, in many a year. But if ever a man was given cause to yowl, it was him and it was at that moment.

The lightning whipped down, parting earth and slicing like a blade that needed sharpening but was forced to hack its way through the task just the same. The earth smoked, flames spat, and fist-size hunks of stone and clods of soil erupted, spraying in all directions.

The jolting, jarring, suddenness of it, along with the rank stink that stank to Regis of gunpowder and burning rock, if there could be such a thing, filled his nostrils. We are trapped between a boulder and a stone mountain, he thought, his heart doing its best to claw its way up his throat and out his mouth.

Ahead, from the rain-slick clot of cattle boiling in a frenzy before him, Regis heard a man's scream, loud and long. Something told Regis it wasn't an utterance of shock at the lightning, but one of terror. Try as he might, he couldn't see anything other than the dark mass of bawling, scrambling beeves. But he had heard it, hadn't he?

He looked to both sides and saw the taller hunched shapes of men doing the same thing he was doing, shouting at the cattle and pressing them hard.

The front of the herd was well into the river by then, and he knew Fergus had been right on every score—keep them moving and get them across before it got any bigger.

And it was already a coursing beast more swollen than it had been minutes before. The air was filled not with phantom screams but with the shouts of men. The crackle and snap of close-by thunder and lightning, which did not want to leave them alone, mingled with the bawling and bellowing of hundreds of head of cattle petrified and being forced to do something their instincts told them not to do.

Fergus rode up, sidling along close. "We have to ease up on them now! They're snagging up front. The cattle need to get their sea legs, or they'll be trampled by those behind! And these at the rear might break and scatter!"

Regis nodded, once more demurring to this seasoned hand's knowledge. And he was soon gratified to see that it was sage advice that worked well.

The herd was spread out wide, ranging both upstream and down, far too spread out for him and his men to continue keeping contained. They would just have to get them all across and then ride the far riverbank in both directions to round up the wandering strays. Which, from the looks of this situation, was shaping up to be quite a chore.

"Where in the blazes is that kid?" growled Regis aloud, eyeing through the rain for Chancy, the non-swimmer.

He shrugged it off and went back to patrolling his stretch of the rear line, urging forth the cattle but not pushing them as hard.

The slowdown began to free up, and the cattle poured forward into the river and beyond, at the front of the line. And then he saw a sight that, for the first time in long, long hours gave him hope—beeves surging up onto the far riverbank. He angled left and saw a rider ahead, close by the bank, waving his arms and shouting, keeping the line from spreading any wider.

Regis held his own corner of the line, slowly walking forward, wishing the cursed animals would get down and across faster. But he knew that Fergus was right—any harder of a push, and they'd risk that the cattle still on this side might rabbit and peel back from where they'd come, or off to the sides. As worked up as they were, they might sprout wings and shoot right up into the air.

He kept on like this, urging the cattle forward, making quick glances to the men ranged to either side of him, and counted what he thought were a half dozen Royle hands.

Had any of the men yet made it across? He guessed they'd have a time gathering the herd once they were all safely there, but that felt like it might take another year yet.

Percy's wagon had been far upstream, but it had grown steadily darker these past twenty minutes. Regis was unable to see anything in that direction save for the boiling river's shape, the hissing sheets of black rain, and closer in, the humped shapes of the cattle and the few riders.

And then, before he could have guessed it, there he was, at the riverbank's edge, staring down into a welter of pocked mud and cattle working hard to make their way through it. The muck was up to their bellies and looked to be difficult for them to slog through.

It seemed to slow them, though now that was of no use. He shouted from the bank, but his presence had long ceased to matter to the keyed-up but exhausted cattle.

Then, as the last of them jumped and slopped down into the river, following those before them, Regis saw several, three, perhaps more, humped forms in the mud, not moving. They were mired cattle. He saw one, then two moving, stretching their necks, bawling in agony.

From their awkward positions, he guessed they had likely

sunk in the mud and then been slammed and trampled by those coming from behind.

Regis bet their legs were broken. He had no idea how to help them. He didn't dare take King down the bank and into that same muck. Maybe he could rope them from the water.

But the river itself, now mere feet from him, was a boiling, brown-black snake. He looked to his left and saw Benito riding up, not twenty from him. Benny stopped and pointed. "Boss! Boss!"

Regis followed the man's arm down along the bank, where the water met the mud, and saw what he had taken to be one of the trampled steers. But it was no steer. It was a horse.

And where there was a horse, there had to be a rider. Regis thought then of the scream he had heard and had hoped he'd not.

He rode over to Benny, who had dismounted and was leaning forward, looking left and right, trying to see without scrambling down into the mire.

"Take my reins!" shouted Regis, jamming them into the stout man's hand.

"What are you going to do?"

But Regis didn't answer. He unlooped his lariat and cinched one end about his waist, then looped the other over King's saddle horn. "I get into trouble, have King pull me out!"

Benito nodded. For a brief moment, they were close enough that Regis saw the wide-eyed look on the young man's face, with fear and exhaustion warring there.

Regis nodded once and slid and jammed his way down the slick slope. Within six feet, he had reached the bottom and leveled off, but then he stepped into the mud and sunk to the tops of his boots. Even through the driving rain, he smelled the raw tang of wet manure, mud, and river water mixed and stomped into this liquid ooze into which he slogged.

It took all his strength to lift each leg and jam it forward again.

He felt as if he'd lurched for hours but had only gone a dozen feet by the time he reached the nearest body, a steer laid on its side, its hide torn and stomped, its legs somewhere below him.

He didn't dare venture closer than a couple of feet in case it was not dead and his presence riled it. He had no interest in getting gored by a nearly dead longhorn.

And then, as he walked by it slowly, its neck and head stretching out along the pocked surface of the slick muck, it jerked its head up and trembled, a pitiful wheeze rising from its parted mouth, its tongue black with muck, a distended thing.

Regis parted the front of his slicker and pulled out his revolver. He cocked it and reached over and shot the beast in the hollow between its eye and horn. "I'm sorry, cow," he said, sliding the revolver back safely in its holster. "For it all."

His words were heard by nothing alive or dead, save for him, and then barely. The wind had, if possible, increased in intensity. He trudged on, slow and slogging, and though he saw other humped forms which he was somewhat certain were beeves, he made for the horse. It was unmoving in a way that the previous beast had not been.

Something about it told Regis that the horse was dead. It was also saddled. He held his breath and edged around its rump as fast as he could, suspecting he was going to find something he did not want to see.

He was right.

The only thing Regis saw of the man was a booted foot and leg up to the knee laid alongside the horse's back, atop the muck, as if he'd been trying to mount up.

"Oh no . . ."

Regis knew it was inevitable that the man would be dead, for he saw little else of the man save for a bunching above the knee of filthy brown slicker. Still, he shoved his way over and tugged on that limp leg with his left hand while his right clawed at the mud. He raked great wads of it up and away, the holes he caused pooling and puddling with rainwater and runoff almost immediately.

The entire time he worked, he shouted, "No, no! Come up out of there!" He cursed the horse, shoving at it with his left knee, jostling it as hard as he could, but it was no use. The man's torso was somewhere below Regis, hidden in the nearly two-foot-thick pack of mud.

What had happened? wondered the frenzied cattleman. Had the horse fallen over on top of the man? Was that even possible? Of course it was, he chided himself. Here was proof!

He dug and dug, his shoulders screaming from the hot, raw pain and from the freakish, cold temperatures wafting off the muck and pooled water. Soon enough, his hand found purchase around a belt. He locked his big fingers tight and tried to draw the man up.

Regis stood spraddle-legged and heaved and jerked and finally was able to budge the fallen fellow a couple of inches. But he realized he was fighting the huge dead beast that had been the man's horse. He still didn't know which of his men this was, but it didn't matter. It was a man fallen, and though Regis knew well enough that the fellow was dead, he worked quickly and frantically, shouting "No! No, no, no!" and shaking his head. Rain poured off his sodden hat and into the holes he kept scooping out with his hand.

Finally he saw the futility of this effort and slogged as quickly as he could around to the front of the horse. If he could get the end of his lasso around the horse's head, he might be able to have King tug it back enough that he could lift free the man.

Then he faced his second problem: the horse's neck was a curve of mud-spackled muscle, but its head was gone, buried, as was the man, beneath itself. The beast had likely broken its neck, either by falling or by being trampled, caught in the mammoth swell and crush of cattle surging forward into the river, forced forward by him and the other men, by their shouts and urgings, by the crash and slam and flash of the thunder and lightning.

From somewhere behind him, up the bank, he heard a shout cutting through the rain, "Boss! Boss!"

"I'm okay!" he shouted, twice in response. He had not quite stretched the full length of rope out between them, and so didn't think the man on the bank, Benito, would take any tugging as a sign to have King pull him back.

He wanted to shout to give him a minute, but then the man might mistake him and haul him in.

Regis operated quickly, once more scrabbling in the muck, working with his bare, frigid hands to find that place below the beast's jaw where he could slick one hand through and meet it with the other, the spot where he could slide the rope through and secure it.

It took long moments, with Regis gritting his teeth so tight he felt certain his molars would powder from the pressure. He was crouched above the man's hidden body, part of him, anyway, and the thought chilled him to the core more than any blast of icy rain might.

He needed this to work, he needed to get the man free. A sense of dread was fast overcoming him, a sense of guilt as weighty as anything he had ever felt that this was Chancy, the young man he'd shouted down not long before, for being a fearful fool.

He'd all but told him that his fear of the water, his having not learned to swim, was of little consequence, and something to be shoved down, bitten off, swallowed back, anything he could think of in that moment that a man might bellow at another, lesser, weaker man to shut him up and keep him moving. The truth of it was that Chancy was no lesser or weaker of a man. He was just a man. A frightened young man. With a long life before him. But that was then.

And if it was Chancy, as he knew it had to be, Regis would never, could never forgive himself.

He worked harder, cursing and spitting, blowing snot and rain away from his face. Finally he wormed his hand where he needed it to go, felt that curve of the horse's jaw, then the hollow beneath.

His growing dread prevented him from probing too hard, too deep, lest he feel something else down there, the face, the cheek, the neck, the brow, the hair, the shoulder, arm, hand of the man he'd doomed to die on this spot, in this gruesome way.

But of the man, he felt nothing in the mud and muck. He untied the rope from his waist and slid it through the little cavity he'd excavated. He tied it, shoved himself up to standing, and jerked hard three measured times on the rope. "Pull!" he shouted. "Pull!"

There was a long pause, and then the rope jerked taut, smacking Regis on the leg, a sharp rap above the left knee. It jerked him, alerted him to move backward a step. Then he faltered, going down on his right knee, lurching to one side, afraid he might be stepping on the buried man.

The horse's head began to rise. It stopped after inching upward enough to reveal one mud-caked open eye. "Pull!" shouted Regis. "Pull!"

After a moment, the tugging continued, and kept on. Benito must be frantic with worry, thinking he was rescuing Regis. But he had no way of telling him otherwise, as shouting in this weather was a fool's game.

The horse rose and rose, inch by inch, and between lashings of rain and the unkillable lightning flashes from the south and east, still too close for any level of comfort, Regis saw what he knew he would see, but what he did not want to.

He bent low, crouching, and saw part of a man's shoulder, flattened, angling toward the river's edge six feet away, still a bit below them but creeping upward.

Regis worked fast, biting back feelings of horror welling in him. He recalled with fingersnap speed the many times over the years they had had to drag free a sailor's body from the clutches of the river or coastal waters, or the bodies of other unfortunates lost to those same waters through accident or ill intent.

He bent low, reaching for the man's bunched, wadded coat, and tugged upward. The man came free with surprising ease, as if he were waiting for this opportunity.

The slimmest flickers of hope bloomed and then died away as quickly as Regis saw a thumb-size clump of mud drop away from the man's eyelash as his head came free of the grime. It had looked for that briefest of moments as if the man were struggling to blink away the filth.

But no. And it was young Chancy, as Regis now saw. And he was dead. He was also possessed of a ruined face, a mashed thing beneath the muck still discernible as the young man's heretofore fine-featured face.

A groan that became a sob burst from Regis's mouth, and he set his teeth tighter and shook his head quick and hard, as if he were afflicted with palsy. This was no time to succumb to foolish emotion and sentiment, Regis Royle, he told himself with a curse.

Time enough for that later. And if you don't get a move on, you will be in the boiling, lashing, foul river right there. He looked up at it and was shocked to see it inching even as he eyed it, closer and closer, now less than a foot from him, and threatening to fill in the hole Chancy now occupied.

The horse had been dragged backward enough that it stood as if a freakish mud-caked statue above him.

It was the first moment since spying young Chancy there beneath the horse that he had looked up at the beast above him.

Then there was a shout from the bank, but not from Benny. It sounded from behind Regis, but eastward. It sounded like Fergus, but who could tell with any surety in such weather.

He glanced that way, while tugging with both hands on the body of Chancy. The young man was becoming freed by degrees, inch by inch, and Regis did not dare let go his grip, slick and sliding as it was, on the crushed man's slathered coat.

Let them shout to him; what did he care? And then the shout came again, but closer this time.

"I'm okay!" shouted Regis. "Too muddy! Stay where you are!"

"Like heck!" shouted the voice, and Regis knew that it was Fergus.

At the same time, the big, flopped horse carcass that loomed with menace above him slipped, seeming to want to drop down on him. Hold on, rope, he told the cursed thing. Don't snap now, or there will be two dead men beneath the beast.

But the horse resumed its slow arc upward, then finally away from him, toward the riverbank, toward King, tugging hard with Benito guiding him.

Regis had Chancy all but dragged free of his mucky death site when something hard, like a branch, slapped and smacked him from behind. His first thought was that he'd been shot, or a snake had somehow wriggled free and slapped him.

He dispelled the absurdity of both notions and glanced over his right shoulder as he struggled to raise his left boot out of the muck. He saw a rope with a head-size loop in it lying on the mud a foot from him.

"See the rope?" shouted Fergus.

"Yes! Yes!"

Curse the rain and wind and dim light and thunder and lightning, every foul thing worked against them today.

Regis held tight with an arm across Chancy's chest, and with his right, he lurched, reaching for the rope. His first attempt fell short, and his hand slapped mud, a hand not recognizable to him as it was as black as cinders, and wet clear through the bone.

The effort cost him his footing, and he slipped awkwardly to his backside, with Chancy flapping across him. He retained his left arm's grip across the man's chest and reached once again for the rope. This time his trembling, clawing fingers grasped it, and he jerked it close, praying there was slack enough to drag them to the bank.

For it was that moment the river chose to rush in on him. Within a drawn-breath of a moment, it filled the hole left by the raised horse, which had completed its journey and flopped most of its body angling back toward the bank.

The water was cold, like ice to him, but he knew that could not be, that it was because he'd been stuck, wedged in this mud, struggling, for so long. At least he still had the luxury of struggle, he thought, using the fingertips of his left hand to help him widen the loop enough that he could slip it over both of them.

He would try this, to have them both saved at once. But if it proved too much to whoever was there, pulling from the shore, then he would shout, beg for slack, and have them drag the dead young man free first.

But Regis didn't count on the river rising even faster than he had anticipated. By the time he got the loop widened and wrapped around them, up under his own arms and one of the dead man's arms up and over the rope, the water gushed, surging against him in waves.

The taste of the river and its insistence at killing him, claiming him for its own, gagged Regis, and he retched. Get it out and away from him, his body and mind agreed. As another surge crested, he turned his head, jerking at the same time the cinch knot. Then, without missing a move, he yanked hard on the line twice, and within moments felt the rope zing taut.

Something had shifted beneath Regis's left boot while he had fiddled with the rope. Perhaps it was the rushing water, he did not know, nor did he much care. But as the person on shore, likely Fergus, shouted, Regis tried to respond in kind. But the water burbled and boiled over him, forcing him to face down-stream and gasp, taking in a stuttering breath half-filled with water. There was no way he could respond.

Fergus shouted again, and Regis realized he was urging on a horse. The man had likely taken a dally around the saddle horn and was now smacking hard on his horse's rump to get the beast to move. It worked. And not any too soon.

The rope did its job and dragged them, lurching step by lurch-ing step, up the mud-slick bank. But the pain he'd felt when they'd first been tugged multiplied, and soon he, too, shouted.

He tried to drag on the rope, tried to shout over the man, to let them know he was going to lose his leg to the cramping, cold. It hurt enough that did not wish to move any more, certain he was soon to feel his leg bones pop out of the socket at his hip joint.

"Gaah!" he yowled and moaned, pulling on the lodged limb himself. To his great surprise, it slid free, but not without a strug-gle and more anguish. And not without him losing his cursed boot. He did not notice this right away, of course, but only as he was being dragged, rapidly, with a dead man flopping atop him and a gouged, manure-and-mud riverbank beneath him.

It was a quick ride, with water sluicing up about them and a trough of muck and mud left behind. Then it came to a stop. His left shoulder wedged beneath a jutting clod of earth at the top of the bank. The tugging ceased, and the rope went slack. As Regis struggled to free himself from the rope, his gruesome burden jostled and suddenly felt heavier than a dead man had a right to be.

"Oh, my stars!" shouted a voice close by his right ear, and then strong hands grabbed him by the shoulder and yanked him up-ward. Another set of hands joined them, and Regis felt himself tugged along, with Chancy, up onto the flat of the once-grassy plain leading to the river.

The rain had, if anything, increased in fervor. It seemed to him as he struggled fruitlessly to help his rescuers loosen the rope, that the storm was a living, vengeful thing, out for some form of revenge.

"It's Chancy!" said the voice of the second man to arrive. Regis looked up; it was Benito.

Regis nodded. "Was dead . . . beneath the horse. Nothing I could do . . ."

"Course not, Boss. Take 'er easy. We'll have you on your feet in a second."

That was Fergus, and he worked to drag the dead man from atop Regis. "Boss," he said. "You have to let him go now."

Regis looked down and saw that his left arm was still curled tight and clamped about the dead young man's chest. He could not seem to unfasten his grip from him. Fergus leaned over and pried Regis's finger away and lifted his arm from across the dead man's chest.

He closed his eyes. Even though he knew the storm was worse than ever, even though he lay face up in it, with the might of the wind and rain and dark skies driving down from above, Regis had suddenly lost all ability to move. He was, he realized, plain exhausted.

"Boss? You okay?"

After a moment, he nodded. "Herd make it?"

"I think so," said Fergus. "Looks to be all across. I think I see most of the men from here."

"Percy?"

"Yeah, he's good, too. Wagon got out okay."

"Who else is over here?"

"You, me, Benito here, and of course, Chancy."

"Okay, help me up, will you?"

They did, and after a moment, Regis looked down at his left boot. Or that place where his boot should be. "Lost my boot." He wiggled the toe of his mud-black sock. "Funny thing."

Neither man could really hear him, but they exchanged looks, and Fergus shrugged.

"I'll take Chancy up on my horse, Boss. You and Benny can ride your own mounts. But we should wait it out here."

"Yeah?" said Regis, just looking up. "Oh, right. The river. Okay, yes, that's a good idea, then."

As Benito and Regis walked to their horses, Benny leaned close to Regis. "You did a good thing, boss. For Chancy, I mean."

"Nah." Regis hooked his head hard, too hard. "Nah, I didn't. Too little, too late. That's all I did."

Benny tried to speak again, to kindly disagree, but Regis was having none of it and shook his head again. "No, I tell you. Now please . . . Benny." He got rein of his emotions, and after a moment, he said, "I know you mean well, but let it be for now."

"Sure, Boss. Okay."

Chapter 16

The storm took hours more to completely pass. By then, Fergus, Regis, Benito, and Chancy, strapped across the back of Fergus's mount, had crossed. They only waited for the slashing, lashing, wind-blown rain to abate, and then they crossed the river, starting a quarter mile upstream and letting their horses have their heads to swim across.

It worked well, and once the three horses made it across, the men found they were but a short distance downstream from the men and herd.

They spent nearly two days more there, alongside the river, long enough to see the flow diminish as they took an accounting of their losses. They'd lost two head, by all counts a surprisingly low number, to lightning strikes, six head to trampling on the riverbanks, and another dozen were among the missing, presumed washed downstream or wandered off unnoticed. And all other men were accounted for, alive and, if not fully well, at least with injuries that would not hinder their work.

They buried Chancy on a bluff about a mile from the river, for several men were fearful that the river might one day overrun its substantial banks and wash out the grave. That notion did not sit well with the men, Regis chief among them.

Though several of the men had been chummy with the dead

young man, Regis insisted that he had caused the man's death. Therefore, he should be the one to contact Chancy's family.

Cyril told him Chancy had mentioned he had a younger sister still at home and a widower father. They lived in Missouri. Regis vowed he'd try to track them down and explain the fact that their sweet young man was indeed a man who died unexpectedly and unhappily. Regis remained inconsolable and brooded openly.

Finally, after a good many of the crew huddled together and learned what details over and over they could about Chancy's death, and why the boss should feel so guilty over it, they elected Fergus to talk with the man.

The rangy cowboy rubbed a hand over his tired, seamed face. "It's not as if he's doing anything wrong, boys," he said.

Though they agreed with him, Benito said, "That's just the thing, Ferg! He keeps on like this, all confused and whatnot, acting as if he caused the whole thing, why, we'll never make it to the railhead at Schiller."

Fergus squinted and toed a well-chewed hummock at his boots. Thing was, he knew they were right. The boss had been acting peculiar since the storm. "All right, then. All right. But look, if I get fired, it's on your heads."

He'd meant it as a bit of a joke, but the funny thing was, it could well be true. Regis Royle was an odd man to begin with, all work-driven and hard to smile, and then you throw a storm and all on top of that, why, you never knew what you were going to get.

Besides, thought Fergus as he walked on over to the boss, he wasn't all that certain the boss didn't hold him responsible for all that happened in the storm. Fergus still thought they did the right thing in crossing the cattle beforehand.

There was no feed left on the old side of the river, and those cattle were skittish to begin with. All that lightning playing up by the time it hit the south bank, why, they surely could have lost a whole lot more than they did.

Regis was secretly surprised they hadn't lost more to those jagged bolts from the heavens. And he was mighty thankful they hadn't, for if that had happened, he surely would have gotten the hard eye over it.

Regis Royle was sipping a cup of coffee on his own, well away from the men, gazing down at the infernal river, at the humped form of that dead man's horse, still there, with Royle's lasso still attached. It would be there a while yet, he reckoned. Even with all the buzzards and coyotes waiting for their turn.

Fergus cleared his throat. Regis turned. "Fergus, pull up a stool." He smiled, and the cowboy saw that the boss's face was looking old, far older than his years should allow. It had been a hard trip so far on all of them, but worse, for sure, for the boss.

"What's on your mind, Fergus?"

"Well, sir," Fergus said, and ran a hand over the back of his neck and squinted down at the river.

"Fergus, we should be past all that 'sir' stuff. You're Fergus, and I'm Regis. If that doesn't sit well, call me 'Royle' or . . ."

"How about 'Boss'?" said Fergus with a wry grin. "Not so much for my sake, but the younger ones yonder." He jerked his head back toward the main campfire, where the handful of men he'd just talked with still stood, trying to look anywhere but toward the two senior men chatting over by the river. They weren't very successful.

"That makes sense," said Regis, nodding. "Okay, then Boss it is. Now what can I do for you?"

"Well . . . Boss, it's about the men. They're concerned."

"Oh? About what?"

"Well, that's the awkward part. See, they're wondering if you're all right."

Regis gazed a few moments more at the river, then smiled. He lifted his boot. "Not too bad now that Cyril rescued my other boot from the mud . . . over there."

He was trying, Fergus saw, to cover up the rawness of the

man's death. And Fergus saw that Regis knew it was a weak attempt.

Regis sighed. "All right, Fergus. Tell the men I'm . . . no, best let me do that. But yes, I'm fine."

"Oh, Boss?"

"Yes, Fergus?"

"I'm sorry about the way things worked out. For young Chancy, I mean . . . I didn't know, you see, that he couldn't swim."

"Fergus, don't think for a moment that you hold any blame in this. Your advice was spot-on. I'd do it all over again the same way. Well, except for young Chancy."

Chapter 17

One day shy of a week after they left the still-muddy river-bank behind, Regis, riding drag and eating dust, saw Cyril ride back into view ahead. He could tell it was Cyril by the long blond hair sticking out from beneath his hat.

He looked beyond the young Englishman and replaced the cork stopper on his canteen and used a corner of his bandanna to wipe the grit from his eyes. Though in two minutes, it would hardly matter. It seemed they were forever traveling in a dust cloud.

He'd tried to cycle the men through scouting forays, in an effort to give them each some time away from the constant dust and grime.

He himself had drifted east and west of the herd to keep an eye on things, and he was surprised each time to find there was a clear, dust-free world beyond what they squinted through day and night.

The country they were riding in seemed to go on forever, though Fergus had assured him and the other men that it was a long, wide stretch of desert that they could only avoid by losing a couple of days' time making either northwest or northeast, before cutting north once more.

Regis had initially said no, no way, that flooded river and all the mess they'd run into there had already slowed them down. That it would be better to move them on through, take the dust and grit for a few days, and then they'd get to good grassland once more.

He had been a little concerned that they hadn't seen much in the way of signs of previous herds before them. On the one hand, he was fine with not traveling paths others had taken. It was a notion that had always served him well in life.

But on the other hand, it made him question his decisions. Did other herders know something he didn't? Of course they did, and he was painfully aware that he was as green as a spring shoot at this trail-driving game.

But once more, he placed his faith in Fergus and the man's senior experience in such matters. Just that morning, Fergus had told him that they could expect to draw near the town of Dennerville quite soon.

The man had rubbed his chin, knuckled back his sweat-stained topper, and squinted northward, as if he could see, in the far distance, the outlines of the buildings of the town themselves. "I reckon it'll be a day and a . . . half." He turned back and smiled. "Give or take a day."

"The boys will be pleased. What sort of town is Dennerville?"

"Oh, typical trail town. A place for the boys to whoop it up, provided they don't get into too much trouble. And as I recall, there's a mighty decent restaurant there, too. Something such as Maude's or Mabel's, can't quite recall. But I do remember the taste of the shoo-fly pie. It was almost as good as mama's." He winked then and strode off for another cup of weak coffee.

Visions of a nice meal at a restaurant—and he didn't much care if it annoyed Percy—carried Regis on through the next couple of dirt- and dust-choking days.

"It's not going to happen, you understand?"

The man's thick, oversize mustaches twitched, spiky to match his bristly demeanor. He was, as he had presented himself to Regis, Marshal Fairborn Tench, the law in Dennerville.

Regis looked down at the small, chesty man and suddenly felt very tired. An argument with a squirt was not anything he was interested in just now. All he really wanted was to help Percy stock up the wagon, buy the other items on the list, and get back to the herd. Then he was going to turn the boys loose, by twos or threes, on the town so they might enjoy themselves a little bit.

"What isn't going to happen, marshal?"

"What you and your foul cowboys are set on doing, which is to tear my town apart from one end to the other! I tell you—"

Regis didn't give the man a chance to continue. "And I tell you, marshal, that we have no such intention. We need supplies, and then we'll mosey on our way!" He was sorely tempted to drive his big poker of a finger into the runt's puffed chest. But he kept that desire in check. For now.

It made little difference to the bone-tired rancher just who was enforcing what in the demure but seemingly booming town. He wanted to make certain that Percy could restock his wares. They were running pitifully low on flour, corn meal, and they were down to their last few pounds of coffee and had about two meals' worth of beans left.

That last fact almost made the boys cheer, for since his encounter with the river, the surly cook had not been up to his usual culinary standards.

Regis had hoped to allow all the men a chance to unwind themselves in the town, but now that Regis had met Marshal Fairborn Tench, he wasn't so certain such a notion would be the best decision.

Regis, well north of six feet tall, and wide at the shoulder and square of the jaw—and his kid brother Shepley would say hard of the head, too—rested his big hands on his gun belt and looked down at the puffed-up, little, self-important man. He'd be damned if he was going to let this runt tell him how he was going to conduct his affairs.

"Percy?"

"Yeah, boss?"

Regis didn't have to turn to try to locate his cook. The man was true and tested. He would be right beside him. And he was. And if Regis dared to look away from glaring at the equally glaring little lawman, he would have seen the same staring, grim look on Percy's face.

"Why don't you go on and finish up that list at the mercantile and feed store. I have to talk with the marshal here, then I'll catch up with you."

Before Percy could respond, the marshal said, "I told you before, mister cattleman, it ain't going to happen."

"Just what is it you're talking about, Marshal?" said Percy.

Regis looked over at Percy and shook his head. The cook gritted his teeth, glared at the lawman for a moment longer, then shook his head and walked toward the mercantile.

"My cook is a man of many passions." Regis offered a slight smile.

"I don't care a thing about him, nor you, nor your cows, nor your men. What I do care about is keeping my town free from folks who wish to upset our apple cart, you hear?"

Regis leant down and put his face close to Tench's, their nose tips almost touching. "You had best get specific, Mister Lawman, and tell me what it is you plan on doing to my people. Or we can have a set-to right here, right now."

To his surprise, the smaller man did not back down a bit. He folded his arms over his chest and spoke in a voice loud enough for the handful of eavesdropping folks behind him on the boardwalk to hear. "If any of your people come into my town and make a ruckus, there is going to be hell to pay. You got me? I will arrest anyone who causes problems."

"Do you always treat potential patrons of the businesses of Dennerville with such disdain, Marshal?"

"Dis-what, now? Don't you go talking down to me, man!"

Regis straightened, looked around, over the head of the man before him, at the townsfolk listening in. He smiled and touched his hat brim, making eye contact with a young woman in a smart hat.

"Folks," he said. "Seems to me your marshal here would rather not make any money off of our modest cattle drive. We aren't desperate for supplies, but we thought it might be nice to stock up, seeing as how we're passing through anyway. But"—he looked skyward and shrugged—"I guess we could just pull up stakes and continue on. Pity, though.

"My men were looking forward to a homecooked meal or two, and some of them need new boots and hats, some shirts, for certain. And I could use a cobbler, myself. Oh, and one of my men might be in the market for a saddle. But"—he looked at the fuming marshal, then at the townsfolk, whose number seemed to have swelled to a dozen or so—"I reckon we'll pass Dennerville on by this time. Don't want to drop our money in a place where we're not wanted, now, do we?"

The marshal uttered a strangled little yelp. Regis noticed the man's jowls and cheeks, cinched tight by a too-tight starched collar, had turned an alarming shade of deep red. Maybe getting on toward purple.

"Now, now, I ain't said that at all! You are not listening, Mister Cattle Man!" The marshal half-turned and flashed a pasted-on smile.

"Oh, I see," said Regis. He raised his voice and smiled again at the now plainly eyeballing and gathering crowd. "My mistake, Marshal. My mistake. I will happily let my men know that they are free to come on into your fine town of Dennerville and spend some of their money." He nodded and smiled to the crowd of townsfolks. "That sit all right with you folks?"

They nodded, smiled, and several of them let out light cheers. One man clapped. And then Marshal Tench turned to face them and glared, his eyes narrowed and his bottom jaw out-thrust.

The sounds made by the group of townsfolk dwindled to fizzled murmurs. Their smiles drooped as well, and they looked away, down at their shoes, anywhere but at the glaring little man who, Regis saw, controlled them far more than he ought to.

What was his hold on these people, Regis wondered. He knew a whole lot of things, had learned a whole lot in his days as a sailor and businessman, and lately as a rancher. And one of the most important, that he learned a long ol' time ago, was that tyrants, in all sizes and stripes, were always outnumbered by the folks they strutted up and over, often trampling them underfoot.

It had always seemed to Regis that if folks got riled up enough and banded together, they could face down the tyrants. And Marshal Tench sure fit that bill.

Tench reminded him that most, but not all, of the cocky, big talkers he'd met or heard of in life were little men. Full of themselves and empty of follow-through and weak as water when they were pressed.

But something, too, told Regis that Tench, regardless of his hold on the townsfolk of Dennerville, had an angle, an edge to him, an inner rod of steel. It was rusting, perhaps, but it was there. He didn't back down when Regis barked and glared at him.

Usually that worked; Regis didn't mind admitting that he had played up the fact that he was a large man and could often back folks down. But his excuse was that he knew it had helped him avoid fights. And any time a man could do that, it was worth the false bravado and growling involved.

As if in response to his thoughts, Tench turned and poked at Regis, almost touching his chest with a stubby finger. In a low, gravelly voice, he said, eyeing Regis through narrowed eyes, "You pull that crap again in my town, and you'll regret it. You and your boys. Now, do what you feel you need to, but you be mindful of what I say. And you best walk on eggshells, if you know what is good for you."

For the sake of the men, the herd, his already wobbly timetable, and even for the sake of the townsfolk of Dennerville, Regis decided to let the little man's threats pass unremarked. If he kept butting heads with the fool, he'd end up with a sore forehead and little else.

The only thing that might have made a difference then was if Tench had indeed poked him in the chest. And then the fool did.

Regis's reactions were viperlike. He grasped the offending digit and the hand it belonged to, engulfing it in one of his big ham hands, and squeezed, pulling the man's hand away from his chest.

In a voice lower and colder than Tench's, Regis Royle said, just loud enough for the lawman to hear, "The last man who laid a prodding finger on me has never quite learned how to go through life without the use of his full hand." And then, without taking his eyes from Tench's face, nor altering his own stony visage, Regis crushed the man's hand, squeezing it as if it were a lemon and he wanted every last big drop of juice from it.

The finger rose skyward, and Regis watched the man's face slide from red-faced rage to eye-twitching agony. The man's mustaches and bottom lip trembled.

"Never lay a hand on me again, and we'll get along just fine. All right?"

The man stared at him, his left eye beginning to tear.

"A nod will do," said Regis.

The man nodded.

Regis smiled. "Good. That's fine then." But he didn't let go. Then he said, almost as an afterthought, "Oh, me and my men will be out of here in short order, not to worry . . . Mister Marshal."

He let go of the man's hand, and Tench gasped and clutched

the wounded limb. As Regis turned and walked toward the mercantile to meet up with Percy, from behind, he heard, "Just you wait, Royle. One false step, just one, mind you, and you'll find I'm not so easy to deal with as you might think I am."

Regis gave up pondering this latest diatribe and walked to the store, not bothering to suppress the grim smile on his face. So help me, he thought, I sure did enjoy twisting that little piglet's fingers.

Chapter 18

Bone McGraw was not impressed with the Texas Ranger situation in Corpus Christi. The office there was a messy affair, papers scattered about the one work surface, an old table with a leg propped with a wooden box of rifle cartridges.

A couple of uncleaned, unoiled rifles leaned in a corner, and a grimy man's shirt, bloodied down the front, lay across the back of the room's one chair. Of Rangers, there was no sign, save for the mess left behind.

Were they called out on an urgent task? There had to be some reason for this disarray.

Jervis Latham, standing just behind Bone in the doorway, but peering over his shoulder, gave voice to the raw notions bubbling in Bone's head. "I don't care how busy a man gets, there is no excuse for slovenliness. My old mama, long dead, rest her, used to say that soap and water are cheap, dirt cheap."

Bone nodded but said nothing. The state of the room annoyed him, and it embarrassed him, too, especially before Jervis.

Bone glanced about the room once again, not wanting surprises; then he ventured farther in. "Might be I have the wrong address."

"No, I don't think so," said Latham. "That barkeep said it was here, and here it is."

"Just the same, I am going to check for proof, in case. Keep an eye on the door." Regis walked over to the table. The papers atop were scattered, as if someone had been searching for something and then either found it or had run out of patience and left. He bet himself it was the latter.

"Where would you go, Jervis, if you had to work in here every day?"

Without missing a word, Latham said, "I reckon I'd be down at the bar. If I was white, that is."

"Right," said Bone. "Come on," he said, pushing past Jervis.

"Where we headed?"

"To find a Texas Ranger in this town."

"How many were you expecting?"

"More than none."

They walked to the nearest saloon, the Greasy Hub, and Bone walked up to the bar. He said something, half-turned, and saw that Jervis was still outside looking in. "What are you doing?"

"What he's supposed to," said the barkeep behind Bone.

"Oh, and what's that? You going to serve him a beer out there?"

"Nope. Not going to serve him a beer anywhere."

"Not even if he's a Texas Ranger?"

"Don't look much like one."

"Do I?" said Bone.

"Not particularly," said the barkeep.

"Well, I am. And I am trying to find the other Rangers in town. You know where they might be?"

"They have an office down the street."

"Tried there. Nobody home."

"Doesn't surprise me. Man who runs the place is Beaudry. If he ain't there, he's likely over at Suzy's."

"Who's Suzy?"

"I thought everyone in Corpus Christi knew who Suzy was." The barkeep smiled.

"Not if they aren't from here."

"Suzy is a whore, down the street, that-a-way." The barkeep jerked a fat thumb eastward. "Can't miss it. As long as you can read."

Bone nodded. "Thank you for the information." He began to walk to the door.

"Hey," said the barkeep. "Ain't you going to buy a drink?"

"Can't," said Bone. "No time. Got to go learn to read, then find this Suzy." He gave the man a quick one-fingered salute off his hat brim and left.

Out on the sidewalk, he walked eastward. "Sorry about that," he said to Jervis.

"Oh, no never mind to me. I haven't got the cash for a beer, even if I was white-skinned."

Bone smiled. "As soon as we find a hospitable saloon, the first beer's on me. But first we have to visit a whorehouse."

Jervis stopped. "Oh now, you never said nothing about such shenanigans."

"No," said Bone, shaking his head. "Not like that. Barkeep said we might find the ranger there. Besides, I'm a happily married man." The thought of that made him feel good, and he smiled as they walked on up the street.

It didn't take long for them to find Suzy's place. It was called just that, on a carved and painted sign hung above the door of a modest and otherwise respectable-looking white painted frame house. Before he could knock, Bone saw curtains in a window to the left of the door part slightly, revealing a dark wedge within; perhaps there had been a face in it.

Bone's big-knuckled hand was poised to knock on the door when it swung open and a woman, average height and with strawberry hair piled loosely atop her head, smiled a dimpled smile at him. Her body wrapped in a no-telling-what-could-be-beneath robe decorated with ornate flowers.

"Why, gents, what can little ol' me do for the two of you?" She beamed at each of them.

Bone's face blushed a deep crimson, and he lowered his hand. "Ma'am," he said, sweeping off his hat. "I . . . I'm Bone McGraw, and this here's my friend, Jervis Latham."

"That's very nice for you both, I'm sure." Still smiling, she stood aside and waved them on past her. Bone led the way, and Jervis, looking wide-eyed and walking slowly, followed.

She touched him on the shoulder. "I'm Suzy, by the way. You all come here for what I hope you came here for?" She slid her hand down Jervis's arm, and he stiffened and pulled his shoulders into a hunch, but did not look at her.

"Actually, ma'am," said Bone. "What we're here for is to find the whereabouts of a Texas Ranger named Beaudry."

"Oh," she said, her hand dropping to her side. She still smiled but now wore a look of relaxed defeat. "Well, you came to the right place, I guess. He's upstairs, sleeping. That's about all he does these days."

"He live here?" said Jervis.

"No, well, maybe sort of, yeah."

"Which is it?" said Bone.

"You're a demanding soul, ain't you?" she said.

"Sorry, ma'am. We've been looking for him for a while now, and it's not a game I enjoy."

"Let me guess, you two are Rangers, and you need him for something official."

"That's about it, yeah." Bone nodded, cutting his eyes to Jervis quickly. "Would it be possible for you to call him on down here?"

"I'm happy to," she said. "He's been sleeping far too long, and I have to get ready for my day's customers."

"Yes, ma'am."

"Set yourselves down there on those chairs, and I'll wake up Chester. Then I'll bring you a couple of cups of coffee. It'll take him that long to drag himself on down, anyway."

She made her way upstairs, and soon they heard a man's loud

yawn, then low talking, then a man's voice saying, "What? Aw, why can't these idiots leave me the heck alone?" His complaint trailed into a wet cough.

Jervis and Bone exchanged glances, and Jervis saw that the Ranger was tense, his jaw muscles tight, and looked to be ready to shout somebody down.

Soon, Suzy walked back down the stairs. "Won't be but a minute or ten now, gents." She disappeared down a dark passage, and soon they heard a stove being prodded, wood being stuffed in and knocked around with a poker.

By the time they'd made it halfway through their cups of hot coffee, heavy steps sounded on the stairwell, and soon they saw a paunched, spindly-legged man descending the stairs. He stopped six steps from the bottom and gazed at Bone and Jervis.

"So," he said, folding his arms. "Two whiny men looking for help from the Texas Rangers. Oh, what fun."

He reached the bottom of the stairs, his robe still hanging wider open than should have been allowed.

Bone and Jervis stood. "You're Beaudry?" said Bone, stepping forward and extending his hand for a shake.

The man sighed and yawned and looked from the hand to Bone; then he shook Bone's hand weakly. Jervis also had extended his hand for a shake, but the man did not look at him at all.

"What do you want?"

"Well, sir, these idiots will leave you alone once we get the information I came to Corpus Christi for. And we'll need to have you swear him in. I can vouch for him."

At that, Beaudry finally looked at Latham. "Why? This is the Rangers, not a plantation."

At that, Jervis looked at his holey boots, and Bone stepped forward. "I've had enough of your lip, Beaudry. I don't care what your newly minted rank is, one more insult to me or my friend here, and you and me, we're going to step outside."

"And just who in the blazes are you to speak to me like that?"

"I am Texas Ranger Jarvis McGraw."

The effect of Bone's words was easy to see on Beaudry's face. "Oh . . . you're . . . Bone McGraw?"

"That's what I said."

Beaudry stared at him for a long moment, then nodded. "Right. Sorry about that."

"It isn't me who needs an apology. It's my friend here, Mr. Latham, you insulted."

Beaudry's eyes widened, and he looked at Jervis. "I am sorry about that, Mr. Latham. It's . . . I ain't had no coffee yet." He turned and ran up a couple of steps. "Now, now, let me get my things upstairs and we can get on over to my office."

"Make it quick," said Bone.

"You bet!"

After Beaudry had thumped his way upstairs, Suzy, who had been leaning in the doorway to the kitchen passage the entire time, said, "Well now, that was something. I have never seen anyone put Chester in his place like that." She leaned closer to Bone. "About time, too."

"It needed doing. There was no call for his rudeness, ma'am."

"Hmm, you might be handy to have around. He isn't the only rude one I get in here."

Bone grinned. "I expect you take care of things just fine here, ma'am."

Beaudry thundered back down the stairs, his shirttails flapping, his braces slopping about his legs, and his trousers poorly stuffed into the tops of his boots.

"Shall we go, gentlemen?" Over his shoulder, as Beaudry swung open the door, he said, "I'll stop by later, Sue!"

"Don't rush," she said, and winked at Jervis, who happened to be looking her way.

The three men left, and she closed the door, then leaned against it in the dim front hallway and chuckled.

Out on the street, Bone and Jervis had a time of it in keeping up with Beaudry. Finally, they reached the Ranger office. It was still a mess and a half.

"You'll pardon me. Been so busy here, I just don't have the time to straighten up." He bustled about the room, his braces slopping against his legs and his hair standing on end. His shaky-hand efforts made little difference at all, and in some instances, the messy piles of papers became messier.

"Leave off of that for now, Beaudry," said Bone. "What I need are reports of the trouble spots where I was told I'd be needed."

"Yes, yes, of course!"

"And while you're at it, I'll need to have somebody sign up Latham here."

"You can do that yourself, Bone."

"Call me Ranger McGraw, Beaudry."

"Yes, sure. Of course."

"And I know I can, but I want you to witness it. And he'll need a badge."

"Oh, we don't have any of those just now."

"Fine. You have one?"

"Yes, but . . . oh, sure thing. You bet."

Bone thrust out his hand. "It'll do, and then you can get yourself a shiny new one."

All the while, Jervis Latham stood by silently, alternating between wanting to smile and wanting to shrink back into the dust outside. "It's all right, Bone," he said in a low voice. "I can get by without a badge."

"Nope," said Bone. "They carry weight, especially where we're going."

"That's a fact," said Beaudry, spreading a map. "Now, see that there stretch?" His pudgy finger tapped, then ran a thin line along the border. "We've been having a devil of a time with three or four bands of border bandits."

He shook his head and smoothed back his hair, looking flushed, as if he'd run a hundred miles to tell them the news. "Word is that they are headed by a woman, of all things! Somebody said they thought it was some woman goes by the name of Valdez. Tina or some such."

"Tomasina?"

Beaudry snapped his fingers and nodded with vigor. "That's it! That's the one. Why? You know who she is?"

"I do," said Bone, looking up briefly from the map. "But I thought she was dead. If it's her, then it's trouble. She was wily and had a pile of men doing her bidding."

"Sounds like she's back in business," said Jervis.

Bone nodded. "Maybe never left it. At least not for long." He stood and sighed, smoothing his mustaches. "Have you been out there yourself?" said Bone, looking at Beaudry.

"Well, no, I . . . I'm fresh in from Austin way a month back, and, well, I'm needed here. A liaison of sorts, you see . . ."

"Uh-huh." Bone slid the map over in front of him and motioned Latham over. "See that country there?"

"Yep."

"You been down that way in your . . . recent travels?"

"Not yet. But I'm ready."

"Good." Bone looked again at Beaudry. "Where are the other patrols you've sent out? Which one needs more men? We'll meet up with them."

"Well, now, that's the thing. There are only a few lone operatives working the field just now."

"What?" said Bone. "I thought the call went out for more Rangers?"

"Oh, it did, it did. But nobody heeded, you see."

Bone sighed. "Well, you have two fools who did."

Beaudry smiled and nodded. "Indeed."

"We'll need to outfit Mr. Latham here, and we'll need to rig ourselves up for the trip. And we'll need a pack animal."

"Ah, yes, certainly."

"Look, Beaudry, I know the call went out a month or more ago. I would have been along sooner, but I had a run-in with a mountain lion."

"Who won?" said Beaudry.

Bone smiled. "You aren't talking to a mountain lion right now, are you?"

"I'm not so sure," muttered Jervis, smiling.

After swearing in Jervis Latham as a Texas Ranger, the three men made their way to the livery, where Bone checked on Bub, procured a solid mount for Latham, and a third horse to pack their goods. The horse was also decent enough for a spare mount. Then they walked to Finkel's Mercantile and watched Beaudry wince as Bone piled new duds into Jervis's outstretched arms.

In addition, he loaded him up with a solid, used, single-gun rig and a nice, wide-blade hip knife and sheath. He also handed him a decent folding Barlow knife and a straight razor.

"The razor and the pocketknife are from me," said Bone to Jervis. "Man should look his best and have a decent blade in his pocket, always."

"Thank you," said Latham quietly, his eyes wide, uncertain what to make of all this sudden good fortune.

"You're welcome. The rest, he can sign for." Bone laid a hand on the bewildered Beaudry's shoulder. "On behalf of the State of Texas. Including the supplies I'm about to list out for the good Mrs. Finkel here." Bone nodded to the portly German woman bustling behind the counter while her husband helped Latham figure out the sizing of boots.

She reddened and fluttered her eyelids at him. "Yah, yah, of course! You go ahead and tell to me. I write it all down and get it packaged for you. Anything for the handsome Rangers!" She giggled and reddened even more.

All the while, Beaudry didn't say a word. But Bone could tell he was silently tallying up the purchases and looking greener the more his lips worked the figures.

Finally, when it seemed to Bone that Beaudry could endure no more, he mentioned to the mirthful German woman that they would be back later to retrieve their order. Then Bone ushered Jervis Latham and Beaudry out the door, its bell jangling.

He didn't pause and give Beaudry time to harry him with fiscal concerns, but instead walked back to the Ranger office and began folding the map they had consulted earlier, and which they had left outstretched on the table.

"We'll be needing this," he said, knowing Beaudry had every right to argue with him over that point. But to Bone's surprise, Beaudry nodded. "That's fine, that's fine. I have two."

"Good," said Bone, miffed that he'd not been able to twist that blade of annoyance a time or two more. "We will ride on down south of here, see what patrols we can come across, and do what we can to foil the efforts of Miss Valdez's border bandits."

"But . . . there are only two of you."

"And others in the field," said Bone. "Unless you're fibbing to me, Beaudry."

"Fibbing? What? No, no. I only meant that . . ." He pulled in a deep breath and tugged down the front of his vest and straightened his shoulders. "I have not been authorized to . . . to indulge individual Rangers in spending so much money, nor in allowing them to venture forth into the wilds without proper and adequate numbers."

"I don't see that you have a choice in the matter, Beaudry." Bone tried to suppress a smile, but did not work too hard at it.

"Now see here, I am technically the commanding officer of this situation. And as such, I demand that you delay your departure until such time as we are able to gather more recruits."

Bone looked to the ceiling, scratched his chin, and said, "Hmm, seems to me that's the sort of thing you can get away with saying to a child or a fresh recruit, but I've been a Texas Ranger likely longer than you've been in long pants, Chester." Bone leaned down until his rangy, grizzled face hovered before Beaudry's.

"Besides, somebody has to do the work of actually rangering. You darn sure aren't."

With that, Bone snatched up the folded map and stomped on out of the disheveled office. Jervis Latham followed, in his squeaky-clean new boots and togs. He paused in the doorway, plopped on his new hat, and nodded to Beaudry. Touching the brim, then smiling, he followed Ranger McGraw back out to the livery.

Chapter 19

Two days after they left the safety of Corpus Christi, having first stopped at a saloon for a glass of warm beer and a plate of bread, cheese, and meats, Bone and Jervis found themselves cutting southward, making for the borderline between Texas and Mexico.

Not that it was difficult to find. But it was the first desolate stretch in many hours they came to that caused Bone to rein up and hold up a hand. He eyed the rolling terrain before them, a mix of sand and grasses and scrubby, stunted trees that looked afflicted with more than too much sun and too little rain.

Even before they had reached Corpus Christi that first day, Bone had been doling out slices of trail advice to Jervis, even before the younger man realized he was being given useful tidbits.

Then he knew that was Bone's way—try not to tell a fellow what to do, but offer examples that had the ring of storytelling to them. Jervis learned that Bone was not bragging of past Ranger exploits, but using those all-too-real adventures as instruction.

He'd kept it up for some time, though Jervis realized it was only while they rode through country that for various reasons—homesteads with folks working, open country with grazing cattle flanking them—that Bone chatted to him.

The closer they drew to the raw border, the quieter and more watchful, more alert—stealthy, even—Bone became. Jervis adopted the same attitude.

So it was no surprise when the senior Ranger silently called a halt to their progress. They were just emerging from a draw. Before them lay a sun-baked flat. Across from them sat a squat homestead—a low line casita, a modest, crooked-rail corral, and a smaller structure some yards from the first that looked to be half-built.

Nothing moved save for a tumbleweed, pinned as it was beneath the bottom corral rail. It wagged with a slight breeze, as yet unfelt by Jervis and Bone. Of livestock, they saw none in evidence.

The younger man looked to Bone briefly and saw the Ranger moving only his eyes through squinting lids. He could well be a lizard, so unblinking did he seem. Jervis looked to their left, was tempted to glance at their backtrail, but did not dare move his head that much. If Bone wasn't, he should not, either.

Bone spoke then, in a low, even whisper. "Something's off. Been by here before; folks who live here have a big brood. No way they'd be gone from here. Man's a mustanger, good at it, too. Fetched ponies from the canyonlands to the south. There'd be horses, chickens, children, something moving around."

Jervis then noticed that the place did not have that look of abandonment so many such homesteads wore like a poorly draped rag. "Should look different if they'd left."

"Good that you noticed that. We're going to ride on in, spread out. I'll go in from westward; you take the east. Slick out your rifle and lay it across your saddle, unthong that sidearm. And if it feels wrong, don't do it."

Jervis wanted to ask how he could possibly know such a thing, but he knew it really was the best advice a man who for so long lived by his gut, his instincts, that he assumed Jervis would feel that way, as well.

And Jervis reckoned Bone was right. Had to learn to trust his own gut.

They split up, with Jervis having tied the pack horse's lead line to the ring on the left of his saddle, just under the cantle.

The land to his left, eastward, sat flat and barren and did not seem as if it would hide secrets that might concern him in the next twenty minutes.

Jervis kept his glance flicking over to Bone, riding slow and measured a good eighth mile westward. The younger man matched his pace and steady demeanor, only angling toward the ranchita proper when Bone did.

Jervis mused that there was something freeing in not caring what might happen to you when you were entering a potentially dicey situation. Now that he felt as if he had accomplished the first part of his debt to his wife and children, a debt he knew he could never set fully to rights, he found that he felt a little different about his life to come. Might be he was beginning to feel that he actually had a life before him that might be worth waking up for.

And on top of that, he had this crazy white Ranger who had taken him under his wing and trusted him, now, with his life. It was a potent situation, and Jervis knew it was one he had to do his best to live up to.

And that was all the time he had for musing, because Bone had begun angling toward the little spread, his rifle now plainly seen as a line of black jutting from either side, across his saddle, above his knees.

A quick gust blew from the southwest, and Jervis flexed his nostrils, trying to do what Bone had told him not but a few hours before—use everything God gave you, from eyes to ears to nose to mouth, and more—to make your decisions. Because one of them alone might not save your life, but two or more together just might. Or the lives of others.

And now, Jervis knew what the man meant. Because carried to

him on that errant, quick blast of breeze, Jervis had detected a sliver of rankness. A thin skin of something foul. Even before he made up his mind as to what it was, his brain knew, and Jervis knew, and he could not help himself, but he gigged that horse into a lope.

He had yet to name the horse, and Bone had said he must do so if he was to share life on the trail with his horse, more so than anybody else.

He glanced at Bone and saw the man sit up more erect and shake his head at him. Jervis tried, but Bone didn't know. He did not know what Jervis knew. That there was something bad in that house. Something that he was in no hurry to find, but that he had to see for himself. Had to know if maybe there was a way to get there faster, to prevent something from happening.

The corral sat east of the house, just right for Jervis to lash up his horse and the pack animal, as well. He was now out of sight of Bone, their sightways blocked by the little adobe home.

Details of the place showed themselves to Jervis—the usual cracks in the adobe walls had been mudded and smoothed with care. Rocks the size of baby heads had been placed also with care along the pathway from the corral on up to the house, and around the house. And there were plants growing there in the shade of the house. Or it would be the shade in the latter part of the day, at least on this side of the little home.

The corral itself had been built with care, not a sloppy affair as he'd seen so many times in his travels. It was something made of gathered bits, to be sure, but robust and lashed and pegged. The other structure they'd seen riding in—perhaps it was an open-face shed for tack and shade—sat to the west of the house and hidden from Jervis's sight. But he suspected that, too, was a tidy affair.

Nothing moved; no sign either of hooves, none recent, any-way, showed themselves to him. He tried to calm himself, knew he would get a chewing from Bone when they met up. Forget about that now, Jervis, he told himself. He licked his perspiring top lip and squinted the sweat from his eyes. Should have done like Bone and tugged his hat brim down lower.

Too late. No wasted movements, the ranger had told him. In a dicey situation, make everything you do count for something.

He knew he was better with a pistol than he was with a rifle, and that this would be a close-in fight if there were foul folks lurking. And he had no reason to think otherwise. Which called to mind another thing Bone had said: "Look at every situation as bad until it proves itself to be otherwise to you."

"Sad way to go through life," Jervis had remarked, and Bone had stopped his horse, looked Jervis in the eye, and said, "Mister, that sort of rosy outlook might work for town folks, but you're a Texas Ranger. Nothing is good until you have proved for certain for your own self that it is. You hear me?"

Jervis had understood, and nodded as the truth of the remark settled on him like a lead shawl. He had signed on for something not a whole lot of folks dared to take on. He couldn't afford to be casual any longer.

And as he walked toward the little adobe casita, with more caution than he'd ever taken in all his days, that notion bubbled to the surface, and he nodded as if finally agreeing with Bone.

That's when he heard a scuffing. It was quick, scarcely audible, but it was there. He felt it, trusted his gut, as Bone said he should in such an instant. And so, it was a sound. And it came from the house. Maybe it was Bone from the far side?

But no, Bone would say, it's not to be trusted until you can prove what it is.

And so, Jervis proceeded, sweat stippling his forehead, leaking down around his eyes. He didn't dare do much more than give himself a quick squint to clear it. He loosened his grip on the rifle, but swung it snout-first toward the house—it was cocked and ready to trigger.

He risked a glance to his left, saw that the way, off to the left of the trodden path, was sandier, less gritty, and he sidestepped there. Might prove to be quieter, though he placed each footstep with care.

It also gave him more of a view to that south-facing side of the house. He saw that, as he had guessed, the entrance was there. He caught sight of Bone, in partial view, also advancing on the house. Bone saw him, too, and nodded once, slow. Bone would have to pass by the half-building first.

And also as Jervis had guessed, he saw now that it was a half-open-faced shed, storage and tools in one section, the rest penned and open to the elements, a run-in shed for critters.

But Bone was right—no chickens, no sign of anything yet that would show this place was the sort of bustling homestead Bone had known it to be.

Bone glanced at him once, then angled over to inspect the shed. It took him but a few moments. The ranger nodded once more to Jervis and resumed walking.

Jervis tapped his left ear with a finger and pointed toward the house, hoping to convey to Bone that he'd heard something. Bone seemed to understand with a nod, and they kept on.

It was still, no sounds, no nothing. And then there was something, that smell again. A whiff of the taint of death. Jervis knew it well, for once a man smells such a thing, it will not let him be. It set to tumbling all manner of memories.

They were painful beyond measure, of his wife and the children, but not as he would choose to recall them, in their fettle with smiles and laughter and happiness in their eyes, but with a grim sadness of the last he saw of them—crying and dying and dead. It was with great effort that Jervis dispelled them.

Each man was within twenty feet of the doorway then, when a sound, more of that light scuffing, rose up. Jervis saw by the shift in the senior ranger's eyes, barely noticeable, that Bone heard it, too.

"Get on out of it now! Get! I got you in my sights, and you're dead if you take one more step in!"

Both men halted. There was a pause long enough for a man to

draw in a deep breath, and Bone said, "Rick! Rick Smithers! That you? It's Bone! Bone McGraw, Texas Rangers!"

This time, the pause was long. Finally a scuffing, dragging sound came to them. "I see you!" shouted the voice.

"Good!' shouted Bone. "Then you know I didn't come here to cause you grief! Me and my pard are here looking to help!"

The response then was immediate. The man laughed. "Ha!" he shouted. "Too little too late, Ranger!"

"I know it, but we're here now. Come on out, and we'll hammer out this thing together!"

"Get on out of it, McGraw! It ain't your affair. Go away from here!"

"Can't do that, Rick." All the while he spoke, Bone walked slowly toward the house. He motioned Jervis to make for the side of the house closest to him. At least that's how Jervis deciphered the ranger's head nods.

By the time Bone reached the door, Jervis was at the house, beside the window facing the corral. It was half-shuttered, and the interior of the little house was dark and dim. Jervis was ready to step into view and draw down on the man inside.

From the front, Bone took one more step, which landed him at the front entrance. He eyed the door, the bottom half of which was closed. The top, as with the shutters on the few windows that Bone had seen, was half-closed, showing him only a dark interior. But within, he knew there was at least one man with a gun. He guessed so, anyway. No reason not to trust Rick Smithers's word about that.

He hoped Jervis was ready for possible action from his side of the house.

"See, Rick! Here I am! Arms are up, no easy way for me to shoot, even if I wanted to. Which I do not!"

There was another long pause of many moments with no sound from within. Jervis didn't dare make a slight move for fear of disrupting whatever it was that might or might not be happening inside the little adobe home. But the smell was becoming more potent and beginning to tickle his nose and mind in ways he did not take kindly to. He hoped Bone would make a move soon.

"Bone McGraw?"

"Yeah, Rick. I'm here. Outside your front door, hands raised."

"Okay . . . I . . . I need help, Bone."

From within, Jervis heard a clunking sound, then a crash, as if something or several somethings made of wood had snapped and cracked and broke.

Bone shifted his rifle to his left hand and snatched at the latch of the lower half of the door with his left. "Rick!" He kept the gun ready, but glanced to his right and saw Jervis shoving his own rifle through the half-open window, too.

They needn't have worried. Rick Smithers was on his back in the midst of a pile of splintered wood. He was not a large man, but he had made quite a mess when he apparently fell backward into a table and chairs.

It was dead weight. Or rather, the weight of a man who was close to succumbing to grievous wounds.

Bone rushed to his side in two strides, taking in the front room. "Jervis! Get in here and check out the rest of the house! Then keep an eye—we don't want any surprise visitors!"

Jervis did as he was bade, rushing around to the front and entering the doorway to see Bone having laid down his rifle. He was clearing away bits of broken table and chairs from the fallen man.

"I think he's just passed out. From wounds, looks to be. Jervis, open those other two windows wide, will you? Then check on the back rooms. Two, I think."

"Okay."

Bone laid Rick Smithers out and checked him over, bending low and patting him all over for sign of wounds. There were two obvious—one on his head, a gash that looked to have bled quite a bit, and another on the man's right leg, a bullet hole in the meaty part of the outer thigh. Both appeared to have been inflicted some time before. Perhaps days.

Jervis returned from checking the back two rooms, small spaces with one tiny window each. They were empty of people, though they had been rummaged hard, with many beds upended and what few possessions the occupants had having been thrown about.

"All clear, Bone."

"Good. See if you can't draw some water from the well out past the little shed."

As Jervis left the house, he noted that the smell that had soured him didn't seem much in evidence inside. It was an odd affair, but he was relieved that Bone and this Rick fellow knew each other. Not pleased, though, to find that the man was unwell. He looked downright awful, to be honest.

He kept his gun raised and moved quickly but with constant alertness, looking as much as possible in all directions. Of unwanted visitors, he saw none. Not even a snake or rat.

The water well, a typical yet tidy roofed affair with an adobe and stone surround, sat where Bone had said. Jervis glanced about once, twice more, then leaned the rifle against the well and reached for the rope that hung taut, tied about a horizontal post below the little well roof. He could use a drink himself.

And then he smelled it—stronger than ever. It was the raw, pungent stink of the end of all things. It stank of doom and death and gloom and disease and rot, of fly-blown corpses greening in the sun, of bad days and worse nights. And then he shook his head. Couldn't be real. This was no good, Jervis, he told himself. You keep on like this, you are of no use to Bone.

But that smell seemed so darned real.

He worked that rope around, hearing the splash of water and feeling the bucket as it weighted and took on its intended freight. Then Bone shouted, "Jervis, hurry up with that water! Sick man in here!"

That set Jervis to moving faster, and he hauled and hauled, and never, it seemed, had he lugged up so heavy a bucket of water. Must be a big bucket, he thought as he yanked.

He knew he was wrong, even before his load jerked up into view from out of the black depths of the well.

The bucket was a large, wooden affair, and there was a doll in the bucket, headfirst and hanging from the waist down out of one side of the tipped bucket.

It was half-slopped with well water, and it was also half-filled with what appeared on closer scrutiny to not be a doll but a child.

It was a little girl, and it was dead.

For a long moment, Jervis stared at the thing. Might it not be a doll? His mind continued to wish, even as he knew it was no doll, but a child in a little light-blue dress. "Oh . . . oh no . . ."

"Jervis!" Bone sounded irate. He had every right to be, but Jervis was still frozen for a long moment, looking at the small child but seeing his own small children dead before him in the bucket.

He shook as he lifted the bucket higher.

The smell that had come and gone, come and gone, before now surrounded him, and as he hoisted the child and bucket up and over the lip of the well, a surge of nausea boiled up his gullet and he retched hard, then again and again, until he was empty.

"Oh, Lord," said a voice behind him. Jervis jerked and spun, still grasping hard the rope inches above the dead girl.

Chapter 20

"What are your thoughts about Dennerville, Fergus?" Regis eyed the man who had quickly become his second in command, and in many respects, the leader of the outfit.

The rangy cowboy nodded in his slow, considered way. "Well, I've been to this town and have fine if brief memories of my time there. But that was a few years back. If it's changed as you say, I don't need to sully my past thoughts with that. But those youngsters on the drive might feel different."

Fergus sipped his coffee and nodded toward Cyril and Benito, joshing each other in line, awaiting their revived fare of flapjacks and bacon and beans. Even with such a simple meal, Percy managed to make it tasty. It had helped that he and Regis had been able to purchase new supplies.

"Yes, I am inclined to give them all time in town, though that lawman does give me pause." Regis mused on his prickly interactions with the man.

"A thought . . ." Fergus glanced at Regis with those bushy eyebrows raised. They looked to Regis to be feathery birds perched above the man's eyes.

"What's that?" said Regis.

"Send them in in twos, threes. And for short stretches of time during the day. Be less apt to whoop it up that way."

Regis was already nodding. "Good thinking."

The first two men, Calvin Scruggs and Pierre Choteau, both were deemed quiet and level-headed enough that though they were both young were to be trusted enough for a brief foray into town.

They returned some hours later, Calvin wearing a new hat, and Pierre, still sporting his flat cap his grandfather had given him before he left New York City for the wilds of the West, was deep into a sack of boiled sweets.

They reported having a fine time, despite receiving sidelong glances from the runty lawman as they went about their business, which included ogling the few young ladies in town, from afar.

They also received scowls from the fathers of the girls, and a tongue-lashing from one frightening and large mother for their efforts. They also, sheepishly and out of earshot of Percy, admitted to tucking into a meal at the diner in town, Mabel's. By meal, they related with half-lidded, dreamy eyes, that they each had tucked into three slices of fresh homemade pie.

That was all the other men needed to hear. Though many of them had a few items they wished to procure for their kits, one man needed a needle and thread, and another hoped to find a book or two, but it was the mention of pie, even though Percy had been known to conjure such tasty desserts himself, that convinced even the toe-draggers among them to sign up for their own visits to town.

It wasn't until later in their second day that trouble poked its head up and eyed the group.

It was the last day they would be there, and Regis had agreed to linger an extra day, for the grazing these few miles east of town had been particularly good. The cattle were fattening and sluggish, the water was free-flowing and plentiful, and the weather, all puffy clouds and blue skies with no sign of foulness on any horizon.

But Regis was anxious to get going. They still had, by his calculations, three weeks to a month on the trail to reach Schiller, where Rupert Preston, the cattle buyer, would be waiting. Regis had corresponded with the man months before, and they had set a tentative price per head, depending on the condition of the beasts, of course.

But Preston had said that his schedule was to be a tight one and that he would be unable to linger for more than two days on the far end of their agreed-upon window of time.

Regis had assured him they would arrive with time to spare. It had all been cordial, and Preston had come recommended by two other members of the Cattlemen's Consortium.

But now, with the flooded river and the mad attack of those rogue thieves, time felt pinched and tight. He had to get those cattle to Schiller, and by his calendar, they didn't have but a day or two to spare, at best.

He was out, riding a slow circuit around the grazing cattle, admiring the sheen of their coats and impressed with the weight they had gained in a few short days of no travel and slow grazing. Then Fergus rode up on his gray, and not from the direction of Percy's cook fire and wagon, which is usually where Fergus could be found when he wasn't working the herd.

"Hello, Fergus." Regis greeted him with a rare grin. It was a good day, he'd sorted the mess with the town's ornery lawman, and early the next day they'd be back on the trail. If all held—weatherwise and without any more mishaps—they just might, *might*, make that meeting date with the cattle buyer. He should have known it could not last.

"Boss, just got word from a rider from town—"

"Is that what that was. I guessed it might be someone curious to see the herd."

"Well, not so much, no," said Fergus.

"Okay, what's wrong?" said Regis.

"It's Benito and Cyril, boss. Seems they got themselves in a scrape in town. The fella who rode out here was sent by the marshal. He's got the boys locked up."

"Locked up?" Regis stiffened in the saddle. "For what?"

"That's just the thing. Fella didn't know quite the full story, but it seems there was something about liquor and causing a ruckus."

"Oh, no."

"Yeah, and while I wouldn't have guessed that from Cyril, ol' Benny, well, he's always had a bit of a wild hair. At least since I've known him."

"What sort of damage did they cause, did the man say?"

Fergus shook his head. "Didn't know. But he did say the marshal's good and steamed. Said something about seeing the boys hang for it."

"Hang? What on earth . . ." Regis heeled King in the barrel, then held up. "Fergus, can you handle things here? I'll go in and see what this is all about. I think it's me that blasted lawman wants."

"Sure thing, boss. I'll tell Percy on my way back down."

"Good, thanks. I hope it won't be long." With that, Regis made straight northwest for the town of Dennerville that had fast become a burr under his blanket. He'd wished now that they had bypassed the town and kept the herd moving. All this foolishness, and for what?

By the time Regis reached the town proper, the day's light was dipping quite a bit into the west. Another hour and a half, and they'd be in early, moody darkness.

"Ah, there you are," said a voice from the shadows to his left as he rode down the main street. If he didn't recognize the voice, Regis might almost think it was an old friend waiting on him. But no. He reined up and looked to his right. There leaned Marshal Tench.

"Tench. What have you done to my men?"

"Easy now, big fella." The man was chuckling. "I ain't done a thing that they don't richly deserve. You see, rancher, those two rascals . . ."

Just then a man and a woman strolling side by side walked

just behind the lawman on the sidewalk. He eyed them with a sneer and waited for them to hurry past before he resumed. "Why don't you drag yourself on over here so I don't have to shout all about your fool men and your dirty laundry to the entire town, huh?"

With that, the lawman turned and walked into the open door behind him.

Regis slid down from the saddle and led King to a nearby trough. The horse had his fill, and then he tied King to the hitch rail before the lawman's office. A sign out front read: JAIL, TOWN OF DENNERVILLE, MARSHAL TENCH.

Regis pulled in a deep breath and tried to steady his rising temper. It would do no one any good to go in there shouting, much as he would like to. Very much, as a matter of fact.

Regis stepped forward, then paused in the doorway. "Okay, Marshal, let's have it. What's this all about? And where are my men?"

The lawman was seated behind his desk in a far corner, a rack of rifles and shotguns to one side, and to the other a table with the lawman's hat, crown down, plus various papers and books stacked neatly.

The desktop held the usual items, such as an oil lamp, a blotter, and an inkwell. Other than that, it looked unused. The man kept a tidy office. Regis saw no other people in there, not that he expected a score of deputies to emerge in a town this size.

Tench leaned back in his chair, balancing it on its two back legs. The chair offered up a few squeaks under the chunky little man's girth. He propped his boots atop the blotter and crossed them and laced his fingers behind his head. He was obviously at ease in his own environs and confident that whatever ills he was about to relate to Regis were to the smarmy lawman's advantage and slight or none to Regis.

"Pull up that chair and get yourself comfortable, Mister, ah, Royle, was it?"

"You know what my name is. Cut to the meat of the matter, Tench. I'm a busy man."

"Oh, I know. I know all about you and your cattle drive and . . . everything." He waved a pudgy hand to indicate the vast sweep of his secret knowledge.

Regis walked over and stood behind the straight-back chair before the desk.

"Okay, okay," said Tench. "So here's what happened. You sent two men here. Well, the latest two, anyway. But see, these two didn't behave themselves."

"What did they do?"

"I'm getting to that. Ain't no call to get huffy with me. You're in my office, understand?"

Regis bit down hard, his jaw muscles flexing and jumping, but he said nothing.

"Those two boys didn't do what the others did. Oh yes, I kept a hard eye on those men of yours. And I will allow as the others weren't awful. They didn't steal or break anything, to my knowledge, though I expect it's only because I didn't see them every second. But these two animals, they made straight for Hasler's Bar and ordered themselves drinks." He shook his head as if he'd never heard of such bizarre behavior.

"First off it was beers, which might have been all right, except in my experience, then a man gets himself liquored up. And then he's a danger to everything around himself. Most important are the lives of those they cross who aren't them."

Regis frowned, trying to decipher what all this meant. "Let me make amends by letting me pay for whatever damages they caused, all right?"

"Well now, see, it ain't all right. Not in the least. They are guilty men who caused a ruckus in my town." The pudgy lawman swept his legs off the desktop, and with an effort, he stood and smacked his hands on the table. "My town!" His newly reddened face shook.

"We've established that, yes. Now look, let me pay you for the damages, and I'll go and apologize to the bar owner. You can come along and watch if you like."

"Nah, that ain't going to do no good. They did the deeds, and they need to pay for them. Work them off or some such. I ain't figured out how I want to do this yet."

Regis sighed. "How about you trade me for them. I know you'd like to see me behind bars; now here's your chance."

"Trade? You mean as in you'd put yourself in the cell back there if I let them two boys get off with nothing but a whistle on their lips?"

"Yes. I'll take on their punishment. No need for them to. They're young men, not animals. And they're good boys, even if they did as you say, blow off a little too much steam."

"Well now, as tempting as your offer is, Mr. Royle, I am not so certain the judge would find that it's legal and all for me to swap one man for two, even if you are the big boss man and all."

"They work for me, and they're my responsibility. So whatever it is they've done is technically my crime, right?"

The lawman thrust out his lower jaw and sucked on his bottom lip, as if in deep consideration. "Maybe."

The man said nothing more, but continued to look toward the ceiling, still mired in thought.

Regis said, "What would it take?"

"What do you mean?"

"I mean, Marshal Tench, what would it take to make this happen?"

The lawman looked at him once more, and this time, he was smiling. "Okay, then. Fine. You will take on the blame, and I will allow them two young beasts to go free. Provided they leave my town and never come back in all their days. If they do, I will jail them so hard and fast they will be crying for their mamas."

"Fine. Now let's get on with it."

The lawman nodded, still smiling a smile that Regis did not

like the look of. But he'd struck a deal, and there was nothing for it now. He had a plan himself. He'd spend a day or so in jail and pay the fine and then he'd ride and catch up with the herd. It was not ideal, but as long as the herd was on the move, it would work out.

The marshal nodded toward him. "You'll have to take off that gunbelt there, big fancy man."

Regis complied; then the man nodded at him once more.

"Got any hideout guns on you?"

"No."

"Okay, I'll take your word for it. But you try anything and I will shoot you deader than dead, you hear me?"

Regis sighed. "I hear you, Tench. Now where are my men?"

"Back here. Right where you'll be soon." He chuckled and unlocked a door that, as Regis had suspected, led to the cells.

"Big jail for such a small town."

"It ain't small. It's the county seat." The lawman puffed up as he said this.

"Oh, my apologies. I did not realize." Regis tried to keep the smirk out of his voice.

They walked down a short corridor and there, on the left, stood two young men holding the bars to a cell, from the inside.

"Boss!" said Cyril.

"Cyril, Benny." Regis nodded toward them, not smiling.

Marshal Tench unlocked the cell door and jerked his hand at them, then pointed for them to get out.

"You paid our debt to society?" said Benito.

"Your what?" said Regis.

"It's what the marshal said we owed him. We didn't do much harm, honest, boss. Some local fella started in on Cyril, here—"

It was then that Regis saw the swollen and purpling right eye on Cyril.

"Enough!" said the marshal, clearly not comfortable with the truth of his paper-thin charges being given an airing.

Regis nodded. "Okay, boys. I've worked a deal with the marshal here." As he said this, he stepped into the cell, and the marshal clanged the door shut with more force than he needed to. He was smiling.

"Boss, you commit a crime against society, too?"

Looking at the marshal, Regis said, "Not yet, no. But the day is young."

This struck the marshal as humorous. He snorted and shook his head he stepped back a pace. "Okay, you have my word, Royle, that your two men will go free." He looked at the two young cowboys. "But if either of you dares to set foot in my town again, there will be no more kindnesses from this marshal!" He thumped his chest. "You got me?"

"Yes, sir!" they both said.

"Okay, Marshal, we all know where we stand in this situation and in your town. But I'd like a moment with the men; I have quick instructions for them."

"As long as it is quick, Royle. You got two minutes. And I'll be right here keeping an eye." He narrowed his gaze and rested a hand on his pistol.

"Cyril and Benny?"

Both red-eyed men looked at Regis with somber, serious gazes. "Yes, boss," they answered, as if schoolchildren awaiting their true punishment.

"I need you to talk with Percy and with Fergus and tell them exactly what I am about to tell you. Word for word, do you hear me?"

"Yes, boss."

Regis leaned in close to the bars, and Cyril and Benny did the same. He spoke in a low voice to both young men. They listened hard, nodding and wide-eyed.

After he'd finished telling them everything he needed Fergus and Percy to hear, Regis pulled out his little notebook and held up a finger, indicating he wanted them to hang on a moment.

He licked a fingertip and thumbed through, up and down the

long rows of figures and dates and such, including the names and ages and pay rates for the drovers. He thumbed through a number of blank pages, then hesitated, then tore out several pages filled with writing, and several more still blank, and tucked them all neatly back into his coat's inner pocket.

He retied the rawhide thong about the covers, then handed the small book to Cyril. "This is for Fergus's and Percy's eyes only. You got me?" He held onto the book until the two men nodded and swallowed and said, "Yes, boss."

"Good. They'll know what to make of it. But if anyone else sets eyes on this, I will hear of it and I will not take it lightly, nor will I deal lightly with whoever is the promise breaker. Now, do you promise me?"

"Yes, boss!"

"But . . ." It was Benny.

"Yeah, Benny?"

"You mean to tell me you're staying here and we're moving on? Taking the herd and all?"

"Yep."

They stared at him. "Without you, boss?"

Regis sighed. "Yes. We are running things way too tight now, and I can't miss that meeting with Rupert Preston."

"Okay, well, all right, boss. If that's what you want."

"It's not what I want, but it's what I have been handed. And kicking up a fuss over it won't help matters at this point."

"Yes, boss. We won't let you down," said Cyril.

"You already have. But here's a chance to make up for it. Man doesn't get many of those in life. Make it count."

"Yes, boss."

"All right, all right," said Marshal Tench. "Enough of this foolish talk. I have me a prisoner to deal with, and you two had best hotfoot on out of my town before I change my mind!"

Both men looked from the Marshal, then to Regis, for a final order.

"Go," he said, nodding.

As they departed, Regis mumbled to himself, "And good luck," realizing his dreams of saving the ranch were all but gone now, powdering to dust and blown off by a stiff breeze.

"Luck," chuckled the lawman—and he clanged the outer call door shut—"is something you don't have, Royle." He slammed the outer door, and Regis heard his outright belly laughter echo down the short corridor and into the office beyond.

In the cell, Regis looked about the shadowed stone and steel cell, then sat down and tugged out the pages he'd torn from the notebook. In the dim light, he reread them, his thoughts directed to Marietta. And one page to Cormac.

He'd not felt as rough as this, so beaten down and emotionally mashed and pulped and ground down, for years. Now it felt as if he would never escape the demons of debt and unfortunate circumstance.

But he knew he had to try.

Chapter 21

It took some time to get Rick Smithers to come around. His wounds appeared grievous at first, and though they were all that and more, Bone knew the man was a tough fellow and, with nursing, might pull through. At least he hoped so. They were far from anywhere that might be of benefit to the man, so they had to do what they could for him.

While Bone tended Rick, Jervis dealt with the poor dead child from the well.

They had set themselves up well enough with full waterskins a few days before, but without being able to use the well—Lord only knew what else the attackers had dropped down there—they would very soon be desperate for water. Bone and Jervis sipped sparingly and saved what they could for the horses, their means of transport on out of that sad place.

Jervis had insisted to Bone that he be the one to tend the dead child. Bone had looked hard into the man's eyes, knowing what he had already been through with his own dead children, but Bone was wary lest Jervis slip into some sort of reverie for the past, a past dead and buried, from which he might not come back as sound as he appeared to Bone to be.

But Jervis seemed to know the cause of the elder ranger's concern. "I'm okay, Bone. I promise you that. But I'll be better when we can tend to things here and then get gone. We need to find who did this."

"And we will try, but we have to get Rick to some place he can heal up."

Jervis nodded. "His body, anyway."

"Yeah," said Bone, looking at the resting man. Bone had tended Rick's head wound. It appeared he'd been clubbed, and the wound in his thigh was a bullet wound.

Jervis found a steel bar and a spade in the shed. Then he scouted the place, and found a slight rise east of the corral that looked to have promise as a burial ground. He walked to it, but it was a rocky knob unsuited to anything of the sort. He looked back to the little house and wondered what life had been like there for the man's family. For Bone had told him that there had been a wife and several children.

Then his gaze once more found the edging of rocks about the house, the spaces where no doubt the woman would have done her best to pretty up the place, a valiant effort in this unforgiving, brutal, and hot place.

It was something his own wife had done, attempted to pretty up the scene. "Bless the poor women of the world," he said, wiping the sweat from his brow. "For they are saddled with men."

But at least he had found a place to bury the child. He walked back to the house and selected a spot that looked pretty enough, off the southeast corner, framed by two valiant cactuses. It didn't take long to work a hole deep and wide enough to accommodate the child.

In the shade of the shed, he laid her out, and washed her face and hands and feet with a wet rag. Then he'd wrapped her in pretty things he found in the house. All the while he whispered soft, encouraging words that he knew well enough did more to soothe himself and tamp down the tight knot in his throat than they did to help the dead child.

Then he told Bone he was going to bury her. Bone nodded and left the side of the still-unconscious Rick and joined him.

They laid the girl in there and, as Jervis didn't seem to know what to say, and as Bone could not recall words from the Bible, the elder ranger said, "Lord above, please see fit to give this child a place under your hand. She did not deserve her earthly fate, but certainly deserves your kindness now."

Bone paused, waiting in case Jervis wished to speak. The man stayed silent, so Bone said, "Amen."

Then Jervis said, "Amen. And Lord, please help us to find those who did this to her and hers. Amen."

The men exchanged glances; then Bone said, "I should tend to Rick. You okay here, or shall we trade duties?"

"No, I will finish burying her."

It was an hour later when Rick Smithers came around. By then, Bone had tidied the little house as best he could. Jervis had scouted the surrounding land on horseback, looking for sign. He'd found tracks leading to the southwest, as Bone had guessed he might. But the tracks were, from what Jervis could tell, with his limited tracking abilities, a couple of days old.

Given that they were going to run out of water before they ran out of life, Bone and Jervis were hoping Rick would be able to sit a horse well enough that they could get him to the nearest town. Then they would dog the killers.

And it was a plan that seemed solid, save for the fact that Rick had no intention of leaving his spread.

"No." He shook his head slowly as if it pained him to think, let alone speak and move. "No, I . . . can't go . . ."

"Well, don't trouble yourself about it just now, Rick. We have time. Best you rest up."

Bone had no sooner said this than Rick's eyes winked shut and his head slipped to one side. Bone checked his breathing and nodded Jervis toward the door.

Once outside, he said, "One of us will have to stay behind with him while the other rides on for help. Since I know the terrain hereabouts, I'll ride on."

He tugged out the map, unfolded it, and pointed a big finger. "Here's where we are. And there's where I'll make for." He pointed to what looked to Jervis to be a jut of land on a river. "That dot there is Diablo Wells. I'll make for that and send someone back. I can't imagine you'll have trouble while I'm gone, but you'll have all the water I can spare and plenty of food and ammunition. And two horses. Keep them close, inside with you if you have to."

"How long?"

Bone tubbed his whiskered chin and gazed at the long horizon southward. "I'd say two days there, two back. Might be longer, won't be any shorter. Unless I sprout wings." He offered a weak smile, but Jervis only nodded.

"When will you leave?"

"It won't gain me much to leave now. It'll be dark in an hour or so. I'll leave before light. Who knows? Maybe he'll come around by then. I'd prefer if we all rode out together. But with a knock to the head, it's tough to tell what condition a man's in."

Jervis cooked up a meal outdoors and, while the two men ate seated by the small campfire, they said little. There was, they realized, not much else to say. It must have been the smells of the food that roused Rick once more. "Delia! Delia, I'm sorry! You should know that—I never thought it would end like this!"

Bone went in and soothed him, gave him a drink, and in a few minutes, he returned and resumed eating by the small fire. "He's not right in his head," said Bone. "Can't blame him. I . . . I can't think about it."

"You are smart not to. It's not a feeling I'd wish on anyone, except on those who did it." Jervis set his bowl to the side and stretched his shoulders.

A tremendous crack and crash from inside the little adobe

home sent both men diving for the earth. By the time he'd rolled and came up on one knee, Bone had his pistol palmed and cocked.

Jervis did the same. They flanked the door and saw smoke wisping out of the open doorway. "Rick!"

Bone peered in, squinting, and said, "Oh, no." He holstered the gun and entered the cabin, emitting a couple of low coughs as he went.

Jervis stayed outside and waited.

Soon enough, he walked back outside.

"Done for himself?" said Jervis.

Bone nodded. "Had a pistol we didn't find." He sighed. "It'll be dark soon. Fetch that shovel, and we'll take turns digging a hole for him. Maybe alongside his girl."

They managed to work in a decent grave for the man and prepped him and laid him out, with the help of lantern light.

"We tend to him now, we can hit the trail south at first light."

Jervis nodded. "I won't be bothered to leave this sad place behind, I don't mind admitting."

"Same here. I feel awful about it all, but the only thing we can do for him now is find his kin, if they're still alive."

"And their killers."

"Yep."

A half hour later found them tamping the earth on the man's grave, and covering it over with stones. They did the same for the girl's grave, and Bone spoke over Rick's grave, similar words as he had earlier. Jervis did the same.

Bone spent the next couple of hours working on a plank with his honed Barlow. On it, he carved: "Rick Smithers, father, and a little girl, his daughter." He carved that day's date and said, "I don't even know the girl's name."

"The Lord does; that's good enough."

"Yes," said Bone, still bothered. "And if we do manage to find his wife and other children alive, maybe taken as prisoners to be sold on the slave market, they might want to come back here. They'll know."

He wedged the base into the earth, with the top leaning against the house, setting rocks around the plank. "It'll have to do for now. We best get some sleep."

"I'll take first watch," said Jervis, who Bone knew had become increasingly silent all day. He could hardly blame him. It had been one grim day, and it wasn't over yet.

Bone slept longer than he anticipated. But it was still full dark when he jerked awake. Jervis sat by the low fire, gazing out into the night.

Coyotes yipped and snarked, it seemed from every direction.

"I've always liked the sound of those odd desert dogs. You?" said Bone, stretching his back.

Jervis nodded slowly. "Lot to be said for the critters who keep on the move, stopping long enough to let everyone know who they are. Fearless, I reckon."

Bone half-smiled. "I never heard of coyotes called fearless, but it makes as much sense as anything I could think of. Anyhow"—he yawned and rubbed his face—"they're comforting to listen to somehow."

Again, Jervis nodded, but didn't respond with words.

Finally Bone said, "You should try to grab some sleep while you can. We need to be fresh tomorrow. Got a lot of ground to cover."

"I hear you. I'm not tired, but I hear you." He stretched out on his blanket and sighed quietly.

Soon enough, Bone heard the man's breathing level off and deepen. He smiled and nodded. He'd lucked into a decent find with Jervis Latham. Now if they could keep that luck rolling and find Rick Smithers's poor family members, alive, before anything more awful happened to them.

Bone crossed his legs and laid his rifle across his lap and listened to the yip-yip-yipping of the coyotes all around them in the cold, dark night.

Chapter 22

"I didn't realize the ranch was so much work," Cormac grinned as he rolled down his sleeves and buttoned his cuffs. He glanced sideways at Marietta to see if she would respond. She had smiled, something a couple of weeks before he would not have seen, as at that point she still wore her veil.

In sunlight, he had been able to see vaguely that she was scarred along one side of her face. But she was an exceptionally pretty woman despite that. And, he wondered, perhaps because of it, too, somehow.

He had realized with a start that he'd admired her shape from a distance; then he had blushed, hoping she hadn't seen him looking. But once you chipped through the stiff, distant way in which she conducted herself, he found her to be a lot of fun. He could see why Regis had been attracted to her.

She was like Regis in a number of ways—forthright, intelligent, decisive, unafraid to speak her piece, and, well, tall. But unlike Regis, she possessed that rare ability to keep her head, to not judge a person with such fiery immediacy as did Regis.

That, oddly enough, was one of the things that Cormac found endearing about his younger partner. But it was also something that he knew caused Regis a passel of headaches—and by relation, Cormac, too.

Yes, if Regis didn't ruin his chances with this woman, she would be of enormous benefit to him in life. And he to her, because Regis, for all his confounding, frustrating ways, was one heck of a good man. Cormac had long suspected that what Regis needed most in life was to season, to mellow a bit. Not too much, for a man needed to retain a keen edge in life, but enough that he knew when to land a solid blow and when to pull back.

"What is it you are really saying, Mr. Delany?"

Cormac had been busy dousing his face with water from the basin, and he looked up at the sudden intrusion into his thoughts. "Pardon?"

She smiled, half-turned to him as was her custom; her veil, he noted, had not merely been pulled to one side, but had been removed fully. This was a new development. For she and he were due to ride out to see the villagers once more to continue helping them with repairs to their fences and garden after the vicious raid by those border bandits.

He dried his face. "Oh, ah, yes, well. I suppose what I meant was that Regis had not let on, at least in conversations with me, just how much work this ranch was. Day to day, I mean. I guess that running the shipping company largely from a desk these past few years has made me soft."

"I don't think so. You have shown remarkable fortitude these past few days. I will be honest, I am uncertain if I can continue at it myself. But I cannot bear to see these people, my people, suffer so because of hateful thieves."

He nodded. "I know what you mean. Some of them are older than me, and they can work twice as hard and twice as long as I can."

"They don't look at it that way, I assure you. They are only too pleased to see that you are like Regis."

"Really. Hmm." He folded the towel and smoothed his mustaches. "I'm his partner in business, and I frequently find myself doubting his choices."

"Ah, yes, but perhaps I have seen him in ways that you have not. Somehow, he is of this place, you see. As if he were born here. But perhaps it is more than that. Perhaps his bond is so strong with this land because he chose it instead of being born into it. It is this I see. And more."

He mused on this while they walked to the stable. "You're certain?" he said.

She surprised him by continuing to speak. She had rarely spoken this much at one time in their weeks working together here at the ranch. She shrugged. "Only certainty born out of love is the truest form of certainty."

He stopped and looked at her. "It is like that, then? Love, I mean?"

"Yes, I am afraid so." She offered a slight smile, her hands held before her as if she were carrying some precious thing of great value.

"Afraid so? Oh, that sounds ominous."

"Perhaps it might well be." Her smile faded. "For in love, there is great risk, too."

"Risk?"

"Yes. Everyone here understands the great risk that Regis may not return from the cattle drive."

"That had occurred to me, as well. But for now, we have no choice but to carry on. If only for the sake of these fine people."

Again, she nodded agreement but grew silent once more.

As they rode toward the village, passing two toiling cowboys working to repair a trampled berm of a new irrigation ditch, she said, "Cormac, there is someone in the village I would like you to meet."

"Oh? Who is he? He need a hand? I'm good on the water, but a learner with these landlubber ways. But I'm game to try." He smiled.

"That's good," said Marietta, riding ahead of him as they approached the first cluster of modest adobe homes. "She will be pleased to hear that."

"She?"

But Marietta Valdez did not turn and wait for him. She was, however, smiling.

Chapter 23

"He said what?" Percy rubbed his head with his hat. "Yes, sir. He said to get the herd out of here as quickly as we were able to and to keep heading north. And that he'd be along in a day or two. And he said to give you and Fergus this." Cyril handed Percy the boss's notebook. "He said you and he would know what to do with it."

Percy's eyes widened. Regis never went anywhere but he had this thing open and was licking his pencil tip and tallying and whatnot. "Well, did the boss say what I should do with it?"

"He said if anything were to happen to him, and he didn't show, that you would need that to sell the herd and take care of things. And we never looked at it! We made him a promise. We swear it, isn't that correct, Benito?"

"You bet. But the boss, he was some certain about two things."

"And they would be?" said Percy, not waiting for the two young cowboys to continue.

"That we were not to wait around for him. And also under no circumstances." Benny looked skyward as he spoke, as if doing so would help him recall everything Regis had told him to relate to Percy and Fergus.

"That neither you nor Fergus was to send anybody else into town."

Cyril nodded. "You are not to try to retrieve him, nor to do anything else in that regard."

Percy was steamed. This was a fix, all right. Put them all in a terrible bind. Even though he was secretly pleased that the boss thought enough of him to make sure all this was in his and Fergus's laps.

Percy wasn't fool enough to think the boss needed him as much as he needed Fergus. But it did put a lift in his stride. Now there was far too much to do. He knew they were leaving the next morning anyway, but this put things in a different light, somehow.

"All right then, you two fools best go find Fergus and tell him everything you told me. And don't tell another soul until you tell him. I'll get busy here, finish up a few things; then I have to talk with him. Tell him if he's over this way, he should swing wide and see me. Easier that way."

The two men stood there awaiting more from the surly cook. But he stood there looking back at them, his hands on his hips. "What? You waiting for me to tell you it's okay? No way, no how. Now git!"

The two men mounted up and took off for the west edge of the herd, where Fergus was keeping watch.

When Cyril and Benito found Fergus, he nodded and squinted as he usually did whenever he got news, good or bad. Nothing ever seemed to rile the man. Cyril and Benny both admired the heck out of him and had talked that one day they'd like to be like him. He was a true cowboy and conducted himself in a true way.

They lingered there while he mulled over what they told him. Then he looked at them in that squint from beneath his hat brim.

"Um," Benny said. "I don't suppose you ever did such a thing before."

"Oh? What would that be, son?" Fergus kept looking at them,

so Benny responded, while looking at his saddle horn. He was feeling mighty laden with guilt over what they did.

"Fighting in town. It was a fool thing, even though I have to say I don't think we really did all that much wrong, Fergus. I know how that sounds, but it's true. Sure, we had a few beers. You know how that is—one tastes so good, you think well, maybe one more, then why not have another. Then before we knew it, that fella come on over and prodded us, saying things about the herd and our friends, and even our mamas."

"No man would have stood for it!" said the normally quiet Cyril.

Fergus nodded. "Go on."

Benny nodded and resumed. "Well, he wouldn't let up. Finally, he shoved Cyril here."

The young Englishman nodded. "Yes, it's true, he did."

"And just like that, the marshal was there, like he was just waiting for something to happen."

"Uh-huh. Well, I suspect he was."

"What do you mean?"

"No coincidence that you were prodded, boys. That fella was likely working on behalf of the lawdog. Now, put it out of your minds. We have work to do. You two keep this west edge from straying. I'm going to see Percy."

"Okay, Fergus. And thanks."

Fergus gave them a finger salute off his hat brim and rode off.

"Man alive, he is a good chap," said Cyril.

"You bet he is," said Benito. "Wish he'd a-been my pappy instead of that no-count old drunkard I got saddled with."

"That's no way to talk of the departed," said Cyril.

"Who said my pappy's dead?"

Percy and Fergus conferred and decided to heed Regis's advice. They were tight for time as it was, and the boss didn't seem to be in any real harm. He and the marshal had been at odds since the start—Percy saw that up close and personal that first day in town—but for all that, he didn't think there was much danger of him not getting out. And the boys hadn't been in any real trouble, just brawling in a bar.

And from what Fergus told Percy, it sounded as if they were set up, anyway.

"Here," said Percy, handing Fergus the boss's notebook. "Full of numbers pertaining to cows. I have enough to worry about. You can read, can't you?"

Fergus looked at the cook with wide eyes. He thumbed back his hat, and Percy got a worried look on his face and took a step backward.

"Percy, if I didn't know you already, I might be insulted. But yes." Fergus smiled. "As a matter of fact, I can read, write, and work up figures. I'll tell you all about my days riding a desk back east in my days before I took to riding horses out west."

"What?" said Percy.

Fergus ignored him and mounted up. "Morning's going to come quick," he said, hefting the little book. "I'll tell the other men to make certain we all know what's what come morning."

"All right, all right. I'll make breakfast ahead of time. Got batches of biscuits and bread going so we can make time and eat like civilized folks. At least for a few days. Although the way these savages eat, I have no idea how long that'll last."

Percy kept mumbling and slamming his pots and pans while Fergus rode off, shaking his head and smiling and thumbing through the notebook.

Chapter 24

Regis was well into the second day of his jail stay, trading his freedom for captivity, his freedom for that of his two young and dumb . . . no, that's not right, he thought. Cyril and Benito weren't dumb, they were just green about life, about most everything.

But on that second day of his captivity, Regis heard voices in the outer office rising and falling, then rising, this time in anger, mutual anger, it turned out. None of this surprised Regis to hear, because Marshal Tench was a little, hotheaded man.

But what he heard set his teeth on edge and confirmed his suspicions. It also told him that it was unlikely that Tench was going to let him loose anytime soon, even if there was a circuit judge due in town in a week.

"Marshal, you gave me your word that if I did that for you, you'd hire me on as a deputy! I need the work. Heck, I told you that already. But now you're going back on your word!"

"Now see here, Simons," said the marshal, still trying to keep his temper even.

But it sounded to Regis as if the man was going to blow at any moment. Go ahead, thought Regis, grating his teeth and enjoying what he was hearing, even while it annoyed him.

"No, I won't keep it down, Marshal!"

Then Regis heard a door slam, but instead of quieting, indicating somebody had stormed out of the marshal's office, the argument picked up steam. Regis guessed that outer door had been open, and the marshal had likely hustled over to close it lest a passerby hear something he didn't want them to hear.

"Now you see here, Simons. I never said I would hire you or I wouldn't. I told you, if you had sense enough to remember rightly, that I would look on it with gratitude should you happen to prod those two young idiots from that cattle drive into a fight. I even paid for your beer, if you recall. And I didn't have to do that, did I?"

"But it ain't a free glass of beer I need, Marshal. It's a job. And you said there was a position open as a deputy and to come around and see you in a couple of days. Well, here I am!"

Regis heard the lawman sigh too loudly, as if he were on stage.

"I never said there was an open job for a deputy, Simons. I said there might be. At some point. Right now ain't some point. You understand?"

"I understand I am being lied to. That's what I understand."

The talk went on for a few moments longer, with lowered voices, but Regis heard all he needed to. The marshal had instigated the arrest of his two men. They'd wanted to tell him that, and he should have known. They were decent young men, and if he hadn't been so steamed up about the marshal and the herd, he might have seen that sooner.

Then voices from the front office rose once more, and Regis heard the lawman bellow, "You dare threaten me? Get out now before I shoot you in the head!"

Bootsteps sounded as a man crossed the office. Then the door opened and slammed loud and hard.

From the now-silent office, Regis heard the lawman sputtering. He hoped the man would poke his head on down the corridor to the cell. He'd like to give him a good . . . and then the stupidity of what he was thinking occurred to him. That would be just what the marshal wanted him to do.

If he was indeed here because the lawman wanted to deal him a blow, just because Tench was a spiteful little man, then Regis had played right into his hands. By giving himself up, he'd acted in haste, just to solve the problem quickly. Anything to get the herd moving. Even if it meant he'd be stuck in a jail cell.

He was foolish, and he felt his face heating up. How to turn this predicament on its head? He sorely needed to get out of here, he thought. But how?

And then he heard the keys in the outer door to the little passageway that led to the cells.

With no further thought, Regis stretched out on the narrow plank cot and pretended he was asleep. If the marshal knew he'd overheard that conversation, he might be even more ticked. And then he'd eye Regis with plenty of scrutiny, and that was not what he wanted.

He wanted the cursed little lawman to believe he was unaware, so Tench would slip up. Just how that might happen, Regis had no idea.

Since he'd been locked up, Regis had only seen two possible times during the daily routine when the lawman might be overpowered. One was when the reeking slops bucket was retrieved once a day. The other was when he was brought a small tray with food twice a day.

He'd not attempted any sort of jailbreak, because he was, after all, a man of his word, and he'd promised the marshal he'd stick with this foolish charge until the judge showed up in Dennerville. But now he even doubted the imminent arrival of any judge. At least he didn't think one was due to show up in Dennerville any time soon.

And now? Now Regis saw the situation for what it was—the runty lawman had lied to him. And as that was the case, most definitely, then he felt no more reason to stick to his end of the agreement.

The marshal was still muttering as he walked down the short, dim hallway toward the cell.

"Huh," said the lawman, coming to a stop before Regis's cell.

The big man didn't move, but kept his eyes closed and kept his breathing low and even, as if he were in a deep doze.

"Useless," mumbled the marshal.

He stood before the cell, and Regis guessed he was looking down at him pretending to snooze.

The duration of it took all the patience Regis could offer, because he was downright ready to jump up, reach through the bars, and snatch the man by the throat.

But Tench was nothing if not cautious. "Hey! Royle!" He kicked the flat-steel bars, and the entire cage clanged and rattled.

Regis sat up and shook his head, eyes wide as if he'd been sleeping off a weeklong drunk. "Wha! What's the matter!"

"You sleeping, Royle?"

Regis dragged a hand down his face and rubbed his eyes. He even worked up a fake yawn. "Not now I'm not. What do you want, Marshal Tench?"

"Just checking on you, that's all."

"Marshal . . . any chance I could get fed?"

"Food? You want food?"

"Yes." Regis nodded and stood. "That breakfast you gave me wore off hours ago. I expect it's time for supper, soon, isn't it?"

"Yeah, yeah, I reckon." Tench tugged out his pocket watch and clicked open the cover. "You have another half hour."

"Any chance we could make it an early meal tonight?"

Tench sighed. "I expect so. I am peckish myself. Been dealing with ingrates and fools all day long, and it has left me hungry. I'll go over to the diner and order up grub."

Regis had to admit to himself that though the lawman was a repugnant little fool, he was pathetic enough to elicit a smidgin of sympathy from him. He thought this because he knew the man was lonely.

As annoying as he was, there was no way the man could be

married. And as for friends, Regis doubted a man alive could stand that fool's company for longer than a couple of minutes.

But each night, when he returned from the diner with the prisoner's meal, Tench also lugged, stacked beneath, a second tray. And that was for himself. He would give Regis his food, and then he'd sit down in a creaky wooden chair outside the cell and he'd eat his own meal. The first time he'd done that, Regis had not known what to think.

Did he not trust that Regis would just eat and not try to make a weapon of the spoon they'd given him on the tray? But then he realized, as Tench began chatting as if they were old chums, that the lawman was just plain lonely. Lonely enough to share a meal with his prisoner, a man he'd gone out of his way to insult and jail.

It had been a little unnerving to Regis, but in its own way, it was endearing. Just a little. Not nearly enough to make him reconsider his plans. No way.

Marshal Tench turned and walked a few paces up the short hallway. "Don't go anywhere, you hear?" He laughed at the same joke he made every time he left the cells.

It hadn't been funny the first time Regis heard it, and it still wasn't. But at least he bit at the first part of Regis's paltry plan. Now he just needed for the rest of the night to fall and darkness to make its way into Dennerville. Then he could, with any luck at all, put the rest of the plan into action.

All he had to do was wait. Wait and do one little thing in the cell.

But waiting was something Regis Royle wasn't any good at all at. For some reason, that brought his brother, Shep, to mind. That kid was another impatient one. "I guess we're more alike than I ever wanted to admit, eh, Shep?" he said in a low voice to the otherwise empty room.

He mulled over the repercussions should what he was about to do go wrong. He would miss out on possibly spending the rest of his life, however long that might be, with Marietta, a wonderful and surprising woman, and someone he still didn't know as well as he'd like to. But he reckoned he had a lifetime to do that.

And then there was Cormac Delany, his partner and oldest friend. He'd be leaving him with a millstone of debt hanging about his neck.

And there was Bone, another longtime friend he'd just gotten to know again, after using him too hard and not appreciating the man. Proof of that was the fact that Bone had married the woman, Margaret, and Regis hadn't even known about it.

And then there was Shepley, a longtime source of headaches for Regis. But a pleasure to know him, too, and to see the sort of young man he was growing into—and he'd make it, too, if he could manage to keep himself from getting killed. Maybe the Army would tighten him up.

And then there were all the folks who worked for him, the ranch hands and cowboys and villagers—they all depended on him. And if he wasn't around, where would that leave them all?

"No," he said. "I cannot let any of that happen. And so I won't."

Instead of backing away from his plan, it made him all the more resolute in his faith in it. More to the point, it made him promise himself he would not, could not fail.

Time after time in his life, Regis Royle had made such secret promises to himself, and then, with the idea in mind that success was the only option available to him, he bulled on through whatever the massive task might be he'd placed before himself, and he'd come out the other end as the victor.

Now was one such time.

He made his way over to the bucket in the far front right corner of the cell and fiddled with the steel handle on the slops bucket. What he had in mind took all his strength, as the bucket and its bail were of thick steel, but it worked. Because he wanted it to. He needed it to.

Then he walked back the two paces to the hard bunk and settled back against the cold stone outer wall and waited for night to fall and for the marshal to return with his feeble evening meal. He hoped the former happened before the latter. And it did.

For the fourth time in as many minutes, Regis held up his big hand before his face to test if he might be able to see it clearly. Each time he tried, he fancied it grew fainter. Good. And then he heard keys rattle in the outer door. That would be the marshal.

Regis stood, diagonally across from the front corner of the cell, where he knew the lawman would make him stand anyway.

Tench would enter the hallway, hang the low-lit lantern on a steel hook outside the cell. Then he would unlock the cell with one hand, and with his pistol aimed at Regis, he'd swing open the door, snatch up the bail on the slops bucket, lift it, and haul it backward on out of the cell. Then he'd set it down outside the cell and replace it with an empty bucket.

He did the same thing just before he gave Regis his food tray each night. Why the man didn't empty the thing during the ample daylight hours, Regis could not guess. But this time it would be useful to Regis.

For in addition to needing time to wait for night to fall and for Tench to return from the diner, Regis had to run through his mind all the things that he needed to do after he was free. There were plenty of them, but getting out of jail was by far the trickiest.

And then there was the lantern glow, the hallway door creaked open, and Marshal Tench said, "Hope you're hungry, Royle, 'cause Mabel, she outdid herself tonight. I could smell the beefsteak all the way back here, and believe me, I wanted to tuck into both our shares right there in the street! And pie, too. I bet you ain't never tasted berry pie like this."

"Try me," said Regis, trying to sound cordial. It wasn't easy, pie or no.

The marshal bent to slide Regis's tray through the low opening in the bars down by the floor.

"Aren't you going to pull the slops bucket out first?"

"What?" said the lawman. "But the food's hot and ready to eat!"

"Oh, I know," said Regis, trying to sound a little disappointed. And he was, but not for the same reason. "It's just that . . . well, it'd be a whole lot more pleasant to eat without that thing in here. For both of us, I mean."

Marshal sighed and nodded. "Yeah, you're right. Give me a second. I got to set down this stuff and fetch the empty bucket."

He did so and returned, moving quicker than he usually did. He also hadn't drawn his pistol.

"Hey," he said, pausing as he unlocked the door. "I trust you to stand back there, right? In your corner so I can swap out this bucket? Faster I do it, the quicker we can both get to eating."

"Okay, okay," said Regis. "I'll stay back here, no worries. I'm hungry, too, you remember."

That comment brought a chuckle up from the lawman. He swung the door open wide enough to sidle through, glancing once at Regis. Then he reached for the handle on the half-full slops bucket, and lifted. It came up; then the bail let go on one side. The contents of the bucket splashed out, right on the lawman's waist and down his legs.

As he recoiled and shouted words of disgust, Regis moved in, quick and sure and with no wasted efforts, and drove a big ham hand into the marshal's near temple.

The blow was enough in itself to knock the man cold. But his head whipped to the side and clanged against the bars.

As soon as the lawman slammed to the bars and then slumped down to his knees, the bucket landing, surprisingly, upright before him, Regis bent low over the man, probing his fleshy neck for a heartbeat. He felt one, strong and solid, and for that, he was relieved.

"Thought for a moment there, Tench, that I'd hit you too hard."

He filched the man's keys, then thought again and slipped off his gunbelt, too. He dragged the marshal by the shoulders of his frock coat into the cell and leaned him against the stone back wall. Then he locked the cell door and picked up the lantern. With the marshal's laden supper tray, he walked to the front office.

With the short corridor door closed behind him, he set down the lantern and the tray atop the man's desk, then greedily gnawed through the food while he rummaged. He found his own gunbelt and rifle, and few possessions he'd brought with him, which the marshal had had brought over from the stable.

Everything save for his saddle, tack, and horse. With any luck, he'd find King, his trusty mount and boon trail companion, at the stable, waiting for him, and then he'd be long gone, hopefully before anyone discovered so. It was a thin plan, he knew, but it was all he had.

With the food gone, his pockets filled with bullets taken from the lawman's stock of them in his desk drawer—he considered them payment for the mistreatment and lies—he wiped his fingers and face with the checkered napkin on the tray. Then he tended to the last bit of his plan within the office.

Standing at the desk, he flipped a sheet of paper over, exposing a blank side, dipped the ink pen in the well, and wrote, in large enough lettering to catch the attention of whoever from the town might come in to see what the lawman's shouts would be about. And Regis did not doubt that the man was going to kick up a fuss.

But the note might quell any future action on Tench's part in tracking down Regis and branding him as a fugitive. He didn't really care, anyway. All he wanted to do was ride on out of Dennerville, never return, and instead find his herd. Then sell up and ride back to Texas, skirting this sad little burg, and resume his life.

"Just try to peel me out of Texas, you smug little man," said Regis as he wrote. When he was through, he laid it square in the

middle of the otherwise whisker-clean desktop. He read it
through once, smiling, as he said the words out loud in a low
voice:

"Marshal Tench: I know what you did. I have proof and two
witnesses who will gladly talk. Let it be, or the town will find out
all about it. Let it be. —RR"

Not poetry, he thought, shouldering his gear. But it would
have to do. He cracked the door and peered out into the quiet
night main street of Dennerville. Not a soul in sight, and very
few lights in the few businesses that were open—two bars and
the café. That made him think he'd need food before long, but
he'd have to make meat on the trail. No way was he going to
stick around this town any longer than he needed to.

Regis slipped out the door and made for the stable, six or eight
buildings down the same side of the street. Nearly the last place
on the lane, and it opened at the back into wide country. He
hoped his horse wasn't out to pasture for the night.

The stable was where he seemed to recall, and one of the big
double doors was not barred from the inside. He let himself in
and looked about the space. It was large and dark, though not
quite black. He let his eyes adjust and began checking the stalls
that lined the two side walls.

They were largely uninhabited and all clean. He'd all but
given up on finding King in the barn when he saw a familiar fore-
lock wagging at him in the near-dark.

"King?" he whispered.

The horse worked his big head up and down like a pump handle. It took longer than he would have liked to locate his saddle,
and he still hadn't laid a hand on his bridle, when a quick scuffing, as if boots on gravel, sounded behind him. Even before he
turned, he heard the throaty metallic clicks of a hammer being
jerked back into the deadly position.

"Hold there, mister."

The voice was low, cold, and even. Regis complied, his hands
half-raised.

"All the way up, big man. Now, turn yourself around and face me."

Regis did, and in the dim glow of early moonlight shafting in through the open back doors, Regis saw that the man who'd gotten the drop on him was half his height and stoop-shouldered. But his grip on that shotgun was steady.

"Planning on stealing a horse, I see."

"I can't steal what's mine."

"You the marshal's prisoner?" The man lowered the gun. "Why didn't you say so?"

"Um, can I put my arms down, then?"

"Course. So long as you don't try to come at me. I'm quicker than I look."

"I don't doubt that, sir."

The man snorted. "Ain't no 'sir' here. I'm Clement. Own this place. Run a good stable, too."

"Yes, you do. And I appreciate you looking after my horse. I need my tack, and I'll be out of your way. But I need to know how much I owe you."

"Hmm," said Clement. "Been what, three days?"

Regis handed him two gold coins. "Will these cover it?" he said, looking for his gear.

"More than. Too much, in fact."

"It's okay. I'm in a hurry."

"I bet you are. Leave that marshal in a sad state, did you?"

"What makes you say that?"

"Because Tench is a lot of things, most of them earned, too, but careless he usually ain't. Don't matter. I'm just glad to see you got on out of there."

"You are?"

"Yeah." The man shoved Regis out of the way and grabbed up the rest of the big man's tack. "Me and the whole town. You getting took by that rascal just because he don't like you. Whole town knows it. He set the whole thing up!"

"I learned that, yes."

"Problem with you is you're too nice. Got to play mean with Marshal Tench. Only game he knows."

"I hope he outgrows it."

That struck Clement as funny, and he grinned and nodded.

"Okay, then. I know you got to git gone, but which way you headed?"

Regis said nothing but offered a half grin.

"All right, all right, I get you. A man's business is a man's business. Only reason I ask is there ain't much in most any direction from here for a whole long time. I ain't got much, but here now." The man stuffed items into a small gunny sack.

"You don't have to do that," said Regis.

"Course I don't. But I am just the same now, ain't I? Here's a small pan, beat to heck, but it'll serve you. And I put in some coffee beans, a few lint-covered sweets, and some of Mother's hard tack—she thinks I like it, but I dole it out to the horses. Too hard on my teeth. But you're young and tough, you can take it. Just don't tell Mother."

"You have my word," said Regis, itching to mount up. The man sensed it and thrust the sack into his hands. "And here"—he tugged out a small bottle, more than half full, of whiskey. "I use it for my rheumatics, but you might need it out there, wherever it is you're headed."

He had also tied a second sack, bulging with corn and oats, for King. "Take care of your horse and you're halfway there. And here." He handed up a horse blanket. "Going to get cold in the nights, and you're not equipped. Oh, last thing." The man scurried off into the dark and returned in moments with a waterskin. "Fill this when you can. Plenty of creeks and rivers in most any direction."

Regis mounted up. "Clement, I don't know how to thank you."

"Thank me? Bah. You done that already. Might be the leverage we need to get ourselves rid of that fool marshal. Got the town cowed, and nobody's quite sure why or how it happened. We was sleeping, I think, and when we woke, there he was. Crazy."

"Time for a change," said Regis, adjusting the reins.

"You bet it is. And none too soon."

Regis touched his hat brim and rode out through the door that the old man held open for him.

"And don't worry," said Clement. "I ain't seen nothing or nobody. Been home sleeping deep. Besides, Mother snores something fierce."

Regis smiled and nodded. "Thanks again, Clement. I won't forget it."

Regis held King to a walk as they made for the west end of the main street. If he'd given any thought to getting caught before he got out of town, he could not have expected it to go as it did.

He swiveled his head all about him as he neared the end of the street. Nobody about. "Time to go, King."

He heeled the big horse, who seemed as eager as he was to put Dennerville behind him. With any luck, thought Regis as they thundered on out of there and made northward, they'd catch up with the herd in a few days. As long as nothing happened between here and there.

Chapter 25

The bullet whistled past Bone's right ear, so close he thought it had been an errant fly doing its best to annoy him. Only a heartbeat later did he hear the percussive, far-off snap of the fired gun.

The reflexive action of long experience kicked in, and he jerked low, sliding from the saddle. His rifle, which had laid across his knees these past many miles since before daybreak, whipped up with practiced ease, snugging to his shoulder and aiming southward, the direction from which the shot had come.

At the same time, he barked a quick oath to Jervis, who had followed his lead and had jumped down out of the saddle.

"Well," said Jervis, sighting down his rifle's barrel. "I guess they know we're back here."

"You think so?" Bone squinted into the distance.

"Let's make for that rocky knob to your left," said Jervis.

There was a sizable upthrust of gray and red rock eastward, perhaps an eighth of a mile away. It might as well be a hundred miles, he thought, squinting south. Where could those devils be? It looked flat and sandy with nary a slope between them and whoever had lobbed that bullet their way.

As they hotfooted their mounts to the rocks, Jervis said, "Don't suppose it was a stray shot from a hunter . . ."

Bone's response told him otherwise. The senior ranger snorted.

"When you're a ranger, you don't assume anything of the sort. Well, you are more than welcome to, of course, but then I'd be working alone again."

"I hear you," said Jervis. "Just trying to sound positive."

"Keep it up, you might be right one of these days. You'll pardon me if I don't hold my breath, though."

No other shots reached them, or were heard in the distance, which suited them both just fine. Once they'd reached the rocky island, they secured the horses on the northern side.

"Might as well make that coffee we never made before light. If you tend to that, I'll climb up and scout. Got my telescope, so maybe I'll be able to catch sight of them before they see the sun reflect off the brass of this thing."

He held up the scope and waggled it; then, keeping low, he switchbacked up the near side of the rocks, using what looked to be some sort of game trail. He supposed even the desert's night visitors had that innate urge that seemed to be deep in all critters to see far.

Once he got up there close to the top, Bone drew down lower and made the last couple of yards on his knees, taking care not to raise too much dust, lest he give away their location. Not that them hustling on over here from being out in the open could be mistaken as anything other than a run for cover.

He found a decent hollow on his side of the topmost boulder and hunkered in, peeling open the telescope full length. He found, because of the long expanse of flat country southward, he was able to see quite a distance while still keeping low. He lay on his belly, eyeing the spot first to ensure there were no fanged discoveries, and elbowed his way forward, snug to the rock.

He propped the spy scope on the fingertips of his right hand and worked the tool until he was able to see, with some clarity, at distance. At first there were no surprises—the wavering lines emanating from the earth, rising up but never so high other bits of interest might not be visible through them.

And then he saw them—blurred, to be sure, but there was no

mistaking the long line of riders moving away, farther southward, spread east to west, some feet apart. They appeared to him through the limited viewing ability of the ground glass lens as dark forms, specters that looked more suited to haunting than anything else.

"Must be the ones we're seeking." Bone eyed them for a few moments more, then sighed and collapsed the telescope. He backed up and leaned against the boulder. One of them had been a bit behind the others, but looked to be riding hard to catch up with them. Must have been their backtrail scout. The one who'd shot at them.

He was good at what he did, for not only did he keep from being seen, as Bone had been eyeing the trail ahead as they rode, but the man had also been close enough to whistle a shot past his ear—surely close enough to have dealt Bone and Jervis, too, a mortal blow.

And yet he'd pulled the shot enough to the side to keep it a warning. Or more to the point, a notice that they'd been spotted.

Bone made his way back down the slope, weaving between boulders, and taking care not to lose his footing on the gritty slope.

He smelled the coffee brewing moments before he descended into view of Jervis and the small fire he'd made. In addition to coffee, Jervis had somehow managed to concoct an entire meal, such as their supplies would allow, of warmed biscuits, dried fruits, and slices of warmed slab bacon they'd cooked the day before.

"I should vamoose more often. Problem is, I've traveled alone so many times, I'd be liable to try to escape on myself, and then I'd come back to an empty fry pan." The notion struck Bone as humorous, but his grin was short-lived. Jervis stared at him as if he'd come back sporting two heads.

"You see anything up there?"

"Plenty. I'd say they're well aware of us. But instead of coming back for us, or at least sticking a bit and watching, they chose to hoof it on out of here and continue their trek south."

Jervis asked a question, but he already suspected the answer. "Long and short of it is that they'll be waiting for us, huh?"

Bone sipped his coffee and picked up a biscuit. "Yep."

They ate in silence, Jervis knowing if there was something Bone needed him to know, the ranger would tell him. And Bone knew the same. For the moment, they enjoyed the hot food and good coffee, about the last hour of the day when they'd be able to enjoy anything hot.

For all that, they did not dawdle. Bone knew they had to keep the distance between them from widening.

As they mounted up and checked their rifles, Jervis said, "Why do you suppose they want us to follow?"

"You tell me, Ranger."

"All right, I will. It's because they want us dead. No prisoners."

"Something like that, yep. Except for the 'no prisoners' part. Vermin like this don't mind prisoners if they can use them, either for personal pleasure or for profit. Or both."

"Do you think—"

"Yep."

Both men rode around the western edge of the broad base of the rocky knob in silence. Jervis was slightly ahead and slowed as they emerged abreast of the south side of the base, opposite of the spot they'd just enjoyed their brief repast.

He held up his left arm and hand long enough to show Bone that he'd seen something unexpected. Jervis waited for Bone to ride alongside, and the two men looked down at a slovenly scene.

It was a camp. Or rather the remnants of one. Close by a large boulder sat a two-foot-wide charred cold fire. When it had burned, it had blackened the smooth face of the big rock beneath which it sat.

Three other rocks, of sizable height and girth, had been rolled here and there a few yards from the fire. Not many unburned sticks lay anywhere, but there were plenty of boot prints. And farther off, ample piles of horse dung, mashed and whole, sat drying in the sun. But the one feature that caught their attention was a dead man.

He lay on his back, hands trussed before him and ankles tied. His skin was browned deeply by the sun, and his black hair and sparse, whispery mustaches and spidery beard told them he was possibly Mexican. His eyes were closed, and he could be mistaken for a sleeping man . . . were it not for the mess a big-handled knife had made of his chest.

They knew it was a knife because the handle still protruded from the center of his breast. "My word," said Bone. "If the size of the handle is any indication, that blade has likely pinned that poor soul to the very earth itself."

"What should we do?"

But Bone was already sliding down out of the saddle once more, handing the reins to Jervis. "Keen an eye. I need to poke around here a minute."

Bone cradled the rifle in the crook of his left arm and walked slowly about the campsite, stopping and crouching often. He palmed the fire, not touching anything, and bent his head forward and sniffed. "Peed all over it to put it out."

He inspected flattened spots where, Jervis guessed, men had lain. Then he returned to the boulders and crouched again, carefully inspecting those flanking the fire. "Captives were set here. Might be women. Barefoot prints of at least one woman, maybe children, lead off from here." He pointed, for Jervis's sake.

There he saw dark spots near two of the four. "Probably women who were abused by these men," said Bone. He felt ill at the sight.

Thoughts bloomed, bruise-colored in his mind, of his Margaret and her awful ordeal in the hands of the slavers and the filth who'd lured her West under false pretenses as a mail-order bride, only to abuse her beyond measure.

He shook himself out of the foul reverie, sending a kind thought skyward for his wife, alone, save for Ramon, at their ranch. He'd give much to be back there with her. But there was a job to do, and he had committed himself to seeing it through. And then, by gum, he was done with Rangering. Done once and for all.

Just now, though, there were likely captives to be rescued and evil, border-hopping, murdering filth to contend with.

"Should we do something with this one?" said Jervis.

Bone returned to the dead man and nudged him with a boot toe. "He isn't stiff, but he'll be there before us."

He patted the man's grimy, thin clothes, eyed his gnarled, sandaled feet, and lifted him a bit on one side, then the other. "I see nothing that tells me more than what I suspected from the first—the man was likely a captive. Border banditos don't usually wear sandals. He looks like an unlucky peasant who got in their way. I feel bad for him," said Bone, straightening and walking back to his horse. "But there's nothing we can do for him now."

"Should we bury him?"

"I'd like to, but we already lost time making coffee and such."

"But . . ."

"Listen, Jervis, it speaks well of you that you want to tend to that poor fellow, but with each minute that passes with us not on the trail, that's another minute another of their captives might die. I can't live with that thought. You?"

"No, I reckon you're right."

Bone mounted up. "Besides, he's far beyond caring. Only thing that really mattered was how he lived his life."

He nudged Bub around and eyed southward, ahead, then proceeded in that direction at a trot. He did not hear Jervis behind. He reined up and half-turned.

Jervis was off his horse and had trotted over to the man. He looked up, saw Bone eyeing him. "Go on, I'll catch you up!"

"That's not how this works!"

But Jervis did not stop what he was doing. And what he did was to place a boot on the man's chest and wrench the deep-sunk dagger from the dead man's chest. He looked at it, then tossed it away. Then he lifted the dead man by the shoulders and dragged him over to the overhang at the knob's base made by the boulders.

He laid him out there in partial shade, and cut his bound hands and feet free; then he crossed the man's hands on his chest and bowed his head and uttered a brief prayer.

He trotted back to his horse, mounted up, and rode the dozen yards to Bone's side.

The elder ranger eyed him.

Jervis said, "I'm sorry for disobeying you, but it would have weighed on me heavy had I not done a little something for the man. Besides, fella shouldn't have to spend eternity with a devil's blade stuck in him."

They rode on in silence for some time, then Bone said, "Thanks for doing that, Jervis. Makes me feel better, too."

Jervis nodded, and they rode on, toward what or who, they knew not. But they were beginning to find out.

Chapter 26

"You ever get one of those feelings that you're being watched?"

Percy looked up from stirring in a handful of roots and greens he'd collected on the trail earlier in the day. "Cyril, that happens to me all the time. But I look up to find it's just some slack-mouthed, drooling cowpuncher waiting for his next feed, and I ignore him."

Percy stared at Cyril until the reddening young man looked away. "My, but you are a rather cantankerous fellow."

"I'll take that as a compliment. Even if it wasn't meant as such."

"I'm serious here."

"And you think I'm not?" Percy almost grinned, then decided he could not let the men see that kinder, gentler side of him. "All right, Cyril, what's going on?"

Cyril looked around, then said, "It's what I haven't seen that is most troubling." He nodded southward, in the direction they'd come. "I swear by all that's holy that somebody is back there."

"Well," said Percy, sampling the stock. "Could be the boss. He said he'd be along as soon as he was able."

Percy wasn't convinced it would be that easy for Regis to free himself of that nasty little town. Or maybe it was just the marshal who was nasty. Anyway, he figured if there was a man who could extricate himself form the clutches of that nasty little man, it was the boss. But *when* was the question. Meanwhile, he and Fergus were sharing the load in commandeering the crew and herd.

"Perhaps," said Cyril, "but I tend to think not." He leaned closer and spoke in a lower voice. "I have what has been called a gift." He nodded.

Percy nodded in reply and leaned in. "My granny had what you'd call a goiter."

"Percy, in light of the brutal attack we all underwent weeks ago on the trail, on this very drive, I'd think you would at least have the decency to listen to me without passing your rank judgment. Let alone take my premonitions seriously."

"All right, all right, Cyril. What have you seen? Or felt? Or whatever it is you have experienced?"

"As I intimated, I believe we're being followed."

Percy regarded Cyril a moment, then stood and smacked his hands against his apron. "All right, then, Cyril. If you feel strongly enough we're being followed, there might well be something in it. Why don't you tell Fergus? He'll be a better judge of such than I am. And if you happen to see anybody else on the way, tell them they can ride on by for grub in half an hour, not a minute more."

"Right, will do, Percy. By the way, what is it?" Cyril leaned forward and sniffed, his eyes closed. "Smells heavenly."

"Thank you. I ain't decided on a name yet, but if you linger any longer, I'm going to call it Cyril Surprise." He hoisted his big chef's knife and waved it with menace at the retreating young Englishman.

He watched Cyril ride off toward Fergus, on the far side of the herd, now bedded for the night. His smile faded as he looked southward. He had hoped there might be no further trouble on the drive. He was plumb tired of all the commotion, and as much as he hated to admit it, he would be relieved when they all rode back into the borders of the Royle Range, so very far south of them.

He turned back to stirring the stew. "If we ever do."

Fergus's meager abilities to prepare for another attack by an unseen, unknown force, were limited to informing the men and putting them on even tighter sleep rotations. They were, of course, all armed, unlike other drives he'd been on when they rarely went heeled whilst on the trail.

Normally their guns rode on the cooks' wagon, as they went unused much of the time and were far too heavy to lug around for no reason.

For all that, the men—and Fergus was proud of them for this—took it on themselves to ration themselves to even less sleep, most of them optioning to doze in the saddle for brief snatches.

It was the fresh memory of the earlier odd attack that put them all, to a man—and perhaps even the beeves—on alert. And for that, Fergus was relieved. he didn't want anyone taking anything for granted, an easy thing to do given the monotony of the trail.

Despite all that, Fergus was downright worried. He'd feel a bit better, of course, if Regis Royle had made it back to the herd, but in truth, not all that much better. Royle was one heck of a capable fellow, but by his own admittance to Fergus, he was not experienced in matters of the trail. In fact, many of the men on the drive were green when it came to such matters. They'd already lost men, and he would do anything it took to keep the rest safe.

He finished the last bite.

"Um, Percy?"

"Yeah, Fergus?"

"Maybe until we're feeling safer, our meals should be something less . . ."

Percy nodded. He didn't want Fergus to feel sheepish in talking to him. If they were going to make it through this drive without the boss and without any more trouble, he needed to at least not be prickly with the man, who saw through him anyway. "I hear you. I got a little careless in making stew tonight. It's not an easy thing to eat quick."

"Or from the saddle," said Fergus, nodding, and visibly relieved.

"Right. Already have a double-batch of biscuits made, and I cooked up a slab of bacon. And we have plenty of jerky, hard tack, fruits, and such. We should be all right for a spell."

"Good to hear. And all your gear . . ."

"Yep, as soon as it cools, I'm going to pack it up, just in case we need to ramble hard and fast."

"That's good, that's good. Well," Fergus said, and slugged back the last of his coffee. "I best be getting back."

"Fergus?"

"Yeah, Percy?"

"You think there's anything to what Cyril said he felt?"

Fergus squinted into the night, as if he could see in the dark. "Well, all I can say is I've known folks who could sense things before they happened. I don't know what you'd call that, but things, good and bad, happened after they talked about them. And they weren't necessarily in positions to make them happen, if you see what I mean."

"I do. So?"

"So," Fergus sighed. "I'd say we'd be fools not to play it safe, which we are doing, and see if we can't come through with something to laugh about and nothing more."

"Can't hurt, is what you're saying."

"Yep, can't hurt and it might well help."

With that, Fergus left the comforts of the campfire and cook wagon and mounted up. It was going to be a long ol' night, and he figured he'd best get at it. No need to dawdle.

The first sign of something wrong slipped in well after midnight. It came in the middle of those hours when everyone was dog-tired and either dozing in their saddles or pining for a smoke—Fergus had forbade anyone to light a cigarette or pipe or such while it was still dark.

It was Benny who found it. Or rather his horse did, by nearly stumbling over it. It being a dead cow. He slipped down out of the saddle and felt the thing, though with ample caution. If it was a sleeping beef and it was one of the many with horns, it could hook him and gore a fist-size hole in him without thinking.

He slid down out of the saddle and toed it a few times. Nope, nothing moved. With his teeth he tugged off a glove and patted the thing, still with caution lest it be as tired as he was. But nope again, the thing was either unconscious—and he'd never heard of such a thing—or it was good and dead.

He made his way up the critter's backbone and felt along its neck . . . and pulled back a hand covered in something mighty warm and mighty thick and sticky. He held it before his face by but a couple of inches and sniffed. His nose wrinkled up. He knew exactly what it was. And it wasn't water.

He held his breath and felt some more. And he found the beast's throat had been gashed open, a deep, clean cut. So deep it went from its skin all the way back and in, nearly to its neck bone.

And the cut was no jagged, accidental affair. This beef was cut with intention.

That's when it occurred to Benito that he'd heard of such things happening to herds on the trail. Usually it was Indians who did such a thing. They would kill off critters, butcher them for the choice bits under cover of darkness, and then they'd rabbit off into the night with fresh meat.

"Oh, Lordy," he said in a low whisper. That meant there might well be Indians about. Maybe closer to him than to anyone else in the herd. Could be this was what Cyril was talking about having sensed.

Benny recalled his own old grandfather, Beaufort, on his father's side. He was a seer, as they called them in the church back home, and Grandpa Beaufort had the ability to see things before they happened. Just like he did when his sister, Elsa, turned twelve years old.

He came to Benny's parents all trembly and said that he'd seen that if the family stayed where they were, right smack dab in Pup's Knob, that Elsa, Benny's sister, would not see her thirteenth birthday.

That was a rum thought and one that Benny's parents did not take lightly. A month hadn't gone by but they'd pulled up stakes on the old homestead and moved house clear over to Wareham's Bluff, nearly ten miles away.

Course, it was well known that Grandpa Beaufort was sweet on a woman who ran a still in the Bluff. And Benny's mama, it turns out, did not last the year herself, worn to a frazzle as she was with gardening and helping to build the new cabin and all.

Sad affair all around, but it proved to Benny that there were some folks who could see and some who couldn't. Trick in life, he'd grown to learn, was to pay attention to them who could.

His other gloved hand still held his reins, and he guided himself back to his horse—after he'd wiped his hand as clean as he was able on the muck-spattered hide of the dead beast—and mounted up. He was tugging it around to his left, hoping to find somebody, anybody from the herd, to tell.

As luck would have it, somebody rode on into sight. The moonlight was scant, but bright enough that he could make out the shape of a rider.

"Who's that? I got a gun!" said Benito, in a half-whisper.

"Easy son, it's only me, Fergus."

"Oh, thank the Lord! I was worried there."

Fergus moved closer. "What's the trouble?"

"Well, sir. I found a dead cow."

"Huh." Fergus slid down out of the saddle. "That why you're

whispering?" He moved over closer to the now-visible form on the ground, squinting to see. "How'd it die?"

"That's the thing I'm worried about. Somebody cut its throat."

"Hmm. That's not good."

"Made me wonder if it's Indians, sir."

"Me, too, Benny. Me, too. And it might account for why Cyril got a bee in his bonnet earlier."

Fergus bent low and did much the same as Benny, feeling the cow's still body. It was warm, but cooling in the nippy night air. The blood, which he barely dabbed with his fingertips, was thickening.

Close by him in the dark, Benny whispered. "You think they're still about, sir?"

"No way to tell, son, but I think if they are about, they'll be back for their spoils. We best leave them to it and keep a sharp eye on the rest of the herd. Tricky in the night like this, but we don't have a choice. And risking a match might be begging for a bullet. I'll ride northward; you round the rear where I came from and make your way back to Percy. Let him know. Don't overdo it, though, Benny. We don't know what's what just yet."

"Okay, sir."

"And Benny?"

"Yes, sir?"

"Enough with the 'sir' business. I'm just Fergus."

"Yes, sir. Fergus, sir. Sorry."

Despite the new and possibly dire situation blooming in their midst, Fergus found the man's flustered response amusing. "Keep your head down, boy. And don't get panicky."

"Okay, sir Fergus." He nodded as he rode on out.

Fergus stayed with the beef a few moments more, hunched there beside it and eyeing the night about him as best he could.

He heard no sounds other than the constant low rumble of big cows plodding in their milling group, many of them down for the night, some of them dozing on their feet, others lowing, still others coughing or blowing snot, as cattle will do, it seemed, at any time of day or night.

Here and there he heard the soft cluck-clucking and low-voiced murmuring sounds his boys made to keep the cattle quiet. He did not doubt that it was Indians, as he'd experienced much the same handiwork by them in the past. They'd sneak up on a herd in the night, kill and butcher what they could, then depart as quickly and as silently as they'd struck.

He couldn't really begrudge them a few beeves. It was their land long before it was overrun by white folks and their herds of grazers. And besides, such losses were always counted on at the outset of a drive. But he didn't want to risk riling the now-placid beasts. They'd had a few small runs and stampedes already. He didn't need another, and especially not at night.

As if in answer to his thoughts, he heard hoofbeats, slow, but measured, west of him, past the dead animal.

Fergus stiffened and waited, his horse beginning to fidget at being so near the stink of a dead beast and unable to flee from it.

Any moment now, he thought, and that fool horse is going to whicker, and then I'm going to get attacked by somebody who can probably see a whole lot better in the dark, if the stories told of Indians were true, which he secretly doubted. But who could tell? Especially at a time like this.

He remained upright, but bent over, his left arm extended and wagging slightly with the movements of his horse. With his right, he reached across himself and lifted free his holstered pistol, hanging on his left side.

One loud crack in the night could set the beeves to running. It could also elicit very little response at all. A fellow never knew where he stood with cattle.

Fergus waited. The hoofbeats continued, moving closer, slow and soft, but they were there.

He wanted to shout, "Who goes there?" and hoist a lit lantern at them, whoever it was, but figured that would only get him shot all the sooner.

And truth be told, as much as he enjoyed the life of a cowboy, he didn't really want to die for it, or in the saddle. He'd always wanted a little place of his own, up in the northern reaches one day, just below the big mountains they were, it seemed, perpetually headed for but never reached.

He'd like a little cabin overlooking a river, a small stable for a horse or two, maybe some chickens for eggs and meat. And room to grow some of his own food. He'd not need much to get by, which was good, for despite having saved some of his earnings over the years, it didn't tally too high.

He wasn't a big drinker, and he wasn't a fool gambler. He had never seen the appeal in wagering hard-earned cash frittered away to strangers or friends, didn't much matter, while staring at paste cards. Dumb didn't begin to define that behavior in his book.

Fergus had no more time for such thoughts, because he sensed and heard the presence of another horse, close in. His horse whickered, and whoever had ridden up and slid down from their saddle halted.

Fergus felt certain he could reach out and tap whoever it was on the shoulder. It was a feeling he did not like. He held his breath. Then, when he could take it no longer, he stood and throated back the hammer on his pistol.

He heard a quick intake of breath and a rustling, then whispers, one voice louder than the other.

Fergus stepped to his right, quick, and said, "Speak English?"

There was a pause; then a hesitant voice, soft, as if it were a woman, said, "No?"

The situation was mighty odd, and Fergus wanted to hop his horse and bolt on out of there. But that was no way for a man to act. Especially one in the boss spot. A man could think anything he pleased, but acting on fool notions was out of the question.

"Hungry?" he said. "Food? Eat?"

"Food . . . eat . . . yes."

If it was as it sounded, a woman, he was talking with, okay then. But there was a second voice, as well.

"Come," he said. "Beef."

And then he heard more whispers. He was convinced one of the voices was indeed a man, given the low husky sound of the voice. They had become emboldened, these two, for he hoped that's all there were. And then he heard another sound, a small voice, that of a child. It was a sob, stifled by a quick hand over its mouth.

"Here now," said Fergus. "Take the beef. Come, come."

It was the sound of the child that made him do something he knew was reckless, but he didn't care. He backed away from them and the dead cow and mounted up, still not entirely convinced he was out of danger, but feeling fairly certain of it with each moment that passed.

He made certain his horse's hoofbeats left no doubt as to the fact that he'd left them. The only other thing he could do for them would be to tell the others to give that stretch of the herd a wide cut for a couple more hours.

Something told Fergus that there wouldn't be more than the one animal killed, and Regis Royle could well spare the loss, but those people could not withstand starving to death.

The rest of the night passed quietly, with no more disturbances to be seen or heard. And as daylight slowly bloomed and the sun poked its head up from the east, Fergus and the men assessed the edges of the herd. There on the west edge, lay the carcass of the killed cow, but it had been skillfully butchered.

Of its takers, there was no sign save for the hoofprints of two horses, both with dragging hooves, as if it took mighty effort just to get there. And their efforts on the trail back the way they'd come, to the low hills a mile or more to the northwest, looked to have been even more demanding.

"Should we go after them?" said Benny, eyes keen despite his lack of sleep. He looked toward the hills.

Fergus looked up from the barefoot human tracks in the dust all about the dead beast—he saw those of a small adult, likely the woman he'd conversed briefly with, as well as those of a man whose right foot was a gimped thing, judging from the bent angle of the print.

And there were more, the tracks of two children, both small. He looked toward the hills as well and wished them all the luck his thoughts could muster.

"Why?" he said finally to Benny.

"Why? Well, they stole from us, and scared us, too."

Fergus looked at the young man, fire welling in his chest. Then he saw that the young cowboy was truly just a kid himself, petrified and confused.

"Tell me, boy, when was the last time you missed a meal?"

The kid shrugged. "Ain't had but biscuits all night."

Fergus shook his head. "Those Indians are more afraid of us than we are of them, Benito. Besides, they're starving and we're not. So think about that the next time you eat a biscuit."

Fergus rode off. He hadn't intended to come across as hard-sounding, but he felt it might be important to let the young man know that despite his fear and discomfort, he was a privileged man living a life of his own choosing.

The natives hereabouts weren't faring too well these days, with all the white settlers moving in and taking game and land out from beneath them. No, thought Fergus, we can well afford a lost beef now and then.

He rode over to Percy's wagon for a cup of coffee. It would be time to move within the half hour, and he needed to be sure everything was in as much order as it could be these days.

He rode the northern edge of the herd, the mass of the beasts already rumbling and horning each other like fool children.

He looked southward, hoping he'd see the tall form of Regis Royle clipping along toward them. He could do with a few less responsibilities. But of the plain behind them, he saw nothing but a long, low purple landscape, just beginning to glow pink here and there with the morning light.

It looked to be a good day and, despite the lack of sleep that had seeped into every bit of him, from his hair down through his toes, and all the bones and gut within, Fergus smiled, ready for whatever the day might bring.

Heck, he thought as he neared Percy's wagon and meager coffee fire. He might just relieve one of the youngsters riding drag. Then again, perhaps he was thinking a bit too rashly. He grinned and slowed his horse, then dismounted by the wagon.

"What's cooking?" he said, by way of greeting the surly cook.

"It isn't food, that's for certain. I'm trying to convince the children on the horses"—Percy waved a scrap of leather he used to handle the coffee pot—"that a cold bit of food is better than going hungry. But I don't think they're convinced."

"You been listening to my talk with young Benny?" said Fergus, pouring himself a steaming cup off the black stuff.

"What? Nah, but I grew up poor as the shadow of a church mouse, and I don't wish that rib-counting experience on anyone. Makes a fellow appreciate a mouthful of food, no matter what it might be, hot or cold!"

"I hear you, Percy. More than you know." Fergus sipped and sighed, and wondered what new lessons he might have to impart today.

Chapter 27

Regis rode well into the day, grateful for the kind stableman's generosity. He mused as he rode that none of this would have been necessary if Marshal Tench had only acted like a decent man instead of a petty little fool with anger clouding his judgment.

Then he realized that he was giving the man more credit than he might have deserved. It was entirely probable that Tench didn't actually carry good judgment, and he was merely an annoying little toad.

The thought, now that he was shed of Dennerville, pleased him. Despite wanting to not even think of the man, Regis found it was difficult, as he was the root cause of all his problems of late.

"King," he said to the horse, who still hadn't flagged one bit since their daring escape from Dennerville. "I think it's high time we stop and stretch our legs." Then he realized what he'd just said and chuckled. "How about I stretch mine and you rest yours. I can't imagine what an unenjoyable task dragging my big carcass around must be."

They rode for another eighth of a mile until they reached the declivity that Regis had spotted earlier. It did as he had hoped, and led in a gentle, long slope down to a shallow but boldly running and clear stream. It flowed westward and looked inviting.

They switchbacked down the banking and reached the water in minutes. It was still early enough that the water hadn't yet had time to dissipate fully, and for Regis, that was great news.

King set to work sipping from the flow, and Regis ground-tied him and roved up and down the bank, eyes always flicking to the skyline to all sides.

He saw little that might bear a second glance, and nothing to incite a wary pose. But that didn't mean, as he well knew, that there wasn't danger about. It came in all sizes, shapes, and intentions.

He had only walked downstream, westward, roughly thirty feet from King, when he felt a prickling up and down his back, as if he were being watched. He paused and held a moment. Yep, it was still there. He spun as if he had just decided to head back to the horse, eyeing the terrain once more. Still, he saw nothing.

Even as he was nearly to King, he saw that the big beast stood with muzzle dripping and head cocked as if he were about to resume drinking, but his ears were bent forward, and he looked across the river at something. Regis also looked across the twenty-five feet or so, but at first glance saw nothing. Then he looked closer, and there was, indeed, something there.

It was the remnants of a camp, if he wasn't mistaken, as a half-scorched circle of stones sat close to the water's edge. And beyond it, up the bank a bit, it looked as if someone had dug in close beneath the overhanging banking.

Grasses hung down and swayed in a slight breeze like hair over eyes. The space behind and within was dark but looked to be large enough to hide something. Or someone.

Regis decided to play it safe and cautious at the same time. He walked over to King and grabbed hold of the reins before the big horse decided against his cooler nature and bolted.

He'd seen it before, and it was a reminder to him not to walk away from a horse doing little more than ground tying him.

"Come on, boy. Time to get moving."

The horse complied, though kept a wary eye on whatever had caught his eye across the water.

Regis walked on the south side of the horse, leading him downstream a couple of dozen feet, and shucked his revolver at the same time, thumbing it back, just in case. He didn't like using King as a shield, but it seemed the prudent thing to do. He stopped and glanced over the saddle at the spot on the opposite bank of the river.

Still, nothing had moved over there. He felt a pinch of relief at having separated themselves a bit from whatever it was. But now he had to either scamper on out of there or face it like a man. He didn't like the idea of poking his sniffer in where it wasn't wanted. But he liked even less leaving something behind him that might pinch off a shot between his shoulder blades as he rode northward. That was one surefire way to not ever reach the herd.

"Okay, King," he said in a low voice. "We're going to cross the river and cut wide, then amble on back. At least I will. You can stay by those trees up above."

The low snag of stunty riverbank trees looked decent enough to hold a tied horse for a bit. But as powerful as King was, he could as easily get riled and tear the thing apart. He'd make it quick. And he'd hobble the horse if need be. He'd read the situation once he got up there.

They crossed the river, making plenty of ruckus, splashing and taking their time. For all his earlier trepidations, King seemed to enjoy the feeling of the river on his feet, and Regis didn't blame him. He'd have to rest the beast well tonight. Pace him or again, they'd not reach the herd.

The last thing he needed was for his horse to go lame. Not only did he not want to lose King and have to put him down, but he did not want to fail to reach the herd or the men.

The notion of reaching them volleyed in his head constantly.

And if he didn't reach the herd, that would likely mean he was killed on the way somehow.

And that would mean not returning back to Texas and the Royle Range, the only place he wanted to be. And he was coming around to realizing that even more important than that was the idea of never again seeing Marietta, of missing out on a life with her.

Up on the north side of the small river's bank, the landscape stretched far, but as he'd noticed an hour or so earlier, there was an increased rolling to the view, with hills blooming the closer they drew to those mountains he and the boys had been spying for what seemed like months.

This, he realized, was the first time he felt as though he was drawing closer to the spine of mountains that loomed ahead to the northwest. The heads of the mountains were invisible behind thick, gray clouds. Might that be a storm that would roll down the long heights and rage its might over him? He hoped not. He'd had enough of brutal storms for quite a spell.

When he figured he'd gone far enough, he glanced back yet again, something he'd been doing as soon as they'd crested the riverbank. Still, he saw nothing.

But that, he knew, didn't mean there was no danger back there. He was certain King had been spooked by something. And he, too, had felt that crawling feeling up his spine. He sighed as he looked back, squinting into the late-morning light. He was about to ride back the twenty feet or so to tie off King to those stunty trees when he saw, or thought he saw, something rise up slightly from the edge of the bank, just about where that old campsite had been.

But no, it was too far to see anything that quick. "Naw," he said aloud, though in a low, quiet voice. "Had to have been a shadow. But we'd better be safe and sure, eh, boy?"

He lashed the horse to the trees, slid the rifle from the boot, and crept forward, circling until he was on the upstream edge of the bank with the spot in question about a dozen feet downstream of him. He knelt and waited. He figured he could give peace of mind a couple of minutes, and then he was going to climb down the bank and get to the heart of the matter, much as his gut told him to do so with caution.

Turned out that he didn't have long to wait. The thing that he hadn't been certain of seeing was indeed real, for it emerged slowly from beneath that shaggy overhang of grass, as a wild creature might from its den.

A coyote? he thought. But it didn't look right, too round for that. A wildcat? He wasn't certain what the denning habits of most critters in the wild were, but in those few seconds, nothing seemed right to his mind.

And then it emerged a bit more. He'd been sighting down the long barrel, his finger resting on the trigger, ready to deliver a shot should the thing prove to be dangerous in any way.

And it kept on emerging, creeping, hugging tight to the bank. It grew taller, turned to face the plain toward where he'd tied King. It appeared to be looking, left, right, moving its head as if to get a better view of him. Or where he had been. It was seeing King, for certain, and it was wondering where Regis was. It stood a little taller.

And then he saw it for what it was. A person. A small person, but it was a person, by gum.

As soon as he got a leg up and over the shock of what he was seeing, he shouted, "Hold right there!"

The effect of his words was immediate. The little person didn't look around for the cause of the shout, but disappeared!

Regis stared for a moment in disbelief. What in the world was going on here? Then he gathered his frayed wits. Still with caution, for the person might be armed, might not even be alone, and with as much stealth as he could muster while not taking his eyes from the spot, Regis clambered and slid down the bank nearly to the river, keeping the rifle trained there.

It took him but a couple of cautious strides to walk nearly abreast of the shady grotto. "Come on out! We all have you surrounded there!"

Nothing.

"I saw you—we saw you—so come on out, or I'm going to start firing bullets on in there!"

"Why would you do that?"

The voice, a high-pitched raspy shout, once more took Regis by surprise. He recovered, "Then come on out of there, I said!"

He heard a scratching, dragging sound, and then from beneath those waving, hanging grasses, something emerged. Regis tightened. Might be a trick, might be a weapon of some sort. But no. It was a grimy hand, small, that of a boy. It was followed with another.

These were followed by a hat, black and foul. It had once had shape but was now a sagged, forlorn thing. And beneath it, an equally begrimed face with two wide eyes settled on him. They quickly narrowed in fear or rage or both. It was a boy.

"Come on out, all the way!"

The boy spat and dragged a filthy hand across his mouth. Then he shook his head and, as if accepting the situation, slid on out of there.

The kid sat in the bank dirt, dust clouding from where he'd slid, his hands to his sides. He stared squinting, up at Regis. "You said *we*."

"What?"

The kid sighed. "You said we have you surrounded. I don't see nobody else."

"I lied."

"Oh."

"While we're on the subject," said Regis. "Are you alone?"

The kid stared a moment longer, then nodded. "Yeah. They took Pap."

"Pap? Your father?"

"Yeah."

"Who took him?"

"Oh, big old group of Indians and others."

"How long ago was this?"

"Some days since."

"I'm sorry to hear that." Regis realized the kid was likely harmless, so he lowered the rifle a bit. He had to find out for certain before he'd ease it off cock. "How have you been surviving?"

"Ain't been, hardly."

"Why didn't you try to walk on out of here, go for help?"

The kid snorted. "Where would I go? There ain't nothing nor nobody for a thousand miles. That's what Papa said. Course, them Indians come out of somewhere. But he wasn't to know that."

"Well, you have to go somewhere or you'll die here."

"I can take care of myself. Been doing all right until you come by."

Regis took a step closer, and the kid tensed. "I'm not going to harm you. Look, have you eaten? I have some food with me. And I'm headed north to find my men and cattle. You'll come along."

"Who said you was my boss? You ain't Pap."

"No, no, I'm not. But if you come with me, you stand a better chance of finding him than if you stay here."

"You really have food?"

"I do. Not much, but we can hunt and cook up some meat. Wouldn't take long."

"Well. All right then." The kid shoved to his feet and walked slowly, as if his feet each weighed fifty pounds.

"You should drink some water."

The kid snorted again. "Water's all I have had. Got my fill of that and then some. Must have lowered the river a good foot by myself."

"Okay, then, let's get up to my horse before he gets bored and leaves us both walking. We can get a couple more hours of travel in. I'd like to reach those hills northward." Regis nodded.

The kid didn't bother looking. He also didn't walk too close to Regis, who let him lead the way up the embankment.

They hadn't walked more than a dozen feet when, thanks to a light breeze coming at them from the north, Regis gritted his teeth and looked to the side. "Hold on, hold on."

The boy stopped and squinted at him, appearing weaker with each step. "What's wrong?"

"Look, you have a natural stink that is about more than a fellow can stand, boy. Now you had best strip off and clean up or we're going to have ourselves a situation. I need to get going, and you need to come with me or die out here alone. And that is not something I'm prepared to allow to happen. Do you understand?"

For a moment, the kid said nothing. Then said, "No."

"No, what?" said Regis, flexing his jaw muscles. "No, you didn't understand me? Or no, you're not going to follow my orders?"

The kid shrugged. "Both."

Regis rolled his eyes. it was like dealing with Shep all over again. Okay, he thought. You didn't do so well with your kid brother in situations such as this, so try to do this differently. He looked over at King, who returned his stare, as if to say, "You're the one who stopped, not me."

"Why don't you want to clean up? If I can smell you, you must surely smell yourself. And rest assured, it's no treat."

The kid stood there with arms crossed, scowling at the dirt. "'Cause I don't know you."

"Of course you don't. I don't know you, either. But we're stuck together. Look, I have to get cracking here."

"Ain't got no others."

"Others? Other what?"

The kid sighed and rolled his eyes, as if Regis were an idiot. "Clothes. This here's all I got."

"That's all right. I have a set of spare longhandles in my saddlebag."

The kid glanced at him again. This time, the scowl was all but
gone. "For true?"

Regis nodded. "For true. And a pair of clean socks. I always
carry clean socks. You never know if you're going to get wet
feet."

"My mama used to say if you're cold, you need to put on fresh
socks, and you'll warm right up."

"I expect you're mama's correct."

"Was. She's dead, too."

"I'm sorry to hear that. What do you mean, 'too'?"

The kid shrugged. "Pap. Those men who took off with him."

"Tell me more about those men."

"You mean the men who took Pap?"

"Yes, but what did they look like? How many were there?
How long ago were they here? And were they headed north?"

The kid stared at him with raised eyebrows. "You ask a lot of
questions."

"And I like answers. So go back to the creek and start in on
them while I get out those longhandles and socks. I don't have
soap, but you can use sand to scrub yourself down."

"Never said I was going to wash."

Again, Regis sighed. "Now look, what's the big deal? I'm a
man, but a long time ago I was a boy, just like you."

The kid turned away, and Regis thought he saw redness
bloom on his neck and ears and cheeks. Finally the boy said,
"Ain't."

Regis thought he'd heard correctly, but no, he could not have.
"Ain't what? Ain't going to wash? Because I can as easily drag you
over there and scrub you down myself."

The kid turned to face him again, this time with narrow-eyed
anger in place of the previous look of fear and pure skittishness.

"What are you afraid of?"

The kid sighed. "Name's Pen." With effort, he tugged off his hat. Long dark hair, matted and greasy from sweat and grime, flopped down. "Short for Penny. And I ain't a boy."

"Oh." Regis did not know what more to say. Finally he said, "Oh. Well . . ."

They stood in awkward silence for a moment; then he extended his hand. "Regis Royle. Pleased to meet you, Penny."

Still eyeing him through squints, she gave his hand a quick but sharp shake, then retreated a step.

"Okay, then. Look, if we're going to travel together, you still have to wash. I'll get those things from the saddlebag. You can use the river. I'll wait up here with King until you're through. And don't do anything foolish like trying to run off."

"Where would I go?"

"Right." He made for the horse.

"You said you have food." She said it in a smaller voice, but he'd forgotten that she must be famished. She certainly was thin enough.

"You bet!" He tried to sound cheerful as he gathered everything he could think of to feed her. In a few moments, he came back and handed her socks and the long underwear and a couple of pieces of the old hostler's wife's hard tack, plus a thick slice of jerky.

She looked at the food a moment, said, "Thank you," as he handed it to her, then not waiting any longer, she crammed it in her mouth, barely chewing, and guzzled water from his canteen.

"Go easy or you're liable to be ill."

If she heard him, she gave no indication, for she kept on wolfing the food until it was gone.

"Hold on a minute." He unbuttoned his own outer shirt and slipped it off. "Here. Take this. I have my undershirt. That's all I need."

"Don't be giving me the shirt off your back, Mister Regis. I'll be fine."

"I insist."

"That another order?"

"Yes."

"You stay right there with your back this way, and don't you move! I catch you sneakin' and I'll brain you dead with a rock, I swear it!"

"I promise, Penny. I promise. Now can you please just get going? I'd like to get at least a couple more hours of travel in today."

"Okay, but you . . ." She pointed a finger at him and kept it up, gnawing a last nub of hardtack until she disappeared down the embankment. Soon enough, he heard the whoop of shock, likely as she began bathing.

After what seemed like a heck of a long time, Regis heard her return.

"Do you want your clothes? You could scrub them out, and we could wrap them up."

"Naw, they're awful. I'm keeping my hat. I washed it out pretty good and it ain't too bad. But the other stuff, that won't never come clean, I doubt. I threw it all back in the hole I was in. Let the critters have them."

"Can't imagine they'd want to smell them any more than I did."

"Hey! I heard you, you know. Just because I ain't got nothing left don't mean you have to talk like that."

"You're right. I apologize." A few moments passed, then Regis said, "Did the men who took your father also take your things? Clothes and food and such?"

"We didn't have much, but whatever we carried they took."

"I see."

"Did you happen to see a cattle drive come through here a few days ago?"

"Yeah, sure did. What a loud mess that was."

"Well, that loud mess is my herd, and those are my men."

"I thought they was a wild herd. I didn't see nobody with them."

That gave Regis pause, as he pondered the possibility that all his men had either been waylaid or up and left. Neither was plausible, or he'd have seen sign of an attack on them, or bodies.

"But then again," she continued. "I stayed hid. I didn't mind saying the noise was like thunder. And I ain't partial to thunder."

"Well, as I said, those men work for me, and I need to catch up to them as soon as possible."

"What're you doing so far behind them? You fall asleep? I bet that's what it was, huh? You fell asleep and they left in the night, hoping to get away from you."

"What? No, no, nothing like that. Besides, why would anyone want to get away from me?"

"Because you're annoying. And bossy."

Regis snorted a laugh. "Annoying and bossy, huh? Well, I've been called both, but not together. At least not to my face."

They rode for several hours, with the girl behind Regis and her hands rarely touching him, only when they trotted or when King picked their way switchbacking up a hill.

They found Pap's body unexpectedly. And from the looks of him, Regis wasn't quite certain how he had died. Sure, he'd been punched in the face, but he suspected that had been when the bandits had nabbed him initially.

As to mortal wounds, he could see none, though the man was dressed, albeit in raggy clothes in keeping with the poor state of Penny's clothes when Regis had found her. But he was relieved to see that the man had not been disfigured in any way, as the man's death was already clearly difficult for the girl.

"I expected this," she said, looking down at the prone form of her father.

Regis said nothing.

"Pap never would work for nobody else. That's how we come to be out here in the first place. It was just his way. And he certainly wasn't about to fall in with law-breaking trash such as them who hauled him away."

Then Penny did something that surprised Regis, and he did not know quite what to do for a long moment. Then he did.

She began to sob quietly and half-turned from him, wiping at her eyes with a cuff of the shirt.

Regis laid a big hand on her thin shoulder. It reminded him of a little bony bird. He was about to say something reassuring when she turned to him and laid her head against his chest and sobbed. He realized all she wanted was a hug, somebody to show her that she was not alone in this hard world.

He let her have a long cry; then, after a few minutes, she pushed away from him and wiped her face once more.

"I know you are in a hurry to get back to your men and your cows, but I would like to bury him. You can leave me here. It's all right. I found my Pap, and that's all that matters."

"No, no. I'll not leave you here, Penny. But we will bury your Pap, good and proper." Already he was wondering just how they were going to do this.

He eyed the surrounding countryside. To the west, about a half mile away, the hills began to rise in earnest. There looked to be a treed glade tucked between two low foothills. With any luck, there would be rocks for topping the grave, and water somewhere nearby, too.

"How about over there?" he pointed toward the spot he'd seen. "It looks green and quiet. A good spot to spend eternity."

She visored her eyes and looked, then nodded. "Yes, I think Pap'd like that. He always talked about having himself a place of his own one day. I reckon he'll be getting it."

"All right, then," said Regis. "We'll wrap him in this blanket. I can carry him, and you can ride King."

"No. He was my Pap; I can help lug him."

"Okay, then."

Hours later, Regis, bone-tired and weary from the past several days of hard travel, leaned against a boulder the size of a wagon and wiped the sweat from his face.

The girl was understandably quiet, and had become more so since they'd found her father. She stood over her Pap's grave, a mound of rocks topping it that represented labor Regis hoped he would not have to duplicate for some days to come.

They'd been fortunate in that there were ample rocks close by the spot they'd chosen to lay the man to rest. The digging had been difficult, as they had only their hands and a couple of stout sticks to help drag the dirt out of the indented grave.

Though it was shallow, barely deep enough to cover the man over again with packed dirt, the rocks topping the grave worked well and would serve to keep the critters—depending on their level of determination—from unearthing the poor man.

But Regis was pleased. The location turned out to be everything he'd hoped for, both for the man's resting place and for Penny's sake. It didn't hurt that not far from there, on the other side of the boulder, in fact, a clear stream burbled out from its course down the long, lazy mountainside.

He'd picketed and hobbled King there, and the horse was nosing out the best of the long lush growth while they toiled not far away. They would camp there for the night. He'd hoped to have been able to scare up a rabbit or small deer by now, but there'd been no time.

Still, he'd seen sign of rabbits in the rocks nearby, with little critter trails here and there. With any luck, he'd be able to provide some meat for them for that night's meal. He would have to be the one to stand watch, and if on his own he'd have skipped hunting, made do with the provisions the old man had kindly given him, then ridden out early.

But Penny was half-starved and had eaten without compunction everything he'd offered her. He could well stand to skip eating much for a few days, but he was afraid, given how thin she was, that she might not have lasted much longer.

As if summoned by his thoughts, Penny walked over to him, dry-eyed.

"Been talking with Pap. Told him I'd say goodbye before we light out in the morning from the campsite yonder. But I'm all cried out just now."

"Are you as tired as I am?"

"You bet," she said, sounding to Regis more like an old ranch hand than a girl that, if he had to guess, since he'd not yet asked her age, he'd put at about sixteen or seventeen.

He offered a slight smile. "All right, then. Let's figure out a fire and food. Maybe you could brew up coffee while I try to scare up a rabbit or two?"

"I can cook anything you care to bring to camp. And that's no lie."

Regis smiled, glad to hear she seemed, if not chipper, at least more relaxed and at peace, somehow. He mused on this as he left her tending the fire and scouted past the spots he'd scouted earlier, when they'd arrived there. He wanted to make certain there weren't sign of those brutes who'd killed her father.

Were they the same men who savaged his herd and men so many weeks back? The direction they traveled likely didn't mean a thing, as when he'd seen them, they'd been eyeing his herd from the northeast and east, and perhaps they had drifted on over to other directions, roving the region in search of victims with easy pickings.

But why kill? Wasn't thieving enough for these beasts?

He realized he was walking without paying attention, a definite poor choice, especially when so much depended on him, including a young girl.

He took cold comfort in the fact that he'd seen no sign of horses or men on their ride here, and so far, no sign anywhere else close by this spot. The only hint he'd seen of others had been the unmistakable sign of a herd of cattle being driven northward. Had to be his.

And from the looks of things, the somewhat fresh dung piles mostly, as well as the tracks of horses and even a wagon keeping pace along the eastern edge of the herd, he was closing in on them.

Until he'd met the girl, Regis had been certain he would catch up with them, perhaps within hours. But he had been forced to admit he was not much for tracking, or at least guessing elapsed time by reading the signs such as dung and hoofprints, boot prints, and wagon tracks. But he was still closer to the herd than he had been back in Dennerville. Maybe they'd catch up tomorrow.

A quick movement, a shadow and little more, flicked at the edge of his right-side vision. He seized in place. Long experience kept him from moving. He'd likely spooked whatever it was, and he hoped it was not a snake.

He did not mind admitting he feared them, especially rattlers. And unfortunately, they were thick on the ground back home at Royle Ranch. And his brother, Shep, chose that moment to pop into his head.

One of the kid's favorite things to say, and likely only when Regis was around to annoy, was calling the spread "Toil Ranch." And while Regis had to admit it was funny precisely because it was so true, it had irked him to hear it. And to see the reaction it drew from the men.

Heck, he knew it was a whole lot of work for little reward, especially in the early days. But they were beginning to see the purple light of dawn after the long dark night of a whole lot of toil.

And if they made it back—no, *when* they made it back, with the cash from selling the herd—things were going to be a whole lot better. Lean, to be sure, and for quite some years into the future, but better for all involved.

Regis held his stiff pose, waiting to see if whatever had caused the movement he'd seen, made a reappearance. His patience paid off. The tawny head of a big desert jackrabbit appeared from behind a low rock, three feet from the spot he'd seen movement.

He waited, held his breath while the animal sniffed, its head moving up, down, left, right, looking for, he supposed, something toothsome that he himself could not see. It seized in place, its head raised, one dark, round eye seemed fixed on him, though he had not moved so much as an eyelid.

Sweat slithered down his forehead and onto his eyelashes. It barred him for a moment from seeing the rabbit, but he had to blink. They were wily creatures, he well knew, because he'd shot many, as had his men. There never seemed to be fewer of them, though. He didn't like to take the life of anything for granted, for he well knew that the rabbit liked its own days and nights as much as he did his.

He'd even given a tongue lashing on this to a young ranch hand named Perez. The man had boasted of shooting anything that wasn't a man or a horse or a cow, dozens of creatures in one day, while in his employ.

Regis had blued the air with choice words, all intended to teach the fool a lesson about valuing life. He was fairly certain the other hands within hearing range had learned a little something. Perez, however, had collected his things and ridden off after breakfast the next day.

Regis didn't miss him.

The rabbit hopped once, twice into clear broadside view of Regis. It stood there, nose twitching, front legs up, held before it as if deciding something.

Sunlight shone through the tall, erect ears. Regis knew the time had come. He'd raised the rifle to his shoulder when he'd first seen movement, and now he sighted down the long barrel.

A headshot would be daring, since the body was larger, but he was close enough to risk it, and save himself the damage the bullet through any potential tasty meat might cause.

One heartbeat, two . . . his fingers tensed. So did the rabbit. It paused, held, turned a quarter turn toward him . . . it was going to bolt; Regis saw the muscles tighten.

He squeezed the trigger.

All the pretty silence of the calm afternoon evaporated with the speed of a bullet. And so did the rabbit's life. But with it, Regis took comfort in knowing that he'd be able to give the girl something nourishing to eat. At least a bit. There was not a large amount of meat on one of these big, bony critters—about like the girl herself, come to think of it—but it would be a start.

The sound would have frightened off others for a spell, so he retrieved it and carried it back to camp by the hind legs.

Penny had the fire going in good shape, not a big one, but large enough to boil coffee without wasting precious wood. She glanced at the rabbit and nodded once, as if approving. He held back a smile at the perfunctory attitude that seemed to have come over her.

She had the campsite arranged as if she'd been doing this for months. The ground about the small fire ring she'd built even looked to have been swept. And indeed, he saw a dry, bristly branch leaned to one side that looked just right to smooth the gravelly earth with.

"You going to stand there or hand over that skinny ol' rabbit?"

"Oh, no, I'm going to skin it out and then go look for another."

She sighed and shook her head. "Give it here and get on about your task, then. I have far too much to do, and you likely will tear this critter all up with those big hands of yours."

"I'll have you know," he said as he handed over the rabbit anyway, "that I have skinned out a fair number of animals, some of them rabbits, and they all came through just fine. Tasty, as I recall. You should meet our cook, Percy, speaking of tasty. He is about as good a cook as I have ever met."

She snorted and shook her head. "Ain't that just like a man, passing judgment on a thing he ain't suited to talk about any more than I am yammering about guns and whatever else it is men waste their time talking about."

He roved back on out toward the lucky rabbit spot, wondering if he'd bag another. He was pleased to hear the girl was coming around, and that she was a bit feisty, too. It suited her, somehow. Though she was a little surly. Reminded him of Percy, and he wondered how the men were faring.

He decided to save that line of thought for later, when he was going to sit up and do his best to stay alert and not to have too big a blaze going once dark settled in. Which it would in another hour or so. He didn't want to be visible too far off, should there be brigands about.

He'd have to check with the girl, see if she could shoot. If it came to a fight, he had a pistol and the rifle, and a sheath knife, which he'd left with her, and his Barlow folder in his pocket. After that, he'd be down to his fists.

Fine enough for him, and for fair fighting. But he'd not yet met someone who skulked and stole from others who ever considered putting up a fair fight. They all wanted to kill and be gone. Unless they could retreat with their cowardly tails tucked first.

He'd met enough damnable cowardly thieves in the last couple of years, cattle rustlers, and he and the Cattlemen's Consortium had run them aground, strung them up, shot them, or dragged them to justice.

He had always preferred the latter to taking the law into his own hands, but sometimes he'd had to take that hard road, and the looks on those men's faces would haunt him forever.

And then he saw another rabbit, and thoughts of the ranch and thieves faded. It hadn't seen him yet, so he cocked his rifle, raising it in one smooth motion.

A voice behind him said, "Hey, mister!"

Regis spun. It was Penny, and she'd said it in a loud whisper.

The rabbit, of course, had done what its kind did best in a dicey spot—it disappeared.

"What's wrong?" he said it in a perturbed growl. He'd been so close to bagging another rabbit for supper.

And then he saw her face—that fear from earlier had crept on her features again. This time, though it was not mixed with suspicion, at least, not directed at him. The girl was worried about something.

She held a long finger over her lips, turned, and motioned to him to follow her.

Regis did, and as they drew closer to their camp, he saw that she had pulled the pot from the fire, and had dragged away whatever wood was still unburned. She was trying not to make smoke.

Then she pointed back toward the plain they'd departed from to bury her father. Her finger aimed northeastward, and he followed it, and saw a line of riders, moving north, angling from eastward.

He saw now that the girl was right to be cautious. For something told him that the riders—there were at least a dozen, perhaps a dozen and a half—were up to no good. How he determined this, he could not say. But he'd been in enough suspicious situations in his life, both on the water and now, as a rancher mixing it up with border bandits, to know to trust his gut feeling.

And his gut was telling him he might have seen these men before. That they might well be the brutes who had attacked his herd and men weeks back. The ones who had seemed to think it was grand sport to kill, pillage, and torment them. And then leave.

And now, there they were—and if it was not them, it was someone else who might well want to cause them harm.

Regis and Penny both crouched, and watched the line of men perhaps a half mile off. They moved steadily and away from them. But if they sniffed smoke or looked their way, they might well follow their noses and make for this spot. And then Regis and Penny would likely have a fight on their hands.

Regis was surprised that they hadn't heard his shot; then Penny said, in a whisper, "I think I can smell 'em."

This sounded absurd, but he glanced at her, and she was sniffing like a dog at the light breeze coming at them from the direction of the men. Maybe there was something to that. Maybe the breeze helped to carry what to them would have been the sound of a far-off shot.

It could also be that there were others who were, even at that moment, sneaking up on them from some other direction, perhaps the south. It seemed far-fetched, but with such folks, you never knew.

He glanced over at the spot he'd picketed King. He didn't want to saddle the horse just yet. But if the men in the distance looked interested in making this way, he would. There was always the chance they could outrun the strangers if need be.

He didn't think they'd stand much of a chance were the men to surround them and lay siege, but they would run or fight if they had to.

"Can you shoot?"

Penny nodded, not taking her eyes from the line of men. "Only if I don't have to aim the cursed thing." This struck Regis as odd, but not uncommon. Most folks didn't use guns as part of their everyday lives, but then again, being out here on the range was not very ordinary.

They crouched lower, and Regis pulled out the pistol, ensuring it was loaded and showing her quickly how it worked. "Two hands," he said, nodding and looking her in the eye. She nodded back.

"Hope it don't come to that," she said, in a small voice, still eyeing the receding line of men.

He nodded. "Me, too."

The thing that bothered Regis most was that the men seemed to be making for the herd, or at least they were headed in that direction. And they would reach the herd before him. He glanced at the girl. Had he not been slowed by her, he might have . . . no, no, it was no good thinking that way.

He was truly glad to have been able to help her. She might have died alone out there. She'd been in the midst of a vast, barely traveled landscape. It might even be months before anyone else came along.

And there was no telling if they would be the sort with ill intent in mind. Besides, she would have perished long before then, anyway. Alone and stuck under a riverbank, starving to death. The thought shivered him. It was no fate for anyone.

They waited like that, not daring to shift much less one of the men glance back and perhaps catch a glimpse of movement. Finally, the line of men evaporated from sight.

Regis stood and stretched, eyeing in all directions, just in case. "I think we can risk a small fire again. But you did well in quelling the smoke."

"I think it was them who took Pap," she said, bustling about the camp once more.

"What makes you say so?"

"My gut. And I felt like I could smell them. They were rank, not the sort to wash themselves."

Regis didn't dare remind her that she had been much the same. But Penny's excuse was not one of wishing to remain slovenly.

The evening passed without incident. The girl slept soundly, and Regis reasoned that perhaps she felt at ease for the first time in a long time. He hoped so.

As for him, sleep tempted him over and over, and sometime in the long, small hours, it won the battle, and his chin met his chest. How long he slept, he did not know. Nor did he know what it was that woke him. But wake he did, with a start and a quick intake of breath.

His eyes popped open wide, and he held his pose, still leaning seated against a boulder, facing the direction those men had taken. From his spot, he was able to remain somewhat concealed and still see most of the camp, the girl, and the tucked-away spot King occupied, seemingly contented.

The sky had begun to purple—the surest sign of dawn—and Regis felt as rested as he was going to get. Enough so that he wanted to make an early start. If he got the girl up and making coffee, he could ready the rest, and they could ride by the time there was enough light to see ahead.

A gnawing feeling in his gut, as if a small, spiny critter churned in there, told him those men would come upon the herd soon. If they were the first band his crew had a run-in with, it wouldn't be a good meeting.

Perhaps he could put up a fight from the rear, though he was uncertain how much damage he could inflict. But that herd was his, every head hard won, and those men and the folks back on the ranch all depended on the sale of the cattle. Depended on him. And so he would fight to whatever end to see that those rogues didn't succeed in whatever their intent was.

He stood and stretched and worked out the inevitable kinks that come with sleeping sitting up leaned against a rock all night.

"Hey, mister."

Even before he turned, Regis smiled. "I told you, my name is Regis."

"Odd name, that. *Mister* suits you better."

"Have it your way. You sleep okay?"

"Sure I did. Like a felled log. I appreciate it, but you should have woke me to help with watch."

"No, it's all right. What do you say to an early start?"

"Good to me. We have time for coffee?"

Regis smiled. "There's always time for coffee."

"It sure was good last night," she said, preparing the fire. "I got me a taste for coffee as a child. Then when me and Pap took to the trail, seems we didn't never have enough money for such things."

"Well, once we make it to the herd, you can have all the coffee you want. Percy always lays in plenty of it."

"Suits me just fine," she said.

In a while, they were sipping hot coffee and nibbling hard tack.

King drank his fill at the little stream, and though he had lost weight, he didn't seem ravenous for a feed. "He can carry us both early on; then I'll hop down and spell him."

"I can walk, too, you know." Penny eyed Regis in the waning dark.

"Right. We'll take turns spelling him. But we have to make tracks—those men are headed in the same direction as the herd."

"Which is also our direction," she said, looking northward.

"Yes. l won't know what to do about it until we get closer."

"That's like what Pap always said—you can't cross a bridge until you get to it."

"Wise man, your Pap."

"If he was, we'd have stayed on the farm in Missouri."

"Ah, so that's where you're from."

But she'd grown silent, and Regis didn't want to pry anything more from her.

Soon enough, they finished and, while he cooled the pot in the stream water and filled the waterskins, she broke camp. He brought water to drown the meager embers well.

"I'll finish up here," he said. "Why don't you say your goodbyes to your father."

"Yeah, I reckon there's no point in putting it off. Only slow us down." She walked off toward the grave, and he mused on the girl and her situation.

With any luck, they'd make it to the herd without incident, and then they could find her a situation somewhere, if that suited her. But there was time to worry about that later.

He still felt bad about not marking her father's grave. He'd volunteered to carve the man's name into a thick branch. He figured they could lash a cross piece and plant it atop the mound. But she'd said no, that wasn't what her Pap would want. He'd want them to use the precious wood for a fire instead.

"Besides," she'd said. "He knew who he was, and I know who he was, and nobody else does, so marking his name there won't change a thing. He's gone and beyond caring. I prefer to recall the good times we had. And there were some of those, to be sure."

Regis thought her response was logical and sound, and not a whit sentimental. It was moments such as this that led him to believe she was older than he had first suspected.

"All right, Regis," she said, returning to the camp and not looking at him.

He wondered why she used his name and not *mister*, but it mattered little. As long as she was satisfied with her visit to Pap's grave.

He thought perhaps her eyes were a bit moist. "You're sure now? We have time if you want to spend more at his grave."

"Nope. He can't hear me any better under them rocks than he can in my own head, which is where he'll live on, so I expect I can talk with Pap most any time."

"Okay, then," said Regis, eyebrows raised. "Here we go."

And they mounted up and rode northward.

Chapter 28

Bone and Jervis hugged tight to the trail the banditos left, easy enough to pick out, as the rogues apparently had no desire to travel light or disguise their tracks. That told Bone that they were unafraid.

The only other thing he learned in tailing them all that way down the southeast border of Texas was that, for all their devil-may-care attitudes, the bandits were not moseying, but moving along at a steady clip. Almost as if they had an appointment to keep.

Past midday of the day after they found the dead man, they held up in the half shade of a crag of rocky overhang. Bone scouted, while Jervis watered the horses.

The elder ranger returned and swigged from his canteen.

"See anything?" said Jervis.

"Plenty of sun and brittle grass and such. And hoofprints, sure, but no sign of the killers."

"One good thing, at least—we haven't come across any bodies in the last day."

"Small blessings," said Bone, with a wry smile.

They came upon a low, but running stream later in the day. There was ample sign of those they were trailing, and it was possible, thought Bone, that he recognized the place. It was also possible that they were gaining on the bandit gang. The tracks looked fresher; the horse dung seemed the same.

"You think they're on to us?" said Jervis, looking southward.

"Hard to say. If I was them, I'd know we were back here." Jervis nodded. "But you're you."

"So far," said Bone, and then a bullet sizzled in.

Both men dropped down. "Guess that answers your question," said Bone. He'd seen a quick cloud of smoke rise up far to the south-southwest.

"What's the plan, then?"

"Jervis, if I knew that, I'd be a whole lot smarter than I am. Just know I'm trying to keep from getting myself sniped in the head. But now that you mention it, I do have a plan. Or at least a good idea of what they're up to and where they're headed."

"It involves skirting to the west. I don't think they're going to go too much farther in that direction, anyway."

"What makes you say that?"

"Because I know where they're headed. And if I'm right, and I know I am, well, it'll take them right back to where they started, in a manner of speaking. Come on; I'll fill you in as we ride."

They mounted up and cut westward, riding at a steadier clip than they had, now that they weren't trying to maintain a healthy distance between them and a sizable gang of bandits.

Half an hour, and much talking, later, Bone said, "And that, my friend, is why we have to get to the Royle Ranch before they do. At least the ranch proper. Especially since Regis is out on the trail with his herd. I'm hoping it has all gone well for him, and with any luck, he'll be back soon with full pockets."

They rode for the remainder of that day, and by the time they made it to their destination, Royle Ranch, both men and their three horses were more than ready to retire for the night.

Bone recognized the tall woman in black from a distance. Or

rather, he guessed who she was, based on Regis's vague, quick description of her. She also had that unnamable quality that seemed to radiate from her. An air of someone who is in charge of a situation, even if she's not fully aware of what the situation is.

He also admitted to himself that he could as easily be full of beans about her. But he didn't think so.

She stood with her back to him, her hands on her hips. Even from his distance of one hundred or so feet, Bone saw that she heard or sensed their approach. She spun, already bending low and making to dart to the cover of a close-by rick of hay. He reined up, held up a hand, and he and Jervis slowed. He held the hand up higher. "Ma'am? Texas Rangers!"

That slowed her. She straightened and stood sideways to them, glancing their way but keeping herself turned. Odd behavior, noticed Bone. Perhaps someone was hiding behind the hay?

"Jervis," said Bone, out of the side of his mouth. "Don't draw yet. We want to keep this friendly. But if there's somebody hiding out there, somebody she might be looking over at, we have to be ready."

"So you're saying don't do anything, but do something. Right?"

"That's about it, yeah. You're catching on."

When they were about thirty feet from her, they reined up. She walked about six feet closer. "You are Bone McGraw?" she said, still not quite facing them.

"I am. Good guess, ma'am."

"Regis has talked much of you."

"Well, I hope some of it was flattering."

"One or two points," she said, without a trace of a smile.

"And I'm going to guess that you are Señorita Valdez."

"We have not met."

"No," he said. "But I am acquainted with your sister."

"Ah, yes, the wayward lamb."

"Hardly a lamb, ma'am. Oh, this here's my associate, Ranger Jervis Latham."

Jervis nodded and touched his hat brim. "Ma'am."

"Welcome, both of you, to this ranch. What brings you here?"

"We were trailing border bandits east of here, and if they are who I think they are, they will likely be making for the ranch very soon."

"You mean you think it is my sister and her men?"

Bone's eyebrows rose. "Well, yes . . . have you seen them?"

"No—well, perhaps. We have been attacked. Several times in the past few weeks. At first, we did not know who it was, but then Cormac Delany brought word that he'd heard in Brownsville that my sister, Tomasina, was still alive, and that she had been threatening to take back the family land. This place." She spread her arms wide. "And that she had gathered men to help her, many of her old gang, and new men, too."

Bone nodded. "That works about with what we found out in Corpus Christi. We've been trailing them and the trail of their dead . . . well, suffice it to say, I don't think she or her men will be expecting a tea party when they arrive."

A broad-shouldered, red-faced, slightly chubby young man walked toward them from the direction of the nearest barn. "And they won't get one!" he shouted, grinning and holding up a shotgun. "Bone, you old devil! Good to see you! You come back to work your fingers to the nub for the enjoyment of it, and little else?"

He walked abreast of Marietta Valdez, and his smiled slipped a little. "Sorry, ma'am. We're, uh, old friends."

"I gathered that. And no need to apologize to me, Mr. Tuttle."

"Mr. Tuttle, huh?" said Bone, dismounting. "You are getting all fancy now that you're the ranch foreman!"

"How'd you know?" said Tut, eyeing Jervis, who had also dismounted and led his horse and the pack horse closer.

As all three men advanced, Marietta Valdez quietly backed away. Bone noticed she still hadn't turned to face them fully, but as he walked closer, he saw part of her face was perhaps scarred. Or maybe it was in shadow.

Then he recalled the story he'd been told. Who by? Cormac? Regis? Something about this lost Valdez daughter being holed up for years in a convent because she'd been kicked as a child by a horse, a bad accident and one that had disfigured her. It certainly hadn't done most of her face, nor her slender body, any harm.

Even as he thought it, he reddened, and felt guilty, because his thoughts flicked to Margaret and her lovely, homey smile. He could not wait to be back in her arms.

"Oh," said Bone. "Rangers always know what's going on. Don't you worry." He tapped his long nose. "We have our ways. And speaking of rangers, Tut, meet my friend, and fellow Ranger, Jervis Latham. Jervis, my old friend, John Tuttle."

The men shook hands and exchanged nods. "Friends call me Tut," said the foreman.

"And where does that leave me?" said Jervis, half smiling.

"It leaves you calling him Tut. Now, if you two young cocks of the walk don't mind, I need to talk with Señorita Valdez a moment. Tut, maybe you could show Jervis the stable. Our mounts are just about done in."

"You bet," said Tut, taking the reins of Bone's horse. "We'll get the horses seen to," said Tut to Jervis. "Then we'll see about a cup of hot coffee, if you'd like."

"Oh, there's never a bad time for a cup of coffee, Tut."

They chuckled and talked as they made their way to the barn.

"Miss Valdez, I don't suppose you've had any word from Regis, or the herd?"

She shook her head.

The next morning, three children ran to the ranch proper from the little ranch village that had been attacked so recently. Two of the youngsters were boys, both crying and barely able to keep up with the third, a girl a little older, and though she had moist eyes, she was stern-faced and stood in the midst of the ranch, shouting in a clear, loud voice, "Señora! Señora!"

Bone and Jervis, Tut, and three ranch hands, who had all been in varying stages of getting ready for the day, some of them just arrived from night duties patrolling the southern and eastern flanks of the ranch lands, made it out to the yard just as Marietta Valdez reached the child.

The tall woman bent low and held the girl by both shoulders; the two little boys held back, but with a quick beckoning hand by the tall woman in black, they hurried to her and clung to her skirts.

She listened to them, nodded, and then turned them over to the care of a woman who had hustled after them. It was their mother. The two women exchanged more words, and then Marietta turned to Bone.

"It seems you were correct, Mr. McGraw. The children and their mother told me that their men and some of the other ranch workers were working in the fields early, to avoid the heat of later in the day, when they saw dust rising to the south—"

Before she could continue, erratic snapping sounds came to them from the east.

"Gunfire!" growled Bone, cursing himself for daring to sleep the second half of the night. He'd been spelled by two vaqueros who, despite his insistence, had not seemed to want to take seriously the threat of the imminent attack by the Valdez gang.

Nonetheless, he had ridden back to the ranch proper to crawl into a bunk for a few hours of rest he'd been desperate for.

Jervis had had an even longer night and had only ridden in less than an hour before the children arrived with their news.

And now it looked like not one of them was going to get any rest.

"I am worried, Mr. McGraw, for Cormac Delany."

"Cormac? Why? Isn't he in Brownsville?"

She nodded. "But he had been dividing his time between there and here to help at the ranch, often bringing some of his dock workers here to help for days at a time."

"Good man. But why are you worried?"

"Because he is due to arrive today."

"And he comes from eastward," said Bone, nodding. "I'll ride the road to see if I can't intercept him, provide some sort of escort. When does he usually get here?"

"He travels early, so as to be of use during the day he arrives."

"Sounds like Cormac. Okay, then, I'd better get to it." He bolted for the bunkhouse.

Chapter 29

By Ferg's reckoning, with help from Regis's little notebook, they were but a week, perhaps less, from reaching Schiller. Indeed, they had seen more folks in the past few days than they had seen since they left Dennerville, nearly two weeks before.

"We get these dogies past that range and across the valley beyond, and we'll have her licked," he said to the men at the campfire. The nods and smiles and murmurs made him feel good. They might just make it through without any more headache.

That didn't mean they were still keeping a sharp eyes on all the horizons. So close, they all thought, yet so very far. They were also all thinking that if they were going to see Regis Royle again, it had to be soon. Each man missed the boss, though they might be hard-pressed to say why, considering he had a reputation among them, mostly earned back at the ranch, as a hard-nose and someone difficult to get along with.

Of course, they knew the reason for that was that he was the boss, and had a whole lot of headache to contend with. But taking Benny and Cyril's place in jail back in Dennerville went a long way with all the men, even if they knew Regis had mostly done it so as to keep the herd moving.

Nonetheless, he had earned a big old wad of respect for it. And now they were all not a little worried that somehow the boss's plan did not work out, and that he might well be stuck in Dennerville's jail. Or worse.

Benny and Cyril brought this up to Fergus and Percy, who had already talked about this possibility. The two lead men had agreed that since they would be cutting pretty much the same trail back to Texas, if Regis hadn't caught up to them, they would slip back into Dennerville and investigate. Somehow.

The rogue Indians were spotted about three of the afternoon clock that same day Fergus had shared his suspected timetable with the boys. And it all happened much as it had that first day, what felt like years before, back on the trail, when they'd first spied the strangers skylined along a ridge.

This time, the ridge was roughly to the south-southeast behind them, and this time they did not have the Greek's excellent eyesight or seeming knowledge of all things. But somehow, each man knew these were the very same rogues who had attacked them in the night, killing and wounding without reason.

The men were justifiably afraid, but more than that, they were angry, weary, wary, and they vowed to fight the demons with everything they had. So close, they thought, armed and droving, and waiting. So close and yet . . .

And wouldn't you know it? It looked like the bandits were going to wait them out and attack once more in the night. Since the bandits clearly didn't care if they were seen, it was probable they also expected the men to take precautions. Fear and anger warred for room on each man's face, but determination won out.

Since they had so few men, Fergus and Percy had decided to split them into two groups. The best cattle wranglers would continue to work the herd, along with Percy and his wagon, keeping the cattle moving, and more difficult to peel away off into the hills by the bandits and their expected stampeding tactics. The rest of the men would hug the southeastern, southern, and southwestern edges of the herd, bristling outward with guns.

And then, about four o'clock in the afternoon, the bandits attacked. It happened swiftly, and no one knew quite how they managed to creep so close without being seen, but there they were. They emerged, spread out in a long line from the southeast, up over a low rise. As they advanced on the men and the herd, they spread out and fired, riding harder with each dust-boiling step, as if they had an unlimited supply of bullets.

They howled and shrieked and growled and yipped, and not a single mouthy utterance deterred the Royle Ranch men from their task. Fergus had warned the men that they must not be unnerved by whatever these attacking fools might do or say or sound like or look like. They were to shoot to kill, no prisoners, no kindnesses to be shown. For they would receive none themselves.

He told them to do anything they needed to—hide behind their horses, behind the random scatter of boulders, sparse clots of rabbit brush, anything they might find.

The fighting came hot and fast. A number of the killers and thieves cut wide and came straight at the herd from up high on the eastern side, straight at Percy. But the surly cook had expected this maneuver and risked sending two men ahead, northward.

They showed up at just the right moment, hammering at the unsuspecting bandits hard from the north, riding straight at them and laying low all but two of the split-away group. The brutes never managed to get close enough to the men or the hustling herd to do any damage.

Back at Percy's wagon, he spied movement from behind, to his right. Something was emerging from behind the boulder that he'd checked not five minutes before, as he knew it might well conceal a man. There had been no one there, but now . . . now he saw, rising into sight, and moving toward him and the wagon fast, the very man he'd held as prisoner weeks before.

"What? You!" growled Percy, clawing for his sidearm. It wasn't there in his holster. No time to wonder where he'd left it, as the past few minutes had been filled with all manner of hasty activity.

He backed up, even as the growling, bald, scar-headed, shirt-less brute advanced on him, a leer pulling his filthy face wide.

Percy made it to the front of the wagon and reached into the boot well. His hands closed around the hickory stock of the sawed-off single-barrel shotgun he kept there. And unlike his missing pistol, he knew this savage weapon was loaded.

He jerked it down as the man halted, not ten feet behind the wagon, about ten feet before the big boulder.

"No sense of gratitude!" growled Percy as he leveled his shot-gun on the man who had been his prisoner.

The little brute had not changed a smidgin. His bald head was still covered in odd scars, and he was still shirtless. But now he had a revolver, and it was aimed, just below his leering smile, at Percy.

Percy tugged the shotgun's trigger, and the gun boomed. At nearly the same time, his former prisoner whipped backward and slammed into the edge of a boulder before sagging to the ground. His limbs twitched and jerked, and then he lay still.

"And I gave you biscuits!" growled the surly cook.

"What can I do to help?" said a voice beside him.

Percy spun, crouching low and ready to squeeze the gun's trig-ger again. But he'd had no chance to load in a fresh shell.

The creature before him was a thin young woman with long black hair trailing out from beneath a homely, misshapen slouch hat. She was wearing a far-too-large men's shirt over a set of what appeared to be far-too-large longhandles. But it was her face he noticed, a face for some reason he could not look away from.

"Hey! Mister! You Percy?" said the face.

"Uh-huh."

"Well, wake up, mister! Regis sent me, said for me to stick with you!"

A volley of three shots slammed in, peppering the wagon's

side and tailgate and spraying glass from a hit bottle. That jerked Percy from his daze. "Regis? You . . . you're here with him? He made it?" Percy spun low and gazed about them.

"Yep, now you going to let me help or what?"

"Where is he?"

"Southward, said he was going to put the squeeze on them from the rear and that you and somebody named Fergus should tell the boys so he doesn't get shot!"

Percy looked at her and shook his head in disbelief. "You . . . how did you get here?"

She shook her own head at him. "What ails you, man?" She smacked her legs. "I run up here from where he's taking potshots at the Injuns!"

"Okay, okay." Percy pointed at her. "Don't move. I've got another gun in here. Can you shoot?"

"Yes, yes; what is it with you men? You think because I'm a woman, I can't shoot?"

"No, I didn't mean that. I . . . it's because you're young-looking. And pretty and all . . ." He had no idea why he said that, but it was too late. Even in the midst of the battle, he saw her try to kill the small smile that crept on her blushing face.

"I can shoot, I tell you!" She said it far too loud, as if making up for what he had said. "And I'm no child—I'll be eighteen before I'm seventeen again!"

"Okay, then," he said, blushing himself as he rummaged for Chancy's spare gun rig. They'd elected to keep the dead boy's weapons, a prudent move as they had found on more than one occasion.

"Here," he said, thrusting the loaded gun belt to her. "It's all oiled and ready to go. I cleaned it myself."

She strapped it on. "You don't say."

Percy thought maybe she'd rolled her eyes. He thumbed in a fresh shell.

She said, "So Regis told me you're the cook, huh?"

He nodded, squinting toward where the shots had come from. "Me, too," she said. "Been cooking since before I could walk."

He looked at her as if she had just said she ate spiders for breakfast.

"Well, it's true," she said; then without warning, she closed one eye, held up the revolver with both hands, and let go a shot.

Percy watched her face the entire time, especially how she'd stuck the tip of her tongue out between her teeth.

"Told you," she said, smiling. "I reckon that one was for Pap!"

Back on the southern edge, the fighting was hotter and more desperate from the start, and Fergus saw one of their men—Benito, he thought it was—shriek from a shot and whip his arms skyward, then topple from his startled mount.

The man landed in a boil of dust, and Fergus could see no more after that. He spun back to the fight and found he was faced with a hard-eyed, nut-brown man wearing a soiled, once-white flowing shirt ripped open to the waist and cinched with a wide brown leather belt.

He wore a red sash wrapped about his head, and his mouth wore a cold sneer. He rode a lunging brown mount of significant size and rode bareback.

But what Fergus found odd was that the man did not utter a sound as he raced forward. He carried a large, heavy-looking rifle, perhaps a Sharps, he could not be certain. It was tucked beneath the man's right armpit, wedged tight, and he jammed the reins between his large white teeth. Then, with his left arm, he balanced the cumbersome weapon by the forestock.

He seemed to Fergus so certain of himself that for a moment, Fergus was unsettled, fear blooming in his breast. Did the man somehow suspect that Fergus's own gun would fail him? He gave in to this odd feeling for but a few moments, long enough for the man to close in and raise the rifle enough to sight along its brute barrel.

Then the seasoned cowboy shook off the foolish jitters the man had unnerved him with and, in a slick motion born of years of practice, Fergus raised his own rifle, sighted, and sent a bullet at the leering brute's head.

The renegade's rifle boomed, a thunderclap of sound and menace that whipped the rifle barrel skyward. The bullet it sent whistled a yard above Fergus's hat. But the cowboy's bullet drove like a lead fist straight into the raider's forehead, coring a tunnel as it punched deep, blooming flesh, blood, bone, and brain skyward in a cloud of pink spray.

As in the last few moments of his life, so in death the bandit uttered no sound, save for the slamming of his body against the hard-packed earth.

Fergus kept riding forward, the man's startled horse avoiding him and his mount by jerking hard to its left and galloping away.

Fergus looked down at the head-shot man and saw the big rifle in the dirt some yards back. He had half a mind to retrieve it, but the sudden sound of hard galloping and high-pitched shouts pulled his gaze up once more.

A rider, bald-headed and wearing long, drooping mustaches, was riding hard at him and barking and yipping. Apart from the mustaches, he reminded Fergus of the man Percy had had as a prisoner. He was certain that rogue had somehow lived and was now among these men attacking them once more.

This time, the enemy had a jump on him and had already leveled down. But he was using a pistol and, as with the last man's big buffalo gun, this weapon looked to be heavy and older. That didn't mean it was any less deadly, but it did slow him down a smidgin. It also looked as if it was going to be less accurate.

Any second now, thought Fergus, jerking his own rifle back into action, and he'd find out just how accurate his foe's gun might be.

In mid-shriek, the bald man fell off his horse, helped by a bullet that shoved at him hard from his left side. He hit the ground, rolled, and hunched up, his head to the ground, wobbling on his knees. A gout of blood sluiced from his side. In moments, he fell over and lay there in the dust, twitching and writhing.

Fergus looked to where the shot had come and saw something, or rather someone, that confused the heck out of him. If he was correct, it was someone he had long wanted to see come riding up, but had about given up hope of seeing the man again any time soon.

"Regis?" he said, in a voice audible only to himself. But the man who'd let loose the helpful shot had already heeled his mount hard and rode toward a clot of three attackers who were attempting to cut southwestward around Fergus, then on up toward the herd.

Fergus saw him ride and, stunned for a moment, could only wonder if it was the man he thought it might be.

The big rider on the big black horse cut wide, not sparing the horse a bit. He wielded his rifle, lodged under his left wing, and his revolver held in a big ham-sized right hand, with deadly ease and laid low the unsuspecting attackers, one at a time. The first two went, clueless, as they thundered toward the herd, yipping and yapping.

The third, however, had caught sight of the big rider from the rear and jerked his horse hard to the left, then rode at his new attacker even as Fergus thundered at him from eastward. Fergus was in a position to drive a round at the man seconds before the big man, and it proved to be a good move.

The attacker did not see Fergus, as he was intent on doling out pain to the man who'd just shot his two friends; the man took the cowboy's surprise bullet as if he'd been waiting for it. The yipping rider screamed and fell to the right side of his saddle, but not off, for his boot fouled in the stirrup. He slammed to the earth, his head banging the hard earth in counterpoint to the horse's frantic stomps.

The big rider changed course and rode straight for Fergus.

The rangy cowboy had not gone two strides when Fergus saw

that it was indeed his boss, Regis Royle, and he'd ridden in just when they needed him.

"Good timing, Boss!"

Regis grinned and nodded. "Let's keep this hand going!"

"What about those behind?"

"None that I know of . . . alive, anyway." Regis nodded northward toward the herd, where the fight still played out in pockets. But so far strung apart had the bandits become that it was obvious to Regis and to Fergus that the Royle Ranch crew had the attackers on the run.

Each man nodded at this unspoken, but obvious to them, fact, and thundered forward, weapons drawn and cocked and nothing in mind but the intention to finish what the evildoers started.

They found Benito a half hour after the last shot was fired. He was alive, moaning, and appeared to have a broken shoulder from his tumble off the horse. He also sustained a wound in his lower right leg that bored clean through his meaty calf muscle.

Other than that, the Royle Ranch crew suffered a dead horse, two dead head of cattle, a few bruises, and one shallow cut from a close-in knife fight between Cyril and a fat Mexican fellow.

Percy and Cyril, who had each counted the brutes as they rode toward them, both swore that the Royle boys had wiped out all of the attackers. The unmoving forms strewn about the plain seemed to verify this notion. Regis and Fergus rode to each one, guns drawn, and made certain they were, to a man, well and truly dead.

And they were, save for one who was, without doubt, mortally wounded in the gut. He would take some time to die. He spat at them, then twitched and groaned in pain. They left him to his last task. Not before they unburdened him of his meager weapons, a pistol and a hatchet.

They did the same with the rest of the dead and hauled a decent stash of guns, gun belts, bullets, and knives back to Percy's wagon. They would divvy up the weapons later among the boys.

Much later, around the campfire, and with several small bottles of Percy's medicinal tincture passing around among the boys, Regis related his story, from Dennerville to the present, and with kindness and respect, folded in Penny's tale, as well.

For once, she seemed uncertain of herself and sat, blushing, not far from Regis, now clothed in a proper pair of trousers and a jacket, courtesy of Percy. Regis told of how her father had been hauled off by the very band of men they'd laid low that day.

Penny interrupted and said, "Me and Pap, we want to thank you all for taking care of this unfinished business. It means a whole lot." Then she fell silent again, looking small and thin as she stared at her drawn-up feet in the hand-me-down boots.

The boys were quiet then, a few nodded, and soon enough Percy cut in with a wry remark about how if nobody was going to bother to eat the beans and biscuits he'd made, he was going to dump it in a hole and call it a night.

"Beg your pardon," said Penny to the cook. "But it was me who made those beans while you were fussing like a hen with your biscuits. Honestly."

Instead of cackling the flustered sounds Percy would normally emit on being corrected in such a manner, Percy blushed himself and nodded. "Well now, that's true, that's true. And finer beans, I have not had." He nodded and looked around the circle, as if daring anyone to disagree. No one did.

When he realized he'd been cowed by the young, pretty newcomer, he blushed an even deeper shade of crimson. Then the boys made *ooh* and *aah* sounds, and somebody offered up a few rounds of smooching sounds, and Percy pointed his big wooden spoon around the group. "Anybody wants a clout, you let me know!"

The evening went on like this, with men spelling each other in watching the herd. Nobody grew too cocksure of themselves, however, because nobody knew for certain if there were other rogues out there, waiting in the dark to attack them. But they felt pretty certain they were in the clear.

The next morning, an especially tasty breakfast was served up by a less-than-surly Percy, surprising given that he slept not beside his wagon but some yards away. It turned out he'd rigged up the inside of the wagon, over which he'd raised its canvas tarpaulin covering and secured it tight, for Penny.

In turn, for the rest of the drive, she acted as his assistant in camp, and everyone agreed that it was a solid match of skills, and of tongues. The two cooks, Penny and Percy, sparred like game birds, but always with blushes and shy smiles.

As they broke camp that first morning following the fight, Regis shouted, "Onward to Schiller!" And they moved the herd northward, on the last leg of their journey, filled with the confidence of victors.

Chapter 30

Bone and Cormac heard shots from southwestward, the direction of the ranch, and then a shot whipped at them from south of the roadway. It pocked Cormac's light carriage. "Drive hard to the ranch!" shouted Bone. "I'll stay; deal with this one!"

"Are you certain? I can help!" Cormac held up his revolver.

"No. You can be of more use there. Marietta and the villagers will need a hand!"

"Okay, then. Good luck, Bone!"

The ranger nodded, but was already cutting back, angling Bub toward the low but sufficient cover of boulders along one stretch of the roadway. He jumped down out of the saddle and with haste lashed the reins about a stunty snag of bushes, then made his way, low-walking, to the rocks.

Another shot peeled close, kicking up dust a couple of feet before the boulders. Bone jerked low and peered around the right side.

Then he heard a hard galloping from a seldom-used north trail that also led to the ranch. It was a man dressed in dark blue, riding an Appaloosa fast toward him. Bone squinted, and as the man drew closer, Bone shook his head. "Can't be," he said.

"Shepley Royle?" bellowed Bone. "What on earth are you doing back in these parts?" He peeled off another shot southward.

"Hey, Bone! Fancy seeing you out here!"

Despite the situation, the droop-mustachioed Texas Ranger smiled over at the young soldier who had also left his horse back near Bub. "What is that getup you're wearing?"

Shep smiled back, but before he could reply, a shot spanged off the knee-height rocks before him. He ducked low and cranked a shot in the dead middle of the puff of smoke that rose up from the shooter.

Both men heard a strangled yelp and then silence.

"I'm in the US Army, Bone. Been escorting my sergeant and his wife and daughter, scouting the region for a base in Corpus Christi, of all places. He wanted his wife and daughter in a safe place for a spell, and we had been making for the home of some of their kin, but they'd moved on. So I thought of the Royle Ranch. Looks like I chose poorly."

Bone shrugged. "Been pretty good hereabouts, save for the usual run of border banditos lately. We'll get them."

"You will now that I'm here." Shep beamed as he said this, and Bone shook his head. "Same old Shep."

"Sort of," said the younger man. "But I like to think I've changed a little, too."

"Oh, I don't doubt that. Why, just look at the way you dress nowadays. Downright spiffy."

"How've you been?" Shep catwalked over and gave the ranger a goofy, affectionate hug. Bone chuckled and patted the boy on the shoulder. "All right now, I can't risk getting shot, son! Too much bubbling on the stovetop these days."

"Tell me all about it, Bone! Hey, where's Regis?"

They chatted for a few more minutes; then, sensing there was nobody else out there, they dropped back, fetched their mounts, and rode to the ranch proper, where they still heard random shots peppering the air.

"Listen, Shep, there's something you should know." Bone gave the younger man the hard stare.

"Oh boy, what's Regis done now?"

"No, not him, not really. It's that Valdez woman."

"Oh." Shep rubbed his tunic and grimaced, recalling the knifing Tomasina Valdez had given him in an alley on his eighteenth birthday. She'd left him for dead, and only by some wonder of wonders had he pulled through.

"Heck, Bone, I imagine she is good and dead by now." Shep remembered how aged and haggard and pathetic the once-pretty Tomasina had been when he'd seen her in the alley that night.

"Well, she isn't dead, and she's running the jackals who've been terrorizing the border. They're the reason the Rangers are stretched so tight. So you tell your sergeant that if he wants to do something useful, he found the right place."

"Not dead?" said Shep. "Oh, my word."

"Yeah, but that's not all. There's another one."

"Another what?"

"Valdez woman."

"What?"

"Yep. But this one's older, the true heiress. Marietta's her name, and she's a keeper. Good lady."

"Huh, who knew?" said Shep. "I leave home for a spell and look what happens."

"That's not all."

"Now what?"

"She and your brother, well, they're what you might call, pals."

"Pals?"

"Yeah. You know," said Bone, dragging a hand over his chin and hurrying Bub along as more shots cracked off. "Fond of each other."

"What?" said Shep, heeling his mount to catch up. "What are you telling me, Bone?"

But the Ranger was already far ahead, making quick time toward Royle Ranch proper.

"It's unbelievable," said Shep to himself, not knowing whether to grin or shake his head. So he did both.

Shep arrived at the southwestern edge of the ranch proper in time to see a tall woman in a long black dress and a black hat, low-crowned and wide-brimmed, standing with her hands on her hips.

Across from her, standing in the midst of four fallen bodies of who were likely her pathetic bandits, one of which still twitched and jerked, stood a smaller woman, but clad in a soiled once-white long skirt and a leather vest over a raggy tunic.

Somehow Shep knew it was Tomasina Valdez. And he also realized she was a poor version of her former self. Her hair, once lustrous and shiny and black, now hung limp and dull gray. Her face, likewise, was a sagged, wrinkled thing. Her eyes were reddened and wet, and she walked one, two steps forward with a limp, toward the other woman.

Beyond the two women, closer in by the near stable and cook shack, Shep saw Bone, and beside him, a lanky black man wearing a badge on his vest. Another Ranger? Emerging from behind buildings walked other armed men and women.

Among them were Sergeant Cowley, Cormac Delany, Tut, and a small handful of other ranch men; as well as Tut's sweetie, the school teacher, Belinda; and Mrs. Cowley and Philomena.

These three women were with other women, villagers, all wrangling the small herd of Mexican village children. They stayed well back, especially as Tut waved them all back and pointed fingers at them to do what he told them.

Only Shep remained on the far side of this scene, with the two Valdez sisters in the midst of it all. He had not been seen by the two women yet, so he stayed put.

Then Tomasina Valdez spoke. "Sister Marietta!" Her voice, a ragged, wet thing, laughed, finding her own comment humorous. Nobody else did. "I see you have yourself a cozy life here, huh? I tell you, these Royle people, they are devils, killers, thieves!" Her voice rose and trembled.

The tall woman in black still stood unmoving, with her hands on her waist. Finally, she said, "Tomasina, sister. It does not have to be this way. You are unwell, and your men are all but dead. Give up this fight. Let me get you help. The sisters at the convent can help you."

Tomasina snorted. "You fool! Nobody can help me! Don't you see that?"

Marietta shook her head. "No, sister. I do not see that. And I refuse to believe it." She held up an arm and walked slowly toward Tomasina as one might toward a growling dog, her hand outstretched. "Come, let us make amends. Before it is too late."

Tomasina watched her sister from beneath her hooded eyes, then seemed to sag as a pent-up breath left her. "Perhaps you are right . . . sister." She raised her arms and walked forward, as if to hug the tall woman in black.

Shep bristled and tensed, ever watchful. As the gap between the two women lessened, he saw something that peeled his eyes wide. "No!" he shouted and, in a blur of a motion, he aimed and fired his revolver.

But it was not the only shot to go off.

Both women dropped to the dusty earth.

Shep ran to them, as did others from the ranch side. Cormac reached the tall woman first. "Marietta!" he shouted, turning her over. She raised an arm just as a stout Mexican woman bustled to Cormac's side and nudged him out of the way. "Cormac, love, help me to carry her."

They made to lift her, but she said, "No, no, I am fine. I am not shot. I . . ."

But though she stood, they realized she was wrong. She had been shot, but only grazed on her left shoulder. The red blood flowed down her dress. "Ah," she said, "it is time I find a new color anyway."

Then her eyes widened. "Tomasina!" She bent to her sister's side, but the other woman would never again draw breath.

Marietta wept in silence, cradling her dead sister in her lap, stroking her greasy, lank, gray hair. "So young, so angry," she said. "Be at peace now, *mi hermana*."

She looked up, and her gaze caught Shep's eye. He stood above her, his revolver still in his hand, but hung limp now at his side. "I'm . . . I'm so sorry, but . . ." He nodded toward Tomasina, and everyone saw then what he had seen: the evil woman had slicked out a small, two-shot hide-out gun.

"Even though I saw it, she beat me to it. She shot you, but I had no choice."

"You did have a choice," said Marietta. Then she offered him a slight smile. "And I am glad that you chose as you did, Shepley Royle."

Chapter 31

One month later

Regis looked across the gaily decorated yard of Royle Ranch proper at the assembled folks, all the people he loved most in the world, all there at once, alive and well. And for the first time in Regis Royle's life, he felt as if he were the grand old gentleman, holding court. Here were all his dear ones.

Of course, he knew he was no old-timer, not by a long shot, but still, it was a fine feeling to see all those he loved, each one he'd thought for a time that he'd never again see in this life. And yet here they all were. It warmed him like no double-dose of Scotch whiskey could.

There, talking with Tut and Belinda, his expecting wife, Percy and Penny held hands and bickered, smiling at each other. And not far away, Bone and Margaret chatted with Bone's Ranger friend, Jervis. There was something odd about Bone and Margaret today, thought Regis. They looked especially happy. He'd have to talk with them more later.

"Yes, that's true," said Jervis to Bone. "I have volunteered to bring Delia—that'd be Rick Smithers's widow—and her daughter and son back to their little spread to tidy the graves, then fetch their things back here. Miss Valdez said that since it was her sister who caused the Smithers family all its grief, they should move on back to the ranch. I think she'll want to do that, but you know, it might be a while."

"Well, that's good to hear," said Bone, looking toward the widow and her two surviving youngsters, standing off to the side with some of the other chatting villagers.

The woman and her children were still saddened by the killings and the terrible mistreatment of them on the trail—everything that had happened to them at the hands of Tomasina and her banditos.

But in time, they might mend, and the Royle Ranch, with the village and school and good, honest work, was a fine place to find out.

"Those two children," said Bone to Jervis. "Will do well to have a man about them for a spell, I reckon. And Delia, too."

"Yes," said Jervis. "I reckon they might be able to use a little help about now."

"Just don't forget your oath, Jervis. The Texas Rangers can use all the good men they can get nowadays, especially seasoned fellows such as yourself."

Jervis smiled at the compliment. "Well, I look forward to working with you more, Bone."

"You'll have to do it on our ranch," said the cowboy, hugging his wife's shoulders. "For I don't plan on ever leaving it again."

"Never?" said Jervis.

"Nope. You drop by in about seven months or so, and I'll show you why."

Jervis's eyebrows rose as he saw the smiling Margaret's hand rub her belly lightly, holding Bone's beneath hers.

"No kidding? Oh, that is prime news, my friend." Jervis hugged Bone. "Prime news."

"Easy now, Jervis," said Bone, patting his friend lightly on the back. "I don't know what's got into folks lately; everybody's hugging everybody else." But as he said it, he smiled and winked at Margaret.

Shep walked over and caught Regis trading a smile with Marietta, twenty-five feet away. She was chatting with Cormac and Jimena.

The latter was a stout woman half Cormac's height who had her arm looped through his. He rested a hand atop hers as they talked with the others. No doubt about it, thought Regis, Cormac was looking mighty pleased today, for obvious reasons. Not to mention that the herd had brought in enough money to keep the ranch alive for a while yet.

But the better news were the lucrative shipping contracts Cormac had managed to land with the Army, largely because of the other man he was now talking with, Sergeant Cowley and his lovely wife. They were two people Regis bet himself he'd be seeing more of in the future.

Regis's gaze flicked back, as always, to his tall Marietta with her long, black hair, some of it hanging down across half her face. She noticed him and returned the smile.

He was pleased to note she was doing more of that these days. He also thought that in her new, light blue, flowered dress she had never looked finer, and he promised himself he would tell her so later.

"I'm sorry again about the shooting, Regis."

"Sorry?" said the big man. "You saved the life of my fiancée. I owe you so much, Shep. More than I can tell you."

"No way. No more competitions between us, Regis. We're even. We're always even."

A few silent moments passed; then Shep clouted his big brother on the arm and smirked. "Heck, Regis, if I didn't know better, I'd think you were about to make a speech or shed a tear. Or both!"

For the briefest of moments, Regis felt a flicker of temper flare in him, the same one that he used to let run rampant like a wildfire whenever Shep bristled him. Now, though, it rose and settled as quickly.

At that very moment, all Regis could do was smile and redden a bit. "Well, no, but I was just thinking that in a funny way, all roads lead to the Royle Ranch."

Shep smiled, a relaxed, genuine smile; then he held up a finger and, still smiling, said, "But they also lead away, too."

Regis nodded. "Yes, I see that now. But that only means you know the way back now. And I hope you know you are welcome here any time, from wherever your life takes you, Shepley."

"Thanks, big brother. That means a lot to me. Especially now." He looked across the yard to where Regis was gazing, and his eyes rested on Philomena Cowley. "I have no idea where I'll be, but I know who I'll be there with."

Regis looked at his younger brother, then at the young woman Shep was watching, a slight smile on his face. "Congratulations, Shep."

Shep turned a red face to Regis. "Oh, but I haven't asked her yet. What if . . . ?"

"Shep, you're a Royle. She'd be crazy to turn you down."

And with that, both men, smiling, returned to the party.

Visit our website at
KensingtonBooks.com
to sign up for our newsletters, read
more from your favorite authors, see
books by series, view reading group
guides, and more!

Become a Part of Our
Between the Chapters Book Club
Community and Join the Conversation